Annie Thomas

Friends and Lovers

A Novel

Annie Thomas

Friends and Lovers
A Novel

ISBN/EAN: 9783337033064

Printed in Europe, USA, Canada, Australia, Japan

Cover: Foto ©Andreas Hilbeck / pixelio.de

More available books at **www.hansebooks.com**

FRIENDS AND LOVERS.

A NOVEL.

BY

ANNIE THOMAS
(Mrs PENDER CUDLIP),

AUTHOR OF "DENIS DONNE," ETC.

A New Edition.

LONDON: F. V. WHITE & CO.,
31 SOUTHAMPTON STREET, STRAND, W.C.

1884.

TO

Daisy, Ethel, and Edith,

THE THREE LITTLE FRIENDS

WHOSE CHARACTERS HAVE SUGGESTED THIS STORY,

I DEDICATE IT

WITH ALL AFFECTION.

CONTENTS.

Contents.

FRIENDS AND LOVERS.

CHAPTER I.

MRS VAUGHAN IS LATE FOR BREAKFAST.

STRATHLANDS, in the parish of Clyst, is a deliciously typical English country home. It is in the heart of a smiling, luxuriant, well-tilled country. It is near enough to a market town to be freshly supplied daily with all the more perishable necessaries and luxuries of life. And at the same time it is far enough removed from any other human habitation for its character as a "place" in the country to be perfectly supported by those essential qualifications, isolation, and distinct individuality.

The family who dwell in it are as typically English country people, as is Strathlands a typical country place.

Henry the First granted it to the Vaughan of the period, who lived contentedly in the then existing house, which was rather of the donjon order of architecture, massive and unpretentious, but certainly neither cheerful nor pretty. But the Vaughans who followed the founder of the family were less easily satisfied than he had been in his mediæval day. So the donjon-like dwelling was effaced, and a building commenced on its site that was begun and nearly finished in the fifteenth century, but was never quite completed owing to various causes, until Queen Elizabeth ordered the Vaughan of the commencement of her reign to set his ancestral home in order to receive her. This act of royal graciousness did more to impoverish the Vaughans even than the building mania had done, and for several generations they were small people though their mansion was vast. But penury taught them prudence, and after a time it came to be regarded as an established and creditable fact that the Vaughans never married any other than wealthy women. Beauty, birth, or brains were all alike powerless to snare a Vaughan. Only well-portioned girls had found favour in the eyes even of the youngest and most impassioned Vaughan for generations.

The present head of the house and owner of Strathlands has been as true to the traditions of his race as any of them. Fifteen years before this day on which we meet him for the first time, he married a girl who brought him a large fortune, which had been left to her by her god-father. That her father was merely a poor struggling professional man, and her brothers and sisters penniless, were matters of no great moment to Mr Vaughan. He regarded them as nuisances, nothing more, and as his wife Annabel made no fuss about wishing to supply any of their manifold wants, Mr Vaughan was well content to let them slip from his memory into the obscurity which he holds to be the proper place for all poor people.

Not that he is a hard or heartless man. On the contrary, he dearly loves the wife, whose income aggrandises his position, and the children, whose good health, looks, and dispositions reflect so gratifyingly on their parents. But the strongest and most lasting attachment of his life is for himself.

He has many good and sufficient reasons for loving himself, and prizing and regarding himself highly. For one thing, he is the chief representative and head of the house of the Vaughans, and it is the habit of the Vaughans to think themselves superior to the rest of the human race. The women they have married have not invariably held corresponding views. But the views of their wives —if unexpressed—are details about which the Vaughans have never troubled themselves.

Another justifiable source of satisfaction with himself is Mr Vaughan's status in the county. Far and wide he is known as one of the wisest employers, justest of magistrates, and most irreproachably-living man that those who converse about him have ever heard of. While he was the heir he was never wild, extravagant, or troublesome in any way. He never sowed wild oats ; but when this is said of him it must not be understood to mean that there was aught of the milksop or molly-coddle about him. His university career was blameless, and he took honours. This young man's home life was so spotless that it was never even questioned in the little shop in Clyst, which was grocer's, draper's, club, and gossip-room and post-office in one. And now that he is the reigning squire, with a handsome wife and four bonnie children, the kingdom might be searched in vain for a more exemplary and admirable character.

He was twenty-five when he married Annabel Lee, and to-day he is forty, and, like most of the Vaughans, he carries his years so gallantly that he might be only thirty-five. Life has rolled on pleasantly with him. He has never been subjected to fretting opposition, gnawing anxiety, crushing grief, or any of the other ills which age men and women more than the years which pass over their heads.

This morning, though it is his birthday, and he has so many excellent reasons for being glad that he was born, there is a frown of dissatisfaction on his ample forehead. The cause of his annoyance is a very slight one. Mrs Vaughan is late for breakfast, that is all. But a crumple on the rose leaf of a Vaughan is never to be disregarded or lightly smoothed. Exemplary and admirable as Mr Vaughan is in all the relations of life, he has a great idea of being in reality what he is in name, the "head" of the house. That Mrs Vaughan should be late for breakfast on his birthday, after having been early for fifteen years, discomposes him.

Not that his breakfast has been spoilt in consequence of her unreasonable absence. On the contrary, Mr Vaughan has satisfied his appetite this morning very pleasantly, for game and wild ducks are in, and the back bones of various birds, devilled to a nicety, form a dainty dish to set before a Vaughan. But he has wanted Annabel to listen to the birthday letters which he has just received from his two sons, who are at school.

"Don's letter would do credit to a lad of seventeen," Mr Vaughan says, glancing at his boy's letter again with pardonable parental complacency, "and little Reggie's catching his brother up fast; splendid boys, both of them to be sure, and will be splendid men."

He does not add "like me," but he means it.

He has risen from the table now, and is standing with his back to the glowing wood fire, looking out through the opposite window upon the fine expanse of well-wooded park that belts in Strathlands House. Far away in the distance other woods clothe a hillside, and midway up this hill is perched a mansion, made after the Italian manner, in which a little girl is growing up who is the heiress to Woodside, and whom he destines for his eldest son Donald.

"When the two properties are united under the name of Strathlands, there won't be a finer one in the county," he is saying to himself, when the door opens and his wife comes in.

Mrs Vaughan is rather tall, rather slender, rather fair, rather elegant, and rather in awe of the exemplary and admirable man who has never since their wedding day been other than kind and good to her, but who has deprived her of the desire almost, and of the power absolutely, of exercising her right to an individual opinion.

"I am sorry to be so late, Edmund," she says, deprecatingly, "but the post this morning has brought me news that has made me feel terribly nervous. I'm so afraid you won't like it."

He is not one of the men who labour under a chronic, irritable half desire to catch their wives out in the receipt of a contraband bill; nor has he so much as a vague suspicion of her corresponding with any undesirable person. Therefore he is rather stoical than sympathetic in his rejoinder.

"Drink your coffee, my dear, and don't think about your disagreeable news till you've read the boys' letters."

He pushes the schoolboys' epistles towards her, and she drops her own letter at once, exclaiming,—

"Don and Reggie! have they written? Dear boys, they will be home for their holidays in another week."

"Meantime they have not forgotten that this is my birthday, though you seem to have done so, Annabel."

She does not regard his remark, being occupied in reading her boys' letters. When they are read, she relapses for a few minutes into abstracted silence, during which he reads the *Times*. At the end of those few minutes he says indifferently,—

"Now for your news, my dear. Are you disappointed by your milliner?"

"Oh, Edmund, it's no joke; indeed, I fear you will think it no joke when I tell you my letter is from my sister Lily—Mrs Arminger. She is coming to Clyst to live."

"To live?"

"Yes. Don't say anything till I have told you all she says. Her husband is dead, and she is not at all well off, but her children are good and promising, and the eldest, Donald, is coming to Mr Dalzel as pupil-teacher, so Lily thinks it will be better for them to keep all together, and she has made up her mind to come to Clyst."

Mrs Vaughan falters terribly as she imparts this intelligence, for the seldom seen frown is gathering ominously on his brow.

"This must be averted," are his first words; "you see

yourself that it will be impossible for your—for Mrs Arminger to live in Clyst—at our gates; this must be averted."

"But, Edmund, it can't be—I don't see how it can be, I mean," she says, the last words apologetically, and Mr Vaughan, remembering just in time that he is a wise, just, good, upright, exemplary, and admirable man, contrives to answer her pacifically.

"Naturally you do not see how it is to be done, Annabel, for I have not yet made up my mind as to the steps I shall use to avert this extremely undesirable—this, I may say, almost calamitous circumstance. But it must be done, and it shall be done."

"Edmund, she is my sister! why do you speak of Lily's coming here as a 'calamitous circumstance?'" Mrs Vaughan gulps out.

"My dear Annabel, you were cut to the core by the notification of her intention before even you mentioned it to me," he says argumentatively. "Your sister Mrs Arminger (pray don't let me hear you speak of her as Lily again) chose to marry badly, and to surround herself with a tribe of little pauper Armingers. All that is nothing to you or to me; but it is much to both of us that Mrs Arminger should foist herself and her unattractive group of children upon us by coming to live at Clyst. Dalzel ought to be ashamed of himself for engaging her son; I have always felt that it is a low thing for the rector of such a parish as Clyst to take pupils, but now when he takes young Arminger as tutor, I shall let him understand that he has done a confoundedly ungentlemanly and unchristianlike thing."

"Oh, Edmund, for many years you have made me forget my family, but your words now make me remember that Lily is my own sister, and that we dearly loved one another once. Why shall she not come here? Why shall she not be as much honoured in Clyst as I am? She may be poor, but she can't have changed so much as to be either troublesome or cringing; she had a high spirit and a lovely face—"

"Good heavens, Annabel ! knowing that, and reflecting on the possibility of her having a daughter like her, can you contemplate the contingency of her coming here, of her children growing up with Don, calmly ?"

"She is my sister, and I will not bid her keep aloof from me."

"I would not ask you to do anything so distinctly ungracious and unladylike for the world," he shudders. "No, no ! such a task is not for you—for either of us. I shall communicate with Dalzel. I shall put the case to him as a gentleman, and ask him to end negotiations with this young Arminger."

"And I shall put the case to him as a Christian, and tell him that, by ending negotiations with young Arminger, he may ruin my sister's son, my own nephew."

Her trembling hand puts down her untasted cup of coffee as she speaks, and her face works as a woman's face is apt to work when after years of repression her feelings are touched beyond control. At this moment she comes nearer to a right estimation of Mr Vaughan's real place in the scale of creation than she has ever done before.

"This is the beginning of the end, I fear, Annabel," he says, with sorrowful dignity. "You receive for the first time since our marriage a letter from one of a group of people whom we tacitly agreed to ignore ; and for the first time since our marriage you array yourself defiantly against my will and wishes, and seem to forget that your paramount duty is towards the house of which your husband is head, your son is heir !"

"Lily is my sister, and I do long to see her," Mrs Vaughan gulps ; "neither she nor her children can hurt or tarnish the dignity of the Vaughans ; besides, Lily is a free woman, she is not like me, tied to you and in subjection to you ! She will laugh at your objections to her coming to Clyst ; she will think of what is best for her son, without regard to her brother-in-law's arrogance."

"The effect of merely a letter from her has been so pernicious that I shall take care there is no personal communication between Mrs Arminger and you," he says coldly.

Then he dips into the columns of the *Times* again, and Mrs Vaughan, for the first time in her married life, leaves the room on her husband's birthday without wishing him many happy returns of it.

"Poor relations are the very devil," he mutters to himself. "The Vaughans never have them, and I won't be the one to establish such a disgusting precedent in the family. A poor, pretty widow, with a troop of healthy, aspiring, well-conducted children trying to tack themselves on to my coat-tails whenever I passed through the village, would drive me into letting Strathlands. Annabel shall know that it is at the cost of her home that she is thrusting her sister upon me. Merciful Providence! Mrs Arminger may have heard of Don! If she has, decent feeling ought to have made her keep her beggar maidens out of the way. I'll see Dalzel at once, and throttle this detestable difficulty in the birth."

Never before in his life has Mr Vaughan allowed himself to act so unjustly and illiberally, for never before has Mr Vaughan been confronted by a contingency fraught with so many unpleasant probabilities as this.

His wife's family have hitherto been such admirably untroublesome people. Her father and mother died without any ado, and her brothers and sisters have dispersed themselves over the world without boring Mr Vaughan as to their whereabouts. He has "been everything to Annabel," he has been wont to say, and he has taken great credit to himself for being it and saying it.

It is monstrous that this Mrs Arminger should suddenly rise up and develop sisterly affection and sympathy for his wife. It is even more monstrous that his wife should develop sisterly affection and sympathy for Mrs Arminger.

Not that Mr Vaughan knows anything against the latter. He carefully and generously impresses this upon Mr Dalzel's mind, even while he is admonishing the latter to cancel his agreement with the widow's son and cast the lad adrift.

" But you understand, Dalzel," he says confidentially, " that members of Mrs Vaughan's family who have not been known to Mrs Vaughan for many years are, perhaps, better away from Clyst. My children are grown up, and these young Armingers are growing up. In order to spare them pain and mortification, you understand, I would prevent their coming here. Young people of different classes had better not be thrown into each other's society on terms of apparent intimacy and equality. I am sure you agree with me."

The hearty old rector looks at his squire in silence for a few moments ; then he chuckles and says,—

" My dear Vaughan, you and I both like regulating our respective affairs without interference from any one. I mean to have young Arminger with me, but I'll put him on his honour never to claim relationship with you till you ask me to do so. He's a fine lad, is Don Arminger—the finest and noblest I ever knew. He will never cross your line of life intentionally. He doesn't even know that Mrs Vaughan is his aunt, for his mother is a diplomatist in a small way, and has concealed the fact from him. Don Arminger will never be a trouble to you, Vaughan."

" It is beyond everything that he should bear the same name as my boy," Mr Vaughan says deploringly. " Mrs Vaughan must have been wandering when she selected the name, and now it may be the means of involving my son in many unpleasantnesses. Young men will be young men, and I fear me much that Mr Donald Arminger's peccadilloes may unfavourably affect the reputation of Donald Vaughan."

CHAPTER II.

DON ARMINGER.

Mrs Arminger's temporary home is in Greenwich. The poor ill-to-do lady has never had anything but a temporary home for the last eighteen years, during which she has been wife and widow to Mr Arminger, of the Inland Revenue Office.

Her husband's life and means of maintaining her and their flourishing group of children came to an end on the same day, and since then she has lived on in a desultory kind of way, on her wits.

She is a very gentle, refined, sensitive little woman, this widowed Mrs Arminger, and underlying that delicate, almost shrinking appearance of hers, there is a vast power of endurance and perseverance. She has three children, a son Donald, about whom the dispute has arisen between Mr Vaughan and the rector of Clyst, aged seventeen ; and Maude and Beatrix, two bits of budding maidenhood, aged respectively fourteen and thirteen.

To see her surrounded by these children is to see a fair flower encircled by buds. However harshly fortune's gales buffet her, she always succeeds in keeping up her normal appearance of flower-like delicacy and sweetness.

Poor as she is, desperately as she has to put her fragile shoulder to the wheel, she always looks—as a little girl of her acquaintance once said—"like a carriage-lady." Her dress may be worn and shiny where it ought to be dull, and dull where it ought to be shiny, but it is invariably well put on and carefully clean. A gentlewoman by birth, habit, and inclination, she never permits any sordid considerations to intervene between herself and the fulfilment of all the gentle practices of her early life.

It is hard lines with the poor little lady very often, but no one thinks of bestowing pity upon her. Mrs

Arminger gets abundance of sympathy and kindly feeling extended to her, but no one thinks of offering her pity any more than they would offer her alms. She smiles and looks cheerily satisfied with the world, even when her larder is empty, and she has not the where-withal to replenish it. And the world in return smiles and looks cheerily at her, kindly ignores her empty larder, and makes believe to think her as well off as she appears to be.

For years she has striven gallantly, and succeeded beyond all reasonable expectation in keeping and educating her children by the hard labour of her brain and hand.

Her work is, artistically speaking, very worthy, but in Mr Vaughan's ears it would sound ignobly if any one were found brave enough to name it to him. She has kept her boy at school, and dressed her little lassies prettily on what she makes by painting lamp-shades and fire-screens.

And now that her speciality is known and appreciated, and that her work commands a fairly remunerative price, she feels herself justified in withdrawing from the vicinity of the Great Mart, and making a home for her son in the village to which he is going as tutor in a school, the very name of which will be a recommendation to him through life.

It is a matter of very little import to her that the rich sister, whom she has never seen since her own real life began, should be living at Clyst in a sphere far above the one she will occupy. Her sole thought is for her son's weal and comfort, and it is only because they shall not have it to say of her that she crept into their midst in an underhand way, that she writes to Mrs Vaughan at all.

But she desires nothing from them, and expects nothing more than she desires. Consequently when Mrs Vaughan's answer comes, Mrs Arminger opens and reads it without an expectant throb.

Fortunate is it for her that she has thus schooled herself to form no bright anticipation of a warm and affectionate response from the sister from whom she has been

alienated for so many years. Mrs Vaughan's letter is a
cautious compilation dictated by her husband. There is
not a touch of tenderness, or even conventional geniality
in it. But Mrs Arminger reads it without a sigh. It
runs thus:—

'STRATHLANDS, *October 20th.*

"DEAR LILY,—Your letter apprising me of the extraordinary resolution to which you and your son have
come, reached me safely this morning. I am sorry that
you should have chosen to make him an usher. It is not
the profession of a gentleman, and his following it will
preclude all possibility of Mr Vaughan ever being able
to offer him any assistance.

"With every good wish, believe me to be, yours very
sincerely,   ANNABEL VAUGHAN."

Mrs Arminger's soft grey eyes sparkle more with
amusement than anger as she reads this frigid effusion.

"I recognise my august brother-in-law in every word.
Poor, ductile Annabel! You never had the vigour of a
caterpillar even, and the little you had has been exhausted in the rarified Vaughan atmosphere. Poor sister,
you needn't be frightened. If we live in different hemi-
spheres we couldn't be wider apart than we shall be when
I'm at Clyst."

There is not an atom of pique, spite, or ill-feeling in
her breast as she puts the letter down, and takes up a
design drawn for her by the skilful hand of her daughter
Maude. From this design an original half grotesque, half
pathetic treatment of a witch on a broomstick flying
through space, Mrs Arminger will make endless combina-
tions for the adornment of countless lamp-shades. Orders
are pouring in fast upon her, and she is in funds and high
spirits consequently.

The little room in which she is painting is the family
sitting-room, but there is no disorder, no shabby subter-
fuges, no air of barren tidiness about it. The hand of a
gentlewoman and an artist is visible in every nook and

corner. The curtains are cretonne, a grey-green ground covered with fern leaves in every shade of brown and dull gold. The floor is polished, partially covered by an old Persian carpet, which, worn as it is, yet retains much of its subdued splendour of colouring. The walls are painted the same pale grey-green as the groundwork of the curtains, and on them are fastened innumerable well-carved brackets which serve to support some good bits of old china, and some exquisitely shaped and coloured modern glass flower vases. A cottage piano stands across a corner with its back to the room, but its back is covered with a beautiful piece of silk embroidery on grey-green cloth, the work of the same deft little fingers that draw the designs for "mother's lamp-shades." There are plenty of books on ebony shelves which rise up on either side from chimney-piece nearly to ceiling, forming a frame for a plain piece of bevelled glass. Clever water-colour drawings hang on the walls and lie on little tables of divers shapes, all of them made by Mrs Arminger and her children. It is the best amusement this hard-working mother and her son and daughters have, this of beautifying and decorating their home with the work of their own hands. Taste in a great measure makes up for the want of money. Mrs Arminger has no rich or rare belongings, yet her apartments invariably give one the impression of beauty and refinement.

She paints on undisturbed for several hours this morning. Then, as the clock strikes one, the landlady comes in to lay the cloth and spread the table for the early dinner, to which the children will come in presently. When they do come in, Mrs Arminger, bright, trim, and picturesque in a becoming lace mob cap and pretty crewel apron with bib and pockets, will show no trace of her occupation, either by fatigue or stain of paint.

She is a proud woman presently when they do troop in, the boy from the school, where he pays for the lessons he takes by the lessons he gives; the girls from their respective drawing and music lessons. It is Mrs Arminger's plan not to have her children crammed with miscellaneous learning, but discover the speciality of each one, and have it cultivated to the best of her ability.

Don's gift of imparting knowledge to others has been worked upon with good and satisfactory results already. Dreamy Maude is studying art under a drawing master, to the exclusion of all other branches of education excepting languages. These latter—German and French —she works at with a will, for she has visions of the Louvre and the Munich Galleries. Little Trixy's speciality has not been discovered as yet, but she avows that she likes music better than most things, and Lily Arminger is as hopeful of her younger child "doing something definite well" as she is satisfied with the others.

Don is just seventeen—a tall, thoughtful lad, slight, but with no signs of delicacy in his firm, upright figure, or in the clear, brave face that is always held aloft with an unconscious air of command. He has his mother's grey eyes—eyes that offer their undefiled depths unflinchingly to your inspection. And he has her composure and self-possession. Altogether, he well deserves the verdict passed upon him by every master and every schoolboy with whom he has been thrown in contact. "Don's a gentleman every inch of him," they all aver, and they are right. He is as brave as a lion and as pure as a girl.

Maude is fourteen, an age that is proverbially unbecoming, but the beauty of Mrs Arminger's eldest daughter is incontestable. There is a dreamy grace in her pale complexioned face, and a good deal of latent pride in her large, grey hazel, longlashed eyes. But she is all a child when she is away from her drawing, and is behind none of them in animation and activity when romping with her playfellows.

Trixy is a little, velvet-eyed brown mouse, brimming over with affection and vivacity—a rosy pretty little brunette, a lump of love, full of tempestuous feeling which sometimes shows itself in a storm of fury, but oftener in a burst of tenderness—idle, mischievous, and bewitching. "Capable of great things, but lacking in perseverance," her mistresses say, but a darling for all that.

These are the young people who Mr Vaughan fears may, by their mere existence at Clyst, exercise a deteriorating influence on his children; and their high-hearted, hard-working, indefatigable, independent spirited little mother is the sister with whom he has forbidden his wife to hold any social intercourse.

Yes, he has brooded over the "calamity" as he terms their promised advent at Clyst, till it really assumes the proportions of a colossal wrong and grievance. Never before has anything so untoward happened in the Vaughan family as that poor relations on the wife's side should obtrude their poverty and relationship upon the observation of the neighbourhood. Never before has Mr Vaughan had such an unpleasant subject so forced upon and kept fresh in his notice.

Through some miserable carelessness, either on his part or his wife's, it soon leaks out that the mother of the handsome young man who has come as usher to Mr Dalzel is none other than own sister to the squire's lady. As Mr Vaughan makes a majestic progress through the village street on horseback, or by the side of his wife in her splendidly appointed carriage, he knows that the busybodies are speculating as to whether he is going to stop at the little way-side house which has been, in the course of a few days, magically metamorphosed from a common-place cottage into a picturesque bowery kind of place, the windows of which give glimpses of filmy cream coloured muslin, from out whose folds hanging baskets of moss and fern and trailing ivy peep.

He knows that these speculations are rife about him, and he cannot succeed in feigning to be unconscious of them. He feels himself turn pale one morning, when just as he is passing, a graceful woman, much fairer to look upon than his own wife, and with an air of distinction about her that compels his admiration, steps out upon the threshold of the metamorphosed cottage door, and he feels his own eyes droop under the careless, cool gaze of his sister-in-law.

It is like her audacity, he feels, to add to the complications of the case, and to embarrass him by being a woman whom he can't denounce as vulgar or underbred. The roughest churls in the village cede her the same rugged homage and prompt respect which they show to the lady of Strathlands. Her very voice is vexatious to him, with its high-bred light intonation, and inflections, when he hears it raised laughingly through her open windows as she talks to her children.

The little girls are thorns in his flesh. He cannot help seeing that his own daughters, and Miss Vaughans of Strathlands, cannot vie with these obscure Arminger girls. And as for Don Arminger, he hates the lad with an intensity that sometimes astounds and alarms himself.

"The fellow must be predestined to bring disgrace on me or mine, or I could not trouble myself to dislike him in this unaccountable way," Mr Vaughan says to his wife one day, when they pass Don swinging along the road buoyantly on his way from his mother's pretty wayside cottage to the rectory, where Mr Dalzel's young gentlemen are awaiting the usher.

"I wonder if he knows I am his aunt?" Mrs Vaughan falters, and her husband, who has been rendered testy by this terrible social calamity, answers testily now.

"Knows that you are, and is prepared to trade upon the knowledge, that I dare swear; however, trust entirely to me and I will keep the whole lot of them at bay."

"Edmund, they don't deserve that you should speak of them in this way," she says, making a faint effort to pluck up something like spirit; "they show no more desire to know us than we do to know them. Oh, it's an unnatural state of things, and we shall be punished for it some day!"

"You punish me already by wailing and whining in this way, Annabel; I really wish you would remember that we have been perfectly innocent of all offence in bringing this extremely compromising complication about. Your sister and you have been strangers for many years; why should you consider it 'unnatural' that you should remain strangers still?"

"I read contempt in my nephew's face as we passed him just now—my heart yearns to him—he is handsome as a star, and he has the bearing of a prince."

"You are uttering greater nonsense than I can conceive you imagining," he interrupts. "He has a fair amount of cheek and swagger for an usher in a second-rate school, I admit, but that only makes him the more dangerous. You have daughters, remember, Mrs Vaughan, and it's your duty to save them from contamination, at the cost of any sentimental feeling you may have."

"Such words to use about my sister's son—my own blood relation!" she cries. But Mr Vaughan pooh-poohs her protest, and argues with her that it is better for her to keep to this line of absolute non-intercourse, than to adopt half measures, and see her sister occasionally in a semi-friendly way.

Meanwhile the Armingers are very happy in their new home, and before many weeks pass over their heads in Clyst, they are well-known and better liked by a vast number of people, all of whom feel impelled to accord kindly and courteous consideration to the Armingers, and many of whom visit in the over-rated Vaughan set.

Once or twice, in a surreptitious way that wins their scorn, Mrs Vaughan waylays Maude and Trixy when she knows her husband is far away at some magistrates' meeting, and tries to apologise herself into their affectionate interest, and to ingratiate herself with tempting offers of trinkets and sweetmeats, fruit and flowers.

The trinkets and sweetmeats Maude resolutely rejects, but flowers she cannot resist; they are as sweet as angel's smiles to her. So it comes to pass that many a choice bouquet of hot-house flowers finds its way from Strathlands down to Mrs Arminger's unpretentious little parlour.

One day, among the other flowers, she finds a pomegranate blossom, and its glorious, flame-like beauty attracts and takes possession of her. For hours she works at reproducing it, but fails till Maude aids her. Then—

"The child's pencil and brush have magic in them!" she says ecstatically, for she means this painted flower to be a message to her sister.

CHAPTER IIL

CONSTANCE FIELDING.

THE little girl at Woodside, who is growing up, according to Mr Vaughan's idea and intention, for the sole purpose of being united to his son Donald, is a very quaint and interesting little girl of twelve, at the time when the Armingers take up their abode in Clyst. She is actually the owner of Woodside already—the little lady of the land ; for her father and mother are dead, and it is under the care and guardianship of a maiden aunt that Constance Fielding is growing up.

She has been brought up on terms of fraternal intimacy with the young Vaughans ; for Mr Vaughan has great faith in the winning power of propinquity, and Miss Damer, the maiden aunt, whose business it is to steer her niece over the sea of life till the latter is twenty-one, desires no better fate for her charge than to see her married to Donald Vaughan.

But no embarrassing ideas of this kind shackle the intercourse of the young people. Constance is to Donald and Reginald merely a girl like their own sisters, to be played with, teased, amused, buffeted, tyrannised over, and petted, precisely as it suits their lordly boyish purpose. And she complains of them, quarrels with them, plays wild beasts or horses with them, and is alternately queen over and slave to them, just as their sisters do and are.

She is a distinguished-looking girl already, young as she is. A well-grown, erect, fearless, blue-eyed, bold-fronted child, with a loud, ringing, merry voice, an

·inexhaustible fund of spirits, and a heart as true as gold. Altogether "Neighbour Constance," as Mr Vaughan is fond of calling her, bids fair to be the heroine of more than one exciting love-chase.

As she sits demurely and reverently by her aunt's side on the Sunday following the Armingers' arrival in Clyst, her musical ear is pleased by a new voice, which rises high and clear above all others when the first hymn is being sung. She has but to turn her head an inch in order to command the rector's seat, from whence this voice proceeds, but she controls her curiosity till the service is over. Then she comes out of church in the wake of the Arminger family, and conjectures at once that the new tenor is the usher about whom Mr Dalzel has spoken to her aunt.

The child is fascinated by the aspect of the whole family at once. The graceful, dainty-looking little mother, the dreamy - looking eldest girl, with her long, fair, streaming hair and glorious eyes ; the piquant beauty of bonnie little Trixy, and the thoroughbred manly look of the son, all exercise a potent spell over the little girl, who has hitherto been strictly limited to' the society of the Vaughans. Constance loiters behind them as they slowly saunter home, laughing and talking freely together. The tones of their voices, something pictur esque in their dress, the happy familiarity that evidently exists between the mother and her children, the unusualness of them altogether, all tend to charm the little predestined wife of Donald Vaughan into an enthusiastic desire to become acquainted with his disowned aunt and cousins.

As she has been accustomed from her birth to have all her requests granted, it strikes her now as excessively hard that her aunt should refuse to "call on those dear people who live in that house, and who don't look like anybody else." Miss Damer, instructed by Mr Vaughan, declines to do this, and perhaps the matter might end there, if she were not weak enough to attempt to defend her refusal, and prove to her far sharper-witted niece that she is right.

"They may be very nice people, Constance, but they do not belong to the class in which you will visit when you are grown up, and if you get to know them now, it will be very awkward by-and-by."

"Does Mrs Vaughan belong to the class I ought to visit?"

"Most certainly."

"And Mrs Arminger is her sister. I know she is, Aunt Emily; I've heard several people say so."

"My dear Connie, you shock me; how can people dare to gossip to you about such things?"

"Such 'things' as Mrs Vaughan, do you mean, Aunt Emily? that's exactly what I call her; a regular mean-spirited old snob of a thing, to be ashamed of her own sister, because her own sister hasn't as much money as she has."

"Dearest Connie, you mustn't speak disrespectfully of our dear friend Mrs Vaughan. She is very much to be pitied, and I consider that this Mrs Arminger shows a spirit of nasty, pushing vulgarity in hunting her sister out in this way, and coming here to disgrace her."

Constance's face flames scarlet at once. She is only a child, and her choice of language is limited as yet, but she has words at command to express her feelings now.

"I call it a beastly shame to look down on people because they're poor; and the Vaughans are stupidly silly too, because the Armingers look ever so much greater swells than the Vaughans do, and so I shall tell Bell and Edith; and, if the Vaughans don't like the Armingers being poor, why don't they give them some of their money, and—"

"Oh, Constance, Constance! what is the use of your learning grammar, if you muddle up your sentences in this way? And wherever have you learned such extremely low and foolish sentiments? It's no use arguing with me, my dear; I know my duty, and mean to do it, and it's my duty to keep you aloof from people who may be detrimental to you in after life; so please let me hear no more about the Armingers, and promise me that you

will never allow yourself to get inveigled into an acquaint.
anceship with them."

"I don't know what 'inveigling' means, but I won't
promise not to know them the first chance I get; they're
as much ladies as we are—any fool can see that."

"Such language as you use, Constance!" Miss Damer
says despairingly.

"I learn to speak like that from Don and Reggie
Vaughan," Constance says a little maliciously. "Whatever they say and do is right, you know; they're so rich."

"It's not their riches that makes them gentlemen;
do understand that, Connie. However poor they might
be, the Vaughans must always be gentle people."

"That's just what I say about the Armingers," Connie
says; and then the spirited little mistress of Woodside
cuts further argument by ringing to order her pony.

"I am going to ride through Clyst, and then round by
Strathlands," she says to her aunt as she turns Peppercorn's head from the door, and, followed by her own
groom, canters down the avenue.

Peppercorn is full of fun this morning, and gives his
mistress all the work she can well do in regulating him.
He is a handsome little fellow, twelve hands high, shaped
like a horse, and full of courage. But Constance has
ridden him for four years, and is an adept in accommo-
dating herself to his wildest movements.

She makes a pretty picture riding down the village
street on this November day in her well fitting brown
habit and little brown billycock hat; and so Maude
Arminger, standing at their open window, thinks. The
two children look straight into each other's eyes with
that interrogating but still trustful look which is characteristic of youth. Then they smile simultaneously, and
in a moment Aunt Emily's prohibition is disregarded,
and Peppercorn's nose is turned over the wicket-gate.

Maude is out by the gate in a second.

"How jolly for you to have a pony," she says, caressing Peppercorn's nose. "Are you the one who walked
behind us home from church on Sunday?"

"Yes. I wanted to speak to you then, only aunt is horrid sometimes, and wouldn't let me. I liked you awfully, and want to be chums. I know your cousins the Vaughans; they're awfully grand, you know, and not half as nice as you and your sister, I am sure. Shall I come in ?"

She waits courteously, in spite of her impetuosity, for Maude to give her a hearty invitation to enter, and then she slips off her pony in a moment, and Trixy comes flying out to see "what it is all about," and with a little disposition to pout because she has "not been in it" from the beginning.

"This is our mother," Maude says, introducing Constance with a certain suave velocity which is so contagious that Constance finds herself directly informing Mrs Arminger of her—Constance's—name, age, place of abode and any other trifle concerning herself which she can remember at the moment; and Mrs Arminger listens to the bold bright child with pleasure and sympathy, and goes on swiftly painting a lamp-shade the while in a way that seems little short of miraculous.

"Do you always do these things ?" Constance asks, pointing to a newly completed shade. "They're awfully pretty, and you're very clever to do them ; but don't you get tired of doing them ? Don't you want to paint other sort of pictures ?"

"Don't you understand," Maude explains earnestly ; "we're very poor, and mother paints these for money, not for pleasure altogether."

"You oughtn't to be poor. I mean, you oughtn't to have to work, any of you," Constance says, with beaming eyes. "Let me come here and learn to paint; may I? Will you, Mrs Arminger ? And let Maude ride my pony. He's called Peppercorn, and he is such a darling."

"My dear little girl," Mrs Arminger says, putting her brush down and taking the child gently by the shoulders, "you shall come here and learn to paint, and Maude shall ride your pony if, after you have seen the Vaughans, and told them what you want to do, you still wish to do it, and your aunt will let you. And now I must send you off on pretty Peppercorn, for it is not right that I should keep you here till I know whether or not your friends will like you to come."

"When I'm older you will be my friends, won't you?" Connie says wistfully, for these people, with their avowed poverty and their impressive refinement, have given her a new outlook into life, and she shrinks from the thought of being cut off from them, and of going back to what and to whom she has always been accustomed.

"Yes, we shall always be friends, I feel," Mrs Arminger says cheerily; "that is, if those to whom you owe obedience allow it; and we shall always like you, even if they don't allow it—sha'n't we, my children?"

Maude assents by a serious nod.

"When I can paint portraits I'll do yours," she says to the little heiress of Woodside, whose face lights up with pride at the thought of having a girl-friend clever enough to paint.

"I should like to ride Peppercorn," Trixy murmurs from the background, and as she is saying this her brother Don comes in.

"This is Constance Fielding," his sisters begin eagerly, "and we're going to be great friends if she's let be; and oh, Don, isn't the pony a love?"

He jumps his youngest sister up in his arms, and kisses her as he says,—

"I'm home for the afternoon, Trixy. Shall it be a ferning expedition?"

The child shouts with delight at the prospect, and as Constance lingeringly leaves the room, she whispers in confidence to Maude,—

"I wish he was my brother too: I like him. He's different to Don Vaughan."

"Not so grand?" Maude questions.

"Oh, grander, ever so much; good-bye," she leans forward and kisses her new friend. "Tell your mother I'm not a sneak; I'm going straight back to tell Aunt

Emily that I've been to see you, and asked you to be my friends."

With this Miss Fielding puts her little foot on the old groom's hand, and is popped up on Peppercorn in a way that commands Maude's willing admiration. There is beauty to the artist-souled child in the breezy freshness, and almost boyish frankness, and general munificence of her new acquaintance. If Maude and her family are a revelation and liberal education to the child who has been nurtured among mediocre-minded but extremely well-bred people, so is this child, Constance herself, a breath of new, enticing, entrancing life to Maude, who has never ridden, much less owned, a pony.

"I shall dream of Peppercorn and Constance," she says, going back into the room where her brother is saying to her mother that they "must be careful not to arouse Vaughan's animus further by ingratiating themselves with this little Miss Fielding."

"Already I fear I've been the cause of Mr Dalzel's losing a pupil. Mr Vaughan was going to send his son Donald there for a term, but the presence of your unworthy Don, dear mother, as an usher in the school, has upset this arrangement; is there anything wrong about Aunt Annabel, mother, that they shun us so ?"

"My dear boy," she cries, laughing merrily, "your Aunt Annabel's one fault in life is that—I am her sister. That is the one black spot in her surroundings. Her husband hates us with a worse hate than he could visit on any sin, because we are poor and independent. If we were poor and needy he could banish us ; as it is, we exist, and make our existence tolerable under his nose, without his aid. Dear boy, does the contempt of your rich relations distress you ? If it does, relinquish your situation, and we will leave Clyst; you shall not stay here to suffer."

"I have no feeling for my aunt, for I've never known her. Does her neglect hurt you, mother ?"

"Nothing can hurt me while I have such children as you about me," she says, tenderly and truthfully.

And then the two girls come leaping into the room, claiming the fulfilment of his promise to go ferning with them.

"It must be nice to have Peppercorn," Maude says, sighing, as they pass Woodside presently, and Trixy cries rapturously,—

"It must be nice to be Miss Fielding, and have a pony, and do as she likes, and have plenty of money to buy sweets, and not have to bother about lessons. Don't you love her, Don? Isn't she a darling?"

"She's little Miss Fielding, of Woodside," he says, taking off his hat in playful, deferential mockery to the hill-side, on which Constance's house is situated. "While you remember that fact, my children, you'll be all right; when you forget it, you'll be all wrong; so remember it."

"Oh, Don, and you'd be the first to forget that she's richer than we, if you only knew her as we do," Trixy says wisely.

"She's but a brat of a child, like you two. Why should I think of her at all?" he says gaily. But he does think of her, nevertheless, and applauds Maude when she makes a sketch of Peppercorn, with his bonnie little rider on his back.

Meanwhile in all honesty Constance has ridden home, and confessed the social enormity of which she has been guilty. But she has not done it in a penitential way.

"I've got to know those Armingers," she says to her guardian aunt. "I blurted right in upon them, and they couldn't help themselves; they had to be civil, you see. Maude's going to ride Peppercorn, and I'm going in there when I like, and oh, Aunt Emily, they are darlings, the little girls as well as Don."

"For the first time in your life you've disappointed and hurt me, Constance," her aunt says severely. "The Vaughans will be more than distressed at what you have done; the inconveniences that may arise from your action will never cease while these people stay here. Half-and-half people are invariably more difficult to deal with than quite the lower classes."

"I shall never want to shake them off; I only hope they'll stick to me as truly as I will to them ; they're the best ladies and gentlemen I ever knew, and the cleverest and the handsomest ; and I don't care what the Vaughans say, or how distressed they are."

"Oh, Constance, how can you turn aside to new friends from such old ones as the Vaughans ? "

" Mrs Vaughan has turned aside from her own sister, and a sister is more than a friend."

" Mr Dalzel would have a more Christian spirit if he had dismissed this young man when he learnt how obnoxious his presence here would be to the Vaughans," Miss Damer says with a heavy sigh, for her prophetic soul tells her that this young man may be a thorn of serious trouble to them all.

The next day an affectionate letter of invitation for Miss Damer and her charge to come and stay at Strathlands for a time arrives from Mrs Vaughan.

The coincidence strikes Constance as rather strange, but the straight-dealing child has no idea that this invitation is the result of an appeal from her aunt to the Vaughans to aid her in breaking off this "pernicious acquaintance."

CHAPTER IV.

VERY INDISCREET.

It must not be supposed that Mrs Vaughan has renounced her sister and the liberty of the subject without a struggle. She has indeed set herself in opposition to her husband's arbitrary decree on several occasions, but she has always done it in a weak way and at the wrong moment. She has, for instance, protested feebly just before going to church against the uncharitable iniquity of being made to slight her own sister in the face of the full congregation, and cried weakly because her protest is disregarded. The effect of this proceeding is that she goes into church with red eyes, and with her complexion mottled by her ill-timed but bitter tears. And Mr Vaughan has the unspeakable annoyance of knowing that people are pitying her and thinking him a petty tyrant, and altogether misjudging him and misunderstanding the situation.

" Why do you think about them? They need not exist for you, for their presence in the place is not a shame to you, as it is to me," he says to her authoritatively.

And she murmurs that it " is impossible to forget that one's own blood relations exist, even if one does fossilise one's heart."

" Nonsense ! " he says conclusively. " A woman with a well-regulated mind forgets all minor conventional considerations if she has a proper sense of her paramount duty towards her husband and children."

" I have never failed in my duty to either," she moans reproachfully.

And her husband assures her that she shall not be tempted to error by being permitted to indulge in intercourse with a sister who has so slight a regard for the fitness of things as Mrs Arminger has shown.

The visit which Miss Damer and Constance Fielding, Miss Damer's highly important young niece, pay to Strathlands just at this juncture is not fraught with much incident, but is productive of serious and important results.

For one thing, Mr Vaughan, who has a manner of authority at command at all times, brings this manner to bear so powerfully on Miss Damer (who is Constance's sole guardian) that she submits without reservation to his decision as to the necessity of there being absolutely no further intercourse between the heiress and the young people of Clyst Cottage.

" There must be no half measures," he says, rather sternly to Miss Damer. " Our dear little neighbour, Constance, is a high-spirited, determined little lady, and it is quite right, in her position, that she should be high-spirited and determined. But in this case you must conquer her will and insist upon her giving up these extremely undesirable people entirely."

"Connie is very wilful; she may defy me," Miss Damer says hesitatingly.

"In that case, sadly as both Annabel and I shall feel parting with our dear little favourite, you must take her away for a time. Change of scene and the knowledge she will soon acquire from the world of her own position, its importance and dignity, will soon work a change in her. At present she thinks it chivalrous to range herself on the side of these people, because she sees that we look down on them. But after a time she will discover that they are not of her world, and that they are better and more at ease if left undisturbed in their own. Speak to her to-day. Tell her that it will be a source of deep sorrow to both Mrs Vaughan and myself if she persists in being familiar with these Armingers."

In obedience to this behest, Mrs Damer does speak to Constance, and does so threaten, weep at, and otherwise badger Constance, that the poor child in despair at length gives an unconditional promise never again to seek the society of her new friends.

"I'll promise not to go to their house, and not to loiter past their gate, and not to try and meet them, Aunt Emily," she says at last; "but I won't promise not to speak to them if we meet by accident, and they stop and speak to me; even Mr Vaughan can't wish me to be such a snob as that."

"Even Mr Vaughan! Why, child, Mr Vaughan has nothing so much at heart as your honour and happiness."

"That's all bosh, as Donald Vaughan says, when his father has been extra grand about something or other; my honour and happiness can't be as much to him as the honour and happiness of his own children; and if it is, it oughtn't to be."

Miss Damer deems it discreet not to enter into any argument on this point. She has a promise from her niece, which though not entirely as satisfactory as a vow to " quite cut " the Armingers would have been, is still better than the defiance she half feared. At any rate, Constance is safe for the present. The future must take care of itself, or rather Mr Vaughan must take care of it for her.

Another result of this visit to Strathlands is that Mr Vaughan and the guardian aunt enter into a solemn compact to unite the eldest son of the one and the niece of the other in matrimony, so soon as the boy and girl shall be of suitable age.

And a third result is that Mrs Vaughan, who has been excluded from these solemn conferences, conceives a fierce jealousy and a hearty detestation of the innocent and unconscious Miss Damer.

The mistress of Strathlands is indeed to be pitied now. Compelled to stand aloof from the sweet-faced, kind-hearted, merry-minded sister of whom she is daily reminded ; with a gnawing sense of injury upon her with regard to her husband ; and cowed by the humiliating reflection that all the neighbourhood must scorn her for her cowardly disregard of the claims of her kith and kin, her reflections are in truth anything but enviable.

Over and over again she almost resolves to be brave and speak out boldly, but the resolve melts away at the first glance of Mr Vaughan's cool, constraining eyes. But though she does not speak out, she frets, and maintains long silences, which have a strong resemblance to sulky fits, and cries, and grows paler and thinner, and more languid and uninteresting altogether than is agreeable to her husband.

Meanwhile, Miss Damer and her charge have returned to Woodside, and Constance, whose heart is yearning for a sight even of the young Armingers, confines her rides and rambles entirely to her own grounds for many weeks, because she will not be tempted to break her promise.

The winter has passed away, and all the land is breaking out with gladness because the boyhood of the year has come.

To the young Armingers, whose lives have hitherto been passed in more or less crowded streets, the coming of spring this year has been a source of boundless joy. From the breaking forth of the first blades of corn in the fields, and the first snowdrops in the hedges, until now when all the banks about Clyst are thickly carpeted with primroses and violets, every day has brought them fresh revelations of the beauty and joyfulness there is in the earth.

Their little cottage home is more like a bower than ever now, for all the climbing plants and shrubs that cover it are in full leaf, and the pink monthly rose at the side of the sitting-room window is covered with flowers. The garden is a mass of colour and luxuriance. Beds of red, yellow, and white tulips and crocuses dot the grass plat, and the borders that run up by the side of the path from the gate to the door are bright with various coloured clumps of cyclamens, primulas, and ranunculuses. Inside the house the air is sweet with the perfume of hyacinths and narcissus.

And the social atmosphere which pervades this little home of taste is as sweet as the air the Armingers breathe. Always busy as the mother and her daughters are, their business hardly assumes the aspect of work in their eyes. If Maude has to labour hard all day at a "study from the round," which is entirely uninteresting by reason of its being a model of an apple or a melon that in its abnormal perfection is a possibility rather than a probability, in the evening she is requited by being allowed to paint some flower or richly-coloured bit of foliage, which Trixy has sought and found for her during the day ; and if Mrs Arminger does find painting lamp-shades perpetually a trifle monotonous, she is amply rewarded for persisting in the pursuit by the knowledge that she is bringing comfort in the present and prospective prosperity to her clever children.

It does occur to them each and all, individually and collectively, to wonder silently, and aloud very often, that they never see anything in these days of the frankly demonstrative little girl who rode into their lives like a princess in a fairy tale.

In vain Maude waits for the hot-house flowers and tropical foliage which Constance, on that eventful day, promised should be frequently forthcoming from the Woodside conservatories. Equally in vain does sanguine Trixy listen for the sound of Peppercorn's hoofs. The eyes of the one and the ears of the other are doomed to disappointment.

But their disappointment does not render them either distrustful or unjust. Whatever else it may be, they are certain of this at least, that it is neither Constance Fielding's fickleness nor fault which keeps her from them. There had been the genuine ring of true metal in her expressions of friendship and regard. The separation has been the work of others, not of her will or caprice. Of this they are sure as they are of their own straightforwardness and honesty.

Still it is hard never to see her except in church, where the extra light that shines in their respective eyes as they catch sight of one another is their sole means of communication.

One never-to-be-forgotten morning in May when the hawthorn is in full bloom, making all the hedgerows round Clyst sweet with its nutty fragrance, Constance breaks through her self-imposed rule, and rides away into the country, with the old groom as usual in close attendance on her.

Nothing has ever happened to the child in the nature of an accident, Peppercorn is such a staunch, thoroughly to be relied upon little fellow. It never enters into Miss Damer's wildest imaginings to be nervous about the little girl who has been perfectly at home in the saddle ever since she was four years old. So some hours passed away after Constance's departure this day, before Miss Damer experiences the slightest anxiety.

Meantime Constance, after having ridden straight away into the heart of the country for many miles, rejoicing in the unwonted sense of freedom, takes a road which brings her home through a large market-town.

It chances to be market-day, and the streets are unusually crowded. Mr Dalzel and his usher, Don Arminger, happening to come out of The Royal yard, where they may have left the carriage, just as Miss Fielding is passing, remark to one another that "it's hardly the day for that child to be here." Then Mr Dalzel goes on rapidly about the business which has brought him here, and Don lingers in the market-place to look at the old cross in the centre of it, and—a little—to watch the busy crowd.

Presently he hears a rush, a roar, and a horrified shout rises up from the mass of people assembled. A huge infuriated bull comes bounding and bellowing down the street in the wake of Constance and her groom. He charges the latter, and the snorting, frightened horse is knocked down as if he had been a thing of straw, while his luckless rider is sent right through a shop window. For a moment the bull stands stamping with wrathful satisfaction, then he lashes his tail, and hurls himself along after Peppercorn.

All in a moment Don finds himself tearing the child who is realising her danger out of the saddle, and has handed her back into safety before the bull discovers that part of his prey has escaped him. Then the bull knows that he has been baulked, and leaving bleeding, mangled, dying Peppercorn, he turns on Don.

It is only one blow, and one stamp, that he has time to give before ropes are over his own wicked head, and he is dragged away. But Don lies perfectly senseless on the pavement, and the little girl whom he has saved kneels tearless and white by his side.

"I know him," she says, when some passing lady stoops down and tries to persuade the well-known little heiress to "come away," "and I know his mother and sisters, and this will kill them, and they're worth a thousand of me."

She stands up and gives directions presently quite quietly and calmly, and so clearly, that when Mr Dalzel arrives at the scene of action, he finds he has nothing to do, save to see these directions carried out.

The poor old groom is hurt a good deal, but he is able to tell where he is hurt, and how much. But for a long time the doctors can make nothing of poor Don Arminger, who is evidently hurt a good deal also, but cannot tell where, or how much, by reason of being speechless and unconscious.

It is a very sorrowful journey back for Constance. She goes in Mr Dalzel's carriage, and opposite to her, propped up by cushions, is the young man who has risked his life and nearly lost it in the endeavour to save hers. The tears dim her eyes whenever she looks, and her heart aches with pity for his mother and sisters.

"How shall I look them in the face?" she asks, clinging to Mr Dalzel's arm. And he tells her to have no fear of their judgment or feelings.

"Mrs Arminger is like poor Don," he tells her, "brave, generous, and gentle-hearted."

"But I'm not worth that," she says, passionately, pointing with her trembling little hand to poor, shattered Don.

When they get into Clyst, Mr Dalzel gets out, leaving Constance in charge of Don, who is regaining his senses a little, and goes on himself to perform that which is perhaps the saddest task that man or woman can be called upon to perform—namely, to tell a mother a child whom she idolises has been struck down. And while he is absent, and Constance with her heart in her eyes is bending forward, tenderly bathing Don's white, pain-lined face with a refreshing, soothing lotion, fantastic fate wills it that Mr and Mrs Vaughan, and their four children, shall pass by.

Without ever having been told to do so, Donald Vaughan has come to take it for granted that little Connie Fielding is more his property than she is anybody else's. The sentiment of love has not informed his young heart as yet. But the sentiment of jealous intolerance of any interference with his pony, dog, fishing-rod, ferret, gun, or friends, has.

Therefore, now when he sees "little Connie," the one

whom he always elects to favour with his constant notice when they are together at juvenile parties, familiarly and rather fondly bathing the forehead of the youth whom he has already learnt to dislike and despise in the double character of his own cousin and Mr Dalzel's usher, Donald Vaughan is enraged.

"Make Constance get out of that!" he says, imperiously, to his mother, but at the same moment Constance sees them, and forgetting their hostility to her hero in her impatience to proclaim him one, she springs from the carriage, runs up to them impulsively, crying out,—-

"He has saved my life from a mad bull, and Peppercorn, poor darling, is killed; and isn't Don brave, Mrs Vaughan? You must be proud of him now!"

Mr Dalzel's timely return averts the necessity of Mrs Vaughan's replying directly to this appeal. But she sheds a few tears which win her partial pardon from Constance, and then at a signal from her husband she tries to detain the child, who is evidently longing to run off to the Armingers' cottage.

"Stay with us, dear," Mrs Vaughan says, softly. "You may be in the way if you go to their house now; if the poor fellow is much hurt, his mother will not want any strangers there; we will take you home."

"Not till I've been to tell his mother that I'll love him all my life for what he has done; but that I would rather have been killed myself than that he should have been hurt," Constance says, impetuously.

Then, to their horror and disgust, she runs—absolutely runs up the street, and is rewarded by a sight of Don, looking more himself again, and by the sound of his voice telling her that he is not so much injured after all.

She is soon captured by the Vaughans, who send for her peremptorily, and taken home with an air of ownership in her, that irritates her for the first time.

"Bulls are nasty things," Mr Vaughan says; "but all that is wanted to tackle them is common-sense and caution. The young fellow wanted to do something melodramatic and sensational, and create a fictitious interest about himself. Dalzel is unwarrantably indiscreet in taking his usher about with him as he does!"

Constance is only a child, and her logical and argumentative powers are as yet undeveloped. But she has strong intuitions and strong courage, and she says now—though Mr Vaughan is a power in her eyes,—

"If you like me, as you all say you do, you must be glad that Mr Dalzel was indiscreet enough to take Don to-day."

Mr Vaughan winces as she uses the familiar abbreviation of his nephew's name, and his son, proud young Donald, flushes angrily.

"We will recompense the young man for what he has done, neighbour Constance," Mr Vaughan says, trying to assume an air of amusement. "He shall not be the loser for having behaved well."

And Donald gets near to his little friend's side, and looks pityingly in her perplexed face, as he whispers,—

"I would have done just the same as he did, Connie, for you; you know that, don't you? It was nothing, after all, for you! Why, I go into the field often where father's Ben Brace, his big white bull is, you know, and I just walk past him without caring a bit, with my stick in my hand; he stamps at me sometimes, but that's nothing; I've my stick in my hand, and I don't care; he doesn't come at me."

"But the bull in the market-place did come at Don," Constance says, reflectively.

CHAPTER V.

COMMON HUMANITY.

It is terrible, but true! That thoughtless, unwieldy, blundering bull has upset matters of far greater moment, in the eyes of Mr Vaughan and Miss Damer, than a mere groom and an insignificant usher.

The bull has, in fact, upset the plans of Mr Vaughan and Miss Damer, by goading Constance, as it were, to insist upon recognising the existence of those exceedingly inopportune people—the Armingers.

Greatly to Mrs Vaughan's jealous chagrin, the strictly private conferences between her husband and Miss Damer become more frequent than ever after the incident of the bull. For Constance is "proving contumacious," Miss Damer declares, and Mr Vaughan's powers of management are being oftener than ever called into requisition for the purpose of subjugating the heiress of Woodside.

Poor little Constance's contumacity after all does not amount to more than this, that she will go daily, laden with fruit and flowers, to inquire for Don Arminger. She does not see the dangerous youth, for, as a fitting punishment for his audacity in having presumed to approach her at all at the peril of his own life, the poor lad is still helpless and suffering in bed. But she sees his mother and sisters, and all her little heart goes out to them in a way Mrs Arminger cannot withstand.

On one solemn occasion, the day after the accident, Miss Damer accompanies her niece, for, as she assures Mr Vaughan, she looks upon the doing so as a duty, which she might perform without compromising herself to the lowest in the land.

" Common humanity takes me there and will carry me through the painful ordeal of an interview with his mother, who will probably think that we are under such an obligation to her son as will justify anything !" Miss Damer says to Mr Vaughan, and the latter knows that his sympathetic friend is hurling a veiled reproach at his wife for having such unseemly relations.

"I think it would be wiser on your part to stay away," he says. "I have done all that is necessary on the part of Constance's friends. I have sent a note down, saying that I will be responsible for a medical attendant and a nurse, in case the young man requires either; you may conscientiously wash your hands of the business."

Mr Vaughan omits to say that his note has been acknowledged by one from Mrs Arminger, declining with courtesy his offers of assistance.

"I think I must go; people in the place will think I ought to go," Miss Damer, says deprecatingly. "You see, objectionable as these people are, they still are Mrs Vaughan's relations."

Mr Vaughan bites his lip and says nothing. Mrs Vaughan is becoming a thorn in his flesh by reason of this sister of hers.

"Besides, it will be perhaps as well that I should see them in their home once, in order to be the better able to point out to Connie the absence of all those refinements and elegances in their lives which are of course lacking. The child sees them at their best in church and going to school. Depend upon it, I shall do more good than harm by going."

Accordingly her esteemed adviser gives her leave to go, and Miss Damer wishes he had withheld it when she finds herself in Mrs Arminger's presence.

For Mrs Arminger's graceful, womanly, honourable pride overtops Miss Damer's miserable, pompous sense of self-importance, and Mrs Arminger's exquisitely arranged little home makes up in refinement and beauty for all it lacks in grandeur and magnificence. It is impossible to patronise "these people," Miss Damer discovers in a moment. So she tries to be haughtily distant, and merely succeeds in being rude.

"Your boy behaved very well indeed, I am sure," she says, watching Constance's manifestations of tenderness towards Mrs Arminger meanwhile with angry eyes. "Anything he may require in the way of wine or fruit shall be sent down from Woodside, and soups and jellies shall be made for him in our kitchen."

Constance's face flames with fierce, righteous wrath as her aunt speaks. But Mrs Arminger puts the rudeness aside as a queen might pass over the insolent observation of a beggar.

"It is my prerogative to make the soups and jellies, and to minister to my son in every way; but in rejecting your offer, let me thank you for all that is kind and liberal in it."

Miss Damer does not stay long after this rejoinder, but she strives to revenge herself for the smart it causes her, by making little thrusts and stabs presently at inoffensive Mrs Vaughan.

" I went to see that young man's mother, in the kindest and most considerate spirit," she says to the Vaughans, with whom she is dining this night, "and, if you can be-believe it, she met my offers of assistance with positive rudeness. It is evident that they will take no small recompense, but will ask for a colossal one by-and-by."

" My sister is incapable of such meanness," Mrs Vaughan says, plucking up a little spirit for a moment; but she is cowed at once by a reproachful look from her husband—a look which glances off her towards the chil-dren, who have come in to dessert.

" Annabel, pray remember; pray restrain yourself," he mutters, and Mrs Vaughan has not the heart to rise up and do battle for her own in the presence of the woman whom she regards as her rival.

But though she has not the courage to do battle for them against her husband, she has at last the courage to look her sins of neglect steadily in the face.

And she goes to bed with part of the burden which she has been bearing lately lifted from her, for, come what will, she will go to her sister in the morning, and hear and speak words of ancient kindness.

She can hardly believe that she is herself as she walks unflinchingly through the village, and stops at her sister's. She is careless as to who may see her, indifferent as to what any one may think and surmise about her now. For at last she feels she is doing right, and the rest may take care of itself.

The meeting between these two women in whose veins the same blood flows, and whose fortunes are so widely different, is fraught with more pain to the wealthy sister than to the poor one. For the heart of the latter is too full of rejoicing at the thought of the probable restoration of her son, to hold anything but gratitude and gladness.

"You can never forgive me, Lily. I can never forgive myself, for the way I have been made to treat you," Mrs Vaughan weeps, and her sister soothes her very sweetly, saying,—

"The desire to be a stranger to me—to me and mine —was not natural to you, Annabel; believe me, I understand what your difficulties have been, and though I've often felt sorry for you, I've never felt angry with you."

"People who only see the outside of things can't imagine what I have to contend with in Mr Vaughan," poor, crushed Mrs Vaughan goes on complainingly. She has burst her bonds, and made a confidante at last. But she is frightened at her own temerity, even while she speaks, and finds a pitiful pleasure in so speaking. "Every one far and near respects him, and has a good word for him, but no one thinks how hard he can be in his quiet, good way. There are times, Lily, when I can't bring myself to ask him to let me have a five-pound note, though he got a fine fortune with me. He chills me till I tremble like a culprit before him. He makes me feel I've been doing wrong when I haven't thought, much less done, anything that can be found fault with in reason. For all my riches, I'm not such a happy woman as you are, my dear; and you must be forbearing with me."

In reply to this long but thoroughly sincere plaint, Mrs Arminger says,—

"Will you come and see my son? Don will teach you better than I can how to endure."

But Mrs Vaughan shrinks from the meeting with her nephew in her newly-recognised capacity as aunt.

"I have had a terrible time of trouble and fainting of spirit," she tells her sister, "and I feel as if a touch more kindness from one of you would break me down to-day; but there are many other days and years before us, Lily, during which we and our children will learn to love and know each other better, and vanquish the oppressor, my dear—vanquish the oppressor!"

She is overwrought, there is no doubt about it. This struggle which she has made in the cause of kith and kin against her cold, unexceptionably-conducted husband's un-written fiat has exhausted her.

Maude and Trixy, her nieces, stand about her, and vainly proffer their childish, affectionate assistance as she rises and staggers, and then gropes her way hopelessly about seeking for the door, which she reaches in a faint-ing fit.

She has a vague idea that she has transgressed in some way or other presently when she recovers, for she mur-murs,—

"Don't tell Mr Vaughan, he will be so ang—sorry, that he mustn't know Tell my children—tell Donald—" She never finishes her sentence, for Mr Vaughan, called hither by an affrighted cry which has arisen through the village, walks in with his habitual air of command, and, waving aside all intervention and intercession, addresses her,—

"My dear, I have come to take you away from scenes and persons who have distressed and harassed you. Our good friend, Miss Damer—"

He is interrupted by a piercing cry from his wife.

"Not that woman, when I am dying! Let my chil-dren, my little children come to me; not that woman, who is no friend, no comfort, no help!"

"Dying! Nonsense," Mr Vaughan says, uneasily, but he loses a little of his self-sustaining power, and looks round for some one to aid him.

Little Maude answers to his unuttered appeal for help.

"My aunt is very ill, sir," she says, standing erect and unabashed before him in the royal, simple strength of her youth and graceful beauty. "Speak to her as if you feel it, and send for my cousins."

He finds himself constrained to do as his little unknown niece directs.

"His wife is very ill. Poor Annabel! He remembers all her good qualities and income in a flash. Her money is settled solely on himself.

"Thank heaven for that! it shows there is both trustfulness and gratitude in her nature," he thinks.

"You will come home with me? I have sent for the carriage," he whispers.

"Let me stay here with my own sister," she replies. "Send my children to me, and let me stay here."

"Her mind is wandering," he says, explaining the state of the case loftily to the cool-mannered lady who stands by so regardless of him, so full of solicitude and sisterly affection for his wife. "Her mind is wandering."

Mrs Arminger has no answer for him. She knows her sister's mind is home at last, and she almost pities the man who is so far away from all that is nearest and dearest to Annabel now.

For when her children come, they, in their affrightedness, turn from their father, who seems ashamed to feel for them, to the genial, graceful aunt, who sorrows and sympathises with them about their mother's illness in a way that makes these children cling to their mother the closer, instead of shrinking from her as from one who more than half belongs to another world already.

The poor mistress of Strathlands is taken home by-and-by at a foot-pace, for her breath is weak and laboured, and the least jerk may stop it.

Mr Vaughan sits dutifully by her side as she is driven home, and refrains, in a manner that appears most considerate and unselfish, from taxing her failing strength by addressing her. But she knows, poor woman, that he is nourishing anger against her, and in her heart she condemns him for a worse sin against herself than one of mere neglectfulness.

"He is tired of me; he is wishing to be rid of me, that he may instal that woman, who has a rich relation, in my place," she thinks bitterly, and in her overtried heart she goes on to accuse him of sins and offences of which he has never been guilty.

"He holds up me and mine to her scorn and derision; he claims her sympathy for having such a weak and useless wife. He will give her the power to teach my children to despise my memory ; he will cease to remember that he owes anything to me ; he will forget to teach my children to call me mother."

So she rambles on for many and many a weary week, suffering, failing, wearing away, clinging to the sister who is unceasing in her attendance and devotion, recoiling reluctantly from the husband who, in the eyes of all Clyst, has led such a blameless course towards her.

It is hard on Mr Vaughan that he should owe aught on account of his wife to this sister of hers whom he has so persistently set aside and snubbed ; but he cannot help himself. Mrs Arminger does not offer her presence at Strathlands, but his wife wails for her, and he is compelled to send for her. So, daily and hourly, the neglected sister waits upon the sick and dying one, and the husband of the sick and dying woman seeks solace for the ignominy of being beholden to her sister for anything in taking afternoon tea and counsel with Miss Damer.

"If I could only feel that this most disastrous intimacy would end with poor Annabel's life I should be happy— that is to say, I should be comparatively happy," he says, pathetically, to Miss Damer, and she shakes her virgin ringlets at him, and replies,—

"If poor Mrs Vaughan only realised the mischief she is doing, she would exert herself to nip it in the bud at once. It is her misfortune that Mrs Arminger should be her sister. It will be her fault if Mrs Arminger is permitted to traffic on the relationship."

"My poor wife is so weak—in health," Mr Vaughan says, and Miss Damer sighs.

"Yes, she is weak indeed—in health."

.   .   .   .

"Don Arminger is better, and able to resume his duties."

The vicar, Mr Dalzel, delivers himself of this sentence in a sonorous voice that seems to ring not only through the school, but through the village. He is himself so unfeignedly glad of his handsome, clever young usher's convalescence that he takes it for granted that all around must share in his gladness. He really expects an ovation for the young fellow who is a hero in his kind eyes, and it more than staggers him when Mr Vaughan bears down upon him in his balmiest and most superior mood, saying,—

"Get this young Arminger the best post you can, away from Clyst, Dalzel. My poor wife's health is too delicate for her to be subjected to the worry and annoyance which the presence in the place of the hero of this melodramatic event will surely occasion. Get the young fellow a post away; my influence and recommendation are at his service."

"Shall I tell you that your offer is *noble?*" Mr Dalzel says, looking him fixedly in the face, "or shall I speak the simple truth, without a word of comment? I'll take the latter course, and tell you that I am justified in refusing your influence and recommendation on behalf of your nephew. Better things are in store for him than either you or I can aid him in attaining."

"I merely made the offer in a conventional way, feeling that I ought to reward him for anything he may have suffered in that affair with the bull," Mr Vaughan says, stiffly.

"Oh, he's getting over that affair capitally," Mr Dalzel laughs. "Don't you distress yourself about any of your undone duties to young Don Arminger, as far as he's concerned; but, take my advice, and let things take their reasonable, commonly human course from this time forth; the lad's of kin to you, and you'll have to be proud of him yet; stretch out the hand of kindness to him and his now—and he'll never forget it."

"My poor wife's state of health forbids my entering upon any discussion of this nature," Mr Vaughan says, with such mournful loftiness that Mr Dalzel feels afraid that he may have been uncharitable and unchristian in preaching peace and goodwill thus inopportunely. "These unfortunate Armingers have been the real source of all the trouble which has come into my family circle lately, and I regret to say the trouble has not been confined to

my house alone. Miss Damer is a fellow sufferer. Little
Constance Fielding is infatuated with these people."

"Brava! little Con!" the vicar cries enthusiastically,
for he is fond of the little heiress, without having any
ulterior views regarding her, and he loves to hear of her
exhibiting right feeling in any direction.

CHAPTER VI.

"IT'S A WRENCH, DON."

THE Strathlands household is a very disorganised, excited,
and uncomfortable one during these spring and early
summer months. Every member of it, from the housekeeper to the crudely formed and minded but withal
kind hearted young person "who does the clouts and
dishes," as she calls the scullery work, knows that the
mistress of the mansion is stricken down and will not in
all human probability ever rise up again. She is waning,
in fact, and another is waxing. But it is hard for de-
pendents to kick off fidelity at the right moment, and so
some show a lagging love for poor Annabel still, and others
undue impatience at the prolongation of her reign.

Her children are not impatient in this time-serving
spirit. But they are not inclined to put any manner of
curb upon themselves, when they see Miss Damer coming
in and ordering things in the same not-to-be-questioned
way in which she orders things at Woodside. She even
attempts to regulate the quantity of beef which has to be
daily boiled down for Mrs Vaughan's tea. And she
scrutinises the housekeeper's weekly account in a way
that makes that worthy vow that she will never render
another to her master.

Through all this sea of disaffection Mrs Arminger has
a troublesome course to steer; love and duty hold her
close by her dying sister's side, while inclination and

taste would carry her far away from the covert incivilities to which she is subjected.

Mrs Vaughan's assurance to the sister who has been so long and coldly neglected that she "is her only comfort now," is not a mere empty one. It is painfully true. For her husband, though he pays frequent visits to her room, is constrained and out of place in it, and is evidently relieved and able to breathe more freely when the moment comes at which he can decently retire. And her motherly heart aches with the keenest anguish when she sees her children and remembers how soon she may be called upon to leave them.

Will they forget her? Will they bury her memory, and turn as gladly to another mother as she feels sure her husband will to another wife? These are questions which she is perpetually asking Mrs Arminger; and Mrs Arminger, eloquent with pity, says all she can to prove how utterly impossible it is for the young Vaughans ever to love their mother less, or to let her memory pass away from them.

It is hard on the industrious little lady to be away from her own children and occupation for such a length of time, and it is harder still to be under the roof of one who detests her as she knows her brother-in-law does. But she bears the hardship of it bravely, for the sake of the poor sister whose "only comfort" she is.

It is a trite but true saying that much comedy and more that is commonplace is mingled with the majority of tragedy in real life.

Even this solemn chamber of death is not free from it. The housekeeper comes in with murmurs against the interference of some one whom she does not distinctly designate, but who is, Mrs Arminger infers none other than Miss Damer.

"Old maids should stay at home and mind their own business, and not come messing and muddling about in gentlemen's houses when their wives are ill in bed," the first lieutenant of Strathlands says sometimes to Mrs Arminger, in one of those whispers which are so constantly employed in sick-rooms in order to make the words uttered be heard in every corner. At this Mrs Vaughan moans and turns restlessly, and asks pettishly,—

"Is Miss Damer here again, Page?"

"Yes, ma'am; she's constant in her inquiries for you; never misses a day."

Page has no desire to hurt the mistress to whom she is really attached, but she cannot resist telling Mrs Vaughan what she knows well it will give Mrs Vaughan heart-sickness to hear.

"Such goings on sha'n't be in any house where I am, without the mistress knowing of it," she tells herself.

Not that she could define even to herself what the objectionable goings on are. She only knows that Mr Vaughan alters the order of things at Miss Damer's bidding, and that Miss Damer has the name in the neighbourhood of being a fussy and stingy housekeeper.

"Coming here with her cheese-paring ways, telling master there's twice too much beef used for poor missus's soup," the cook says, indignantly, to her fellows, when Page has conveyed her master's dictum as to the quantity of meat henceforth to be used to the incensed queen of the kitchen.

"Actually telling master yesterday, when she didn't know I'd just come into the room, that unless he had a check-book against me, he'd never know how the wine went," the outraged butler says to Mrs Page, when they are supping comfortably, winding up their repast unostentatiously with a bit of excellent Stilton and a glass of something very choice.

"It's my opinion she'd burn farthing dips," the house-maid says to the cook. "The master complained to-day there was twice too many lamps lighted every night, and it's not him to be mean, unless he's brought to it by her."

"My belief is she'd have the stones in the courtyard and the vegetables we give to the pigs boiled down for poor missus rather than master should buy a bit more meat than she thinks proper; and who's she, I'd like to know, to do it; she'd be nothing if it wasn't for little Miss Fielding."

"And she'll be nothing when little Miss Fielding grows up and marries," the footman chimes in oracularly.

"Ah, no such luck ? Long before that day she'll have stepped into poor missus's shoes, and then no more Strathlands for me," the housemaid replies.

"Not she," the footman says, scornfully ; "she'll never catch him at that game ; why, she's no figure to look at, and she's getting up in years, and she's no money."

"But she've got Miss Fielding," the housemaid cries, triumphantly ; "and if she was a 'ag or a witch, master would marry her to get Miss Fielding for Master Donald by-and-by."

So the motives of the exalted Mr Vaughan and his irreproachable friend are discussed in that universal parliament—the kitchen.

Meanwhile Constance, who is essentially human, finds considerable solace for the honest sorrow she feels about Mrs Vaughan's illness, in the frequent and prolonged absences of her maiden-aunt guardian.

For during these absences she has the joy of receiving her little friends, Maude and Trixy Arminger, in her own house, where they frequently play at giving dinners and receptions, in the smallest and least pretentious room in the house.

But on other occasions she feels proud to take Maude through the picture gallery, where generations of brave and fair Fieldings look down with various expressions on the little artist-child who appreciates any beauty they may have so keenly.

They make a fair group, these three children, standing in the rich light which is streaming through a grandly-painted oriel window at the one end of the gallery, one June afternoon.

Constance—the little mistress of all they survey—with her beauty set off pleasantly by a fashionably-made dress of simple material, and her golden hair neatly braided back, and tied by a ribbon of the same colour, is a type of carefully pinned and trimmed true aristocratic modern beauty ; while Maude and Trixy, with their long hair across their foreheads, and their supple little figures dressed in round-bodied frocks with puffed sleeves and deep falling collars of lace, look like "little Stuart Princes," Constance is just saying, when a shout of joy from Trixy makes them all look out of the window, when they see with astonishment Don making rapid progress up the avenue to the house.

"Something must be the matter," Maude says, for though they often come to Woodside now (Miss Damer having her own reasons for keeping Mr Vaughan anxious) their brother has never been to this enchanted hall which holds his princess yet. "I will go and meet him; you stay with Constance, Trixy."

They watch her as she runs along and meets her brother, and turns, clinging to his arm.

Then Constance turns away, and with a tone of pain in her voice says,—

"It's a little hard to see you with your brother sometimes. All mine died."

"Take him for yours too," Trixy says, with prompt generosity. "He'll always feel like a brother to you since the bull, you know."

"Isn't Maude pretty?" Constance says, abruptly turning the conversation.

"Well, not so much 'pretty' as like a pretty picture," Trixy says, critically. "She was lovely, but now her face is only graceful-looking. Her pictures ought to be nice by-and-by, oughtn't they, if she can make them anything like herself?"

"Oh! she'll be a swell in painting," Constance says, seriously.

"And then she'll be grand, and every one will want to know her. I shouldn't wonder if the Queen wants to know her then," Trixy says, with calm conviction.

"I wonder if she'll care to know me then?" says the little heiress of Woodside.

At which remark Trixy comes down from the sphere of exalted anticipations in which she has been dwelling for a few moments, and with many a hug and kiss assures

Constance that she will always "be more than the Queen
to them and Don."

Don comes in presently, and explains to them briefly
why he has broken the unwritten law which has excluded
him from Woodside.

He has come to say good-bye to his sisters. He is "off
within the hour," he tells them gleefully. A great piece
of good fortune has befallen him. By the death of a
cousin of a lad called Divett (one of Mr Dalzel's pupils),
the father of the lad has become the Earl of Timerton,
and Divett himself has merged into Lord Sylvertre. His
father, hitherto a poor major in the line, has now consented to gratify his son's yearning for travel, and Don
Arminger has been chosen to be his tutor and companion.

"We are going to Mexico first, to the land where
Montezuma reigned magnificently, and was magnificently
conquered by Cortes. Maude, my darling, I wish I
could take you with me. Mexico would put colour into
your soul. Trixy, I'll send you a set of gold ornaments
and feather trimmings that will make you like a gorgeous
foreign bird."

"And gather every kind of flower you see, and press,
and send home," Maude cries.

"And catch all the humming-birds and butterflies and
parrots and send home," says Trixy.

Only Constance is silent. He is going away, and he
is full of pleasure at the prospect, and she is not his
sister, and must not expect him to care for her, or to
think of her.

But Don is a gentleman, and does not forget her for
more than the first five minutes of jubilee with his sisters.
Recollecting her, he says at once,—

"Give me a commission, Miss Fielding. What shall
I bring to you when I come back from Mexico?"

If he brings himself safely back that will be enough
for Constance, but she will not allow herself to tell him
so. Her little girl dignity is as true and sensitive as if
she had already crossed the brook where womanhood and
childhood meet.

"Bring me a tiny little model of a Mexican bull," she says.

"What! in memory of our little adventure?" he asks, with a gay laugh, that makes Constance draw her golden-haired head up an inch higher as she answers,—

"No; but because Mexican bulls are handsome, and I want a model of one."

He must go now, he must be off at once. They have been all smiles and brightness till this the supreme moment of parting. Maude sobs quietly and convulsively. Trixy cries aloud, and feels it in her heart to "punch Constance" for being so quiet. Don himself has to get over this part of the business very quickly, or his newly-acquired manhood would desert him.

He is gone!

"You're unfeeling not to kiss him when he went, and he saved your life and all," Trixy storms out reproachfully to Constance, and the latter takes the reproof mildly, and kisses Trixy instead.

The same night, just after the tidings of Don's departure having reached Strathlands, Mrs Vaughan is declared by her medical attendants to be "so much worse that Mr Vaughan will need all his powers of endurance and resignation."

To do him grudging justice, Mr Vaughan does endure the thought, and does resign himself to the probable loss of his wife, with cheerful obedience, not to say alacrity.

His wife is going from him for all time, at last! But it is much more important to him that Don Arminger is going from Clyst for a term of years!

For Mr Vaughan, in spite of his hard, selfish crust of habit, has that within him which teaches him to feel that little Constance Fielding has elevated his scorned and neglected poor nephew to a place in her regard which his son, the heir of Strathlands, will never attain.

"So, the lad is best out of the way," he says; "the lad is best out of the way."

It wounds and surprises him when his own sons, Donald and Reginald, for whom he is striving and scheming, lament their young cousin's departure, and admit that they have sought every opportunity of cultivating his acquaintance since that adventure with the bull.

The proud man owns with secret pain that he is being set at nought by fate and his own family. Still he will not abate one jot or tittle of his pride and pretension. For he knows that he holds a strong card in his hand in the blind devotion and allegiance of the exemplary lady who is the aunt of little Connie Fielding—the guardian of the heiress of Woodside.

The parting between Don Arminger and his mother is a bright and characteristic one. She comes down from her sister's sick-room in a softly-falling, noiseless garment of peacock-blue flannel, looking so sweet that he tells her he longs to be ill to be nursed by her.

Then while the smile called forth by the compliment is lingering in her eyes and on her lips, he changes her aspect by telling her he is going.

She will not chill his light-heartedness at the outset of his career by one doleful look or word. Her face is full of hope and promise, and her son nearly worships her for that self-control which enables him to bear himself as a man should.

"It's a wrench, Don," is the only pathetic sentence she permits herself to utter, and she qualifies the pathos instantly by adding—" How you will have altered for the better before I see you again, and how Maude and Trixy will have grown! I almost wish the three years of your absence over; your children will be so much nicer for each other when you're older; only I cannot quite do it, you see, for you'll have such a splendid time in that gorgeous land."

" Let them alter, but you be just the same when I come back," he says, and then he asks for his aunt.

" Dying, Don, dying fast, and their father has not taught her children what her death means."

" We learnt that of ourselves about you," he says, clasping her fast; then it is a wrench—he kisses his mother, and is gone.

CHAPTER VIL

GROWN UP.

EIGHT years have passed away since Mrs Vaughan died, and Don Arminger departed from Clyst. And still in many ways Clyst remains unaltered, though Mr Vaughan has married again, and Don Arminger has made a name for himself.

A name in which his mother revels, not so much because it gives him fortune, as because his fame justifies her maternal judgment. She has not lovingly overrated the great abilities of her boy. Her boy in every respect justifies her pride in him.

He is well and widely known as a traveller and a writer. For a time after leaving Clyst with Lord Sylvertre, Don Arminger determined to devote himself entirely to tutorship. But after the publication of his first book of travels, authorship became his only vocation.

He has not established himself in a home of his own yet. His periods of sojourn in England are at long intervals and of brief duration, and he divides his time pretty equally between his mother's house at Clyst, and any residence of Lord Tiverton's at which Lord Sylvertre happens to be staying at the time.

The friendship which commenced between the boy and the young usher at Mr Dalzel's school is unbroken still, and there is no guest more welcome to the whole of Sylvertre's family than handsome, clever, famous Don Arminger.

His mother's house at Clyst is a very different one to the pretty little cottage in which Constance Fielding first made the Armingers' acquaintance. They have a beautiful home now, standing in the middle of a quaint old garden, with a terrace and a sun-dial, and long alleys bordered in the summer by sunflowers and tall white lilies, and holyhocks interspersed with sweet-williams, and mignonette, gillyflowers, and rose-bushes bearing roses of every shade of colour, all growing in wild, old-fashioned luxuriance.

The Grange, as Mrs Arminger's house is called, is just such a home as it is well for an artist to dwell in. Maude revels in it, and in its quaint, time-honoured beauty.

The two girls and their mother have been quite in unison as to the furnishing of it, and the result is that every room makes a picture from every point of view.

Maude has been no less industrious than her brilliant brother during these eight years. No less industrious, and little less successful. A pupil at the Slade schools, she has had the advantages of the best teaching, the most careful supervision, and the most valuable suggestions from the various accomplished visiting academicians.

And she has profited by these advantages, and after years of incessant work and study, she has realised her early dream, and has painted a picture which has been accepted by the Hanging Committee of the Royal Academy. It is a powerful picture for a girl to have painted, and on this score of power it may fairly lay claim to attention, independently of its clever drawing and finished, careful, and conscientious painting.

Oxen are still employed in ploughing about Clyst, and Maude has made a grand pair yoked to the plough the subject of her picture. Boldly and skilfully she has delineated the rich, brown soil, which seems to be falling away as the ploughshare parts it. Cleverly and vividly has she portrayed the stolid countenance and the slouching gait of the ploughman. But the triumph of the painting, its highest merit, is to be found in the magnificent modelling of the oxen.

It is late April now, and the whole Arminger family are preparing to go up to town to be present at the opening of the Royal Academy. Maude and Trixy are full of girlish excitement about dresses and bonnets, and other weapons of feminine destruction, for Don is to meet them in town, and they have already received invitations to a grand ball to be given by Lady Tiverton, and to a series of "at homes" which she also purposes having.

They have fulfilled the promise of their childhood physically as well as mentally. Two pretty or more graceful girls it would be hard to find than Maude and Trixy Arminger.

Maude is distinguished by a sweet, serious grace of face and manner, and Trixy by a brilliant vivacity that is always refined. Endowed with slender, well-set-up figures, and perfect hands and feet, always well dressed, and thoroughly well-bred in their unconscious calm self-possession under all circumstances, it is no wonder that the "pretty Miss Armingers" should be much in the minds of all the young men who have the fortune ever to see them. In no one's mind more than in Donald Vaughan's, rather to his own despair and intensely to his father's disgust.

The relations between the two families have not altered in the least, bitterly to Donald's chagrin, for Maude's graceful beauty has won all his heart, and, well satisfied as he is with himself ordinarily, he is hopeless of ever winning hers in return.

Moreover, the scheme of marrying him to Constance Fielding is still cherished by Mr Vaughan, who is meeting now with opposition to it from a quarter where opposition seemed least to be expected.

As had been surmised by all when the first Mrs Vaughan died, the lady who was Miss Damer now reigns in her stead.

During Mr Vaughan's period of decent mourning, Miss Damer's demeanour had been discreet to a degree. She showed just the right amount of sympathy. She ceased to visit Strathlands. She always appeared pleased, almost honoured, when he came to see her at Woodside. And above all, she was ardent and unceasing in her protestations as to the intensity of her desire to see her niece eventually become Donald Vaughan's wife.

But when a full year had elapsed, and still Mr Vaughan made no sign of wishing to make her the legal partner of his joys and expenses, Miss Damer changed her tactics.

She assumed a reserved demeanour that spoke more of sorrow than anger, and threw out dark hints as to the probability of her finding it necessary, for the preservation of her health and peace of mind, that she should leave Woodside, taking Constance with her. She threw out even darker hints respecting the absolute ascendency which she had over her young charge's mind, and gave Mr Vaughan to understand that, if present circumstances continued, she should not throw her influence into the scale in which Donald's merits and claims to her niece's hand and fortune were being weighed.

On this hint Mr Vaughan spoke. He liked Miss Damer as a friend and as the patient recipient of all his plans and perplexities. He had a certain sort of esteem for her, founded, not on appreciation of any good qualities of which she might be possessed, but on the belief that she looked up to him as a superior being, and stood in admiring awe of him. But of either admiration or love for her he had not a particle.

Nevertheless, as his wife she would, he felt sure, be of service to the cause which was nearest to his heart— namely, his son's marriage with Constance Fielding. So at least he believed, for, acute as he was about most matters, he was entirely credulous in this. He really believed Miss Damer when she, weak sister that she was, told him that she had unlimited control over the mind of her clever, high-spirited niece.

Confiding in this statement, he asked Miss Damer to be his wife. And when we resume acquaintance with Clyst and its inhabitants she had been his wife for nearly eight years.

Mr Vaughan has had many a bitter disappointment in his married life with her, but none so bitter as this—that she has grown lax in her desire to see her niece married to his son.

In many ways, indeed, Mrs Vaughan differs from Miss Damer. Miss Damer had been humble though interfering; Mrs Vaughan's hauteur becomes a proverb. Miss Damer had been diffident; Mrs Vaughan allows no judgment but her own to be exercised in the management of things at Strathlands. Miss Damer had seemed to adore him—to esteem him and bow down to his opinions; Mrs Vaughan does neither the one nor the other, but pursues her own course without consulting him in the slightest degree.

She is not a sensitive woman, therefore the airs of displeased reserve which broke down the spirit of his first wife are utterly thrown away upon his second. Nor is she a grateful woman, for undoubtedly she has much to thank him for, since she is of far higher account as the mistress of Strathlands than she was as the merely temporary ruler at Woodside. But she is not a grateful woman, and will not recognise this fact.

She is, now that a sense of power and security develops her real nature, merely a selfish, mean-spirited, overbearing, stolid-minded woman, who cannot take a broad or enlightened view of anything on earth.

If the world had been searched, a more inefficient guardian and directress could not have been found for Constance Fielding, who realises this fact as she grows up, and takes the guidance and direction of herself pretty much into her own hands.

On the marriage with Mr Vaughan, the establishment at Woodside was broken up, and Mrs Vaughan's frugal spirit led her to advertise it as "to let." But Constance, when she heard of this, asserted herself indignantly and decisively. The rooms in which her mother had lived and been happy, the furniture that was sanctified to the child by the thought that her mother had looked upon it and touched it, and perhaps loved it, should never be desecrated by the presence of strangers who might conceive they had the right to treat it carelessly because they paid for it. So Mrs Vaughan, who had intended the rent—"the trifle the place might let for," she termed it—for her own pocket, had to forego her plan, and submit to Constance's decree.

"I shall have to live at Strathlands, but I'll keep my right to go to Woodside every day, and to take any one I like there," Constance says to her friends the Armingers, and so it comes to pass that these three young girls spend most of their time in happy, innocent liberty in Constance's old home.

The child insists on retaining the services of several of her father's old servants, who keep the place in the same beautiful order in which it was kept while "the family" lived there; for Mr Vaughan, though he disapproves of all this, and is steadily antagonistic to her intimacy with the Armingers, finds that he cannot control Constance in these things.

She is very open in her defiance of these illiberal and unjust wishes of his.

"If you make me seem to give them up while I'm a child, I must," she tells him; "but as soon as ever I'm a woman I'll go to them, and tell them that you made me seem mean and ungrateful while I was young."

"Little neighbour Constance, I will never be a tyrant to you," he says, deprecatingly, but Constance knows that he would be if he dared, and is not moved from her purpose for a moment by the tone.

As years rolled on, and the Armingers established themselves in a home that "really gives them quite a standing," Mrs Vaughan said, that lady evinced what her husband considered an unpardonable desire "to know them."

"They visit everywhere," she said. "They're dining at the Dalzels' to-night, and I hear those girls are most accomplished—quite an acquisition to any society.

"The Dalzels have had the good taste not to ask me to meet them," he said, pompously.

He had never forgiven Mrs Arminger for the generous, self-forgetful spirit which she displayed when his wife was on her death-bed.

"You will find you have made a mistake with all your nonsensical proud notions," she said.

"Mrs Arminger is your sister-in-law, and her children

are your nephews and nieces; and it's my belief that
Constance and young Don Arminger will make a match
of it. She's as proud of the name he is making as his
own sisters are."

"I hold you responsible for Constance, and I shall
think you have deceived me very basely if she does not
marry Donald."

"She's a free girl, not a slave."

"You said you had unlimited influence over her."

"So I have, but I'm not over well disposed to use it
in behalf of Donald. Neither your sons nor your
daughters have ever shown affection or respect for me,
and I don't see why I should try and sacrifice my niece's
affections to Donald's ambition."

"If I could have believed that you would ever have
acted so perfidiously, I would not have made you my
wife," he said, angrily.

But his anger had no effect whatever on a lady who
cared nothing whatever for his pleasure or displeasure—
who cared, indeed, for nothing on earth save her own
social status and bodily comfort.

Truly Nemesis had overtaken him for the polite
tyranny which he exercised over his first wife, who
brought much to him.

.   .   .   .

It is a lovely spring day. All the hedgerows round
Clyst are thickly covered with primroses and violets, and
the woods are full of the graceful waving wood-anemone,
or "wind-flower," whose pendant blossom waves so grace-
fully in the breeze. In the garden clumps of daffodils,
Lent lilies, and narcissus are making the borders gay
already; and in the Grange drawing-room a dozen
varieties of ferns, a tea rose, and several pots of lilies-of-
the-valley show themselves as the advanced guard of the
grand army of flowers which is marching on.

A delicious old room it is, this Grange drawing-room
—long, with a recess close to one side of the fire-place,
which is in the middle of its length, and above which a
window looking out over the old-world garden is placed.

At the end of the room there is another recess, formed by a large bay-window. This is divided from the rest of the room by a full, long curtain of dark olive-green, of a softly-falling material, which has been cunningly embroidered in a device of peacock's feathers by Trixy's skilful fingers.

This recess has come to be considered almost sacred to the youngest daughter of the house, and is always in a sweet confusion of embroidery silks and loose sheets of manuscript—for Trixy holds another gift in her hand besides the one of doing dainty needlework. The art of graceful story-writing for children is hers, and she exercises it continually.

Afternoon tea is going on now. It is served in dainty cups of blue-dragon china, and is set forth on a long, low table of carved oak, which savours more of her Dutch predecessor than of good Queen Anne. Trixy pours out the tea. Mrs Arminger lies back in an easy arm-chair, and reads out some gossip about art and literature from one of the weekly society papers. Maude, seated on a low stool, rests herself comfortably against her mother's knees. Constance Fielding occupies herself in cutting thin brown bread-and-butter, in a way that shows how thoroughly at home she is in this household.

Neighbour Constance has developed into a very striking, aristocratic, and handsome young lady, with more sparkle about her than is the portion of dreamy Maude, and less piquancy than is characteristic of Trixy.

Though she is sweet and twenty now, she is still quite fresh and unworn by society's usages. She has only had one season in town, and has not been allowed to indulge in too many of the dangerous delights of that one by Mr Vaughan, who has guarded her more jealously for his son than his son has cared to guard her for himself. She is over here to-day with the Armingers, discussing a plan which has formed itself simultaneously, and without collusion, in the minds of all four here assembled; and this is nothing less than that Constance shall come up and spend some weeks with them in town.

"There will be consternation in the Vaughan camp when you tell them; but no matter; if only you can come," Trixy says, and Constance answers,—

"The consternation will be confined to Mr Vaughan; for some inscrutable reason or other Aunt Emily always opposes him about me now; she opposes him about most things, but about nothing so much as me." Then the girl pauses for a moment, and presently adds, with a little blush, "It sounds conceited to say so, but I owe the immunity I enjoy from Donald Vaughan's attentions and worryings to Aunt Emily; at one time she wanted to make up a match between us, but for the last two or three years she has done all she can to keep us apart, and to set me against him."

"He looks a very nice fellow," Mrs Arminger says.

"And he's very handsome; don't you think so, Maude?" Trixy puts in.

"Not half as handsome as our Don," Maude replies.

"He's as vain as Narcissus," Constance says, "and for all he's so scrupulously courteous and gentlemanly on the surface, he's not a bit above implying that nearly every girl he mentions is or has been in love with him."

CHAPTER VIII.

REBELS IN THE CAMP.

EVER since the dawning of the day of prosperity for the Armingers, Mrs Vaughan had been vigilantly on the look-out for a suitable opportunity of making, or as she chose to phrase it, resuming her acquaintance with them.

During the years of the growing girlhood of Maude and Trixy Arminger, their mother had, without exactly living a secluded life, unquestionably abstained from going into society. But this was from no unsocial motive. It was only that she realised the fact that her work was the first condition of her children's present comfort, and possible future success. By her "work" they all lived and were being educated. Therefore, as her strength was not as the strength of ten, she gave all she had to the fulfilment of the obvious duty that was set before her.

But this order had been changed since the day when, proud and happy, Don was first enabled to smooth away all pecuniary difficulties from the path of his still prouder mother and sisters. Now that it was no longer necessary to toil unceasingly, Mrs Arminger showed that she was as well fitted to take her place on the holiday side of life as on its labour slope. And as they had been well known and better liked in the neighbourhood for years, they soon found themselves in the full swing of the best society the neighbourhood afforded.

Now, all this is bitter to Mr Vaughan, who is not, for all his pride, at all above permitting the most puerile jealousy to gnaw his vitals.

That these people whom he elected to ignore, and thought to stamp out of all recognition when they first came to Clyst, should be now sought by his own set under his nose, is more than his patience can endure. He feels as if his sovereignty were being disputed, and girds in spirit against his first wife's relatives more in their day of prosperity than he had done in those of their poverty and obscurity.

Oddly enough, it is not the celebrity which Don Arminger has acquired in letters which goads Mr Vaughan nearly to madness every time he thinks of his lost wife's "poor relations." It is rather the popularity and place which Don's mother and sisters have made for themselves in the narrow world about Clyst, of which Mr Vaughan believes himself to be a great head-centre.

"I dislike self-made men," Mr Vaughan says to his spouse, when she applies her little lash to him of lauding "his nephew's success." "I dislike self-made men; as a rule they are made after a pattern that gentlemen are not cut by; but I don't grudge the lad anything that he

may have gained by his success, such as it is; he is out
in the busy mart, and I have nothing to do with him.
But I do object to being forced into familiar association
with his mother—a woman who came down in a state of
humiliating penury in order, as I firmly believe, to trade
on her remote relationship to me."

" Holding those views, you can surely never wish to
trade on your even more remote relationship to Constance," his wife says, tartly, in reply to this exordium.

" You will please to refuse Mr Dalzel's invitation to
meet Mrs Arminger at dinner," he says, stiffly, ignoring
his wife's reference to Constance.

" Mrs Dalzel has not made the vulgar mistake of asking us 'to meet' any one at dinner. I simply happen
to know through Connie that the Armingers will be
there, and as there is nothing to prevent Constance and
me going, I shall be delighted to resume my acquaintance
with them."

" Nothing to prevent your going, excepting my desire
that you do not go. I will not have Constance en-
couraged in this pernicious path; I can't control her,
but I shall think that you strangely forget your duty as a
wife if you make it easy for her to see these people of
whom I so strongly disapprove."

"She would see them whether I made it easy for her
to do so or not; she must have companionship, and it
says much for her taste and discretion that she has
chosen the most cultivated companions the neighbourhood
affords."

" If she wants companions there are my daughters."

" Your daughters are no companions for Constance,"
Mrs Vaughan says, with so perceptible a sneer that Mr
Vaughan in a moment of irritation condescends to notice
it, and so loses more ground.

" Upon my word, Mrs Vaughan, you forget yourself,
and what is due to me in a way that is—that I cannot
conceive a gentlewoman doing; no sweeter, gentler girl
ever lived than Grace, and few cleverer ones than Ada,
I fancy."

"It's your misfortune to be blind to the weaknesses and defects of your own family," she says, coolly. "Grace's 'sweetness and gentleness' are but other words for silliness and inanity; and what you consider cleverness in Ada, I call mere pertness. They haven't an idea in their heads excepting about dress, and they have no taste in that. Constance has a very different order of intellect, and has been very differently brought up. You can't expect her to talk on the exciting topic of the Miss Vaughans' ribbons, and frills, and artificial flowers by the hour."

"They are quite well educated enough to be able to talk on any subject that may be discussed in good society, and they will never be in any other. My daughters have not been brought up to be governesses, or 'professionals' of any sort."

"What an undignified allusion to your niece, Miss Arminger, being likely to make a name as a painter," his wife says, tauntingly, for the secret ill-temper which so effectually tamed his first wife, has only made his second hate him. Then seeing that he winces at this, she goes on, "Take care how you say slighting things of Miss Arminger; it may make ill-feeling between you and your son Donald, if you do."

"Donald!"

"Yes, Donald; vain and empty-pated as Donald is, I give him credit for this, that he has fallen head over ears in love with the prettiest, cleverest, and most charming girl who has ever crossed his path."

"Who has dared to put this girl in his path, madam?" Mr Vaughan asks, almost foaming with fury, and striking his wife's work-table with his clenched fist in a way that makes it totter.

"Pray, don't be so foolishly violent," she says, calmly. "Constance introduced Donald to her particular friend yesterday at his special request."

"I'd have that woman and her family drummed out of the parish if I could," he says, with such concentrated wrath in his tone that, for the first time, his wife realises how very terribly vindictive he can be, and how long he can nurse anger.

"You can't do that, and you can't snub them, for they're quite indifferent to your notice ; and you can't ignore them, for every one who is worth knowing about here is seeking them."

"Who has told you all this ?" he asks, in bewilderment, for he knows that the language she is using is not her own.

"Constance and Donald have both told me so. Donald is furious at finding that the way you have behaved to them for years, may, and probably will, be the means of barring their doors to him now ; he was speaking about it to-day after you left the luncheon-table, and I couldn't help feeling that his anger was a judgment upon you, for the way you have behaved to your wife's family."

"He will never be mad enough—wicked enough, to give up Constance for this girl," Mr Vaughan says, with quivering lips ; but his emotion wins him no pity from his wife.

"I must remind you," she says, sharply, "that Constance has never given herself to Donald, therefore the question of his giving her up need never be raised. Constance, frank as she is about all other matters, is very properly reserved about the state of her heart ; but I have formed an opinion about it, which I will give you if you care to hear it."

He feels sure that whatever opinion she has formed, will be adverse to his hopes and wishes. Still he finds himself drawn into asking for it.

"I had better know what is hatching," he says, sullenly.

"Just as well. The shock will be less when what I am anticipating comes about. If Constance ever enters your family, it will be as the wife of your nephew, not as the wife of your son."

"Of the fellow who was Dalzel's usher ?"

"Of the man who has made such a name for himself as must make you proud of him, though you won't admit it yet."

"I have no appreciation of literary distinction," he says, sneeringly. "You certainly have no ambition for your niece, if you are inclined to throw her at the head of a fellow who has managed to make a little noise in a little world through the fortunate fact of having been bear-leader to a lordling. I have more respect for her, and for the family she represents. So once more I mu entreat, or rather command, that you endeavour to check the folly which seems rife around me with regard to these Armingers."

"You can hardly expect me to go down to the Grange and tell Mrs Arminger that you forbid her son to ask Constance to be his wife, before he has shown any desire to do so," she retorts, provokingly.

"From what you said just now, I thought he had shown some such desire."

"Not at all. I was speaking of what I believed to be the state of Constance's feelings towards him. I've had no opportunity of forming any conjecture as to the state of his towards her."

"These humiliations will shorten my days," Mr Vaughan says, dejectedly. "But I'll take care of one thing—that girl shall never be mistress of Strathlands. If Donald marries her, the property shall pass to Reggie, and Mrs Arminger shall find that her plotting has ended in her daughter's marrying a pauper."

"And perhaps Reggie will marry a barmaid or a ballet-girl. Judging from his photograph album, his chief female friends belong to one or other of these classes."

"I would as soon see him marry a barmaid or a ballet-girl as see Donald marry that other girl," Mr Vaughan says, excitedly. Then he adds, "I will not sit down to dinner till I have spoken to Donald, and crushed this cabal against my honour and happiness."

He goes away gustily from the room, and presently Mrs Vaughan hears the front door bang, and understands that her husband is gone to have it out with his son, who, as usual during this hour before dinner, is having a cigar in the harness-room.

For smoking in the house is strictly forbidden at Strathlands, and is only done surreptitiously in the harness-room by day, and in the kitchen at night by the two sons.

"They have both of them such evil tempers that I'm glad they're going to clash," Mrs Vaughan says, contentedly, to herself. "The idea of Mr Vaughan thinking, after all I have seen of him and his family, that I should give Constance to his son!"

Mr Vaughan has no difficulty in finding his son; but he does not find the other part of his programme so easy to carry out.

Donald Vaughan is a good-looking, well-mannered, moderately-educated, and intensely self-satisfied young fellow, whom circumstances have combined to spoil, considerably. The heir to a large property, he has been brought up with the notion that a life of pleasant, amusing idleness is his portion by right. The lesson that he need do nothing for his living has been well learnt by him, and though he is not utterly void of ambition, it is not ambition of the right sort which animates him.

For example, though the prospect of a seat in the House has a fascination for him, he will not be at the trouble of mastering the merest rudiments of the politics of the day. But he rides well, few can live with him after the hounds in his own country. He is a capital shot, and deports himself very creditably in private theatricals. These accomplishments, together with a certain quiet, easy assurance, and a remarkably self-possessed address, make Donald Vaughan a popular man in society.

But underlying this quiet, indifferent, easy manner of his, there is a deep stratum of obstinacy. And to-day, when his father broaches the subject of the Armingers, this obstinacy develops itself at once.

"I hear from Mrs Vaughan that in disregard—I may say in defiance—of my known wishes on the subject, you have made acquaintance with those people at Clyst," Mr Vaughan begins, overbearingly.

Donald has sauntered out into the stable-yard with his father in amiable unsuspicion of what is about to follow. But he checks himself when his father says this, and answers rebelliously,—

"I don't know what 'people' you are speaking of, but I'll tell you at once that I shall make any acquaintance I please, quite irrespective of you."

"I am speaking of those people at the Grange—the Armingers."

"My aunt and cousins?"

"I have never admitted that any relationship exists," Mr Vaughan says, intemperately.

"Then you repudiate my mother?"

"I didn't come out here to listen to insolence or to nonsense. I came to speak on a matter of vital interest to us both. Is it true that you are thinking seriously, or indeed at all, of that girl?"

"Do you mean Maude Arminger?"

"I don't know her name—"

"Your niece's name is Maude."

"But I mean the eldest girl, who is to be an artist, or something of the sort. Good heavens! Donald! I should have thought the instincts of your caste would have saved you from the snare of a girl to whom some amount of publicity may attach ; her name may be in the public journals. Any little cad of an art critic will have the power and the right to pat her on the back in the press ; the idea of it is appalling, revolting to a degree."

"I'm neither appalled nor revolted by it," Donald says, smothering his wrath as well as he can.

"You mean that you will persist in seeking this girl— in making this ignoble and most ruinous marriage ?"

"I shall be a better man if I can get her than I shall be if she won't have anything to say to me, father ; my only fear is that Maude Arminger will feel that she's worlds too good for a fellow like me ; she'll compare me with her own brother, and—"

A snort of futile, supercilious rage from the father interrupts the son's speech here.

"Compare you with her brother!" he gasps out. "Donald, have you forgotten that you are my son? Do you remember that these people are outside our social circle?"

"They are what my mother was."

"They are not, I tell you," Mr Vaughan snaps. "Your mother took my status when I married her; it was her misfortune that these people should have had any claim of kith or kin upon her; it is to her credit that she never admitted such claim."

Donald groans.

"Don't try to make me as much ashamed of my dear mother as I am of you, sir," he says, striving to deport himself after the manliest pattern he can remember.

"Don't bandy words with me and try to make me forget that you are my son," Mr Vaughan says, letting his fury become ungovernable. "Strathlands shall never be yours if that girl is your wife; she shall be warned that in marrying you she will marry a pauper, for not a shilling of my money shall ever find its way into your pocket. If you defy me in this way it will be to your own destruction."

In answer to this Donald murmurs something relative to his readiness to resign Strathlands, father, and every shilling that father may be possessed of, rather than give up the sweet hope and possibility of eventually winning his cousin Maude for his wife.

But though he murmurs this, the thought of losing Strathlands for her sake, makes him feel that she ought really to consider him a very heroic creature.

At dinner this day Constance openly announces that she is "going up to town with the Armingers, who will leave the day after to-morrow." And Donald resolves to follow them without delay, and meet his fate in London.

CHAPTER IX.

LADY ELINOR'S EYES ARE RED.

DON ARMINGER has done all that a man can do, and provided all that a man's foresight can suggest as necessary or desirable for the well-being of his mother and sisters during their stay in town.

He has taken apartments for them in a house in Norfolk Street—fair-sized, fairly-furnished, indisputably well-situated apartments, in which they are well served and waited upon. His efforts on their behalf would probably have ended here, but they have been supplemented by the efforts of another.

This other is one for whom Don's mother and sisters have a subtle fascination which she cannot define to her own satisfaction, but to which she succumbs with willing grace—Lord Sylvertre's only sister, Lady Elinor Divett.

For eight years she had been thrown into frequent and intimate association with Don, and she had passed through various phases of feeling respecting him. For the first few years of their acquaintance she regarded him as a sort of brotherly being—as one, indeed, who owed her fraternal duty and allegiance to the same extent as Sylvertre did, but to whom she owed naught in return, and over whom she had an indisputable right to exercise all the imperial airs of which she was mistress.

But these years of affectionate negligence passed away, and there came another day, in the light of which she saw him as he was—neither brother nor friend, but something infinitely nearer and dearer.

She is a very handsome girl, this young patrician— tall and stately, with clean-cut features and manners, and a strong inward conviction that whatever she sets her heart upon ought to be hers—a conviction which is fostered by one of the best-hearted and weakest- minded mothers on record.

All the world knows Lady Timerton, and nearly all of it likes her. In the days of her youth, she had been spoken of by her compeers as "a sweet, stylish-looking girl," just as her daughter is spoken of by the present generation as a "jolly girl, and good form all round." But this attractive past is only a memory now, and the present Lady Timerton strikes the eye as being rather overblown, and the ear as being rather of the garrulously given order of womankind.

She has hobbies without end, and she rides them with much awkward indiscretion. Her endeavours to ameliorate the condition of standing shop-girls, starving dogs, street-performing children, and the unbeneficed clergy, are arduous and incessant; but little good results from these endeavours, for the reason that she forces her hobby, for the hour, right into the heart of the most incongruous society, where it gets rebuffed and cast down, simply because it is inopportune.

But, in spite of her want of tact, Lady Timerton is a popular woman, for she is the soul of good-nature, and this dominating quality of hers asserts itself forcibly when she hears that Don Arminger's mother and sisters are coming to town.

Everything she can think of that may add to their comfort she sends to their furnished lodgings, in order, as she expresses it, that they "may feel at home through having home comforts about them. Books, bottles of perfume, hothouse plants, bouquets of exotics, magazines, and such things, she scatters over the tables with a lavish hand, and then she looks at her daughter, and exclaims,—

"Elinor! how could we? We've forgotten the brougham!"

"You can't put that in the drawing-room," Lady Elinor says, laughing, but secretly overjoyed that her mother is showing such kindly forethought for Don Arminger's people.

"No more I can, but I can leave a note saying that the coachman shall call for orders to-morrow at ten. I can't do less, as I shall tell Mrs Arminger, feeling almost as if Don were my son,—as I do."

"Oh, mamma! you mustn't say that, indeed you mustn't," Elinor says, blushing vigorously.

" But I shall say it, because I feel it," Lady Timerton cries, in an ecstasy of good feeling ; " he's like one of us, and his mother and all the world may know that I say so." Then she writes an effusive note to Mrs Arminger, and bustles away on one of her countless missions of philanthropy.

Now it is a fact that though Don Arminger may be "like a son " to Lady Timerton, he is not in the least like a brother to Lady Timerton's daughter Elinor. From the day of his first coming to Barrowgate as Sylvertre's friend, Don has been the supreme object of interest to Lady Elinor. And there have been times when, as far as the engrossing and exciting natures of his pursuits would admit, he has seemed to return this interest.

With all the power of machination that is in her guileless soul, Lady Timerton has schemed and plotted to bring about a union between her handsome favourite and her only daughter. But Don, though he has neither seemed to see nor to avoid the scheming and plotting, has not profited by it to any extent beyond this—that he has suffered himself to fall into almost fraternal familiarity with the sister of his former pupil. He calls her " Nell," just as Sylvertre does, and treats her generally with such brotherly, affectionate kindness, as sometimes makes her heart beat with pleasure, and at others throb with pain.

She has a hard part to play, both in her own family and in society, this rich, well-born, pretty, highly-placed young lady. Her secret is no secret to her brother, who, though he sympathises with her, jokes her about it occasionally in a way that makes her hate Don Arminger for half-a-minute, and be cold to him for the following few hours.

On the other hand, it is not even suspected by her father, who would as soon believe her capable of entertaining a *penchant* for the butler, or the best-looking groom. "Arminger is a capital fellow " in his lordship's estimation, a valuable acquisition to the home party, either in town or country, and altogether a most satisfactory familiar friend for them all, and companion for Sylvertre. All these worthy merits of Don's are freely admitted by Lord Timerton. But as a possible husband for his daughter, his lordship has never been enlightened enough to regard Don Arminger for a moment.

Regarding his noble spouse as an extremely silly and gushing person, Lord Timerton takes very little notice of the wild enthusiasm with which her well-meaning ladyship dwells on the fact of Mrs and the Misses Armingers' approaching visit to town.

"I suppose you'll have them here?"

"Have them here! I hope they'll be here perpetually," she replies. Then she goes on to say flurriedly that as she regards Don "quite like a son, it will be only natural to be most intimate with his family."

"Nonsense! Ask them here to dinner, and have done with it," he says, sharply. "Don's having the run of the house is a very different thing to giving it to his people."

"Don has the run of plenty of houses that are quite as good as ours," Lady Elinor puts in injudiciously, colouring up, and obviously taking the slur on Don's dignity and importance to herself.

"What have you to do with it?" her father asks, with stiff politeness. "I scarcely conceive it needful to receive instruction from you as to the tone I may adopt towards your brother's friends."

"Don Arminger is my friend, too."

"Really!" her father says, sarcastically. "When young ladies become demonstrative about their friendship with young men, it is time for a little parental advice to be given. You'll get misunderstood, my dear, if you flare up about Arminger in this way; not only the world but he himself may fall into the fatal error of imagining that you are in love with him."

Her face is in a moment dyed with a scorching blush that is a revelation to him.

"And if I were, papa?" she asks, as firmly and dauntlessly as if she were not shivering inwardly at the expression of horrified incredulity which is rapidly overspreading her father's face.

"If you were! But that is incredible. I should be compelled to ask Mr Arminger to at once resign a position which he has so grossly abused."

"He holds no post under you, papa; he is no servant of yours, nor of any man's, to be dismissed; he is my brother's friend, as good a gentleman as any I know, and much better than most," she adds, indignantly.

"And it is really cruel of you to speak in such a way to the dear child about dear Don," Lady Timerton says, half crying and wholly flustered by this very unexpected scene.

"Elinor must learn to hear home truths when she makes a fool of herself, and Don Arminger must bear the brunt of my displeasure, since he has chosen to forget what is due to me."

"Papa, you'll kill me if you talk like that to him," Lady Elinor says, trying to force herself to be brave enough to state the case fairly. "Don has never hinted or looked or done a single thing that could lead me to suppose he cared for me or could vex you in any way. If you charge him with having done so it will kill me."

"Then I am to understand that the folly is entirely a spontaneous growth on your side, and has been quite uncultivated and utterly unreciprocated by him? Upon my word, Lady Timerton, you have brought up your daughter nicely! That she should throw herself at the head of her brother's tutor speaks well for her training."

"Is it a disgrace to have taught Sylvertre to be what he is?" Lady Elinor asks, with a mingling of pretty pride in her brother and half shame-faced idolatry of Don Arminger, that is infinitely touching.

"It is a disgrace to us all that I should have been led to speak in such a way," Lord Timerton says, liberally dividing the error between them. "No one likes Don or admires and respects him more than I do; but I'm not going to have any romantic nonsense about him, and I'm not going to let my only daughter throw herself away."

"You may say what cutting things you please to me, papa, but please spare Mr Arminger, who knows nothing of my—I mean who is quite innocent of having given any cause of offence," the young lady says, proudly.

Then she goes away and cries, and hopes when they next meet that Don Arminger will know for whose sake her eyes are red.

.   .   .   .

"Have you any reason to think that Arminger is sneaking into Elinor's good graces?" Lord Timerton says to his son this same night, when a note comes from Don excusing himself from dining with them as usual, on account of the arrival of his mother and sisters.

"Don wouldn't sneak into anything."

"Don't quibble about a word, Sylvertre. Do you think he has been taking advantage of the trust and confidence reposed in him to try on any humbug with your sister?"

"I think my sister is quite capable of discriminating between humbug and genuineness," Lord Sylvertre says, with far too much of an air of taking it all for granted to be agreeable to his alarmed father.

"I meant you to understand my question in this way: have you any reason to suppose there is anything—any nonsense or secret engagement between them?"

"Not the slightest reason in the world for supposing that Don likes Elinor more than as one of the family, nothing more; but rather a strong suspicion," he adds with a merry twinkle in his eye, "that Nell has flopped—"

"Has what?" the Earl of Timerton interrupts hurriedly.

"Has gone down like a shot partridge before one of the nicest fellows in the world, before he has even aimed at her," Lord Sylvertre says, with cool candour.

"I wish you would speak intelligible English," Lord Timerton says, testily.

"Well, I think Elinor likes him so well that she would marry him to-morrow if he would only ask her," Lord Sylvertre says, cheerfully ; "but there's the rub, you see. Don's a deuced proud fellow, and though he can't help seeing, if he looks, that Elinor likes him, he doesn't care to make a sign that may get him called to account by you."

"Do you mean that he sees your sister's infatuation and has the insolence to disregard it ?" Lord Timerton asks, in an inconsequent rage at the very result being brought about which he himself desires.

"I can't say whether or not he sees it, but most certainly he disregards it," Lord Sylvertre says, laughingly ; then seeing that his father looks annoyed, he adds more seriously, "I thought you would prefer hearing my real opinion as to Don's sentiments, since they so entirely coincide with your own, sir."

"It is in ill taste to canvass these delicate possibilities concerning your sister."

"I agree with you entirely in that, sir," Sylvertre cries out heartily ; "but you opened the subject, and I—"

"Pursued it to its bitter end," Lord Timerton says, savagely. "These are pleasant things truly to be told me on the same day ; first, that my only daughter is in love with an underling ; and secondly, that he hasn't the grace to make the poor amends of returning her regard."

"Poor Nell! it's hard lines on her," Sylvertre says, compassionately ; and then, to his father's wrathful indignation, he goes on to explain that he feels it hard his sister's fancy should be unrequited, and utterly refuses to sympathise with his father as to the enormity of Don Arminger's conduct in allowing himself to be loved within the prohibited social degree.

.   .   .   .

"I say," Sylvertre says to his sister the following day, "the mother and you call to-day on Don's people, don't you ?"

"Yes, one has to do it."

"Exactly; but you needn't try to come the governor over me, Nell, for I happen to know better; you want to go, it isn't that you have to do it.　But a word in your ear. They've brought a lovely young heiress up with them, a local professional beauty, and the heroine into the bargain of a romance wherein Don and a bull played prominent parts.　Now it strikes me, unless I am prepared to sacrifice myself to her, you had better relinquish all ideas of sacrificing yourself to him."

"How silly you are, Sylvertre," she says, gaily; but he sees she is pained, and so he drops badinage, and says,—

"Seriously, Nell, look to yourself now; I'd give my life for Don if I were a woman, but I'm not a woman; and being a man, I don't want to see my sister give her life to him, do you see? You have it in your hands still to recover—you're blighted a bit, but not blasted."

"Not even 'blighted' yet," she says, proudly.　"Who is this girl—what is she that I should shrink before her?"

CHAPTER X.

THE CLASH.

"You must forgive me if I am not with you much by day, mother," Don says to Mrs Arminger at dinner on the night of their arrival; "the preliminaries of this new Central African Expedition take up my time, unfortunately, just when I want to give it all to you."

"Does that mean that you are really going to explore Central Africa, or that you don't want to bore yourself by exploring London in the company of country friends?" Constance asks.

"It means that the conduct of this new expedition is entrusted to me by Government, but if my mother looks so terribly disappointed, I'll resign it, and go with her to the Tower and the Thames Tunnel instead."

"But you really will do the pictures, Don? Maude pleads.

"And go with us to all the theatres?" Trixy puts in.

"And take us under your protecting wing at Lady Timerton's ball, or we poor little unknowns will be swept into utter obscurity," Constance adds.

"I am afraid that in spite of the claims of Central Africa, you will find I shall become monotonous, Miss Fielding. As for Lady Timerton's ball, I shall probably not win a word, much less a waltz, from either of you there; she tells me she has secured all the best waltzers in town."

"What's Lady Timerton like?" Maude asks.

"A good old soul, always in a good-natured fume about something."

"And what is Lord Sylvertre like?"

"One of the best and best-looking fellows breathing," Don says, heartily.

"And his sister—the 'Nell' you used to talk about when first you went to Barrowgate?" Mrs Arminger asks.

"Lady Elinor? Oh, she's a capital girl, devoted to Sylvertre, and not half as much spoiled as you would expect to see a London beauty of two years' standing."

"Don't you call her Nell now, Don?" Trixy asks, with inopportune curiosity, for her question causes Don to look a little embarrassed, and he is conscious that Constance Fielding's eyes have involuntarily fixed themselves on him.

"I call her Lady Elinor," he says, gravely, but he does not add, "on rare occasions," which would have been the whole truth.

"I thought you were all like brothers and sister," Trixy says, in disappointed accents. "I don't call it at all fraternal to address her as 'Lady Elinor;' do you, Connie?"

"Not at all fraternal," Constance says, slowly; "but perhaps—"

Then she checks herself, remembering that he does not call her "Constance," and fearing that a personal feeling and meaning may be ascribed to any idle words she may utter about this unknown Lady Elinor.

It is a fact that Constance Fielding has cherished the image of the handsome, gallant boy who risked his life for hers, very tenderly and jealously in her heart during all these years of non-intercourse. Now that she meets him again, it is, perhaps, a little unfortunate that the cherished memory should fade and pale before the reality. Don as a man is grander in her eyes even than the ideal Don whom she has been thinking about all these years; and Don as a man has an intimate friendship with a Lady Elinor, a London beauty of two seasons' standing.

There is not a particle of vanity about this girl, who is an important little queen in her own country. It does not occur to her to think of herself as a beauty who would have been one of London's famous ones if only London had been allowed to see her.

Lady Timerton's little note relative to the brougham has been found, read, and acted upon. It is to be at their door at half-past two, but at two Lady Timerton sails in upon them herself, her daughter leisurely following in her wake, with an air of indifference that is in reality assumed to cover the agitation she feels about meeting Don's people for the first time, and that is erroneously set down by them all as a supercilious affectation of superiority.

Lady Timerton is full of enthusiastic pleasure, not to say of emotional gush, at this opportunity of becoming acquainted with Don's family. Regardless, or rather forgetful of her husband's strictures on the subject, she with lively zeal seeks to identify them with every form of entertainment in which she and her daughter are involved during the ensuing fortnight.

"Whenever you have a free evening you must dine with us, just as dear Don does," Lady Timerton declares; and Lady Elinor with cheeks aflame, reminds her that,—

"Mr Arminger gives more of his free evenings to work than to dining with us, mamma."

"No, my dear, I contend I'm right: when he's at work he is not 'free;' and I will repeat that I hope Mrs Arminger and her daughters "—her ladyship looks round approvingly on the three girls as she speaks—" will make our house their home as Don does."

"This is not my daughter. I must apologise for not having introduced Miss Fielding more distinctly," Mrs Arminger says, and Lady Elinor owns to herself liberally that the heroine of the bull adventure is well worthy of being the life-romance even of Don Arminger.

Lady Tinnerton has a scheme for the furtherance of their happiness even this first day of knowing them.

She tells them that at four o'clock a meeting has been convened to be held in her own drawing-room, which will be attended by all the influential members, and many more well-wishers of the Anti-Vivisection Society, and addressed by a lady whose pen, purse, voice, and talents generally are exclusively devoted to the cause.

"It will be most interesting," her ladyship assures them. "Do come and be converted to our side,—to the side of humanity."

"I don't think we, or any of us, need conversion to the cause of anti-cruelty," Constance says; and Maude murmurs something relative to her anxiety to see certain famous pictures which are on view separately in Bond Street.

"I should like very much to attend the meeting, but you see my girls have other plans," Mrs Arminger says, apologetically.

"I'll go with you if you like, mother," Trixy puts in, "and Don can take care of Constance and Maude."

"Mamma never takes into consideration that other people are not so intensely interested in these meetings and lectures as she is herself," Lady Elinor says, coldly, for the programme as arranged by Trixy does not please her.

"Dear Elinor, I wouldn't press it if I didn't feel sure that Mrs Arminger will be well repaid for sacrificing any other engagement to come and hear Miss Angel Ormond.

You will be horrified! your flesh will creep, and you'll feel faint and sick at the things she will tell you," Lady Timerton adds encouragingly to Mrs Arminger and Trixy.

Then she goes on to describe some of the diagrams illustrative of the vivisection tables and instruments, and of the helpless, agonised, living creatures which are stretched upon them in the cause of "pure science."

"I've been anxious, ever since I've read at all, to see Miss Angel Ormond," Trixy says, kindling up. "I read every article of hers that I meet with; she has the heart of a woman and the head of a man, and I always feel that her name describes her."

"She is an angel of mercy and tenderness to every living thing," Lady Timerton says, and tears that are caused by no especial feeling, but which flow as freely as if they were, well into her amiable eyes, as she pays tribute to the goodness of her friend.

Lady Timerton and her daughter have scarcely taken their departure when Don comes in. He has tried to resist the inclination which has led him hither, has tried to force himself to do something which he knows ought to be done. But the desire to see more of the girl who is as a sister to his sisters has been too strong for him. He knows how steadily she has held her own, from her childish days until now, in the matter of being loyal to his family in the face of all opposition.

He remembers how frankly she told him she "would love him all her life," when he was nearly done to death in her service. And knowing and remembering these things, and seeing her as she is now, fair and sweet as any woman that ever blessed a man's life, he does desire to see her again, he does desire to be warmed by the sunshine of her presence before he goes off to the damps and swamps, the disagreeables and dangers of Central Africa.

It is not fair to say that the re-introduction to Constance has blotted out the recollection of some thoughts which have at intervals flashed through his brain respecting Lady Elinor. There have been times when it has seemed to him that he is so identified with Lord Timerton's family as for it to be only in the natural order of things that he should fall in love with and marry Lady Elinor. And there have been times, too, when he has very nearly fallen in love with her—very nearly, but not quite.

At such times as it has happened, something has always intervened to take one or other of them away, and by the time intercourse has been renewed between them, Don has forgotten how nearly he had been over the border a while ago.

To-day, as he walks from his club to his mother's rooms in Norfolk Street, in spite of all his keen desire to see and know more of Constance, he finds himself thinking of Lady Elinor.

"She likes me, I'm sure of that. I wonder how she'll like Constance?" he thinks, and an involuntary, doubtful shake of the head proclaims that he, for some reason or other, fears that these two ladies may collide.

But he forgets doubt, fear, and Lady Elinor when he comes in and finds Maude and Constance ready and anxious to go out, both of them frankly expectant of his appearance, both of them delighted to see him.

"Your friends, Lady Timerton and Lady Elinor, have been here, Don, and have been more than kind," his mother tells him. Then she goes on to explain to him what they are going to do, and why they are going to do it.

"Miss Fielding and Maude wouldn't get entangled in Lady Timerton's humane net; they want you to go to the pictures with them, Don," Trixy says; "but I'd rather hear Miss Angel Ormond than see all the pictures in the world."

"Lady Timerton's a dear old soul! but she does shove people on to her hobbies, without much regard as to whether they care to ride them or not," Don laughs.

"I don't think Lady Elinor is exactly what I should call *sympatica* as far as her mother is concerned," Maude says; "she gave me the impression of shrugging mental shoulders whenever Lady Timerton grew enthusiastic."

"Nell hears a lot of it, you see," Don says, good-naturedly, and directly he has said it he wishes he had not spoken of her as " Nell," and does not know how to recover the trip.

"I can hardly fancy Lady Elinor Divett being sympathetic with anybody or anything that did not conduce to her own honour and glory," Constance says, and she regrets her petulant speech immediately, quite as sincerely as Don is regretting his familiar one.

"Oh, Connie! that's unkind," tempestuous Trixy cries out. "She was as cordial and friendly as any one could be to us all; she doesn't gush like her mother, but I felt that she was well inclined to make friends with us; didn't you?"

"Indeed I didn't, and indeed I don't see why she should," Constance says, with a flushed and vexed sense of being in the wrong in having uttered disparaging words about Lady Elinor.

"I move that we get to the pictures as soon as possible, before Trixy discovers more merits, and Miss Fielding more demerits, in Lady Elinor," Don says, and there is a little confusion and bustle while Mrs Arminger and Trixy are being sent off in the brougham, and a cab is being fetched for the others.

The remaining hours of the afternoon are hours of pure and perfect delight to Maude. But they are not hours of pure and perfect pleasure to either Constance or Don. For being thrown together, and, by reason of Maude's abstraction, cast upon themselves, they keep on coming near to a clear understanding of one another, and then sheering off as if such understanding were contraband.

"How tame all this must be to you," Constance says to him, waving her hand in a way that is meant to express that she is referring to London life all round.

"Then I must plead guilty to liking tame things in preference to wild," he replies, and he means it thoroughly, for if companionship with her is one of the consequences of civilisation, then civilisation has it in his estimation over Central Africa.

"How Lady Timerton and all of them will miss you. She spoke to-day as if she looked on you as one of them."

"I think she does, dear, kind woman that she is ; but Sylvertre is the one who will miss me, unless he makes up his mind to go with me."

"Don't his family wish him to go ?"

"His father and mother have some natural parental qualms about the dangers and diseases he may encounter ; but Ne—his sister, Lady Elinor urges him on."

"Why didn't you finish her pet name, 'Nell,' as you began it, Mr Arminger ?"

"Because I remembered in time that I was speaking of her to a stranger, who would not know to whom I was referring."

"And she wishes her brother to go out with you ?"

"Yes, she's rather an adventurous girl."

"I suppose reading all your travels and explorations has made her wish to travel and explore too ?"

"I don't think I can lay claim to the honour of having formed the taste ; I think it was born in her. In fact, I believe that if it wouldn't give a shock that might never be recovered to the home social system, she would propose going with Sylvertie !"

"Oh ! from your tone you evidently don't sympathise with her desire to knock about the world ?"

"I certainly don't sympathise with her conventional scruples about gratifying it."

"If I had a brother going to the torrid zone or the North Pole, and I wanted to go with him, I'd go, and the social system might get over the shock as best it could."

"You see you speak as an absolutely independent young lady. You are in a position which is above all power and control, save your own sweet will. Lady Elinor Divett is not in a position to exercise independent judgment and will."

"Is she very fond of her brother?"

"Yes, I think she is."

"And is he very fond of her?"

"Yes, and very proud of her."

"Then I think Lady Elinor Divett will be able to do as she likes about travelling and everything else; for her mother is wax to receive any impression her daughter wants to have. Am I not right?"

"Yes, but she is not marble, to retain it. I pity Lady Elinor sometimes; she has a fine nature, and it must hurt her to feel how far she is superior mentally to her mother."

"Maude and Trixy are sure to get fond of Lady Elinor, as she is so clever," Constance says, meditatively.

"I don't say she's 'so' clever; I don't think her 'clever' in the ways that Maude and Trixy are. She hasn't thought half as much as Maude or read as Trixy has, and she hasn't the natural vigour and brain power that they have; but she is a brightly intelligent and very fairly well-informed girl."

"And she's very, very pretty, and has charming, polished, graceful ways," Constance says, with a mighty effort. "What a grace she would lend to your expedition if she could persuade her father and mother to let her go! How she would be guarded and waited upon and watched by the whole camp! Why, it would be the romance of the period, Mr Arminger."

"It will never be enacted, Miss Fielding," he says, smiling at her earnestness.

"Why? Don't you wish her to go?"

"Most decidedly not."

"Poor Lady Elinor!" Constance says, smiling freely and brilliantly. "She is doomed to disappointment then, I feel, for yours is the will that must be carried out. If I ever set my heart on going into savage countries, I won't ask to be personally conducted by you."

"If it were your wish to go, you need never fear my answer," he says.

And they both feel relieved, and, as it were, extricated

from a precarious position, when Maude comes to them, saying,—

"I'm not tired, but I'm merciful, and I know you two are sick to death of being here. Oh, Don! I'm feeling myself such a dauber at this moment; no one will ever stand before a picture of mine, and feel as I felt before that just now."

"Then the want will be in those who pass before it, not in your picture, Maude," Constance says, forgetting Don, herself, and all minor jealousies in her earnest desire to soothe and comfort the artist, who is artist enough to feel her own defects.

"How could I dare to send a painting of mine to be looked at by thousands?"

"Your mother, Trixy, the Dalzels, and I looked at it with pleasure, Maude; are we more tasteless than the majority?"

"No, but more fond of me."

"My dear little sister, you may never be a Rosa Bonheur, or a Miss Thompson, but—"

"She may and will be something equally fine," Constance cries, with such perfect sincerity, that Maude's fainting spirit revives, and she retracts the vow she has mentally made—never to paint again.

CHAPTER XI.

"HOW SHALL I MY TRUE LOVE KNOW?"

IT is a curious fact that this reunion with Miss Fielding makes Don Arminger think more of Lady Elinor than he has ever thought of her before. Whenever for an unguarded moment—or shall it be said a moment not occupied by literary business or other more important considerations?—the image of his old child-friend grown into perfect womanhood arises before him, straightway recollection of Lady Elinor obtrudes itself.

As he walks away from the door of his mother's lodg
ings this afternoon, having refused to go in with them,
the remembrance of Lady Elinor is very vividly upon
him. He cannot but remember—now that he is thinking of her, and contrasting her with this peerless Constance—how she has always singled him out above all
others to be the recipient of the smiles and favours which
it behoves her to dispense to her father's guests. He
cannot but remember that she has shown more interest
in his exploits than she has in anything else, save her
more important society engagements; that she has asked
for his advice, taken his opinion, adopted his professional
views unhesitatingly about things which she does not in
the least understand. All these things he cannot but
remember that Lady Elinor has done, now that he has
met Constance Fielding again, and finds himself thinking
her charming.

He tells himself that he will dine at his club to-night,
in order that he may see one or two men whom he feels
sure will be there. But there is a latent desire in his
mind to get out of the Timerton home-circle for a day or
two, until, in fact, his quiet student habits have resumed
their sway over him, and the thoughts of Lady Elinor
and Miss Fielding have ceased to jar, and have become
customary and commonplace.

But just as he is finishing dressing, and has sent for a
cab to take him safely into club-land, a note is brought
to him from that excellent well-meaning blunderer, Lady
Timerton.

"You must dine with me to-night. Lord Timerton is
out, and I have something very particular and private to
say to you.—Yours, JULIA TIMERTON."

"She is going to say something about Nell!"
This is his first horrified and bewildered thought, but
he puts it away from him. Lady Timerton, devoid of
all tact as she is, is not wanting in maternal pride and
feeling. He is safe not to have unmanageable mention
made to him of Lady Elinor by her mother.

When, after a moment's debate with himself as to the wisdom of it, he does go to Lady Timerton's house to dine, he finds that lady waiting for him in the ante-room, and his partially assuaged fear that she may be going to tackle him on the subject of her daughter returns in full force.

For her ladyship looks fatigued and pre-occupied, and is dressed sombrely, not to say dowdily. However, she explains without delay why these things are, and relieves him considerably.

"Dear Don," she says, "I have had a most delightful afternoon. Our anti-vivisection meeting—you can't think how your dear mother and sister enjoyed it—was not over till six, and then Lady Kenwyn came, and we've had a most satisfactory *séance*."

The Countess of Kenwyn is Lord Timerton's sister, and is most cordially hated by that nobleman for the way in which she exposes herself to the sneers of the scoffers in the matter of spiritualism. Hence her visit during his absence for the purpose of conducting a *séance*.

"You must be bored to death," Don says, unsympathetically.

"Bored! No, Don, far from that. Awe and perplexity are my pervading sensations, for Lady Kenwyn assures me that if I persevere I shall become a medium. I can hardly believe it myself, but a voice told her, while we were sitting in this room not an hour ago, that I was in process of development, and that I should soon be in a higher star-circle, when I should both hear and see."

Don laughs at the glib way in which Lady Kenwyn has taught her guileless proselyte to gabble out the jargon of the craft.

"Did Lady Kenwyn give you any hints as to how you were to accelerate the process of development?" he asks. Then before she can answer, he adds, "My dear Lady Timerton, don't let Lady Kenwyn's miserable hallucination affect you. She was originally a clever and agreeable woman. See what she has become since she has been the dupe of a lot of charlatans—a laughing stock to society, and a nuisance to her friends."

"She lives surrounded by higher interests, that make her indifferent to society and—"

"Indifferent also to her friends. That's not a wholesome state of affairs."

"It's too mysterious altogether for me to discuss it with you," Lady Timerton says, vaguely. "I only know this: she has a dual being—she told me so herself; she holds constant converse with Catherine de Medicis, who, it appears, was a most interesting and elevated character, and who has been terribly—oh, really terribly maligned. But what I want you to do to-night, Don, is to take me to a spirit-circle that is sitting in some place. I don't quite seem to know it, but here's the address."

"It's a loathsome little purlieu between Holborn and Fleet Street. I'm afraid you won't find Catherine de Medicis there. Besides, you're too late, Lady Timerton. It's eight already. By the time you have dined—"

"I'm not going to dine," Lady Timerton puts in eagerly. "Lady Kenwyn has given me a few rules for self-development. For one thing, I am to abstain entirely from shell fish. They are evil spirits. In fact, she says the sooner I bring myself to strict vegetarianism the sooner I shall—"

"See Catherine de Medicis?" Don laughs.

"No," Lady Timerton says seriously, "she will only reveal herself to Lady Kenwyn, who tells me, do you know, that she never derived such happiness from intercourse with any earthly creature as she does from her intercourse with 'dear Catherine,' as she calls her, for they are as familiar as sisters; but I'm chattering and wasting time as usual. Are you ready to go with me to-night?"

"If you command me, I have no alternative."

"Oh, Don, don't put it in that way," she says, half crying at the possibility of being baulked; "it's my only chance, now that Timerton is away. I asked Sylvertre to go, and he roared with laughter. So if you won't be kind, I can do nothing."

"My dear Lady Timerton, I'll go anywhere to please

you, but I can't bear the idea of taking you with me. These wretched people who hold special circles will have made it their business to find out everything concerning you and your family before you go in to-night, and they'll not scruple to astound you, and perhaps frighten you, for the sake of obtaining an influence over you. What does Lady Elinor say to the expedition?"

"She is dining, and going to the theatre with her cousin, Lady Vic Gardiner, and knows nothing about it; come, Don, be the kind, dear boy you've always been, and come. I shall feel hurt if you refuse me, for I feel quite an impulse to go; Lady Kenwyn told me if I felt that, to obey it unhesitatingly."

"And forthwith you felt it," Don says; but, in spite of his disapproval, he finds himself offering his arm to Lady Timerton when her carriage is announced.

It is a grimy, unpleasantly odoriferous dwelling into which they finally enter. Apparently neither the spirits, nor those mortals who have formed a circle for their reception, are at all fastidious on the score of dilapidated appearances, or evil smells.

They pass along a passage permeated by the fusty aroma of a number of coats and cloaks which hang up on one side, and after ascending a dark and raggedly-carpeted staircase, arrive in a meagrely-furnished, dimly-lighted room, where a number of men and women of various orders of semi-gentility are sitting solemnly round in a circle, which is now made perfect by the addition of Lady Timerton and Don Arminger.

Presently the medium, who is to open the night's proceedings, pushes aside the black curtain which occupies the open square left by the doors which have been taken down between the front and back rooms, and with a broad and business-like smile says, "Good evening to all assembled friends," pulls towards her a square table, on which are a lamp, several tambourines, and other musical instruments, and some blank paper and pencils.

Seating herself by it, and resting a corpulent hand and arm on it, the medium, who is an obese person of forty-two or three, begins her exalted mission by stating that the spirits had just sent a message to her to say she must not be rash.

Urged by an ardent member of the circle to ask the spirits what they meant by this, the medium, after a minute of deep abstraction, followed by a few spasmodic contortions, comes round sufficiently to say, in that soft voice which is an excellent thing in woman,—

"Dear friends, the spirits say that unless the medium is built up, there will be no further manifestations to-night."

"Their ain't been none yet," the unbelieving husband of a believing wife shouts out.

But the gentleman is quickly hushed down by a group of sympathisers with the medium, who press her to "name" what she will take to build her up.

A slight delay arises owing to her apparently uncontrollable human aversion to have resort to "stimerlants" as she calls them. But eventually the spirits are too strong for her, and with a shudder that it is indicative of her dislike to the course to which she is driven, she feebly cries out,—

"Champagne is what they will go on ordering."

"Champagne be it," says an advanced member of the circle. "All the ladies and gentlemen here present will, I am sure, gladly give towards a pint of the best fizz for our esteemed medium."

At this moment, while the purses are being taken out for the laudable purpose of contributing towards a pint of the best fizz, for the medium's immediate and their own ultimate advantage, the medium is again seen to struggle, subside, gasp, and recover.

"They will have it a quart; they say I need it worse than ever before," she gasps out ; and the same gentleman who previously alluded unfeelingly to the lack of manifestations, now says,—

"They should supply your drink, if they're not content with beer."

"A quart" the medium is heard to murmur in a far-off voice, and Lady Timerton, her face flushed with generous emotion, says to Don,—

"Poor thing! how weak she is; Lady Kenwyn told me it was most exhausting sometimes when the spirits didn't quite like the circle. Put in half-a-sovereign for me, Don."

The champagne is announced as being ready in a retiring room presently, and the medium, who has been apparently in a state of coma until now, rises up and totters off to partake of it.

A quarter of an hour elapses, and some of the circle get impatient. Then the medium's husband comes forward, and announces with many regrets that his wife is suffering so severely from the effects of some strong antagonistic element in the circle, that "there will be no further manifestations to-night."

There is a good deal of grumbling from the doubters, but this has no sort of effect whatever on the medium's husband, who perhaps thinks the manifestations of the half-crowns on entering, and the champagne later on, ought to be quite enough to satisfy any reasonable beings.

"How very disappointing and sad!" kind-hearted Lady Timerton says as they stumble out through the murkiness, and get into the carriage. "Still it has not been time wasted; it has been a wonderful experience!"

"Wonderful!" Don says, briefly, refraining from wording his hope that the medium and her husband may quarrel in their cups, and dash out one another's unworthy brains.

"How beautiful and touching it is that the dear spirits should think of the fleshly weakness," Lady Timerton goes on, "showing such sympathy! Lady Kenwyn told me that I should be quite astonished at the way they entered into our feelings and understood our wants."

"I think they would have contented themselves with suggesting small beer, if they had not known you were there, Lady Timerton," Don says, impatiently.

But Lady Timerton disregards the impatient tone, and is very glad that dear Don's opinion so entirely coincides with her own.

"Isn't it extraordinary that they should have been *en rapport* with me so soon?" she says, delightedly. "I think Lady Kenwyn must be right, and that I must have the mediumistic power. I was conscious of there being quite an unusual atmosphere around me in that room."

"So was I," Don says, with strong distaste.

"Then you felt it too?" she says, joyfully.

"I felt it, smelt it, was choked by it," he says, in disgust. "I thought I had never got into such an evil-looking, evil-smelling place in all my travels in savage lands. I hoped you were coming away loathing it all— the beastliness and mendacity, the shallow trickery and blasphemous pretence—as heartily as I am myself."

"Lady Kenwyn has prepared me for all this style of argument," she says, complacently. "When Catherine de Medicis first came into spirit intercourse with her, Lady Kenwyn unguardedly spoke of it in the world, and was scoffed at, and, I'm sorry to say, not believed even by me. Lord Timerton frightened me, you know, Don —said because his sister was mad I needn't be a fool, and I was weak; but what I have seen and heard to-night makes me very strong."

And to this day Lady Timerton looks upon the ordering of the champagne for the medium as proof incontrovertible of the truth of spiritualism.

Weak, well-meaning, womanly Lady Timerton has a strong hold, from long association, on Don Arminger's heart and consideration. Only "the folly of it" would strike him if any other woman showed herself ready to be so transparently humbugged and cajoled. But "the pity of it" is prominently before him now that Lady Timerton is the victim.

"It's too low and feeble a fraud altogether; I'd like to have the whole gang of them up for common swindling and obtaining money under false pretences," Don says to Lord Sylvertre later on, when Lady Timerton, exhausted by the remarkable manifestations she had witnessed, has retired to her own chamber to try if she can persuade

Helen of Troy or good Queen Anne to come and treat her with the familiar regard of a sister. "I'd like to have the chance of breaking every one of their "conditions," the mere imposing of which is an insulting proclamation of their belief in the idiocy of their "circle" at one fell swoop. I'd like to give that woman who craved for strong drink to-night ten months at the treadmill, and I should feel delighted to carry out the theory of selection by exterminating every one of the upper-class fools who make themselves cork jackets for this contagious imbecility."

"Including my aunt?" Sylvertre asks affably.

"Yes, including Lady Kenwyn; the mischief and misery she has brought into her daughter's life stamp her spiritualistic practices as accursed, if they're anything. Gardiner is a vicious brute, and there's not a more miserable—there will soon not be a more weakly forlorn woman in town than Lady Victoria."

"I don't like her, but I'm sorry to see Vic Gardiner going so fast," Sylvertre says, and then he adds, with a big air of impartiality, "but I don't quite see what his going a-head in his way, and her going adrift in hers, has to do with Lady Kenwyn's spiritualism."

"She excited and benumbed her daughter's reasoning faculties alternately at these confounded *séances*, and then told her that the "dear spirits had declared that she must marry Mr Gardiner," and Mr Gardiner aquiesced in the swindle because he was in debt, and Lady Victoria's fortune would square him. Now they're going apart as hard as they can, and—I hope Lady Vic won't get any influence over your sister, Sylvertre."

Don words his hope as he feels it, warmly, and Sylvertre falls headlong into error.

"It's the interest you feel in Nell that's setting you up about Vic Gardiner? Look here, old man, don't you alarm yourself, Elinor is all right; Vic can no more influence her than I can the Irish members! I can't give you a better idea of her firmness—or obstinacy."

His manner is so cordial, so almost fraternal, his words

are so unmistakable, that Don Arminger feels impelled to say,—

"I do take an interest in your sister; how could it be otherwise—"

He is going to add something relative to his warm friendship for Sylvertre himself, but the latter cuts in injudiciously, and having fallen headlong into error, now flounders about in it.

"I know it all, old fellow, and I'm delighted; I'd rather see Elinor married to you than to the best duke on the cards."

He holds his hand out heartily to Don as he speaks, and Don takes it, and feels the while that the boy he had trained, the man who is his best and dearest friend, has unwittingly drawn him into a trap, and sealed a monotonous, loveless fate for him.

CHAPTER XII.

AT THE BALL.

THERE is nothing more said between the young men relative to Elinor at this time. But when Don gets himself out of the house, pleading fatigue as a reason for leaving before Lady Elinor comes home from the theatre, he does devoutly wish that he had stuck to his original intention and dined at his club.

It comes home to him that he has shown a great deal of liking for, and a great deal of interest in, the girl whom he has known so intimately for eight years. That he should have done so strikes him as being untoward now, but he admits that Sylvertre, from the common-sense and friendly point of view, is quite justified in having said what he has.

"He thinks I'm holding off because of her father," Don tells himself; "whereas I wouldn't let her father stand in my path for an instant if I wanted her. But it's past thinking about now. Sylvertre having said what he has must have the satisfaction of feeling he hasn't offered me something I don't care to take. I wish with all my heart I hadn't seen the other one again."

His disquietude and uncertainty, and fear of hurting the proud, sensitive feelings which he himself has been partly instrumental in implanting in Lord Sylvertre, keep him away from the Timertons for two or three days. And each member of the family misconstrues the reason of his absence. Lord Timerton thinks that the "young fellow, in whom there is a great deal of good, has seen the folly of aspiring to a girl who might be a countess to-morrow if she pleased." Lady Timerton thinks that he is "hardening his heart against the sweet influences of spiritualism, and staying away, fearing her arguments in favour of it may be too strong for him." Sylvertre fancies that "it's fear of the governor" which keeps Don aloof. And Lady Elinor takes it for granted that he is in constant attendance on "that Miss Fielding."

"That Miss Fielding," meanwhile, is seeing no more of him than her rival is. In vain his mother sends him a little note each day entreating him to give some portion of it to them, and offering to dine at midnight nearly if no other hour will suit him. He is always engaged on work, and cannot come.

His sisters openly lament, rail at, and repine about his staying away. But Constance is not a sister, and will not avail herself of the sisterly privilege they proffer so freely. She "has no doubt Mr Arminger is much better employed; of course, he has seen all the things they take pleasure in seeing on account of their novelty, or if he hasn't seen them, he doesn't care to do so; for her part, she prefers being independent and dawdling about by themselves. Escorts are so apt to wax impatient, and are so intolerant of shop windows."

So Constance says, and she acts up to her words. She is the foremost of them all in seeking out whatever is best worth seeing. She is apparently inexhaustibly delighted with every form of pleasure, and untiring in pursuit of it. A walk in the park every morning to look at the riders in the Row is one thing that she insists on, and each day she goes there more than half expecting to see Don riding with Lady Elinor Divett.

But Don, as we know, is abstaining as assiduously from Lady Elinor as he is from Miss Fielding.

One lady, whom they look out for eagerly, after seeing her once, without knowing her name or aught about her, is that very Lady Victoria Gardiner of whom and her husband Don Arminger permitted himself to say some rather hard things. " Lady Vic," as she is familiarly called by every one in society, is a beauty of a luxuriant and loud order. Her complexion, eyes, and figure are faultless. Her habit always looks as if it were moulded upon her, and indeed it is buttoned after she is settled in her saddle. She is popularly described as " being up to everything," and is in the fastest set in society. She is known to smoke! She is said to swear! She is seen alternately in the society of all the most dissipated men in London—always excepting her own husband. And she is the only daughter of that Countess of Kenwyn, whose whole heart, soul, interest, and attention are given up to a star circle and intercourse with long-deceased royal sinners who, after having been filtered through several spheres, are now in the highest ones, and are to be regarded as saints.

Lady Kenwyn, absorbed in the pursuit of spiritualism, hears nothing and heeds nothing of the vagaries of the clique to which Lady Vic belongs. The intimate friend of Catherine de Medicis does not hear of her daughter's way of living with lords and ladies of high degree, of her own way of thinking and acting.

It would really grieve Lady Kenwyn for ten minutes if she observed what every one else who knows them sees plainly, namely, that Mr Gardiner is a scoundrel who is always ready to give his wife a slight impetus, if she is inclined to check herself on the downward path.

But Lady Kenwyn observes little else save the progress her pupils make in the society of the spirits who are in respectable spheres. Consequently Lady Vic goes on her way unchecked by maternal counsel.

There is a great talk about Lady Vic in these days, for she is playing for every charitable institution in London nearly, in company with the best amateur actors of the day. The other "leading lady," though a finished actress, highly trained and thoroughly experienced, is a little hard and dry in certain parts. She is past her first youth, in fact, and though she has subdued all tendency to superfluous flesh, she has run to bone a good deal, and does not contrast favourably with Lady Vic's soft curves and slender outlines.

But for all her charm and gracefulness and good-nature, Lady Vic is a woman for whom Don Arminger has an unconquerable horror. He does not like her, and he does not believe in her, and all his loyal blood boils in his veins when he sees her two or three times with Lady Elinor Divett, and hears their names coupled carelessly together.

It is the night of Lady Timerton's ball, and half London is going to it, for Lady Timerton prides herself on her talent for bringing people together and making them happy.

His sisters have entreated Don to go with them.

"If you don't, I know how it will be," Trixy pleads. "We shall arrive, and after a struggle we shall reach Lady Timerton, who will smile and say something kind, and then we shall pass on into the unknown crowd and be no more seen."

"Sylvertre will look after you, and I won't be late," Don says, shrinking from the idea of going to Lady Elinor's home in the company of the girl who is her rival.

"And when you come, you'll know heaps of people, and you'll never get to us three maidens all forlorn," Maude says.

But Constance says never a word.

If Don will not come with her without being asked, then he may stay away.

He has dropped in for the first time for several days

at his mother's just as afternoon tea is going on, and both Mr Arminger and her daughters cannot fail to perceive that there is great restraint in his manner to Constance, which manner Constance is quick to reflect. But they prudently refrain from noticing it, mistakenly supposing that Don is so absorbed by Lady Elinor Divett that he can give neither time nor attention to the old friend of his boyish days, the heroine of his gallant adventure.

Their fate at the ball is far less gloomy in reality than in the fancy picture painted by Maude. They are far too pretty in the first place, and far too highly distinguished by Lady Timerton and Lord Sylvertre in the second, to pass unnoticed even in a brilliant London ball-room. Their cards are full before they have been in the room ten minutes, and it is with a thrill of satisfaction that Constance feels she "hasn't one left for him," when she sees Don coming towards her through the crowd.

But his progress is arrested before he can reach her by Lady Elinor herself, who pulls herself up as she is revolving past him to say,—

"I am charged with a message for you, Don. My cousin, Lady Vic, says you're to ask her for the tenth. That's a waltz."

"I can't go fast enough for Lady Vic," Don says rather grimly.

"Never mind; she'll sit it out with you. She really has something to say to you, so you must do it."

Lady Elinor does not add, "for my sake," but her eyes say it, and Don feels angrily sure that there is some folly afoot, in which Lady Vic is seeking to involve Lady Elinor.

Meanwhile Constance has vanished, and so has Lord Sylvertre, and Don's jealous fancy connects the disappearance of the two, and the pleasure of the night is poisoned to him.

It does not occur to him, being Trixy's brother, to speculate as to sparkling, piquant Trixy's whereabouts. Other men in the room are missing the girl who is pleasantly ensconced in a far-off corner of the conservatory, with Lord Sylvertre by her side. He has attracted her interest, first by talking about Don, and now he is chaining it by talking about himself.

"The relations of tutor and pupil didn't exist very long between Don and me," Sylvertre says. "We became fast friends before we had been together a month, and now we're like brothers, and shall continue on these terms till the end, I trust," he adds warmly.

"Or until you both marry, and your wives either absorb you away from one another, or are jealous of each other," Trixy suggests. "I'm rather like a bird of ill-omen to throw such a leaden possibility over your rosy vision of the future relations between Don and you, am I not?"

"You're a very realistic young lady."

"I'm a very prosaic one."

"Yet you write romances?"

"No, I don't. I write stories of the real life I know, and there's very little romance about that."

"I don't know; I've always thought your life at Clyst by way of being a poem. Your home is beautiful and picturesque to a degree, and your mother, sister, and yourself all are employed in beautiful artistic work. Then you have for a friend a lovely young lady who is a little princess in her own land, and all the people round wonder at you for having such a celebrated brother, and for still condescending to walk the earth. Yes, I still contend your existence is a poem, and a poem that I am learning by heart."

He drops his voice as he says this. But Trixy, as she says herself, "is too prosaic" to fall to low tones and honeyed words.

"It would serve you right if I made mother invite you to Clyst on the strength of the nonsense you've been talking to me about our lives, and let you bore yourself to death there."

"I wish you'd try that form of revenge. You would find that I should bear my hard fate bravely."

"Here comes my partner," Trixy says, feeling relieved at the prospect of escaping from the seclusion of the conservatory, for she is beginning to find it strangely pleasant to listen to Lord Sylvertre, and she has no intention of surrendering at the first appeal.

"The supper waltz is mine, remember," Sylvertre says as she is moving away ; and as she assents with a bright, heart-free smile, Sylvertre feels that the man who is taking her away, and who will presently be clasping her closely in authorised fashion, is a presumptuous brute.

Meanwhile Don Arminger has been captured by lovely Lady Vic.

They have only swung half round the room when she stops and backs out of the revolving masses.

"Come out on the stairs, we can breathe there, and can speak without half a hundred old harridans hearing what we're talking about."

"As far as I am concerned, the harridans are quite welcome to the instruction or entertainment, whichever it may be, that will be afforded by our conversation."

"That's so like you ; you're always up aloft about everything. Now I'm of the earth earthy, and being that, I do like baffling and puzzling, and generally putting out my fellow-worms ; so, out on the staircase if you please, and hear what I have to say."

His repugnance to the office to which she is hilariously appointing him is very strong. But it is weak compared to what it would be if he knew what her real object is.

"You know my place, The Keg, at Barnes ?"

"I do not know it."

"Nonsense, Mr Arminger. You've heard of it often enough, and disapproved of it oftener, as I know very well. Now I'm going to be nice and forgiving, and beg you to come and honour my poor place with your presence for three or four days. I'll have nothing but fun and sunshine. I've not asked a single man or woman without grave deliberation, and I've succeeded in getting together those who most want to meet each other ; in fact we're all paired in perfection."

"And Mr Gardiner and you play the Darby and Joan in this domestic Arcadian light comedy?"

"Nothing of the kind,' she says, laughing; "Mr Gardiner would spoil everything by being the unwanted one in the first place, and wouldn't come in the second. No; The Keg is sacred to me and pleasure."

"And I should be strangely out of place in it," he says coldly.

"Oh, I know you think I ought to be stoned," she laughs carelessly, "but I'm very forgiving, and never quarrel with any one's opinions. I want you to come because my cousin Elinor will feel safer in her prudish little soul if you're there; she is not exactly in my set, you know, and some of them frighten her."

"Lady Elinor going!"

"Why not?" she asks haughtily. Then wishing to carry her point, and feeling that she will gain nothing by a display of temper, she resumes her coaxing tone. "Don't interfere to prevent her coming, there's a good fellow. I really am fond of Elinor, and it doesn't do never to be seen with one's own people; really, I'm not half as mad, bad, and dangerous to know as people make me out; so, come to The Keg, and be convinced that it's perfectly proper Elinor should be there; no one will try to flirt with her; we married women will take care of that."

"Why do you say this to me?"

"Because—it's no secret, is it?—you'll carry your point and sweep all poor Lord Timerton's silly objections into outer darkness, as I did when he remonstrated with me about marrying Cecil Gardiner. I'd better not have done it, she continues, shrugging her shoulders; "but Elinor and you will probably get on better."

She is saying this in the light, ringing tones which she rarely thinks it worth her while to modulate, when Constance Fielding passes by.

"Who is that?" Miss Fielding asks of her partner.

"Lady Victoria Gardiner. Arminger has kept clear of her up to now, but I suppose from what she said, that he's going into the family, and feels he may as well be on cousinly terms with Lady Vic."

"I suppose so," Constance says quietly, and when Don does free himself from Lady Vic's net, and reaches Miss Fielding at last, he meets with an iron welcome.

CHAPTER XIII.

AFTER THE BALL.

"I can only vouch for what I heard Lady Victoria Gardiner say to your brother as I passed them, and I am only telling you because I thought you would be glad to have Lady Elinor for a sister-in-law," Constance says to the two Misses Arminger as they are about to part for a few hours' rest, before facing the pleasures and business of the new day.

"I don't feel a bit glad," Maude says definitely. "Lady Elinor will be deadly dull to live with, unless she can go on living in the set, and living as that set lives, in which she has been brought up; and so Don will find if he marries her, and Don can't stand deadly dulness well."

"You can't judge her properly any more than I can," Trixy says eagerly, for Lady Elinor is Sylvertre's sister, and Sylvertre has been the reverse of deadly dull in Trixy's opinion during the last few hours.

As a rule, the youngest Miss Arminger does not permit her fancy to run away with her reason, but to-night's experience has been unlike the experience of all other days and nights of her life. Words have been spoken to her in tones that will ring for ever in her ears, and she does think all manner of good of the one who has spoken them, and of all to whom he is dear from the family point of view.

A double marriage! Don and herself wedded the same day to another brother and sister! As the vision of this possibility flashes through her mind, she blushes furiously, and feels half guiltily that she would pronounce any other girl a fool for jumping to the contemplation of such an extreme improbability.

"Honestly, Constance, wouldn't you think Don was throwing himself away if he were to marry a girl who is just an innocuous society puppet—nothing more?" Maude persists, and Constance replies with more acidity than she usually employs to flavour her words,—

"Under Lady Victoria's auspices, Lady Elinor may soon cease to be innocuous; but I'm too tired to talk about them now. Good-morning, dears. Oh dear, how I wish myself back in the country! These hours kill me, and make me cross."

"Wish yourself back with the Vaughans?" Trixy asks, with surprise.

"Yes—why not? I know the Vaughans so thoroughly that I am never deceived in them. I expect to find self-seeking, and unkindness, and selfish forgetfulness in them, and I'm not disappointed; I find it."

There are tears in her eyes and a pathetic strain in her voice as she says this, and Don's sisters read these signs aright, and mercifully permit her to depart without remark.

"Poor Con! I always thought she'd be our sister; didn't you hope so too?" Maude says, yawning, for other people's love affairs are rarely exciting enough to banish sleepiness.

"I don't know about 'hoping.' Lady Elinor may be quite as nice," Trixy says.

"Yes; only she has never been presented to us in this light until a few minutes ago; and I liked the contemplation of the old possibility best," Maude mutters sleepily.

Then she kisses her sister, and is soon in a deep restoring sleep, while Trixy is in a happier dreamland than she has ever visited before. A waking dream is Trixy's, but it is as full of sweet mysteries and subtle perplexities as any sleeping one could be.

Constance Fielding does not subside into a restoring

sleep; nor is she in a happy, waking dreamland. She is wrestling with the first, worst, bitterest disappointment of her life. The knowledge, namely, that she has given her heart to one who has not wanted it, and who has given his to another.

"If he doesn't suspect the truth already, he shall never see a sign of it now; anything would be preferable to being the object of his half-pity, half-contempt."

Then she remembers having told him, when he saved her from the bull, that she would "love him all her life," and her contempt for her own candour on that occasion is prodigious now.

It is a satisfaction to her now, in these her hours of angry mortified repentance, to remember how coolly she has been deporting herself to Don Arminger during these latter days, and how cuttingly indifferent her manner was when he did at last find her out, and solicit from her the honour of a dance.

Yet with the remembrance of her manner on this occasion comes a sense of degradation. The man who had been her last partner was still with her, well pleased to be seen in close attendance on a girl whom he saw was a beauty, and heard was an heiress. And this man she instinctively felt was one from whom Don Arminger would revolt. Yet though she shrank from his over-bold, too confident, too caressing manner, she would not rebuff it to-night, because Don Arminger should see how little she cared for his approval of her companions and conduct.

He is not an attractive man in many respects, this one whose *empressé* manner towards her caused Don's soul to kindle within him this night. He is an earl, fifteenth of his line, with a magnificent family history and an equally magnificent rent-roll. He is in the bloom and strength of his youth too, for only a quarter of a century has rolled over his head. But his steps are tottering as an infant's frequently, and his voice at the same time thick, and his words incoherent as a very old man's.

In fact he is doing his best to obliterate the noble marks of high-born manhood which is set upon him by too copious libations of every form of alcohol that can either stimulate his often flagging spirits or drown reflection.

But for all this the Earl of Charldale is the object of almost universal charity in the world he lives in.

"Such a fine young fellow—so full of noble impulses, and so easily led !" they say. "Kind to every one who approaches him. After all, what are his follies but the follies of a boy ?"

It is the prevailing opinion in the breasts of all the high-placed matrons in town who have marriageable daughters that a "good wife" will be the saving of Charldale, and will be able to lead him from the brandy and wine bin to the five o'clock tea-table with a silken thread. There is great unanimity of feeling about this. But here the unanimity ceases. For each mother feels that her own daughter is the predestined good wife, and each has no toleration for the schemes or hopes of other daughters' mothers.

But this night of Lady Timerton's ball further unanimity of feeling prevails among the mothers, who one and all combine in denunciation and detestation of the audacious young invader from the remote country who is so unconcernedly allowing herself to be the object of Charldale's devotion.

It is true that she makes no effort to monopolise his coveted attentions, nor does she respond to them encouragingly. But even her quiescent acceptance of them is offensive in the eyes of those who regard her as an interloper. Charldale has not only been "sought," he has been coursed and hunted and stalked, till at times he has been compelled to seek safety on the broad ocean from the fair sportswomen who have nearly brought him down.

There is accordingly something irresistibly attractive to him in the way in which Miss Fielding just tolerates him. He is even fascinated by the look of weariness which overspreads her face when he persists in pouring his uninteresting sentences into her ear.

"Not another girl in the world would have the honesty to look bored when I spoke to her, whatever she might feel," he tells himself rapturously, and then he sets with ardour about the easy task of bringing another rebuff upon himself.

"You ride and all that, I suppose?" he asks.

"I ride; but I don't know what 'all that' means, so I can't tell you whether I do it or not."

"May I hope to see you in the Row in the morning?"

"Indeed, you may not. I have no Row-riding blood in me."

"Where do you generally go? Tell me, for I am sure I should like it better than the Row."

"I have no horses in town."

"May I—will you—"

He is about to proffer the loan of one of his horses, but Constance stops him with a look of such unmistakeable surprised indignation that he is spared the actual commission of this offence.

"You are staying with Lady Timerton, aren't you?" he says lamely. "Lady Elinor would mount you, wouldn't she?"

Constance shudders at the idea of the favour of a mount being offered her by Lady Elinor. Then collects herself, and replies haughtily,—

"I am staying with Mrs Arminger."

"Arminger's mother?"

"Yes."

"Don't like Arminger myself," Lord Charldale says confidently, for the wine he has taken at an earlier stage of the evening is beginning to tell upon him. "Don't like Arminger myself; he's too much of the cultured cuss about him; but Sylvertre and the rest of them in this house think him perfection. I think Lady Elinor is throwing herself away.'

"I must ask you to take me to Mrs Arminger," Constance says coldly, and Lord Charldale, feeling that he has offended her, and not having the most remote conception of how he has done it, grows more sober through contrition and fright.

It is after this that Don comes to her. Lord Charldale is still hanging round about her, and as she declines to give Don the honour of a dance, Charldale feels that, for all her refusal, this Arminger, whom he dislikes already, is his rival.

Events march rapidly in a London season. People who mean to do anything during it soon realise that they have no time to lose. Two days after Lady Timerton's ball, Lord Sylvertre, in the course of an hour's stroll in the park with Mrs Arminger and her daughters, gives Trixy to understand that she can accomplish her fate at once if she will.

They are five or six yards ahead of the others, when he asks her suddenly to marry him. And Trixy, who has been hoping and wishing him to do so for the last three days, does not express any surprise.

"I'm so glad you've said it before I have to go home," she says frankly. "I shall go back to Clyst quite contentedly."

"But, my dear little girl, I hope you won't go home at all, till I take you as my wife," he tells her.

"I am sure Lord Sylvertre is proposing to Trix at this very moment," Constance whispers to Mrs Arminger; "the tips of her nose and chin both beam with satisfaction, and his profile looks so happily silly."

"How very angry his papa and mamma will be, I'm afraid," Mrs Arminger says unconcernedly.

And then a vexed shadow crosses her face as she recognises in a young man who steps forward eagerly from the rails doffing his hat low to Miss Fielding and Maude, her nephew, Donald Vaughan.

She does not desire to have aught to do with him or his. She is not a woman in whose heart a corroding sense of injustice or injury can find a place for any time. Still, she cannot but recollect how persistently the Vaughans have tried to press down and crush out both herself and her children. Still, though she is human enough to remember this, she is generous enough not to feel disposed to resent the sins of the father upon the son. Moreover, though she is sorry to see him at all, and more than sorry to see the eager, enamoured air with which he takes his place at Maude's side, he is her sister's son, and blood is thicker than water.

But she is glad when the Row and chairs begin to thin, and she has a fair excuse for breaking up the party and getting her own charges home.

"I shall call upon you at four," Lord Sylvertre says, as she is shaking hands with him. And maternal instinct teaches her that he is coming to ask her to surrender the first right in one of her cherished daughters.

"Why could not this man have waited a little longer," she thinks half angrily. Then she looks at Trixy's love-lit face, and chides herself for her selfishness.

It is an aggravation of the unpleasantness of the situation to her that her nephew Donald takes it for granted that he may walk home with them. He is so intimate with Constance Fielding in such a perfectly free and fraternal way, that, on the face of it, nothing could be more natural than that he should do this. But Mrs Arminger's heart is a little rasped about Trixy already, and there is no balm for this soreness in the sight of Donald Vaughan by Maude's side.

"I hope my own dear Don will come and see me before that man calls at four," she says to herself, and in her secret soul she accuses Lord Slyvertre of having been unwarrantably hasty and impatient.

The happy young girl makes full confession the minute she gets home.

"He has asked me to marry him, mother darling, and I'm more than happy."

Mrs Arminger does not dash this happiness by uttering the words, "More than happy in the thought of leaving me for this stranger," but she thinks them, as probably most mothers do when a daughter, who has been a mother's chief consideration from her birth, signifies her readiness to flee from the love-sanctified safety home, at the first note of an untried, untested lover's voice.

"Remember he has parents, darling; don't raise your hopes too high till you know how they look upon his project," Mrs Arminger says very tenderly. Then she adds more brightly, "Don't think me a croaker, dear Trixy, for reminding you of them ; very few marriages take place without opposition from some quarter; may yours be one of the exceptions."

Trixy's face flushes partly with pride and partly with love.

"If his people oppose his marrying me, never fear for me, mother; I will not fight for what is held to be too good for me."

Don does not come. He stays away to-day as he has been staying away for so many days, because the earth seems to have been shattered under his feet, and he no longer knows where is safe standing-ground. The way in which two members of Lady Elinor's family have seemed to relegate him to her fetters perplexes him horribly. For the first time in his life he adopts a hesitating, faltering, half-and-half policy. Instead of making an opportunity and going boldly to Sylvertre with a frank declaration of having no other intention than friendship in his intercourse wtih Lady Elinor, he waits for an opportunity which does not come.

The fact is, Don stultifies himself by recalling and reflecting upon every act of kindness which has ever been shown to him by the Timerton family. He piles these up, and contemplates them, until he is overwhelmed by the thought of the colossal debt of gratitude he owes them. And then the image of Constance Fielding rises, and the ring of the tones in which she told him that she would "love him all her life!" And altogether poor Don is in a situation of dire distress, not to say danger.

As he does not come, Mrs Arminger has to pass through the ordeal of an interview with Lord Sylvertre, unaided by any counsel from her son.

"It's like preparing to have a tooth drawn, isn't it, mother?" Trixy asks, when four o'clock is about to strike; and Mrs Arminger says, sighingly, that they had better all three go down to the dining-room, and leave her to receive Lord Sylvertre alone.

"If it were only a tooth to be drawn, I shouldn't send you three girls away; two should hold my hands and the other one my feet, in order that I mightn't be able to scratch and kick the dentist if I felt inclined," she says, trying to laugh.

"As it is there will be no one to prevent you from scratching or kicking Lord Sylvertre," Trixy says. "Dear mother! how it does love its cubs."

The visitor's knock is heard, and the girls fly, all of them excited out of the usual calm of conventionality on account of the one.

"I wonder how he'll begin?" Constance says, when they are regaining their breath in the dining-room. 'Your mother isn't like most mothers, and so ought to be approached differently; she's been so much to you, hasn't she?"

"She'll go on being more and more to us all her life," Trixy says, with a laugh that has a sob in it.

And then the girl bursts out crying, makes a dash from the room, and soars on frightened wings past the drawing-room to the sanctuary of her own chamber.

"Trixy is the first of us to want to go, Con," Maude says, meditatively. "I haven't seen the man I could marry yet—have you?"

"Yes," Constance says bluntly; 'but I sha'n't tell you who he is, and—I sha'n't marry him."

CHAPTER XIV.

LORD SYLVERTRE'S SUIT.

LORD SYLVERTRE wins his case with Mrs Arminger the minute he enters the room. He comes in, looking so extremely dubious of his reception, that the mother of the girl he has been wooing feels satisfied that he will not think that girl has been lightly won.

"You know what I have come here for, Mrs Arminger? Don will be able to tell you better than I can myself what sort of fellow I am, and if he satisfies you, will you give me your daughter?"

"Don is sure to satisfy me as far as you are concerned," she says cordially. "I think I know you well through my son already; but I know my daughter better. Before you ask my consent, you have, of course, obtained your father's?"

"Well, no, to tell the truth, I have taken that for granted; my father has never thwarted me in any reasonable thing."

"Lord Timerton may be justified in considering this an unreasonable thing. My child is very precious to me. Before I agree to giving her up I must be well assured that the one to whom I give her will secure for her all the tender regard, all the delicate consideration by which she has been surrounded from her cradle."

"I love her as much as even you can desire," he says simply and earnestly.

"I believe you thoroughly; but your family—how will they take this wish of yours? For it can be nothing but a wish of yours to be engaged to Trixy till your side has spoken."

"My mother will adore Trixy, and as for Elinor, Don's sister will be the most welcome sister-in-law I can give her."

He laughs a cheery meaning laugh as he says this. But Mrs Arminger steadily ignores his meaning. Whatever there may be looming between Don and Lady Elinor, is a veiled mystery to her as yet. Her son has not yet confided it to her, therefore she will not notice any allusion to it.

"And your father? You don't say a word of the one who must be the real arbiter of your destiny with my daughter."

' I admit that my father is crotchety, but I am confident of being able to talk him over, even if he objects, which I don't anticipate, at the first blush.'

Unconsciously Mrs Arminger's head settles itself into a prouder pose.

"My dear Lord Sylvertre, I am pleased as a mother must be that you have thought my daughter the one woman in the world best fitted to be your wife; when you bring me your father's consent to your marriage with her, you shall have mine. Until then there must be no engagement."

"May I see Trixy?" he asks anxiously.

"Certainly," she says heartily. "I can trust you to tell her my terms, and I can trust my child to keep them. I will tell Trixy to come to you."

Trixy, waiting in a tempestuous state of mind in her own room for the summons which seems to her so very long in coming, answers her mother's knock presently with flying feet and a trembling inquiry,—

"Mother dearest, are you satisfied?"

"As far as he is concerned, yes, dear. But he has a father, remember, and till that father endorses his son's request, you cannot be engaged. Remember that, Trixy. And now go down and see him, as I have promised you shall."

The gilt is off the gingerbread, the bloom off the plum; the sweetest odours of the roses of love must not be inhaled by them yet.

"The happy prince with joyful eyes," who is waiting for Trixy, longs to clasp the girl to his heart, and press the diamond ring he has brought for his affianced on her finger; but he does not dare to offer either the ring or the embrace in defiance of Mrs Arminger's unwritten law.

"I'm as sure of my father in the end as I am of myself," he says, and Trixy, who is trying to seem interested in a wonderfully intricate piece of silk embroidery, replies,—

"But you're not sure of him in the beginning—is that it?"

" He never thoroughly likes a plan until he has looked at it all round, and viewed it in every aspect. · In fact, he likes to keep up our habits of obedience, but I know how to manage him, and invariably get my own way in the end."

" I shall be glad when you've got it in this matter," Trixy says, half laughing as she speaks, hoping to conceal the nervous agitation which has possession of her.

Assuredly the girl's is a trying position just now. Her mother has set a task, which Trixy finds a hard one to perform. She has, in fact, to keep her lover aloof from her on an undemonstrative friendly platform, though she has accepted him for her future husband, and promised to be his loving wife.

" I shall have to choose an auspicious hour to break the news to him," Sylvertre says, unconsciously letting her perceive that he is more in doubt and fear of his father than he has professed to be ; " but I suppose in the meantime I may come here and see you ?'

" I think you had better not."

" Trixy ! won't you care to see me ?" he asks, in pained tones.

There is a spice of the unjust selfishness of his sex about Lord Sylvertre, and it seems hard to him that he may not see the girl of his heart as often as he likes, though he can't consult her dignity by proclaiming her as such at once.

" Perhaps I might get to care too much, and then, when your father has looked at the case in every aspect, and failed to find it pleasing, you might never come again ; then there would be nothing for me to do but to put my head under my wing, poor thing, and be a very disconsolate bird indeed."

" Fifty fathers would fail to keep me from you, Trixy. No human power will detach me from you, if you are staunch."

" Fifty fathers might reasonably be expected to fail— theirs would be such divided authority ; but I shall not defy Lord Timerton if, after 'looking at me all round,' as you say, he finds me wanting."

"At least you will let me call on Mrs Arminger every day? It will only be two or three days at the utmost that things will be unsettled. When I bring my father's consent, as I shall in a day or two, you will think you have been too stern to me, Trixy."

He has risen and come near to her as he says this; and now he is bending down, and his lips almost touch the soft, nut-brown hair that waves over her brow. But Trixy, though her whole heart yearns towards him, knows that, if she keeps faith with her mother, no kiss must pass between this man and herself till he is her affianced husband.

She looks up unflinchingly; it is hard to throw a shade of rebuke into her manner when all the while she is loving him so well; but a promise spoken or implied to "mother" is a very sacred thing in the estimation of these Arminger girls.

"You have come to shake hands and say 'good-bye' for a time; haven't you, Lord Sylvertre?" she says quietly, holding out her steady, slender hand.

"This is a cold parting," he murmurs, but Trixy rises now and draws herself up.

"If you knew how it tries me that you should seem not to understand the reason why, that you should seem not to wish to help me," she says falteringly.

And as she says this, he resolves more earnestly than ever to have this woman and none other for his wife.

About an hour after he is gone Trixy goes back to the drawing-room, and finds her mother there alone.

"You have just missed Don," Mrs Arminger says; "he loitered on here till nearly six, hoping that one of you girls would come in."

"You haven't told Don about me, have you?" Trixy asks quickly

"Yes, dear. We have never had mysteries or secrets in the family yet; we won't let the love-affairs be the means of introducing them."

"You're right, I'm sure," Trixy sighs, "but I feel so uncommonly like being rejected by Lord Timerton as unsuited to the character and requirements of his family; and if that's the case, Sylvertre and I will have to go on for years, maybe for ever, attached but not united. I've told him I won't defy his father myself, and given him to understand that he mustn't do it either; but I am sorry that I have to be approved and chosen by another man besides the man who wants to marry me. It's so very unlikely that both father and son will prefer me to any other girl in London for Lord Sylvertre's wife and the future Countess of Timerton."

"Whatever comes of this, Trixy, remember we are powerless to avert disappointment from you, but we are powerful in the perfect rectitude of our conduct. They may cut us, but they can't censure us."

"What does Don say, mother?"

"That you must be prepared for opposition from Lord Timerton, who has what Don calls an almost besotted sense of the magnitude of his position; but Don says Sylvertre will conquer in the end."

"Conquer—I don't like that word; I don't want to be fought over."

"You're worth fighting for," the mother thinks, and something seems to tell her that Sylvertre will fight for Trixy very manfully and well.

Meanwhile two or three things have been happening at Timerton House, which have not been conducive to Lord Timerton's peace of mind or sense of greatness.

In the first place his sister, Lady Kenwyn, has been quoted, and worse than this, sneered at and derided in the public press as being either an arch-duper in the cause of spiritualism, or a dupe and tool of the first water. Her ladyship is in the habit now of introducing paid charlatans who are professors of spiritualism in all its branches, into good society at her own house, and the orgies which take place under her noble auspices are making her a laughing-stock in the world to which she belongs.

In the second place his niece, Lady Victoria Gardiner (whose gay and *débonnaire* way of kicking her heels over all social traces, has been a thorn in his flesh since her childhood) has carried off his daughter Elinor to Lady Vic's own little *bijou* nest, The Keg, at Barnes.

And, in the third place, Lady Vic has committed the cruel and unpardonable indiscretion of assuming in a pretty little note to her uncle that he can't possibly be annoyed at Elinor's being with her, as his favourite, Don Arminger, is of the party.

"What the deuce does that precious niece of yours mean by writing such a letter as this to me? Coupling Elinor's name with that fellow Arminger's, in a way that I'd like to whip her at the cart-tail for doing," Lord Timerton says one morning, striding into his wife's private room, and flinging the letter down on her table, as if it had been a torpedo which he trusted might explode and demolish her.

Lady Timerton flurriedly picks the letter up, and without meanly reminding him that Lady Vic is his niece, not hers, proceeds to read the combustible epistle.

"Well?" he says, with rather a savage and alarming note of interrogation when she has finished it.

"Victoria always expresses herself so prettily," Lady Timerton says cheerfully, not having the faintest idea which way the wind is blowing her lord's temper.

"Does she!" he exclaims with such ferocity that she jumps in her chair; "and it's a pretty subject that she expresses herself about, isn't it? And it's a pretty prospect that you are preparing for your daughter. I solemnly declare that whatever evil or misery may come to your children in after life, it will be your own doing, it will be you they have to thank for it all. You encourage them to set themselves up against me; you encourage Sylvertre's extravagance, and Elinor's idiotic and disgraceful feeling for Arminger, and now you actually approve and applaud your niece's indecent conduct in getting my daughter to that den of iniquity, The Keg."

"You make my blood run cold, Timerton," the poor lady says tremblingly.

"You and your tribe make mine run hot enough," he roars. "Victoria Gardiner is a woman who—"

He is raving out his denunciation with such volume and force that he does not hear the door open and a servant announce "Lady Kenwyn," and so he declares Victoria Gardiner to be a woman who is unfit to enter a decent house, in the presence of her astounded mother.

When he does awake to the situation, it is to see his grand Juno-like sister confronting him with the port that possibly may have been one of the queenly attributes of Catherine de Medicis.

"Were you under the dominion of an evil spirit, Timerton, or did you know you were speaking of your niece—my child?" she asks in her low, soft, placid accents. But her blue eyes flash proudly as she speaks, and Lord Timerton wishes that his subjective wife only had been the recipient of his opinion concerning his niece.

"I was under the dominion of a spirit of fatherly indignation, that my daughter should have been persuaded by yours to go to The Keg in the society of men and women of whom I highly disapprove," he explains rather shufflingly.

"Oh, is that all?" Lady Kenwyn says indolently, accepting the explanation, for her mind is full of a revelation she has just received through the mediumship of an accomplished American, who is in such a highly rarified "circle" that he is enabled to read clearly the closest secrets of all who approach him antagonistically. As the secrets and thoughts he attributes to these unwary ones are in all instances the reverse of praiseworthy or even reputable, his power is becoming widely acknowledged, and he is much respected, and has great reliance placed in him by the faithful who believe in and take council with him.

"Oh! is that all? Really, I think you may be quite satisfied that Victoria has no second-rate people with her; indeed, I consider her painfully fastidious and worldly

Her manner to dear Mr Mott "—Mr Mott is the new medium—"was really most repellant when I took him to one of her at-homes."

"I give her credit for objecting to receiving cads, but she is anything but particular enough—anything but particular enough," Lord Timerton says, phrasing his censure much less harshly than he would do if Lady Vic were listening to him instead of her mother.

He is still smarting under his sense of having been cowed into comparative silence respecting her daughter's indiscretions by his foolish sister, and lashing himself into fury at the thought of Elinor's name being coupled with Don Arminger's, when his only son Slyvertre rather solemnly requests an interview with him.

"I suppose it's the old story ? You've been imprudent and extravagant, and now you come to me to free you from the fruits of your folly," Lord Timerton says gruffly.

For it is true that on two or three occasions, excellent fellow as Slyvertre is, he has found himself compelled to apply to his father to relieve him of debts which, in all integrity, he ought not to have incurred.

"No, it's not money ; in fact, it's nothing disagreeable in any way this time, sir," Slyvertre says, trying a gay laugh. which catches his breath before he can bring it to a natural conclusion, and causes him to gasp in an undignified way.

"It's something you're in a great hurry about, apparently," Lord Timerton says dryly, "for you've run yourself out of breath, it appears, and now you're tumbling over your own words. If it's not the old story, what is it. may I ask ?"

"Well, it's the old, old story, 'love,' not money, sir," Slyvertre says with a certain frank shyness that is very becoming to his young manhood, but which his father chooses to seem to regard sarcastically. "I have asked the dearest girl that ever lived to be my wife, and now I want to ask you to consent to my marriage, and also to ask you how I am to live when I am married."

"The best way you can, is the only answer I can make

to that last question, until I know who the lady is, and what her people can settle on her."

"The lady—" Slyvertre is beginning, when his father looks up with such angry suspicious interrogation in the eyes that gleam under the bent and bushy brows, that the young man pauses involuntarily.

"The lady is—a great fool if without a large fortune of her own she thinks of marrying you. Out with it all —who is she ?"

"Don Arminger's sister; the second one—the very pretty one, and I don't fancy she has any fortune."

"I don't fancy she has, either," Lord Timerton says savagely; "and deuce a bit of my consent will you gain to have any nearer or further connection with Don Arminger or his family."

The old man throws himself back in his chair as he speaks, fuming and foaming in a frenzy of passion which makes his son fear he is going to have a fit. But the paroxysm passes away without anything fatal happening, and rather to Slyvertre's relief, his father brings the interview to a close with these words,—

"Don't look so frightened, my boy : I've had one or two of these attacks, but I get over them quickly when I'm left quiet and to myself; you must leave me to myself now."

So in obedience to this desire Slyvertre leaves his father, feeling disconsolately that he has not made much headway towards gaining the object which is now nearest to his heart, and knowing that he does not dare to take the tale of delay and discomfiture to Trixy and her mother.

"The poor old governor ! he looked awfully bad for a few moments. I should never have forgiven myself if anything bad had come of that struggle. If he had only listened to me, and heard how determined Mrs Arminger and Trixy were to abide by his decision, he wouldn't have got into that way ; but he never will listen."

As day after day passes, and still Lord Slyvertre does not come near the Armingers, and still Don stays away from them because he does not dare to trust himself near Constance Fielding, a longing to get back to Clyst again comes upon Mrs Arminger.

It is evident that Maud is the only one of the party who is perfectly at rest in London. Her picture has made a great sensation, and has been sold for a corresponding price. She is hard and heartily at work on another, and when she is not working she is employed much to her own satisfaction, in finding out the latent good that is in her cousin Donald.

"Altogether would we were safely back at Clyst!" Mrs Arminger sighs.

CHAPTER XV.

"GLADLY, DEAR DON!"

In spite of Don Arminger's sense of responsibility about the expedition of which he has the organisation, and which has been deferred; in spite of his uncertainty as to his relations with Lady Elinor, and his hopelessness as to Miss Fielding; in spite, too, of his never long dormant disapprobation of Lady Vic and her clique, Don cannot help finding his visit to The Keg pleasant.

The Keg itself is the prettiest thatched cottage of the picturesque nondescript order of architecture that may be imagined. It stands on a rhododendron and rosebush decorated lawn, round which a little river runs nearly all the way. Its rooms are light and airy, small and numerous, and are furnished with every conceivable luxury in a miscellany of styles. There is no Queen Anne severity about any of the furniture or decorations. Yet such an exquisite taste presides that nothing looks florid, though a good deal of colour is employed; and though everything is of refined beauty, nothing looks too fine for constant use.

There is refined beauty too in the women who lounge

upon and about these things, which, for all their comfortable luxurious appearance, are so perfectly adapted to the place and the people who use them, that even Don Arminger cannot bring himself to denounce them as sensuous superfluities.

"Now, Mr Arminger," Lady Vic says in her sweet, saucy, challenging tones to him when he has been there two days, and is surprised, and a little sorry to find he likes it. "Now, Mr Arminger, you're quite ready with book and bell, I know. Have you found the demon you came to exorcise?"

"I came at your invitation, and you made no mention of any demon."

"I believe I mentioned a few of my friends," she says, laughing the ringing merry laugh which seems to belong to the sunshiny side of life, but which frequently is at its loudest when a woman feels the shadows darkening over her. "I believe I mentioned a few of my friends; knowing what you thought of them, I didn't go into exhaustive descriptions of them; but there's one coming to-night on purpose for you, Don"—she grows beautifully eager and confidential as she speaks— "Charldale, Lord Charldale, you know him, don't you? He has a thousand good points, and two thousand faults and follies to balance them. I want you to get him on your expedition, and save him from—himself!"

"Himself means alcohol, unlimited, doesn't it?" Don asked, remembering that Lord Charldale was the one apparently preferred to himself by Constance at Lady Timerton's ball.

"Charldale is a man you will take the greatest interest in when you come to know him well."

"May I be defended from such knowledge," but he wishes he had bitten his tongue out before it had spoken such words, when she says,—

"Oh, don't say that; redeem him from this one sapping, ruining fault if you can, not only because he's a good fellow when he's himself, but because he's going to marry your mother's friend, that lovely Miss Fielding."

"Is that so?"

"It's said so in good places, and it's paragraphed in two or three of the society papers to-day; but as the same papers say I've eloped with a baby-peer who won't attain his majority till I am in the sere and yellow, perhaps it isn't true. Meantime, do your best for him. You'd like Miss Fielding to have a husband who can keep himself straight, and look the world in the face, I'm sure; and you'll please Elinor by doing it. Elinor's so superior to all littleness that's she's quite delighted to hear the country beauty is likely to carry off the match of the season."

"I'm always glad to be able to please any member of Lord Timerton's family, but why do you make a point of my pleasing Lady Elinor especially?" he says boldly.

But Lady Vic only laughs and walks away to join some other guests, saying,—

"Oh, don't be so sly, Don! I'm not to be deceived, either by Elinor's faint protests or your assumed unconsciousness."

He is vexed with her for not crediting him with being as innocent of all lover-like designs on Lady Elinor as he seems to be; but the more important subject of Constance's engagement to Lord Charldale takes his thoughts away from himself.

That Constance—the sweetest, bravest, truest-hearted, clearest-minded girl he has ever known—should have freely promised herself to the aristocratic young sot, whose besetting sin is a by-word and scorn in society, shocks and astounds him.

That she of all women in the world should have been snared by rank and position! That a title should have caught her independent, unconventional soul!

"There's absolutely nothing in the fellow's appearance to catch her fancy even for a day; young as he is, he's bloated and coarse; he can't converse for five minutes on any subject but race-horses and yachts; he'll outrage her purity and pride by making himself a laughing-stock in his cups; he'll neglect her; and I must stand by and see this sacrifice consummated, because, forsooth, I'm not her brother, and have no right to speak. Oh, little Constance, better that the bull had done for me that day, than that you should have told me you'd 'love me all your life,' and that this should be the end of it."

He despises himself for letting the thought of the woman who is leaving him for such an one as Charldale haunt him as it does. But he cannot lay the ghost of the happy possibility that came across him only the other day.

Then he remembers that he has no right to feel the faintest touch of anger, or even of disappointment. He remembers that the peculiar relations into which he has been thrust with Lady Elinor through Sylvertre's unguardedness and precipitancy, have made him hold aloof from and seem to shun Constance.

What other could she think than that he had grown as careless of her in reality as he was in seeming? If, that is, she thought of him at all!

Still, she ought to have been more loyal to the promise of her beautiful, independent, high-spirited childhood than to have given herself to a man who would never be able to take care of her, since he was rarely able to take care of himself.

"I'd rather see her dead than ever hear her name bandied about," he tells himself passionately, and he almost makes up his mind to go the next morning to his mother, and beseech her to use her influence with Constance to break off the match with Lord Charldale.

But on what plea or pretext can he interfere? Constance has relations and guardians, a clear judgment and a strong will. If all these are in favour of Lord Charldale, how can he (Don) come with objections and reasons against the match, however well-founded these may be? Possibly his own mother may deride him for cavilling at what is so distinctly an advantageous match in society's estimation, for contact with the world makes people very worldly. Or even if his mother is on his side, Constance may very likely resent his absurd presumption in attempting to preserve her in peace and safety.

He can't risk that. Constance's contemptuous resentment would be the final crushing straw, so he determines not to bring it upon himself, but to let what is inevitable take its course.

It is rather unfortunate and detrimental to the course of his true love that Lady Elinor should be the one to break in upon his miserably resigned meditations. For she has known him so long and well that insensibly she adapts herself to any mood he may be in.

Unfortunately, too, it happens that Lady Elinor has just had a brief and hurried note from her brother, telling her that he has spoken to his father about his love for and hopes respecting Beatrice Arminger, and adding,—

"Though the governor looks blackly enough upon the project now, he'll come round in time, I feel sure of that; meanwhile we must wait."

Elinor comes in with her head full of this news which she has just had from her brother, and without consideration she takes it for granted that Don must know what is going on between her brother and his sister. Accordingly, without prelude of any kind she says out of the fulness of her heart,—

"Oh, Don! Sylvertre is quite sanguine about papa giving his consent in time; in the meantime, Syl says, ' we must be patient.'"

She speaks the last words in inverted commas, meaning Don to understand that she is quoting Sylvertre about his own case. But the misfortune is that "spoken" inverted commas are not visible to the naked eye. In this case, too, Don's mind is clouded with the foregone conclusion, that the only love affair about which Sylvertre is likely to speak to his father is the one Sylvertre erroneously imagines is going on between his sister Elinor and Don Arminger.

Driven to bay, feeling disheartened and disgusted with the fate rumour is assigning to Constance Fielding, remembering all he owes, or imagines he owes, to Sylvertre and Sylvertre's family, Don Arminger succumbs to the fate that seems to be forced upon him.

"I have no right to ask you to share such a lot as mine," he says gravely, and with such emotion, that Lady Elinor feels satisfied he must indeed love her wildly and well to be so utterly overcome; "but if Sylvertre has half won your father's consent, may I hope to win yours?"

"You mean—do you mean my consent to—to—"

She pauses in confusion and perplexity, and he is chivalrously desirous of not leaving her in doubt a moment longer.

"Your consent to be my wife."

"Oh, Don, gladly, gladly, dear Don," she says, bending her stately head, and stretching out her hands towards him, half in protection, as it seems to his uneasy observation, a little in appealing surrender. "Gladly, dear Don, but it's not papa's consent to our marriage that Sylvertre has been fighting for, don't you understand? It's his own affair with your sister Trixy. I thought you knew all about it, or I would have been more lucid."

"With Trixy!" he says, taking advantage of the opportunity of expressing the deep surprise he feels at this revelation to conceal the deeper chagrin which is his portion for having blundered into a trap which has not even been laid for him.

"Yes, with Trixy," Lady Elinor says, seating herself in a lounge-chair opposite to him, and complacently fanning herself; "but now please leave Sylvertre and Trixy alone, and tell me what peace-offering you'll take to papa when you propose to rob him of his daughter. He'll flame and flare at first, of course, I warn you of that, but when he finds you are determined, and what's more to the point, that I am determined, he'll give way."

She gives him an encouraging glance as she says this, but it is unheeded by him. He is resting his elbow on the table, and his hand supports his forehead, and half covers his eyes. Anything more unlike the picture of a successful lover can scarcely be imagined.

"You're not cast down by the prospect of a little opposition, are you, Don?" she asks rather sharply, presently, for there is something about Don's frigid acceptance of the situation which palls her pride.

"I promise to meet the opposition in any spirit you desire," he says a little too courteously.

Her head gives an impatient toss involuntarily.

"Meet it in the spirit you would meet anything else that was adverse to your honour or your love," she says, and then she rises slowly, very slowly, and saying something about its being time to go and think about dressing, she gets herself gradually out of the room without her lover making an effort either to detain her, or to embrace the tips of her fingers.

What has made him do it? What has led him on to conduct himself like an ass—like such a precipitant ass? Why had he acted on the impulse to save her from humiliation at such a heavy cost to himself? And after all, if he had only waited another minute it would have been made clear to him that there was no humiliation to her involved in the matter! It would have been shown to him that she was speaking of her father with reference to her brother's case, not to her own.

What evil genius had presided over the inauspicious moment of his making an offer which he must always regard as a sacrifice of himself ("heart" being merely another word for "self" on these occasions), and which the lady's family will always regard as a piece of presumption, however tolerantly they may treat it.

As for Lady Elinor being the slave to anything approaching to a violent or intensely romantic attachment to himself, he is not weak enough to imagine anything so absurd for a moment. He understands thoroughly that Elinor has grown fond enough of him to accept the position of his wife, partly because she is fond of him, and partly because she will not have it said that she is trammelled by her father's prejudices. But his prophetic soul tells him that though she will accept the position, it will fail to satisfy her

His prophetic feeling is even more correct and true than he thinks it. In a thousand little intangible ways, and by myriad signs Lady Elinor, if she becomes his wife, will unwittingly give him to understand that she is remembering and regretting.

However, upbraiding himself for what he has done will not avail him now. He has done it, and he must bear the consequences as manfully as may be. Retrospective lamentation is but a currish and cowardly thing at the best, and there is nothing of the cur or coward about Don Arminger yet. What an uncongenial wife may make him by-and-by, remains to be seen.

While he sits where Lady Elinor left him, trying to think out the manliest and best course, and strenuously purposing to pursue it, Lady Elinor herself has made her way to her cousin's room, where Lady Vic is alone, according to promise, waiting for her.

"Well, how did he take Sylvertre's news? Did it embolden him to speak the clenching words?"

"He spoke them, but under the influence of a mistake, I honestly believe," Lady Elinor says laughingly. Then she tells Lady Vic how she had begun to quote Sylvertre, and how Don, misunderstanding her, had applied what she was telling him of her brother to his own case.

"So he's taken heart of grace at last, has he?" Lady Vic muses. "I'm not a bit in love with Don Arminger myself; but as you are, I suppose I must congratulate you. dear. My own impression is that you will find you won't like it altogether; but then no woman ever does like it altogether, so you won't be singular. When is he going to face your father?"

"I don't know. Now, please, Vic, don't make a joke of it, for when papa hears it, it will be no joke. I'm not going to be crushed out of shape like mamma, though. I know beforehand that papa will talk as if I wanted to marry the footman or the groom, but if Don sticks to it I will."

"I wonder if any one is worth sticking to?" Lady Vic says meditatively. "I'm sure my worthy spouse isn't.

Oh dear, dear, dear! what nice young men you and I used to plan we'd marry in our nursery days, Nell, and now I've married a brute, and you're going to marry a prig."

"He's not that," Lady Elinor says warmly.

"Yes, he is, in a way. He's so disgustingly superior to all the little venial faults and follies of our world that he'll either make you ashamed of belonging to it, or afraid to say you're not ashamed. But never mind, Nell; cheer up. Very likely you'll be safe, and that's something."

Lady Vic is serious for half a minute as she says this, and her cousin looks at her uneasily.

"What do you mean, Vic?"

"Never mind what I mean now; you'll learn that soon enough. I wish I hadn't called Don Arminger a prig. He's the best man I know, and if ever he tells you I'm not fit to speak to he'll be right. Now, Nell, my child we must dress. I do hope Charldale will keep straight till we go to bed. It's so unpleasant when he lurches against little tables in the drawing-room. Let us hope Miss Fielding will redeem him."

CHAPTER XVI.

"THAT GIRL'S MOTHER."

WHEN Lord Timerton comes quite to himself after requesting his son to leave him alone, in order to recover himself, his first impulse, naturally enough, is to send for his wife, and accuse her of being accessory to the evil and and corrupt deeds of her son.

She comes to him breathless, panting, and flushed, and Lord Timerton hates a woman whose circulation and complexion are not always in good order.

"What is it?" she begins excitedly, as she waddles down the room towards him. "They said you were not well, and I fancied there had been words between Sylvertre and you."

"I wish you wouldn't puff so; you raise such a gale that I shall be having neuralgia in my head," he says, putting his protecting hand over the ear that is nearest to her, "and I wish you wouldn't employ 'fancy' with regard to Sylvertre and me. The boy and I are on the most friendly terms. No one can say I don't love my boy, and haven't dealt liberally by him, but when you encourage him to go out and entangle himself with people of whom I can't approve, I suppose you will grant me that it is time for me to speak."

"Oh, Timerton, what have I done now?" she asks tremulously, and as he cannot worry anyone else at the moment, by reason of his inability to get at them, he resolves to worry her.

"You've been conniving at this affair with that girl!"

In a moment all Lady Timerton's maternal instincts are aroused! Her son is her son! And if it can be shown that he has gone beyond the border in search of a wife, then, indeed, is her lot a weariful one, and she a sorely tried woman.

"Is it about Sylvertre?" she gasps.

"It is about Sylvertre, you needn't doubt; it's about Sylvertre's wanting to disgrace himself by making **a** low match; and I say you're at the bottom of it."

She plumps herself back into a chair, more flustered, flushed, unbecomingly agitated than ever at this cruel accusation. Her heart is quite in the right place, though she does not look nice. If Lord Timerton could only understand it, he would know that not a heart in the universe beats with more full, true, and loyal wifely allegiance than does hers for him at this moment. She forgives the rough words, and the injustice to herself, out of sympathetic consideration for the way his paternal pride and affection must be wrung, if indeed Sylvertre has declared himself determined to make a low match. The ready tears rush from her eyes and flow down her cheeks as she sobs out,—

"It can't be that our boy wants to break our hearts in such a way. I've been so proud of him all his life;

it can't be that he is to become a grief and a shame to us."

"Don't you know anything of it ?" Lord Timerton interrogates sharply. "Haven't you been encouraging him, and throwing the girl in his way ?"

"I throwing a low girl in his way !" she says indignantly. "What can you be talking of, or thinking of, to suggest such a thing ?"

"You can't deny that you have thrown Don Arminger's sisters in his way."

"Is it one of the Armingers ?" she cries, beaming with delight. "How could you frighten and deceive me by pretending it was some one objectionable ?"

"There you are ! Just like you, to want to see us all disgraced and lowered for the sake of opposing me. I tell you, madam, no girl in the kingdom could be more objectionable to me than this Miss Arminger, not only with regard to Sylvertre, but with regard to Elinor ; as sure as Sylvertre entangles himself with her, Arminger will have the presumption to propose for Elinor. And as she is fool enough to be in love with him, there'll be a nice kettle of fish."

"We might well be proud to welcome him as our son, and to give the dear girl into his safe keeping," she says deprecatingly, and in all her life she has never been nearer having a book thrown at her head by her irate lord than she is at this moment.

"Don't talk such confounded twaddle to me, Lady Timerton !" he shouts out. "If I find you abetting or encouraging either of these pair of fools, I'll send you down to Gatley, and take Elinor abroad till she's cured of her idiotcy. Sylvertre I can't compel to leave the country, but I shall see that girl's mother, and put it very plainly to her that a marriage with her daughter will completely separate my son from me ; if she has any decent feeling after hearing that she'll put a stop to it."

"You can't insult Mrs Arminger in such a way," she says appealingly.

"Can't I indeed, Lady Timerton ; who is to prevent

my speaking for my son's good?   I tell you it's as much my duty to save him from this if I can, as it is yours to keep a sharper look-out on your daughter than you do. I'll have Elinor home; you shall go down to The Keg to-morrow to fetch her."

But despite this order, when to-morrow comes, Lady Timerton manages to evade it. She is one of those weakly, indulgent parents who cannot put themselves to the pain of depriving a child of any present pleasure for its future good. So now, though she does feel that there is something pernicious in the atmosphere of The Keg, still as dear Elinor seems to be enjoying herself, she allows dear Elinor to remain.

Two or three days pass, and Lord Sylvertre, hoping each hour that something will occur to soften his father, weakly stays away from the Armingers, not liking to go until he can appear in the character of a successful and acknowledged lover. And this course of his, dictated as it is by warm love for Trixy, and jealous consideration for her pride and self-respect, causes grave doubts to arise in Mrs Arminger's mind, and stinging fears in Trixy's.

At last the mother, seeing the look of anxious expectancy deepening on the lovely face that is so dear to her, breaks down the little barrier of silence and restraint which has been raised during the last few days, and says,—

"Have we all had enough of London, my children? If we have, the garden at Clyst is full of roses by this time, and only the servants are there to enjoy them."

"Oh, mother, yes!" Trixy cries vehemently; "enough of London! I should think so. I've had a good deal more of it and its ways than is good for me; let us go home, and forget all that has happened here."

When she says this they know that Trixy is teaching herself a great lesson of resignation, and that she has brought herself to believe that her lover has failed her.

To the surprise of the Armingers, now that they are really preparing to go back to Clyst, Constance Fielding betrays a certain amount of unwillingness to fall in with the scheme.

The fact is the girl feels that she cannot go back and live the old life at the Vaughans, now that the unnamed intangible hope which made that life endurable is dead.

How will it be possible for her to go on proclaiming her pride in and admiration for Don Arminger, while her heart is burning and aching with jealousy of Lady Elinor? And if she keeps silence about him, the Vaughans will guess the reason why, and triumph over her. No; she cannot go back to Strathlands, now that the dreams and visions and unuttered hopes which have irradiated her life for so many years, have perished. She cannot go back to Strathlands, and Woodside is not ready for her, and there is no longer peace and perfect pleasure in intercourse with the Armingers. They will of course go on constantly speaking of Don as of old, and perhaps they will take to praising and extolling Lady Elinor, and this is the one straw too much for Constance.

The girl is wounded, disappointed, heart-sore. She is impulsive by nature, impatient of control, apt to take desperate measures. What further can be urged in her excuse? Alas! little. The record which must be written of her here will not have much sympathy or toleration for her it is to be feared. But as lenient a judgment as can be accorded to her is prayed for. In the bitterness of her spirit she believes that if she takes a new duty and obligation upon herself, she will, in the full and honourable discharge of them, find balm for her wounded spirit, peace and rest for her torn and restless heart.

The opportunity, the temptation comes. The Earl of Charldale offers himself and his almost fabulous fortune to Miss Fielding, and there is no one to tell the girl what manner of man this is whom she is promising to marry.

She is of age, and there is no one to say her nay. Moreover, who would have the courage or the folly, the unworldliness or the blundering stupidity, to prevent her making the best match of the season. On the contrary, she is fiercely and savagely envied and abused for her great good luck, and no one knows how she despises her self for having availed herself of it.

Mrs Arminger has a glimmer of the truth that if her son Don had come to the fore, Constance would not have been Countess of Charldale. But even Mrs Arminger is a little dazzled by the brilliancy of the position and the *bonhomie* of the gallant-looking young man who offers it to Constance. And as in these days of his courtship Lord Charldale gives his enemy a wide berth, all looks fair and promising on the surface.

The forthcoming event is duly announced in the society journals, and Constance suddenly finds herself the most-talked-of girl in London. And then Don comes up, and gives his mother two staggering and altogether unpleasant pieces of intelligence.

The one is that Lord Charldale is in plain language a confirmed drunkard ! The other is that he, Don, is en-gaged to Lady Elinor Divett.

"Whichever way I look I see nothing but misery," poor Mrs Arminger says despairingly for once in her life. And then she tells her son of Lord Sylvertre's apparent abandonment of his suit.

"He hasn't given it up, he isn't thinking of giving it up, but Lord Timerton's 'kittle cattle to shoe behind.' Sylvertre is only waiting to get his father's consent; he has written to his sister telling her so."

"And his father will not give it ?"

"Time will show, mother ; Sylvertre's plucky and honest enough. Trixy must be patient, and have confi-dence in him if she loves him ; he won't do anything rash, but he'll be very determined."

"Then there's Maude giving me anxiety for the first time in her sweet life."

"What about ?"

"About your cousin Don Vaughan ; they're falling in love as fast as they can, and what can I do ?"

"Nothing ; why should you ? My sister is too good for him ; I know that as well as you do, mother ; but then Maude's too good and sweet for the majority of fellows, he ought to feel himself the luckiest fellow on earth if Maude cares for him."

"His father will be furious."

"That's a very minor matter. Maude is a girl who can command respectful consideration. If my sweet, stately, clever sister gives herself to Donald Vaughan, it will be on condition that his father is grateful to her for doing it. Don't distress yourself about them, mother; Constance is the one you ought to be most anxious about now."

"She is not my child, and all the world thinks her a woman to be envied."

"Don't you take the world's opinion, and the world's tone, mother; tell her what I have told you."

"Then I must quote you, Don; she will naturally ask me to give up my authority. Do you wish to appear to be putting obstacles in the way of her marriage?"

"Yes, even at the cost of her thinking me an impertinent, jealous, interfering fool," he says. "She shall not marry Charldale in ignorance of that fearful vice of his, which will make life a hell to her if she becomes his wife. I tell you, mother, I know it from men who have known him from a child. His is no common case. Drink is a madness with him. Temperance is useless to him. He must rigidly and totally abstain from every form of alcohol. A glass of wine so excites him that he can't restrain himself from drinking off a bottle full at once—and then he's mad! You must impress this upon Miss Fielding. Good heavens! her marriage with this man will be her heart's murder. Insist on her making it a condition that he takes the pledge and keeps it. Persuade her to test him for a term; do anything to stop this awful sacrifice."

"Oh, Don, my dear, dear son, you could have stopped it, but I can't," she says sadly, and then, with interest and fear, she asks him a little about Lady Elinor.

"I would rather that nothing is said about it until I have seen Lord Timerton," he says, in some embarrassment.

"And Lord Timerton will, I suppose, be decidedly opposed to it, as he is to Lord Sylvertre's engagement to your sister?'

"I don't know, mother. I shall ask for his consent as soon as possible, and if he refuses it I shall offer Lady Elinor her freedom. It will be hers to resign me or retain, just as she thinks proper."

"I wish you were all little children again, with no thought of marriage in your heads," his mother says, half laughing; but there is a good deal of seriousness underlying the smiling manner.

Then Don goes away, and Mrs Arminger tries to perform the task he has laid upon her of offering counsel to Constance.

As delicately as she can, Mrs Arminger approaches the obnoxious subject, and as she proceeds she sees Constance's colour fluctuating a good deal, and an uneasy expression coming into her eyes.

"It would be too awful if it were true, Mrs Arminger; but I think your informant, whoever he or she may be, has maligned him. Lord Charldale told me that I must expect to hear him run down now; he has disappointed so many unscrupulous mothers about their daughters by proposing to me."

"Constance, it's not like you to say that, or think it?"

"No, I know that. I'm not a bit like what I used to be. Something has changed me to all the world excepting you and Maude and Trixy. My love for you three will never change, but as for others—"

Mrs Arminger has hardly recovered from the perturbation of spirit which has been caused by her interview with Constance—an interview which ends in Miss Fielding declining to believe Lord Charldale to be addicted to the vice with which gossip is now accrediting him—when she is compelled to face the fact of the Earl of Timerton being within her borders.

The mother's chief anxiety, when Sylvertre's potent father comes into the room, is that Trixy may not know that he is here. For the furtherance of this end, she leaves him for a few moments with a hurried apology, in order that she may go and consult with Maude as to the best way of keeping Trixy in ignorance of the presence of the arbiter of her destiny within their own territories, and Maude undertakes to manage the situation by getting her sister out on a shopping expedition.

"Gone to get her daughter to put on her most becoming war-paint, and bear down upon the cruel father in it," he says, chuckling to himself at the futility of the scheme he is imagining.

Then he goes on to tell himself that "the girl's mother" is a wonderfully good-looking woman, but just the sort to keep a tight grip of Sylvertre if he, Lord Timerton, does not wrench his son out of her designing hands.

He is rather surprised, therefore, when Mrs Arminger comes back with the simple statement, spoken by way of explanation of her absence, of having been engaged in "giving her daughters several commissions, which they are just going out to execute."

Lord Timerton feels almost disappointed as she says this, for he has felt a good deal of unacknowledged curiosity to see the girl who has won his son.

Moreover, now that Mrs Arminger is sitting opposite, looking at him so calmly, and without any sign of impatience or annoyance, or even embarrassment in her face or manner, he feels that his mission is an awkward one, and begins to regret having come upon it.

However, hard as it is to break the ice, he knows that the onus of doing so is upon him, and that, unless he says a portion at least of what he came to say, he had far better have stayed away.

"Probably my son has prepared you in a measure for my visit?" he begins, and Mrs Arminger answers quite cheerfully,—

"Indeed, no; I have not seen Lord Sylvertre for some time."

"Am I to understand that you have not seen him since he spoke to me about the exceedingly ill-advised engagement between your daughter and himself?—an engagement which you must feel I can never countenance in any way."

"No such engagement exists," she says quietly; "but if your son were engaged to my daughter, which he is not, I certainly should not wrong my child by feeling that you could never countenance it."

"I am speaking of the case irrespective of the young lady altogether. I have other views for my son, and my object in calling on you to-day, was to ask you to strongly advise your daughter to relinquish the affair before it takes deeper root, and may possibly affect her happiness."

"My daughter cannot relinquish what does not exist; there is no engagement. If you had not come here to-day, I should probably never have mentioned the subject to her again; it was closed between us from the moment she bid him bring your consent before she could consider his offer. You see, my lord, you have been attacking a grievance which has no substance save in your own brain; and in coming to me you have sought to make me punish my daughter for what is solely the act of your son."

"I am sorry to have offended you," he says.

"Your offence has been against good-feeling and good taste; I will not take it as against myself."

"I should like to give you some of the reasons which make me desire to see my son make a—a different marriage to this we are discussing."

"Pardon me, Lord Timerton, I have no interest in your reasons—they are for your son's good, no doubt; but allow me to correct one of your expressions; we are not 'discussing this marriage,' there is no possible marriage to be discussed between—"

Even as she speaks she remembers Don and Lady Elinor, and the thought of them makes her nervous. She is not on such sure and dignified ground with them as she is with Trixy.

"I have come in all kindness, as far as kindness is consistent with prudence," he says, and she replies,—

"And I have listened in all patience, as far as patience is consistent with my respect for my daughter.".

He rises slowly.

"If I had known you before I came, as I know you now, I should not have dared to come," he says bowing low to her.   And then he goes away, not feeling at all sure whether he has gained a victory or sustained a defeat.

The next day they go back to Clyst without having seen anything more of Lord Slyvertre.

CHAPTER XVII.

POOR VIC.

CONSTANCE is welcomed back to Strathlands by her aunt with as much deferential affection and ecstatic pride, as if a coronet already graced her brow and never a single murmur against the man who is to place it there had reached Mrs Vaughan's ears.

The wife of the man who married her solely in order that she might induce her niece, the heiress, to marry his son, has not a jot or tittle of sympathy with the bitter sense of disappointment and chagrin which overwhelms that man now.

On the contrary, Mrs Vaughan openly laughs at her husband, and scoffs at that feeble, faulty diplomacy of his, which has been unable to avert an end so full of annoyance and mortification to him.

"Don't expect me to throw cold water on my niece's happiness," she says to him when he tells her that a rumour has reached him that Lord Charldale is so addicted to habits of intemperance that no woman with a spark of self-respect can expect peace or comfort in a union with him.   'Your motive in collecting all the common vulgar gossip you can get hold of against the Earl of Charldale is too well known to me, for me to feel uneasiness for a minute."

"Whatever my feelings as Donald's father may be about this proposed marriage, they would never lead me to hint a word against Lord Charldale that is not well authenticated," he says indignantly, and his wife only laughs, and tells him that if he wanted her influence with her niece to back up his wishes, he ought to have let her remain Miss Damer.

"Since I've been your wife I've known too much about you! I've seen to much of your selfish overbearing temper, and fathomed too many of your schemes, to wish to see Constance the wife of a son of yours," she added defiantly; and though he hates her, and is her husband, he feels that he is powerless to bring her into subjection or to make her miserable.

"I shall speak to Constance myself," he says despairingly.

"Do! I've prepared her for your ill-natured interference. It matters very little to me what undignified things you do, or what petty low gossip you scrape together and repeat. I am not like your poor crushed first wife, who really thought you a great and good creature, and let you break her heart. I can laugh at your blunders, but I'll tell you beforehand that you'll make a really pitiful mistake if you asperse the Earl of Charldale to my niece."

Mrs Vaughan takes a malicious delight in rolling out the full title of the man who has successfully rivalled Donald Vaughan and baffled Donald's father. She knows that the sound of it makes Mr Vaughan's ears ache, and Mr Vaughan is the one person in the world for whom his wife has no mercy. She can never forgive the slight and insult he offered years ago to her egregious, ill-founded vanity, in letting her clearly understand that he married her solely because he thought she would forward his views with her niece. She can never forgive this, and whenever an opportunity offers of making him smart, she takes that opportunity eagerly, and makes the most of it.

She glories now in the great match her niece is going

to make, chiefly because it will be the climax of Mr
Vaughan's disappointment. She revels in making the
social circle around them, in which the Vaughans have
hitherto been paramount, feel how little important the
Vaughans are in comparison with her own niece. She
delights in feeling that the approaching marriage is the
one topic which is being discussed in the neighbourhood.
Go where he will, the magnitude of the match is always
being prominently held up before Mr Vaughan until he
loathes the subject.

And all the while Constance goes on as if she were in
a dream, hoping against hope and probability that Don
will come one day and save her from this marriage, as he
saved her from the bull! If he does not care to do so,
no one else shall.

Lord Charldale comes down and stays at Strathlands,
and Mr Vaughan is compelled to tolerate and entertain
him, because his wife threatens that, if he does not do so,
then will she remove to Woodside and proclaim to all
the world that it is because his scheme on Constance's
fortune has failed that he will not exercise hospitality
towards the man Constance has resolved to marry.

While he is at Strathlands, Lord Charldale orders his
ways with commendable weariness and discretion. He
knows that if he slips now he will lose Constance for ever,
and his passion for her has become the dominant power
of his nature.

If she were an hair's breath less cool and reserved
than she is to him her influence would be less. As it is,
he always has the dread upon him of losing the hold,
slight as it is, which he has on her. His sensations
are aught but agreeable when (against his will) a vision
of how she would look at him ; how she would turn
away from him with averted eyes for ever, if he once
offended in the way he is wont to offend, before her.
He starts and shivers with horror as the vision presents
itself. And, out of dread of the vision becoming a reality,
he draws the reins of self-government with a firmer, more
manly hand than he has ever had on them before.

This effort of self-command is all lost upon Constance. She has no idea of the strain there is upon him to maintain it. She has no consciousness of the hideous gnawing desire which almost overcomes him now and again; the desire to drink, drink, drink, till delirium mercifully steps in, and he is not in a condition to ask for, reach or swallow any more.

And during these two or three days of his stay at Strathlands, bored as he is by all his surroundings, save the lady of his love—of whom he is half afraid—he subdues this desire, and conducts himself with that air of superior calm indifference to most things which is his distinguishing characteristic when he is sober.

Constance is compelled to admit to herself that she is satisfied with him. He is neither very interesting nor very intellectual, but he is up to the level of the great majority of men of his caste. Riches have no great charm for a girl who has plenty of money of her own; but the prospective possession of halls and castles which have been in the Charldale family for centuries has a charm, and Constance freely acknowledges that she feels this charm.

Moreover, since the man she has loved from her childhood has turned aside from her—has slighted her for a girl who is far less attractive than herself, after she has unadvisedly let it be seen that she prefers him to all others—since these things are, it is well that her interest and pride should be founded on a rock, however it may be with her heart.

And marriage will be that rock to her. Whatever Lord Charldale may develop into, if she marries him, Constance will be a star of the first magnitude in the firmament of matrons. She will look to her shining, and in the perfect way in which she will fulfil every duty, from the highest to the lightest, she will find her soul's happiness, even if her heart's delight is denied her.

She says very little about her approaching marriage, or about the man she is going to marry, to the Armingers, but she indentifies them with every future plan of hers which she discusses before them.

"I wonder if we shall become enthusiasts about catching salmon and shooting stags when we go up to Scotland?" she says one day. "Trixy will, I feel sure; but I rather fancy that you and I will take to tamer things, Maude."

Another time she will remark,—

"Before we go to Crownistown for Christmas we must make out a programme for each day's and night's entertainment—something binding, that must be adhered to—mustn't we, Maude? Otherwise we three will be too severely exercised when we find ourselves with a number of bored and dull guests on our hands."

But though she speaks to them in this way, taking it for granted that the union between them is to be preserved in all its integrity so long as they live, the name of their brother Don is by tacit consent never mentioned.

Accordingly she is left in ignorance of a general hewing down and uprooting of some of Don Arminger's arrangements, amongst others of his intention of conducting the exploring expedition, of which mention has been made in a former place.

In order to get hold of the facts of the case, and gather together all the connecting links of the chain that is around him, it is necessary to go back to The Keg, and tell the story of the break-up of the party assembled there.

One night, while they are lingering in idle, happy fashion over the latest portion of the late dinner, sipping liqueurs and sweetening the hour by recounting all the enormities that their (absent) dearest friends have ever been guilty of, the master of the house, or rather the husband of the hostess, walks in.

"I thought you'd gone to Ireland, or Iceland, or some place of the sort," Lady Vic says, coolly disregarding the look of fury that is in his face.

That something more than usual has occurred to disturb her lord's usual diabolical spirit, she sees plainly enough. But the sight does not discompose her in the least. She is accustomed to see him in every stage of savage ill-temper.

"No !" he says with a smile that is worse than a blow or a curse; "I've deferred my journey to Ireland till to-morrow, when I mean to take you with me."

"I am sorrow you should have taken so much trouble," she says slowly; "for I have no intention of going."

"The intention will be formed in your mind in the course of the next few hours," he says sneeringly; "or I'll know the reason why," he adds with a glare round the assembled company, which makes more than one guest register a vow never again to accept the hospitali-ties of The Keg.

"Our little differences of opinion will hardly be inter-esting to my friends," she says, rising haughtily, levelling a look of such scorn and hatred at him as she speaks as no one present has ever seen on lovely lady Vic's face before.

Her coolness and composure desert her as soon as she reaches the drawing-room. All the women in the room —all save her cousin Elinor—know how deep her resent-ment is, and fear the form it will take.

She speaks freely.

"He has driven me to bay; he knows that there isn't a blood-thirsty beast of the forest that I wouldn't rather be alone with than with him; he knows that already I've endured that from him that I'll kill myself rather than endure again. Well, Elinor, the carriage shall be ordered for you, and you must go home to-night. This is no house for you now he has come to it. Tell uncle and aunt that I've broken up my party; that's all you need say. Now, Nell, go. I'll explain to Mr Arminger, and he'll bless me for sending you away, if he never blessed me before."

She hurries Lady Elinor out of the room as she speaks.

"There'll be a tragedy before this night is over," she says, addressing two or three of the intimate friends who have always been with her at The Keg. "He has never

dared to follow me here ; or, rather, he hasn't followed
me, because he was content to just stop short of driving
me to desperation.   Now his object is to have done with
me ; he knows I can't help myself ; he knows—'

"Dear Vic, it's not worth while saying this to us," one
of her friends, who wishes to keep square with the world,
interposes gently.   "We all know what wonderful powers
of endurance you have, and we all feel that you will bear
to the end, and keep your place in society."

Some time after this, when Lady Vic's conduct is
quoted in the world, and quoted against her, this diplo-
matic little lady friend of hers sighs tenderly, and says,—

'How I argued, how I pleaded, how I implored her to
be strong and "suffer to the end" that last night at
The Keg ; but poor Vic was always too daring and im-
petuous ; she could not control her impulses, and they
generally led her wrong, poor darling ; no woman should
leave her home.   And there's no place left like The Keg,
after all."

A little against her judgment, and entirely against her
affectionate will, Lady Elinor allows herself to be hurried
away from The Keg this night.

One or two words she does say to Lady Vic when the
latter comes flying in to bid her good-bye.

"Vic, dear, you're looking feverish and ill ; come
home with me, instead of staying here to quarrel with
Mr Gardiner to-night."

'I sha'n't quarrel with him, and I sha'n't stay here !"
cries Lady Vic.

"Where will you go—to your mother?" Elinor asks.

"I shall not tell you where I am going, Nell.   You're
not good at keeping a secret, and while his wrath is hot,
Mr Gardiner might thing it worth while to follow me."

"Poor Vic !" Lady Elinor says feelingly.   But she
has not the faintest conception of the desperate urgency
of the case which her cousin is thus pitifully stating.

There is quite a long carouse in the dining-room at
The Keg this night, for Mr Gardiner has assumed the

post of host, and will not permit his guests to move till the hours grow late, and the wine has passed freely round.

When at length he does give the signal for a dissolution of this vinous parliament, he says, sardonically pointing to an empty chair,—

"When did Mr Vanheldt give us the slip?"

"An hour ago," one or two men say unadvisedly.

Thanks, gentlemen, for your accuracy," Gardiner says, civilly; then he adds, "Mr Vanheldt being no friend of mine, I hadn't missed him, you see. An hour ago he went away, you say? An hour is a long time for a man to be missing; we'll see if we can find him."

It is late night, or early morning rather, when Mr Gardiner, after vainly trying to open it, knocks loudly at his wife's dressing-room door.

In a second she flings it open, and stands before him, ready dressed for travelling, her trunks and boxes packed and corded.

"I am ready to go to Ireland with you," she says, before he can speak.

"The devil you are! I'm not ready to take you. Has your lover cast you off?"

"I am ready to go with you, sir. Am I to go, or am I not?" she says sternly.

"Go to the devil!" he cries. "So that sneaking coward has cried off, has he? So—'

His hand is raised, but he never finishes his sentence. A hand that feels like iron descends upon his head, and when he gathers himself up a bruised and aching heap presently, the same hand of iron collects the fragments of him, and flings him on to a sofa in the corner.

Then Don Arminger's voice says,—

"It was time to stun and stop you; you were going mad. Mr Vanheldt left The Keg three or four hours ago. You were assaulting your wife when I knocked you down!"

Then Mr Gardiner's currish face brightens up again,

and he calls faintly to all the servants to come and save him from this miscreant. When they have come, chiefly out of curiosity, he says, turning a mournful glance on Don,—

"You are the man who has wrecked my home; it was not Vanheldt I came down to expose, it was you. If you have human hearts in your bosoms," he continues to the servants, "turn that man out of my house this instant; he has abused my hospitality, and he has tried to murder me. Anyone who sides with him after this declaration of mine shall be treated as his accomplice. Now throw him out."

But the servants know better than to attempt to throw out stalwart Don. All they do is to run backwards and forwards between the scene of action and Lady Vic's room, conveying intelligence of what is passing to her, and bringing back her comments thereon.

Later in the day, just as Don has sent a final appeal to her to put herself under his charge, and allow him to take her to Lady Timerton, this note is put into his hand,—

"I shall have been gone two hours when you get this. Don't trouble about me any more; I can't live to be 'pitied' and 'forgiven,' so I've gone. Let the man who struck me last night go unpunished.

"Vic."

"Poor Vic!"

He cannot bring himself to censure her save by the pity in his tone.

As soon as Mr Gardiner can collect his scattered and shattered physical and mental forces he goes to Lord Timerton, and nearly breaks that gentleman's heart by giving a garbled account of Lady Vic's flight.

CHAPTER XVIII.

"I AM CONQUERED."

WHEN Don Arminger, later in that day, an hour or two after Mr Cecil Gardiner's communication, entered the Timertons' house, it was with the uneasy humiliating conviction in his mind that he was about to beg for a blessing that he did not want, to be grateful for a favour that he would much rather were denied him, and to play a sorry and ignominious part for the first time since his appearance on the stage of life.

He was determined not to see either Lady Timerton or Lady Elinor before he had encountered the arbiter of his destinies. Plainly and straightforwardly he resolved to ask for the Lady Elinor's hand in marriage, and if her father refused it to him, plainly and straightforwardly he resolved to act still, by abiding by the paternal decision.

But somehow or other Lady Elinor managed to waylay him, or rather to have him waylaid for her.

"Such awful news, Don? Vic Gardiner has run away."

He was startled. Somehow or other, though he had never liked Lady Vic, he did feel surprised when he heard that she had cut the last rope which bound her to society. Yes, that was his feeling. He did not give her any credit for possessing any instinct of goodness, but he marvelled at her for the mixture of weakness and strength which had enabled her to put herself outside society's pale.

"It's the most fortunate thing in the world for us," Lady Elinor goes on, "for mamma has told papa that it was you made me come home last evening ; so out of evil comes good to us, Don. He's so grateful that you may wind him round your finger."

The selfishness of his bride-elect strikes him smartingly. The probability of winning her without any very great effort is singularly devoid of charm for him.

"It will be rather heartless of me to intrude on your father at such a moment as this," he suggested.

"Nonsense! Now's the very moment to do it. He doesn't really care for poor Vic, you know; it's only his pride is hurt, and he thinks we're all disgraced. As far as we are concerned, Don, nothing could have been more opportune, though of course I'm sorry for my cousin."

"Why, I thought you loved her?" he said.

"So I did—of course I did; but this sort of thing shocks one's sympathies. While she stayed with Cecil, bad as he is, it was all right; but now, as she has left him, it can't be all right, can it? Now, Don, papa will be going out soon. Do get it over; it's so awful for a girl to sit and wait for a decision like this."

Don was in the room with Lord Timerton before another minute had passed over his head; but in the course of that minute he had time to ask himself if it would not be for Elinor's weal as well as his own—if it would not be best for them both, in fact—that he should turn back and counsel Elinor to break off the alliance, instead of asking her father to sanction it.

Unfortunately he had not time to answer this question in the affirmative.

The tale told to Lord Timerton to-day by his niece's husband had plunged Lord Timerton into a state of the deepest distress. Unpleasant and disgraceful things happened in other families—of that he was quite conscious, and to it he was quite resigned. But now it had come near to him—terribly near to him; for, to do him justice, he did not attempt to dissociate himself from his sister, Lady Kenwyn, at this juncture. It had come terribly near to him, this disgrace, and it crushed him.

In his trouble he turned to Don Arminger. Don's loyalty, truth, and honour were such comforting things to have about him now.

"You have come to speak of what all the town is ringing with by this time, I suppose?" he began. "Has anything been heard of that wretched girl?"

"I had not heard a murmur of it till I came here just now," Don says; and he is about to add that it would be wise to wait for a little further information before such wholesale condemnation is uttered, when Lord Timerton puts in,—

"I must go and break it to my poor sister. With all her follies, Lady Kenwyn is a most affectionate mother; and I shouldn't be surprised if this is the death of her; I feel it will be of me. Still, odious as the duty is, I'll fulfil it, and it certainly is my duty to break it to my sister. Come with me, Don, like a good fellow."

"Willingly; but what have you to tell? Lady Victoria has left The Keg, without leaving her address with her husband. Is that extraordinary, considering what he is?"

"If she wanted a home and protection from that villain, I wish she had come here. Poor little Vic! I wish she had come here."

Lord Timerton quite believed that he meant this when he said it; though if his oppressed and ill-used niece had presented herself at his gates as a suppliant for safety, he would have bidden her remember her marriage vow and her wifely duty, and have driven her back to the dubious protection, and the merciless mixture of slavery and freedom, from which she had fled.

"I don't doubt for a moment but that Gardiner is much more to blame in the matter than she is; but then, you see, his ill-conduct does not reflect upon us in any way, whereas hers—Heaven only knows how it may affect my own girl! By the way, I find I am indebted to your influence for my daughter coming home last evening."

He paused here, and looked at Don with such trustful interrogation that Don felt there would be downright deceit in leaving him (Lord Timerton) in the dark any longer.

"It is about Lady Elinor that I have come to speak to you to-day, sir; she has consented to be my wife, provided you give your consent."

He felt as he uttered the words that there was little or no heart in them—felt that he was speaking in cold and measured terms, respectful enough, but lacking in warmth and reality. Would not her father miss the genuine ring of the metal, and rebuke him for it?"

"You have spoken to my daughter?"

"I have. I admit freely that I was wrong in asking her if she would marry me before I had asked you if she might."

"That's not a very rapturous speech," Lord Timerton said somewhat, grimly, "but it's a sensible one. You certainly ought to have given me the option of forbidding you the house before you persuaded my daughter to pledge herself to you."

"Conditionally; her promise is conditional on your sanction of it," Don puts in.

"Supposing I refuse to sanction, are you ready to yield my decision?"

"We are both resolved to abide by it," Don replies, getting hot with reactionary feeling.

It appeared for a moment or two as if Lord Timerton were about to knock off the shackles which fate and Don himself had bound about his own feet.

There was a long pause. During it, dark and disappointed thoughts had possession of Lord Timerton's mind. Lady Vic was Elinor's cousin. Lady Vic's conduct would probably mar the more glorious matrimonial prospects which he had hitherto fancied were in store for his daughter. After all, was it not a better thing that Elinor should be safely anchored with a man she loved, a man possessed of good, noble, and honourable qualities, who would take care of her, than that she should marry brilliantly and perhaps follow in the footsteps of her cousin? Or—there was another alternative—was it not better that he should make his only daughter happy by giving her to a man she loved, than that she should remain unsought, unwedded by any of her peers because of her cousin's dereliction from duty?

If Lord Timerton had not been unduly shattered by

the hard and cruel words Cecil Gardiner had spoken of his wife that morning, these considerations would not have obtained with him for a moment. But, as it was, they greatly influenced him, and so he told Don that if in twelve months, without any engagement existing between them during that time, Elinor and he were of the same mind as they were at this present, that the paternal consent should be given, and they should be free to marry. But mind you, Don," he added, "your case is no precedent for Sylvertre and your sister."

"He must fight his own battles."

"But you ought to exert your authority over your sister, out of gratitude to me for having conceded the point to you."

"I have no authority over my sister," Don said, and he might have added, "and I feel no gratitude to you."

"You had better let me tell Elinor my ultimatum," Lord Timerton said, presently. "I know what girls are; if you go to her, she'll be suggesting means and ways by which you may soften me, the inexorable parent; but she won't try any nonsense of that sort on with me."

"That must be as you please; you have refused me the right to demand to see her."

"For twelve months only, if you both keep in the same mind. Man alive, surely that's reasonable enough! I'm not a tyrant though, so if you think she would like to hear my decision from your lips instead of mine, go and tell her; but get it over quickly, for I want to see Lady Kenwyn."

Honestly and honourably Don did as he was told, and fulfilled his mission briefly. When he had clearly put her father's terms and his acceptance of them before her, she grew angry and impatient.

"You had no right to consent without consulting me; I could have managed papa much better."

"You agreed to leave it in his hands."

"Don, how cool, how horribly cool and indifferent you are about it; a semi-engagement of twelve months' duration! I wonder at you for submitting to anything so derogatory."

"Your father is distinctly right; he will not have you hurried for life into a station so inferior to the one to which you were born."

"That's all nonsense. What more shall I know about the station I am to fill as your wife twelve months hence than I do now, if I'm not even to be engaged to you?"

"You shall have all its advantages and drawbacks clearly pointed out."

She looked at him in bewilderment and anger.

"I cannot think that you mean it. Why, if it is so little to you that I marry you, have you asked me to be your wife?"

He could not tell her that the asking had been more on her side than his, but he remembered it.

"I wouldn't trap you into a situation that you possibly may not like with your eyes open. Lord Timerton's decision gives you time and freedom; and you will find me unchanged at the end of twelve months."

"Is that all you have to say to me, Don?"

"It is all I may say honourably."

"Won't you make me vow that I'll be staunch too?"

"Certainly not," he said hurriedly; "my doing so would be distinctly to break faith with your father."

"You must remember that other men will be about me, and that, with your consent, I am exposed to any attentions they may choose to pay me."

"I leave the matter of their attentions and your manner of responding to them to your own good taste," he replied, and then to his relief a servant came to say that "My lord is waiting for Mr Arminger."

Piqued, disappointed, feeling that all the excitement was over for a time—for so long a time!—Lady Elinor made her farewell as cold as a spring day on the north coast of Cornwall, than which nothing colder, clearer, or better calculated to take one's breath away can be desired. And Don departed from her, feeling well contented that it should be so.

"She will never hold out for twelve months to fidelity and me against the fascinations of marrying men," he said to himself, as he went out from her presence ; "but what a state of suspense to be living in—twelve months rolling slowly over a man's head, leaving him in doubt as to whether at the end of them he will have to marry or not!"

His meditations on the subject were set flying abruptly by Lord Timerton.

"Have you made my daughter clearly understand my resolution ?"

"I repeated your words as exactly as I could."

"And gave her to know that you have given me your word of honour to abide by my decision ?"

"She could not doubt that for a moment," Don said hastily ; "that was clearly understood between us before —before I spoke to your lordship."

Lord Timerton smiled—the first smile that had crossed his face since Cecil Gardiner's visit.

"Is she as sensible as you are about it, Don ?"

"Your daughter is as obedient as you can desire, sir," Don says, frowning slightly, for he is too loyal to admit that Lady Elinor objects to the delay much more than he does.

"Obedient, is she? I wish the other pair of fools were half as tractable," Lord Timerton said ; and then they got themselves into Lord Timerton's brougham, and were driven to Lady Kenwyn's door.

Lady Kenwyn was alone in a room that is half-study, half-boudoir, and that is enriched with countless relics of Catherine de Medicis. The maligned royal lady smiles or frowns down upon them from various portions of the wall. Jewels that belonged to her, and that have been collected at a vast cost by Lady Kenwyn, gleam from a cabinet that history says stood by her bedside, and sometimes contained phials of her pet poisons. Tapestry that was worked by some of the ladies of her court hangs over the door. Lace that adorned her person now decorates a shrine in the corner of the room, over which a marvel lous mosaic portrait of her, framed in richly-wrought gold studded with jewels, is suspended.

Lady Kenwyn, with pen in one hand and forehead supported by the other, was evidently deeply pre-occupied when they came into the room. But at the sound of her brother's voice she rose, and throwing her pen aside, held out her hand to welcome him.

Her perfect-featured calm face, framed with its wealth of still luxuriant golden hair, looked too placid to be lightly disturbed. Still her brother nerved himself to the task.

"In Sylvertre's absence," he said, "I have brought our friend Arminger to help me in breaking very bad news to you, Victoria."

She folded her arms gently over her breast, heaved a sigh, and waited for him to proceed.

"Won't you ask me what it is?"

"I can wait for all things, Timerton, even for bad news."

"Arminger," Lord Timerton gulped out, breaking down after the manner of the commonest humanity at the sight of his unconscious sister's patience, "Arminger, tell her—tell her what Gardiner has told me! I can't do it."

She bent her head slightly forward in an attitude of more intense attention when her brother said this, and a faint additional colour came into her face; but she said no word to make it either harder or easier.

"Mr Gardiner has seriously alarmed Lord Timerton by telling him of the disappearance of Lady Victoria Gardiner from The Keg. I have tried," Don went on manfully, "to make Lord Timerton feel that there is nothing mysterious or even surprising in this; the wonder to me is that Lady Victoria remained in the house a moment after her husband entered it."

Lady Kenwyn shone a grateful smile full upon Don, and then turned to her brother.

"Is this all, Timerton?"

"All! Merciful heavens! isn't it enough that your

daughter has run away, we don't know with whom yet, and that we are all disgraced?" he cried out, relapsing into his original inconsequent excitement. "I have seen it looming for long. You, absorbed in your nonsensical spiritualism, were blind and deaf to what every man and woman in London saw and heard; but now the blow has fallen, Victoria, and I thought you would feel its weight even more heavily than I do myself, and, Heaven knows, I am crushed by it."

His voice rose high, and then sank to a whisper, and his head drooped on his chest as he sobbed out the last words. His sister regarded him with a gentle, wistful, unexcited air that was very wonderful, Don thought, under the circumstances.

"Come with me," she said, rising up and putting her hand very gently on her brother's shoulder; "you too, Mr Arminger. Come with me."

She crossed a large hall, and led them down a long passage. At the end of it she paused before a door hung with green baize.

"This was Vic's school-room," she said pathetically; "come into it now, Timerton, before you say or hear another word about my child."

She opened the door, and they followed at her bidding. The old school-room was neater than in Vic's childish days, but in all other respects it was unaltered. And to make the resemblance to its own self complete, there at the table, writing, sat Lady Vic herself.

She jumped up from her seat in haste as they came in, and rushing over to her uncle, exclaimed,—

"Don't be angry! I have borne everything else; but when he gave me a blow I came back to my mother: and now I suppose you'll believe all the papers say of my leaving The Keg?"

"Elinor shall come to you at once—at once, my dear," Lord Timerton said, fumbling with his handkerchief. And he was nearer going down on his knees to his sister and her child at the moment, than he had ever been going down to living woman before.

"I am conquered—I am conquered!" Lord Timerton said to Don when they were walking home; the brougham had not been kept for fear gossip should arise between the servants of the two houses; "conquered by you and Elinor this morning, by my sister and her daughter now. Don, I swear to you I'm so relieved in my mind, that you may marry Elinor in a month if you both wish it."

"This is mere emotion; we must abide by your lordship's first decision," Don said.

CHAPTER XIX.

SEVERAL PEOPLE " NERVE " THEMSELVES.

"I'm better out of the country than in it while these testing twelve months are trailing themselves over our heads," Don Arminger said, in extenuation of what Lady Elinor called " his heartlessness " in determining to go to South Africa, and write a work on the industries, the social and spiritual advancement, and the general prosperity and outlook of the great "diamond fields " tract.

"It will be virtually giving me up, after having pestered papa to give his consent to our marriage," Lady Elinor said, inflating her nostrils, and giving him the impression that she regarded herself as one who might claim the royal prerogative of giving the initiative.

"But as your father has not given his consent to our marriage, and won't have the topic touched upon for twelve months, I'm better out of the way for that time. I should feel like a tame cat about the house now—a tame cat whose tenacity in clinging to the place was rather a tedious thing to the inhabitants."

"Don, you know your presence is essential to my happiness," she said reproachfully.

"You mustn't try to flatter me into the belief of anything so improbable," he told her, and then she went on another tack.

"Surely you will wait for the wedding! Such a brilliant affair I hear it's to be."

"Do you mean Miss Fielding's wedding?" he asked, looking her fixedly in the face.

She nodded assent, and smiled triumphantly. At this period Lady Elinor felt herself to be the moral superior of Constance Fielding; for the latter, with her eyes open, was going to marry Lord Charldale, who unquestionably was not without reproach, even in society's eyes, whereas she—Elinor—was secretly pledged to marry Don Arminger, who was above suspicion.

"I wouldn't see Miss Fielding cast herself down, as she will that day, to save my life," he replied, so sadly that Lady Elinor's sense of triumph over and superiority to Constance strengthened itself mightily.

"My dear Don," she said earnestly, "I believe really that it has been my respect for your opinion that has saved me from marrying brilliantly several times. Even before you let me see what you thought of me, I shrank intuitively from sinking in your estimation. If I had married a man whom you could despise, I would never have seen you again."

"Miss Fielding's descent is the more appalling to me because she has always been on such a height," he said meditatively, and rather ungallantly. "It's impossible to describe the nobility and goodness of that girl's character. Surrounded by time-servers and sycophants from her cradle, the object of Mr Vaughan's selfish scheming, and of her aunt's weak, ill-regulated affection, Constance never came in contact with a single ennobling influence till she met my mother and sisters; yet, child as she was then, she had a character and qualities that compelled respect and love."

"I never could feel sympathetic with paragons; they generally do something dreadful in the end, as she is going to do", Lady Elinor said coldly.

Something dreadful, as she is going to do! Yes, Don acknowledges the truth of this derogatory aspersion. This thing which Constance Fielding is going to do fills

Don Arminger's soul with horror and despair every time he thinks about it. For she is going to ally herself to a man whose conduct will surely soon make her an object of pity, and himself one of contempt.

"I must be out of the sight and beyond the hearing of it," he said to himself, when a few more days had passed over his head, and gossip told him that Miss Fielding's wedding-day was drawing very nigh.

And so it came to pass that he had pushed all his preparations so far forward, that he steamed away from Plymouth for South Africa just a week before the day that was to transform Constance Fielding into the Countess of Charldale.

The wedding programme had been arranged, re-arranged, modified, altered, revised, and improved out of all resemblance to its original self. Constance herself scarcely knew how it was to be. At last she was told definitely by her aunt that on such a day she, Constance, was to be married to Hugh Lanford, Earl of Charldale, and that Maude and Trixy were to be among the bridesmaids.

The Earl of Charldale's relatives, the few that is whom he had consulted on the subject, had signified their desire that the marriage should take place in London, where the due pomp and ceremony could be the more easily displayed and observed; and Constance, having grown indifferent to the "how" of it all, had consented, greatly to Mr Vaughan's delight.

But Trixy Arminger unexpectedly threw an obstacle in the way of the fulfilment of this plan.

"If we go up to town now, Connie, Lady Timerton and Lady Elinor are sure to seek us out, they'll do that for my brother's sake, and then Lord Timerton will say that I am running after Sylvertre. He sha'n't have that to say about me, so as you're to be married in London, I'll stay here; I can't be one of your bridesmaids."

"Then it shall be here," Constance said promptly. And so all the arrangements had to be remodelled again.

Miss Fielding's own home, Woodside, was put in order

for the reception of the wedding guests, as she herself was to remain at and be married from Strathlands. Accordingly a goodly party took possession of the place late on the eve of the wedding-day, and among them was Lord Charldale himself.

The local papers, as is their wont, were indulging in fits of preliminary ecstasies over the splendour of all the bridal arrangements and wedding gifts. The names of the titled wedding-guests already assembled in the Clyst were printed in the best type in the leading columns, and some reporters, anxious to take time by the forelock, had already written out a full account of the ceremony, containing several pithy passages descriptive of the demeanour of the lovely bride and noble bridegroom.

The dinner at Strathlands on the night before the wedding was a triumph of decorative and culinary art. Even the old Countess of Charldale, the mother of the reigning man, was resigned to the inevitable glide into dowager countess-ship when she saw how admirably "these people of Miss Fielding's did things."

Lord Charldale was rapidly getting to find the wholesome moral restraint which was upon him a wearisome and almost unendurable thing. For some weeks past he had been acting a false part under the fear of losing the beautiful woman who would so grace and dignify his position. Now that the time had nearly come when she would be his for better or for worse, so long as they both lived, the tension of "keeping straight," as his advisers called it, seemed to him a desperately over-strained one.

He felt himself being narrowly watched at dinner by his mother and two or three of his more intimate friends. But the time was so short now! The hour that would make Constance his own, to whom and before whom he could do as he pleased, had so nearly come. Champagne was all very well now just to keep the ball rolling during dinner, but he would take something stronger by-and-by just to nerve him when he got away from these observant doubtful friends.

So by-and-by, while Constance was kneeling and praying that she might prove to be a good, staunch friend as well as faithful wife to this man whom she was to marry on the morrow, while she was denying herself even the dear companionship of Maude and Trixy Arminger because she would concentrate herself entirely on the subject of the great responsibility she would assume in a few short hours, while she was doing these things with all her pure heart and womanly strength, Lord Charldale was " nerving " himself for the event of the morrow in a widely different way.

He had spent the earlier hours of the evening decorously as has been said. At dinner there had been no unseemly hilarity in his manner, and in candour it must be conceded there had been no equally unseemly depression. Mrs Vaughan thought his demeanour " perfect. More fitting the occasion than she had ever witnessed before in any man similarly situated."

Not only did Mrs Vaughan think this, but she expressed her thought to every one in the room, until Lord Charldale became the object of universal approbation.

Constance, quiet, resigned, strangely calm and self-contained, with much of old Constance *verve* and vigour gone from her, but unaltered in other respects, marked her future husband keenly, and frankly told herself that he would command her respect, though she might never be able to give him her love. Manly, clever, and amusing in a way about which there was no suspicion of drawing-room buffoonery, he might become the object of her pride and ambition, though love, such love as she knew herself to be capable of feeling, might for ever be out of the question. She would sympathise at any rate with him, and take such a hearty interest in his political career, that for her sake he must make it a grand one, and so justify her acceptance of him in the eyes of—" the world," she said, but she meant Don Arminger.

Yes, when Mrs Vaughan said to her,—

" Are you satisfied now, Constance? Any girl might well be proud of such a man. H.s mother tells me ' as you have seen Charldale to-night, so has he been from his boyhood; isn't it too heinous that disappointed women, whose daughters have failed to catch him, should have given my boy a bad name?'"

"Did Lady Charldale say that, aunt?"

"Well, her words may not have been exactly the same as mine, but I have given you the meaning of them."

"Then her words either to me or to you are false, for when I asked her this morning if she had ever known or ever heard that Charldale drank too much sometimes, she vowed to me that she had never heard a murmur of it. Oh, who is there left that I can believe or trust?"

"It was a delicate question to put to a mother, Connie, and I must say that it didn't show your usual tact to put it. Lord Charldale is evidently a man of whom every-one connected with him has reason to be so proud, that the least aspersion on him is painful to them; I shall have you flaring out at me in a few months if I un-guardedly remind you of the fears and doubts you once felt about him."

"No fears, scarcely a doubt, aunt; if I had a strong doubt of him even now, I would break off the marriage; but he has given me no reason to doubt him—he has left me no excuse for not keeping my freely given promise.

"It's like my dear, honourable, noble-minded Connie to say that," Mrs Vaughan, said with an air of mingled relief and emotion.

To tell the truth the good lady had been living in a state of suspense and dread for weeks, feeling that it was quite in the order of things that some rumour so strong that it would have to be relied upon might reach Con-stance's ears, and justify the girl in breaking off a match that was very dear to the heart of her aunt.

But now this painful period was past, and the noon of the next day would see Constance safely ensconced for life in the ranks of the aristocracy! Breathing a brief but fervent prayer that all would go well with the guests and the breakfast, Mrs Vaughan bid her niece good-night, and returned to her own room

Lord Charldale's suite of rooms at Woodside consisted of a study, dressing-room, and bedroom, and one of the study doors opened through a conservatory into a winding laurel-bordered path that led to the stables.

In this study Lord Charldale and two other men settled themselves for a quiet smoke before going to bed on the night before the wedding. The men who were with him were about the best companions he could have had from among his own set. They were men who were considerably older than he, men who had sown their wild oats. Their influence and example would both have been good for him if only he had followed either.

After one cigar, with an accompaniment of Apollinaris water on their sides, and of brandy-and-soda on his, they rose simultaneously, declaring that "bed was the proper place for them now."

"My fellow is waiting for me in the next room," Lord Charldale replied, as he bid them a cordial "goodnight." Then he added, as they were leaving the room, " I shall only stay here for a little while, but I feel that I want a few minutes to myself to-night."

As the friends mounted the steps together, one said to the other,—

" I wish we hadn't left him till he went to his room ; he's straight as an arrow now, but you know what Charldale is, and if he breaks down now, the lady will hate him for life.'

"He'll be all right ; he's too proud of what he has half won not to make the effort to win her wholly," the other man said. But still the other one, who knew Charldale best, wished he had stayed with him till he was ready to retire for the night.

Meantime, Lord Charldale had tinkled a silver handbell, which summons was responded to by his man, bearing in his hand a small tray, on which was a small bottle of brandy and a claret-glass.

Then his lordship began to " nerve " himself, and after some hours spent in fruitless attempts to do so he was borne to bed by his valet.

At eight o'clock the following morning Lord Charldale was senseless as a log.   At nine he was the same.

At ten his man, with a vivid recollection that the marriage was to be at eleven, went to the friends who had seen Lord Charldale the last thing before the fatal introduction of the brandy, and confided to them the state of affairs.

They went and looked at him, and then told the countess, his mother, who had come from Strathlands in a fright, on account of a rumour which had reached her privately, that she had better allow it to be said, "that the earl was taken seriously ill with congestion of the liver, and advise that the marriage should be deferred till the following day."

"If it's deferred for an hour, it's deferred for ever," the old lady said, rising in her anxiety to a spirit of prophecy. "I know Miss Fielding's spirit; if Charldale is not waiting at the altar at the hour appointed to meet her, he need never be there at all. Rouse him; surely something can be done to rouse him!"

She looked round appealingly at all who knew him best as she said this, and they proceeded to undertake the task assigned to them.

But for many valuable minutes the Earl of Charldale remained log-like.

At last they got him up, and, as his valet said, "A bath did wonders for master." Then they got him erect upon his hind legs (in speaking of him in his then condition, it is difficult to remember that he was not an animal), and he allowed himself to be dressed, but could not remember what studs he had determined upon wearing. Indeed, if he had remembered them, the remembrance would not have been worth much, as he could not word it. His lordship's speech had become incoherent.

In this state he was conveyed to the church, where his bride had been baptised and confirmed, and was now awaiting him.

———

CHAPTER XX.

A PAINFUL RELEASE.

CONSTANCE FIELDING woke on her wedding morning to the sound of church-bells pealing, and a great many other joyous noises. There was, for instance, a good deal of rush and tumble going on between the bridesmaids and their attendants. Mrs Vaughan was almost hysterical over the successful aspect of the bridal breakfast. And everybody was quite cordial and outspokenly friendly with the sun, who had done his best to outshine other things that day,

Maude and Trixy Arminger came early by appointment; no hands but theirs were permitted to aid the bride in dressing. No eyes but theirs were allowed to rest upon her, until the moment came for her to emerge from her room and go down to the carriage which was to take her to church.

By Constance's own desire her aunt was to give her away, so that Mr Vaughan was not called upon to endure this crowning pang of bestowing what he had meant for his own son upon another man.

The whole party were assembled before Constance, by whose side Mrs Vaughan walked with an air of exultant pride, came up the aisle. No, not the whole party. The most important member of it had not yet arrived, and consternation at the extraordinary absence of Lord Charldale was depicted on every face.

For at least twenty minutes Constance, motionless as a statue, knelt at the altar, while messengers went and came to and from the laggard in love! At length she rose, and for the first time seemed to be conscious of the indignity that was being offered to her by this delay. Meantime, the expression of consternation on the faces of Lord Charldale's best friends had changed to that of despair.

Suddenly, there was a commotion at the church-door, and on the appearance of the bridegroom an air of relief spread over his party. But this was but of momentary duration.

"He is not very well, but quite able to go through the ceremony, my dear," old Lady Charldale bent forward and whispered soothingly to Constance, for the look of horror and loathing which swept like a storm over Miss Fielding's face, made the mother fear that the marriage, which was to be the making of her son, would be marred after all.

Constance faltered for a moment, and those nearest to her thought she was about to faint. But as Lord Charldale lurched nearer, and with a foolish smile strove to articulate a few words, she drew herself up with such a concentrated expression of repugnance to him, that he was almost startled into sobriety.

"You must take me home again at once, aunt," she said, in a low, firm voice. "No power on earth will make me marry that man."

Horrified, Mrs Vaughan, who felt that a little more liberality should surely be shown towards an earl—especially so wealthy an earl as this one—than might reasonably be claimed by a commoner, still found herself powerless to resist her niece's will. Before the bewildered lady could offer a word of expostulation, she found herself hurrying out to the carriage by Constance's side, and in a moment the mob had got hold of the facts of the case, and instead of jubilant cheers, shouts and derisive laughter greeted them.

"Even the people who have known me all my life won't spare me, now they know how near I have been to marrying a drunkard," Constance said sorrowfully. "Oh, aunt, for once feel for me! Rejoice over my deliverance from that fate."

"It is terrible that it should have happened this morning," Mrs Vaughan sobbed. "The poor young man was overcome."

"As it was to happen at all, it is a mercy for which I can never be grateful enough that it did happen this morning. I am saved!"

"But—but you don't mean that the marriage is anything but postponed?" Mrs Vaughan stammered, in tones of anguish. "Oh! Constance, Constance! you only mean that it is postponed."

"What do you take me for?" Constance asked, with fine scorn. But her aunt, as frequently happened, misunderstood her.

"I thought you were too good and sensible a girl to break off such a solemn thing as a marriage on account of a slight though most painful—I admit, most painful slip on the part of the one to whom you have pledged yourself," Mrs Vaughan said, breathing more freely. But her hopes were dashed to the ground by Constance at once.

"Cease to believe in my goodness and sense then, aunt; when I have returned Lord Charldale's presents, I have done with him for ever."

She bounded upstairs and into her own room at Strathlands, and was stripping off dress and veil with trembling hands, but an untrembling heart, by the time Maude and Trixy and the rest of the bridesmaids arrived. And then she went down on her knees and gratefully and humbly thanked God that she had been saved from the snare, and escaped the danger.

"My soul would have been in daily peril through the disgust I should have felt; a stronger, a more forbearing woman than I am may save your son still, Lady Charldale; I should only have lost myself," she said to the Countess of Charldale, who is with tears trying to get Constance to reconsider her determination.

"The shame, the disgrace of this will kill my boy! Spare him to his mother's tears and prayers."

"Lady Charldale, your words cannot alter my purpose; your son is dear to you rightly enough; win him from his ways if you can. He would become hateful to me, with a hatefulness I couldn't endure if I ever saw him again as he was this morning."

"He is quite himself now. Do see him," Lady Charldale pleaded.

"Not for anything you could offer me. He and I had

better never meet again. It would only be humiliation to both of us."

Then Lady Charldale left her, and a raid was made upon her by others, by her aunt, by Lord Charldale's friends, by countless acquaintances, who did not like this cruel abbreviation of the wedding festivities.

But nothing moved Constance from the position she had taken up. Nothing would induce her to marry Lord Charldale now, therefore it would be better that she should not see him again.

The wretched cause of this was nearly beside himself. Completely sobered now, but shattered and broken by the shock, he was at one moment vowing that he would drop his title and income and go abroad into some wild country, where civilised man would never hear of him, and the next declaring that he would shoot himself.

"Let me see her, let me hear it from her own lips," he kept on raving; "she can't be such a stone as you're making her out to be. Let me see her, I say; she'll shrink from having my death at her door."

But they could not drag the young lady down to see him, nor could they surprise her, for she kept her door locked. Accordingly, towards nightfall, after taking bitter counsel with his friends, Lord Charldale took his departure, pursued by hoots and yells from the excited and disappointed roughs of Clyst.

The rest of the wedding party dispersed rapidly and sadly, Maude and Trixy remained with Constance, and Mrs Arminger sat up late that night writing a detailed account of all that had happened during the last two days for Don's benefit by-and-by when she should know where to address him.

So the great Charldale alliance came to an end, and Constance Fielding prepared to live an independent unmarried life in her own beautiful home at Woodside.

"I have made two ventures, one for love, and one for position," she said frankly to Maude and Trixy. "The man I gave my heart to didn't want it; the man I was going to give my hand to forfeited my respect fortunately before he had taken it. I shall never make a third venture, but I mean to lead a happy life."

"And so do I," Trixy said stoutly; "though I have had my chance and lost it too. I shall always be glad Lord Sylvertre liked me, though he hadn't the strength to prove it quite, but he's spoilt me for smaller men. What do you say, Maude? Will you join the guild of old maidens?"

"I don't think I shall," Maude laughed; "I'm contented with 'no hero but a man,' and I've found him. Whether Mr Vaughan likes it or not, Donald and I are going to fight the world together."

The two girls who listened to this announcement were far too fond of Maude to give a word or look that might show disapprobation of her intention; but they felt it. Trixy knew that it would always be hard for her mother to treat as a son the son of the man who had treated her with studied insolence and contempt during the whole term of her residence in Clyst.

"And Maude will feel hurt if mother doesn't take Donald to her heart and love him next best to Don," she said to Constance when they two were alone.

"And Maude will do all the fighting as far as fighting is represented by work," Constance replied. "Maude will paint beautiful pictures, and make much money, which she will humbly hand to her husband, who will take it graciously, and counsel her not to be extravagant in the use of what he will allow her to retain. I know Donald Vaughan well. I made a careful study of him when I knew that Mr Vaughan designed me for his son. Donald is the best of his family, but he has faults which will pinch Maude by-and-by."

"I don't suppose any man is without faults—at least, hardly any," Trixy said, a timely remembrance of Lord Sylvertre tempering the sweeping severity of her judgment.

"But Donald Vaughan's faults are such as affect those of his own household only. He doesn't in the least mind spending money, but he likes to do it entirely in his own way, without regard to others, and he'll like his wife to do it in the way that seems best to him, and if Maude doesn't yield she will not have a pleasant time with him."

"Maude is quite capable of yielding" Trixy laughed.

"That's what I'm afraid of for her; she is so much the higher, stronger character of the two that his weakness will conquer her. However, she'll be happy in her own way, I trust, and we'll be happy in ours; won't we, Trixy? You industrious girl! I envy you the gift which enables you to get away from real life and its many bothers and troubles, into a region that you can fill entirely with pleasant people and agreeable things, if you please."

"I'm afraid my most natural characters are anything but altogether pleasant," Trixy said. "Now that I've made studies of mother and Maude, and Don and you, from every point of view I can think of, my readers demand a change, and lo! I find I have exhausted my list of pleasant people."

"Trixy, I believe if Lord Timerton could only see you and hear you for half-a-minute he'd become importunate in his desire for Sylvertre and you to marry," Constance said, looking with admiration on the brilliant, pretty face that was so eloquent and true.

"That's a page of the past that we won't turn over again," Trixy said gravely. But in her gravity there was nothing morbid, nothing sickly nor sentimental. It was evident that she would always stand fast to the memory of the man who was dead to her. But she would not do it sombrely, so that others should see and be depressed by the sight.

Clyst was anything but a united little village in those days. Intercourse between Strathlands and Woodside was of the most limited kind, and was only kept up on Mrs Vaughan's part at all to save appearances. The disappointed lady could not get over or forgive the obstinacy which had deprived her of an earl and countess for her nephew and niece. If only Lord Charldale had deferred his escapade until the wedding-breakfast even Mrs Vaughan would have been a happy woman, whatever her niece might have been.

Extraordinary rumours got into the papers as to the real reason of the rupture at the altar of a marriage in high life. Some had it that the lady from her childhood had been subject to epileptic fits under the influence of any strong excitement. Others that just as the service commenced she caught sight of an old lover hiding behind one of the pillars. Only one or two hinted, and that in very guarded language, at the real disgraceful truth.

It was several months before Don saw a newspaper version of the story, and in all that time his mother's true rendering of it had not reached him. Being the most important it was unfortunately the only letter from home which had miscarried. And as in his replies he made no allusion to the occurrence, his mother and sisters thought the topic was a painful one to him, and so did not touch upon it.

The first report he read was one of those which ascribed the breaking off of the match to physical infirmity on Miss Fielding's side. This filled Don with indescribable feelings of sorrow and pity. But soon a second and more veracious account reached him, and then his heart bounded high with joy at the thought of Constance free.

But his elation was of brief duration, choked as it was by the remembrance that it was in the bond that at the end of the twelve months he was to go home and marry Lady Elinor if she would have him. Still, there was a great deal of happiness and satisfaction in the thought that Constance was released from what would have been a direfully ignominious fate for her, and was now at liberty to marry some better man who—lucky fellow!—was free to win her.

For a long time he debated with himself as to whether or not he would write and congratulate her on her narrow escape, and at last he decided to do so. He tried to think of her only as the dear, grateful, enthusiastic little girl who had hugged him and told him she would love him "all her life." But visions of her shy stateliness towards him in London sadly marred the lines of the mind-picture he tried to paint, and a timely recollection of Lady Elinor chilled the ardour with which, but for her, he might have expressed himself.

However, he wrote, and this is what he said :—

" KIMBERLEY, *February 20th.*

"MY DEAR MISS FIELDING,—I have just read with inexpressible delight that you bravely freed yourself at the last moment from a fate which I am sure would have been a hideous one for you. Will you forgive me for venturing to express that delight to you directly instead of conveying it through my mother or sisters ?—Always yours truly,   DON ARMINGER."

" He was never 'mine truly,'" Constance said pathetically to herself, when she read the letter. But there was not a particle of pathos in voice or manner when she told the Armingers of it.

"I've had a letter from your brother congratulating me on not being married. He writes as an old governess might be expected to do to a former pupil who had abstained from picking and stealing something which would have led to transportation for life."

"I dare say it's difficult for a man to write to a girl with whom he has been very intimate, when he's not quite so intimate any longer," Trixy pleaded ; and Constance said,—

"Lord Sylvertre doesn't seem to experience that difficulty at any rate, judging from the length and frequency of his letters. Trixy, you're a heartless little thing to hold out against him as you do."

" I'm not holding out against him ; it's his father is holding out against me."

" But you won't see him, and you won't say you'll marry him."

"Because I won't marry him till his father says I may; if that day ever comes, then you'll see how little I can hold out against Sylvertre; but if it never comes, I had better keep a firm footing where I am."

"Does he ever say anything about his sister?" Constance asked.

"Yes," Trixy said, blushing furiously as she did not blush when her own love affair was under discussion. "He says he doesn't know whether she has given up thinking of Don, but she certainly has recovered her love for society."

"How I shall hate her if she undervalues him and forgets him," Miss Fielding said slowly.

"But, Connie dear, if she does that, Don will be free," Trixy said, considerately looking another way.

"With his freedom I have nothing to do," Constance said, her head involuntarily settling itself into a prouder position, "but I should be angry if after winning him she threw him over."

"I am afraid Lady Elinor is not nearly so noble and good as her brother," Trixy said.

Whereat Constance only smiled.

CHAPTER XXI.

SLACKENING THE CHAIN.

It was in September that Don Arminger had left England, and now it is May, and still he is in suspense as to whether Lady Elinor will cling to him and her un-written troth to the bitter end of the twelve months or not. No word or hint has reached him which would justify him in showing jealousy and "throwing up the whole thing." It comes upon him like a nightmare sometimes that she is going to be beautifully faithful. And he could so readily find it in his heart to forgive her if she were faithless.

But still he has striven hard, as these months have

rolled over his head, to bring himself into subjection to such an extent as may enable him to find peace and comfort in his own fate, and to make her happy as his wife. For one thing, his love and regard for her brother will aid him greatly. Lady Elinor will not be alienated from her "own set" by her marriage to any great extent. That is to say, Don Arminger hopes that she will consider herself sufficiently "in it," though there is no intention in his mind of setting up an establishment in London for the season, unless she will consent to live in a modest way in London altogether.

Meanwhile the lady, whom her unbetrothed but still probable future husband regarded as a too-perfect model of constancy, gathered her roses, made hay while the sun shone, improved the shining hours, and generally enjoyed herself.

It was in October that Lord Charldale defeated himself and lost Miss Fielding, and it was at Christmas that Lady Elinor went, with her father and mother, to stay at Lady Kenwyn's place in Cheshire, which was only a couple of miles from Crowniston, the Cheshire seat of the most noble Earl of Charldale. At Crowniston this year Lord Charldale was keeping Christmas with his mother and two or three old family friends only, very quietly, as his guests.

His lordship had neither shot himself nor dropped his title and exiled himself, as he had threatened, but he had sulked and sequestered himself a good deal; and now that Christmas had come, and he had no "house party" about him as usual, he found it very dull.

Ever since the day that the unfortunate man had so disgraced himself, his mother had been "hard and uncomfortable to him," as he phrased it. The proud old lady and loving mother could not bring herself to forgive "her boy" for having thrown away the chance of becoming a better man which had been offered to him in a union with Miss Fielding. She was not exactly angry with him, but she was angry, beyond the power of words to describe, at his weakness.

"If he had only restrained himself that one night, he would have become Constance's husband the next day, and she would have saved him from himself," she said to herself.   To her acquaintances she said,—"That unhappy girl's loss of temper because Charldale was a little late at the church has cost her a coronet.   He will never seek her again; of that I am sure.   Deep-rooted vanity and ungovernable temper are things that a man does well to avoid in marriage."

Gradually people (though they didn't believe it) affected to take this view of the case; and three months after that baffled wedding at Clyst, Lord Charldale found himself white-washed so completely that he began to think himself a grievously-insulted man, and to bestir himself about another wife.

He was in this mood when he came down to play host at Crowniston to his mother and two or three familiar friends.

Old Lady Charldale had adopted the moody manner with her son, under the profound conviction she had that it would not be well to allow him to rely upon her powers of soothing solely at this juncture.

" He must be stimulated by the apparent want of sympathy into seeking a sympathetic wife," she said to Lady Kenwyn, just before leaving London.   " Your Vic would have been the very girl for him if she were younger and free.   Is she going to get a divorce from that brute who struck her ?"

" She is going to live on with me whether she gets a divorce or not," Lady Kenwyn said gently; and Lady Charldale, who wouldn't have had Vic for her daughter-in-law for the worth of her own diamonds, smiled resignedly, and wished Lady Kenwyn would let the subject drift on to her niece, Lady Elinor Divett.   For Lady Elinor was known to have not only a fair face, but a fine, firm will of her own also, and to that will the anxious mother was desirous of committing her son.

" We shall meet in Cheshire.   I am going to Crowniston on the twentieth ; shall you be starting about that time?" old Lady Charldale asked, and in reply got the information she had been seeking.

"No; Vic and I go earlier. Lord and Lady Timerton and Elinor spend Christmas with us, and I have not been down at Scallow for so long, that I expect to find things greatly out of order."

"Is yours merely a family party, like my own this year, Lady Kenwyn?"

"With the exception of Mr Mott, yes," Lady Kenwyn replied.

"Mr Mott is the spirit-rapper, isn't he?" Lady Charldale, who had a wholesome contempt for all such people, asked abruptly.

"He is the most powerful and advanced medium it has ever been my happiness to meet," Lady Kenwyn said softly, but at the same time she registered a vow that Lady Charldale should not have many opportunities of offering the cold shoulder or slight of any kind to the illustrious American medium.

However, in spite of this vow, when the two families found themselves in Cheshire, under rather dull conditions, a habit of intimacy was set up between them which had not existed formerly.

From the time the party assembled at Scallow, Lady Elinor became the object of a couple of schemers, each one of whom fathomed the motives of and resolved to defeat the other if possible.

Lady Charldale's scheme was a good and honourable one in the main. In Elinor, as has been said, she recognised the "will" which might, if brought to bear upon Lord Charldale, dominate and save him from his besetting sin. Hers was a motherly and worthy machination. The same, in honesty, cannot be said of the other plotter.

This second one, whose mind was bent to the task of upsetting Lady Elinor's unavowed fidelity to the absent Don Arminger, was none other than Mr Mott, the medium, whose thoughts were supposed by Lady

Kenwyn to be wholly given to the higher sphere, with which he held endless communications.

It seemed to the powerful medium that this fair English girl with a title and a large fortune would repay him far better for wooing and winning her than the spirits did whom he was perpetually invoking. And as he was endowed with perseverance, plenty of self-esteem, and an unlimited stock of audacity, he went in for the work with vigour.

His position in the circle was against him certainly. But handicapped by that even as he was he entered himself with a good heart for the race for " her lady-ship," as he always called Lady Elinor.

He talked an immense quantity of mystical trash to her, which half fascinated her (as it had wholly fascinated her aunt) when she had nothing better to listen to ; and he looked a great deal of adoration at her, which she accepted since there were no other men to adore. Poetry of the intense, pathetic, simple, yet love-laden American order he quoted to her by the yard, generally giving her to understand that it was his own, which it was not ; but as she was not deeply versed in American literature that did not signify. His spirit friends served him in good stead too, for he continually made those who were possessed of the loftiest sentiments and highest-sounding names, send him messages about her soul being in unison with his own, though she had not discovered it yet. These messages he scrupulously delivered to her, and altogether, after a few days of assiduous work, he gained her attention and interest.

" How can you let that odious humbug, whom mamma retains on the premises to delude her, make love to you, Nell ? " her cousin Vic asked her, in accents of utter disgust.

" I really find a great deal more in him than you would suppose, Vic. And if he has been silly enough to fall in love with me, that won't hurt me, you know," Lady Elinor laughed.

"How you can stand his vulgarity and his awful assumption as you do, puzzles me," Lady Vic said impatiently; "and you all the time engaged, or half-engaged, to Don Arminger."

"One can't keep on thinking of a man who is thousands of miles away," Lady Elinor said, shrugging her shoulders, "and one must talk to someone, and Mott is the only man here."

"I know the creature thinks it will end in your marrying him, and I can't endure that he should dare to think it; he would no more plump himself down on a sofa by me and begin spouting his maudlin poetry, than he would seat himself on a bee-hive."

"I don't mind being liked," Lady Elinor said languidly; "and the lies he tells me about what the spirits in the best set—I mean the best 'sphere'—say of me, amuse me. I can leave Mr Mott off at any moment; don't be alarmed."

"We dine at Crowniston to-night, and Lady Charldale wouldn't ask him, I'm happy to say, though mamma gave her broad hints enough to have made most women ask a baboon," Lady Vic said, with glee, for the sight of her cousin surrendering ever so lightly to Mr Mott's attentions was sorely distasteful to her.

"I don't care; I shall have Charldale to-night," Lady Elinor said indifferently. "His mother told me yesterday that she had never seen him so bright since his illness as he is with me."

"Blows the wind from Crowniston, does it?" Lady Vic laughed, and Elinor held her fair head up with affected unconcern, but coloured faintly.

That night after dinner at Crowniston, as the ladies huddled over the drawing-room fire, the topic of Charldale's brightness came to the fore once more.

"I have never seen my dear boy so lively and like himself as he is to-night since the day that horrid girl treated him so basely," Lady Charldale said joyfully, and sounds expressive of happy commiseration emanated from the lips of the other ladies.

" There was always something about that Miss Fielding that I disliked extremely," Lady Elinor said truthfully enough.   There was always something about Constance's beauty and charm which her rival had disliked with all her heart.

"Oh, but her conduct to Charldale puts her outside the pale of all toleration," Charldale's mother went on warmly ; "there can be no doubt about it that there was some other man in the case."

Lady Timerton faintly ventured to state that her friends, the Armingers, couldn't speak too highly of Miss Fielding.

"Ah, I'm afraid your friends, the Armingers, have a very pernicious influence on the unfortunate, misguided girl," Lady Charldale replied ; "the mother is a terribly gushing, presuming woman, Mr Vaughan told me, and she wants to secure Miss Fielding's money for her own son, the author."

"Don Arminger will never look at Miss Fielding," Lady Elinor said, tossing her head.

"Besides, Don Arminger is engaged," Lady Timerton said excitedly, in spite of a warning frown from her daughter.   But just then Lord Charldale and his guests came into the room, and further disclosures were arrested.

"I think Crowniston is the very dearest place I ever saw," Lady Elinor said to Charldale later on in the evening.   They two were apart from the others, looking at a portrait of the earl when he was little Lord Crowniston, and a very pretty little boy.

This portrait hung in an ante-room, or rather a passage between the dining-rooms.   The colour of the room was warm terra-cotta.   The looking-glasses were framed in glowing chased copper.   The fender and all the fire-irons were of the same metal, elaborately wrought.   Everything in the room was suggestive of warmth and beauty and comfort, to say nothing of riches and splendour.   Lady Elinor liked the look of things, and the suggestions made by them.

"I had the whole place done up under one of the best men in the town last year when I was going to be—"

The word "married" choked him, and he did not say it, but Lady Elinor glibly went on, and spared him further embarrassment.

"And it's done up in such exquisite taste. I am sure you had more to do with it than anyone else."

"Well, I had, because I wanted it to be very perfect in the eyes of the one who was to have been its mistress," he said rather sadly; and Lady Elinor said quickly,—

"I felt sure your influence predominated. Now we must go back; Lady Charldale asked me to sing."

"Will you sing something for me?"

She smiled assent.

"Will you choose the song, or shall I choose the one for you?" she asked, and he, feeling that he might safely leave the delicate matter in the young lady's hands, said,—

"You shall choose it."

She went back into the room where the others were, and Lady Charldale looked up with irrepressible anxiety, hoping that the sequestered situation had seduced her son into speaking definite words. But Lady Elinor's fair unruffled face and mien tell no tales.

"Did I hear you say Don Arminger was in Kimberley now, Elinor?" Lord Timerton asked somewhat sarcastically, as he saw his daughter slowly unbutton her long gloves, and then hand them to Lord Charldale to hold for her while she sung for him.

"No, papa," she said, with a little faint air of surprise, that did not escape her father. "It was Sylvertre; but you always will mix Sylvertre and me up in everything."

Lord Timerton said nothing; but he laughed. It was clear to him that he need have no further fear of his daughter on account of Don Arminger.

"I always thought Nell was a girl who would take care of herself; and, by Jove! she can be trusted to take care of Charldale too," his lordship thought with much self-satisfaction, as he saw his daughter singing

at the best match in the country with considerable
success.

"Oh, that we two were maying,"

was the lay which Lady Elinor chose to sing for Lord
Charldale, and the words, sang very feelingly to an air full
of languor and sweetness, carried him on in imagination
to the spring still buried in the depths of Nature. And
we have it on high authority that "in the spring a young
man's fancy lightly turns to thoughts of love."

"You sang that song for me?" he whispered, seating
himself comfortably by her side on a lower chair.

"Because I am so fond of it myself," she said quietly,
taking her gloves from him. Then there was a general
request from the others that she should sing again.

"For me again," he whispered, and Lady Elinor, who
liked Crowniston very much, and had no reason to doubt
that all Charldale's other places were equally admirable
in their way, sang for him again.

This time she consulted his sporting tastes, and sang—

"Drink, puppy, drink, and let every puppy drink,'

with much spirit.

It ended in Lord Charldale's proposing to take her for
a ride the next day if there was a thaw, and Lady Vic
Gardiner could go with them.

"What does it mean?" Lady Vic asked, when her
cousin propounded this plan to her in Lady Vic's dressing-
room that night.

"It means that I like Crowniston," Lady Elinor said
simply.

"And you'll give up your hero, Don Arminger?"

"Dear Vic, there's no 'giving up' in the case. Papa
was very wise; he wouldn't allow an engagement?"

"When you see Don Arminger again you'll just
loathe Charldale—yes, you will, Nell. He may have
reformed under your strong hands by that time; but the
mere sight of Don Arminger will make you wish that
you hadn't cared so much for Crowniston."

"There's a good deal about it besides Crowniston that I like," Lady Elinor said calmly, "and perhaps I shall never see Don again. If I do, he will have the good feeling to forget there has been anything between us."

But though the ride came off under the most respectable auspices, Lord Timerton being of the party, the offer was not made then: and for a day or two, as Lord Charldale secluded himself again, poor Lady Elinor was compelled to fall back upon the devotion of Mr Mott.

He indeed was a man of whom it could not be truly said that he lacked energy. He possessed the quality to a redundant degree, and therefore contrasted favourably for the moment with the absentees. Still Lady Elinor held herself aloft, and never deemed for a moment that he would dare to dream that she would deign to marry him.

"There's no one round, and so I'll take my chance of speaking to you now, right off," Mr Mott said, coming upon Lady Elinor suddenly one afternoon, as she was lounging back in an arm-chair before the library fire, reading a novel, and thinking of Crowniston.

She opened her eyes at him; but unabashed he went on,—

"When I came to the old country first, matrimony was just the farthest way round to where I meant to go; but since I've seen you, that's just become number one notion in my mind—"

He was compelled to stop, for Lady Elinor had risen, and was walking with her grandest step to the door.

"Pray pardon me," she said; "but I never do listen to people who have 'notions' about anything, especially matrimony. I should recommend you to speak to the object of your affections, and not to attempt to introduce the subject to me again."

"By the holy poker, her ladyship doesn't think small snakes of herself!" Mr Mott muttered, when he had recovered his breath. "I'll take her advice, you bet; for these are right down the cosiest quarters I've ever been in."

Then the daringly soothing idea took possession of him that perhaps he might invoke the spirits, and get them to persuade or threaten Lady Kenwyn into thinking smaller snakes of herself than her niece thought of herself.

"And the old lady'll do for a windy day; poor fortune wouldn't have much chance of blowing me into nasty places if I had the handling of the countess's dollars."

So he overlooked Lady Elinor's snub as utterly as if she had never offered it to him, and set himself to storm the loftier fortress.

The question of what he would be called if he married Lady Kenwyn soon became an absorbing one. He was in doubt as to whether he would be a count or an honourable; he hoped the former, because it would strike the deeper envy into the hearts of his relations, who kept a dry-goods store in New York.

Lady Elinor took good care not to let Lady Vic know of the indignity that had so nearly been offered her. Indeed, at this juncture it was easy enough to leave Mr Mott off, as she called it, without exciting suspicion as to the real cause; for Lady Charldale invited Lady Elinor to stay with her at Crowniston, and Lord Charldale, whose wounded pride and bitter mortification were not quite healed yet, found her presence and her graceful flatteries soothing as oil.

Still there was nothing definite done during the visit, and even in May, when the Timertons and their friends were back in town, Lady Elinor's allegiance to Don Arminger was still unbroken. But Lord Charldale had confided to his mother that, if no younger beauty threw herself at his head early in the season, he would marry Lady Elinor Divett about the middle of it. Now the middle of it had nearly come.

"It's a pity to defer it," old Lady Charldale said to her son; "while you do, that horrid girl down at Clyst will think you're wearing the willow for her."

"I wish Elinor were as good-looking as that girl down at Clyst," he grumbled.

"Do you know, Charldale, I think she could be if she tried. Not one of the new ones is to be compared with her."

But Lord Charldale still hesitated, waiting on for the possible " fairer she."

CHAPTER XXII.

ELINOR BALANCES THINGS.

THE necessity for himself seeing his book through the press brought Don Arminger back to London in the mid-season. He arrived by one of those uncomfortable trains which land you at your destination when it is much too early for breakfast, and much too late for bed. Accordingly he took a bath, and then went out for a stroll through the squares, where the atmosphere was fragrant with the breath of mignonette and the countless other flowers with which all the windows were brilliant.

It was not any intense impatience to behold the casket which contained his jewel which led him past Timerton House.

It all looked very familiar, just exactly as it had looked a hundred times when he had gone home in the early morning soft summer light with Sylvertre. Familiar, and yet with an air of comfort and luxury and perfection about it to which he had been long a stranger. The upper windows with their red silk blinds and creamy lace curtains; the flower-boxes decking every window-sill right up to the top of the house ; the crystal clearness of the glass and brilliancy of the brass knocker all spoke in a pleasant way of wealth and a well-ordered establish-ment.

A desire to go in by-and-by and breakfast with them, and get a hearty, loving welcome from Lady Timerton and Sylvertre, and perhaps a few surreptitious sweet glances from Lady Elinor, seized him. The prospect of going back to his hotel seemed a dull one after his observation of Timerton House, and his revived recollections of its interior. Accordingly he loitered about, and amused himself by watching aristocratic London wake up.

He managed to be at the door with the milk, and the servant who took the latter in suspected him on the spot of being a gentleman burglar. She was on the point of a scream, but suppressed it, when Don told her to go to the butler and tell him that "Mr Arminger was at the door."

And soon he found himself in the library with a cup of cocoa, and (now that he was committed to the situation) a regret in his heart for having acted with what would look like ardent precipitation.

" Elinor will think that I was eager to see her, whereas in truth it was those home-like red blinds and flowers that lured me in," he said to himself. But there being nothing for him to do now but go through with it, he drank his cocoa, felt refreshed, and waited.

From the butler he had heard that all the family, Sylvertre included, were at home, and so at a reasonable time he sent Lord Sylvertre's man up to tell his master that Mr Arminger was below, and the result of this was an immediate request that Mr Arminger would go up to his lordship.

" Don, old boy ! if I shouldn't look too ridiculous I'd jump out of bed to greet you," Sylvertre cried when Don went in. Then they shook hands reasonably, as became a brace of Englishmen, and for the next hour talked over the majority of things concerning themselves and each other.

Except Lady Elinor ! Oddly enough both her brother and her lover forgot to say anything about her.

" We'll breakfast in my den ; the others never turn up till mid-day," Sylvertre said. So they breakfasted together, and had another long happy conversation, during which Don gave Sylvertre an invitation to go down to Clyst, which invitation Sylvertre accepted with avidity, never hinting to Don that Trixy had forbidden him to go to her till he could carry with him his father's consent.

But suddenly Don remembered.

"How about Trixy and you, though; have you buried your dead, and got over any awkardness, about meeting?"

"We've no dead to bury; I write to her frequently, awfully amusing letters, too, Don, I assure you, posting her up in everything, and gently keeping it in view that I mean to marry her by-and-by; and all I get in return is a beautiful line about once a month :—

"DEAR LORD SYLVERTRE,—Thanks for your kind and clever letters.—Yours truly,   TRIXY ARMINGER."

Don laughed.

"Trixy's right.   I think children owe absolute obedience to their fathers, especially in your position."

"Do you! Nell didn't like your advising her to knock under to the governor that time just before you went away."

Don winced at the recollection, not of the knocking-under, but of Lady Elinor; for his suggested visit to Clyst had brought back vivid visions of the old child-friend who had volunteered to "love him all her life."

"I hope your sister is quite well?" he said.

"Wonderfully! I don't see it myself, but they say she has become a beauty; how women do that after they have been grown-up, and merely good-looking for some years, I don't understand; but Elinor's got the trick it seems. I drew the line at her being shop-windowed, but she has managed all the rest of it. I think she did the trick this year at the Academy private view. Went in rather late, marvellously dressed, made no pretence of looking at a single picture, but just walked round the rooms twice with Charldale. The next morning when we turned into the Row, the crowd turned to look at her, and it has gone like that ever since."

"Oh, she walked round the rooms with Charldale, did she?" Don asked, with a guilty feeling of intense relief. And then Sylvertre proposed an adjournment to his club.

Just as they were leaving the house and getting out beyond the shelter of the broad awning into the fierce blaze of the sun, three or four riders clattered up, and Lady Elinor, the foremost horsewoman of the group, recognised Don Arminger with a fainting spirit. By her side was Lord Charldale, and behind them came Lady Vic Gardner, and a group of acquaintances.

But it was evident that Lord Charldale had constituted himself Lady Elinor's cavalier.

"I thought you were in Africa, Mr Arminger?" Lady Elinor said, leaning over to shake hands with him with her easiest air of self-possession.

"I was; but I thought to-day I would just look in to breakfast at Timerton House," he said, laughing, and then Lady Vic, who was enjoying the situation, rode up and said,—

"I believe Elinor had a presentiment you were here, she has been so singularly lively this morning. Now, Elinor, didn't you, 'by the pricking of your thumbs,' or by what your Mr Mott used to call 'spiritual affinity,' feel that Mr Arminger had come back?"

"My thumbs never prick, my pulses are too well regulated," Lady Elinor said calmly as she slipped out of her saddle. Then, after a parting word with Lord Charldale, she went into the house, and the cavalcade moved on.

"That's my impassioned lady-love of eight months ago!" Don thought, as he went on to the club with Sylvertre.

"Charldale's not the brother-in-law I should have chosen, but as a rule fellows can't choose their brothers-in-law," Slyvertre said. And then, presently finding Don made no rejoinder, he went on: "But I suppose I shall have him for one unless Nell and you swear unalterable affection at the end of twelve months."

"Are they engaged?" Don asked, steadily ignoring the reference to himself.

"Engaged. my dear fellow! no. Probably now you've come back, Nell will cut him short."

"I wouldn't wish for a moment to stand in the way of Lady Elinor's brilliant prospects," Don said so blithely that Sylvertre felt he spoke the truth.

Lady Elinor, her pulses still in their usual admirable order, but nevertheless a trifle perplexed, went in and divested herself of her habit, and then sat down to think of a method of precipitating matters.

If Don had only stayed away a few days longer, she firmly believed that she would have been able to have her engagement to Lord Charldale announced. As it was she might now have to go through the fuss and disagreeableness of an explanation with Don. At any rate his arrival was inopportune and inconsiderate in the highest degree, and she felt that it was an act of injustice on his part towards her to reappear when she was forgetting him so comfortably.

At luncheon she said to Lady Timerton,—

"Don Arminger is back; did you see him this morning?"

"He has not been here, has he, Elinor? It was selfish of you to keep him to yourself when you know how I'm longing to see him. Our dear Don!"

"Indeed, mamma, I only met him on the doorstep as I was coming in, and he and Sylvertre were going out. The sun was blazing down on my head, and that you know I never can stand, so we didn't say much. I told him I thought he was in Africa, and he said no, he had been here to breakfast, and there it ended."

"Oh! there it ended!" Lady Timerton said, looking vaguely at her daughter.

"Don't invite him here often, it will only annoy papa; and, do you know, we must be careful about doing that, for I am sure papa is not well. I think he has those attacks oftener than we know of. Any excitement would bring them on, and naturally it would excite him if he saw Don Arminger here, when he wishes not to see him here."

"I don't know what to do, Elinor; I know it will be dreadful for you not to see a good deal of Don."

"Oh, don't think of me," Elinor said politely; "please don't; think only of papa."

So Lady Elinor got rid of the Don difficulty at home, but it was obstructing her in another direction of which she had no knowledge yet.

Lord Charldale had nearly brought himself up to the point of openly consoling himself by taking for his wife the lady who had got herself taken for the beauty of the year, when ill-conditioned circumstances brought Don Arminger out under the awning. Now this was annoying, to say the least of it, for Lord Charldale; for a rumour relative to Don and Lady Elinor had reached him, and he felt that it was due to his noble self to take the beauty of the year without any encumbering associations.

"'I feel that I shall cut the whole concern, and go off in the *White Squall* for a cruise to heaven knows where!' he said to his mother, after he had narrated the Don under the awning incident. 'The fellow looked so perfectly indifferent to my presence, that Elinor is safe to flirt with him again, if it's only for the sake of paining him, and I won't stand that."

'The dear girl is incapable of doing anything so foolish," Lady Charldale said with energy, for the idea of her son going off in his yacht, the *White Squall*, for an indefinite period, with unlimited alcohol on board, was abhorrent to her. "She has just sent me a little painting of the passage-room at Crowniston, painted on a terra-cotta plate—the sweetest thing!—painted from memory."

Lord Charldale laughed.

"You needn't think that I doubt her affection for Crowniston, mother, and I know she thinks the diamonds and herself will do each other justice; but I won't have her if she's going to make mental comparisons between Arminger and me."

And then Lord Charldale grew sulky, and for the first time for some months retired to his own room with that fatal little tray and bottle.

No wonder that his mother grew more and more

anxious to bring this great good thing of a marriage with Elinor about. Intuition told her that under that graceful, sometimes indifferent, and always rather languid manner of Lady Elinor's was concealed a will so impregnated with selfishness that it was indomitable.

"Her amiable resolve that everything shall redound to her own credit will be a shield to Charldale," the old lady told herself.

And then she went and called on Lady Timerton, and took the opportunity of Elinor being at home to let fall several hints as to Charldale's sensitive jealousy.

"If I could only meet him before I see Don Arminger again I'll make him bring things to a climax; but if he finds out that Don is about the house in the meantime, good-bye to Crowniston and the Charldale diamonds," Lady Elinor said to herself.

She was thoughtfully dressing for a "small and early" at Mrs Vibart's, and Mrs Vibart was a niece of the late Lord Charldale's. It was more than possible that Lord Charldale might be at his cousin's. It was almost a certainty. Lady Elinor weighed the chances, and dressed herself with care.

On her way down to dinner she met her brother rushing up two or three stairs at a time.

"I've got Arminger to say he'll dine here to-night," he said as he passed her, and she vouchsafed him no answer, but went on to the drawing-room where Lady Timerton was alone reading.

"Is Sylvertre going with us to Mrs Vibart's?" she asked.

"I think so, dear, and Don Arminger too," Lady Timerton said cheerfully.

"What a drove from one house; I shall stay at home, and I will ask you to give a little note for me to Lady Charldale; will you?"

"Of course I will, but what a disappointment for poor Don," Lady Timerton said pathetically.

To which Elinor replied that Don "ought to have stayed in South Africa honourably till the twelve months were up."

With the announcement of dinner Mr Arminger walked into the room, and almost at the same moment a diversion was made that would have been blessed by Lady Elinor had it been caused by anything less untoward. Lord Timerton's own man came forward, and with much agitation and a little consequent incoherency made them understand that his lordship had been " taken strange " suddenly a few minutes ago, and that he was now lying back in his chair, speechless.

They flocked to his room, and as they entered he opened his eyes, and his lips moved, but no sound issued from them then, or ever again. There were a few struggles, a few wild directions given by the frightened group, a cry for " Sylvertre," who had not come down yet, and then the end came.

When Don Arminger's former pupil joined them, he was the Earl of Timerton.

There was deep sorrow in the house that night, and for many days—sorrow upon which Don felt that it would be more than unseemly for him to intrude; but though he stayed away, he wrote both to Lady Timerton and to the young earl, and from her mother and brother Lady Elinor learned that he was still in town.

The young lady who had felt herself within a hair's-breadth of being Countess of Charldale, was in bitter uncertainty as well as deep grief now. That Lord Charldale, whose fickleness was proverbial, might forget his fancy for her, and either go off in the *White Squall,* or after some brighter, happier beauty, during the period of her enforced retirement, was quite upon the cards. In that case would it not be well to be faithful to Don? After all, Don was the only man to whom so much as she had of heart had ever warmed. But after Crowniston, and all the other places, and the diamonds, had been almost within her reach, it would be hard to come down to a single establishment, and that not too magnificently appointed.

This much must be said for Mr Arminger: he did not in any way actively add to her difficulties. After the late lord's funeral, he called on the widow before she left town, and saw Lady Elinor for a few minutes. He made no reference to the agreement which existed between them about coming to a decision for life at the expiration of the specified twelve months, but spoke as easily about his plans as if it was not contemplated that she might have a share in them.

"If you'll come down to us by-and-by with Timerton, we shall be very glad, Don," Lady Timerton said, her eyes filling with tears as she spoke of her son by the title which could not be his while his father had lived.

"I am going down to Clyst to-morrow, and shall be there for some time, I think," he said. "I have seen but little of my mother and sisters for the last few years; a quiet month with them will do me all the good in the world."

"Is that girl who behaved so abominably to Lord Charldale living at Clyst now?" Lady Elinor asked coldly, for though she was ready to throw Don over, she was not ready to resign him to a rival.

"I don't know of any girl who behaved abominably to Lord Charldale."

"I mean Miss Fielding."

"She lives at Woodside, not at Clyst."

"Oh!"

That was all that was said between them, but Lady Elinor made up her mind that if Lord Charldale went off in the *White Squall* without speaking, she would summon Don back from Clyst without scruple.

Day after day she managed by some means or another to delay their departure for a week. At last Lord Charldale dropped a P.P.C. card, but did not ask for admission; then Lady Elinor, feeling greatly discomfited, went out of town with her mother, and gossip said "the projected match of the season was off."

Lord Charldale went off to Norway in his yacht, but his mother took measures to have herself kept well informed as to his movements. She made up her mind that when he came home he should find her at Crown-iston, and that Elinor Divett should be with her.

Meantime Don had gone down to Clyst, feeling him-self as tightly bound and as unable to speak openly of his bonds as ever.

He found his sister Maude carrying out one of the old childish dreams—painting a portrait of Constance Field-ing, namely, and painting it in a way that would satisfy even a lover. What wonder, this being the case, that his sister's studio became his favourite haunt?

He found his mother sweet, sagacious, active, and in-dustrious as ever; he found Trixy flushed into brighter, softer beauty by the glory of an intensified happiness which she knew was coming to her. Only Constance was changed towards him. She had grown wiser and colder.

CHAPTER XXIII.

A LESSON LEARNT.

THERE was still about Constance Fielding that straight-forwardness and outspoken boldness which had character-ised her in her childhood, and his lively recognition of this quality made Don feel sure that she would before long speak to him of Lady Elinor.

And what, if she did so speak, had he to tell her?

One morning when she came to give Maude a sitting, Constance found herself with Don alone—Maude being engaged in pacifying Donald Vaughan, who had come to vent the rage he was in with his father, who had just refused to advance him a large sum of money, in her safe atmosphere.

For Donald Vaughan was engaged to his cousin Maude openly, in spite of his father's fury that such should be the case, and in spite also of Mrs Arminger's milder disapproval.

"I needn't hope to see Maude for the next hour," Constance said, when she came in and found what the reason of Maude's absence was. "Your mother is hard at work, as usual, and Trixy's writing something that must go off to-day, so you and I must make the best of each other for a time, Mr Arminger."

"I shall have no difficulty in fulfilling my part."

"Don't say things that sound like compliments; they don't suit either of us." Then there was a pause for a few moments, which she broke by asking in her downright way, "Why do you never speak to me of the lady you are going to marry? It would be so much more friendly and like you, if you would."

"Because, Miss Fielding, I don't know that I am going to marry any lady."

"I shouldn't like to think that you prevaricated—no —I couldn't do that," she said, looking at him thoughtfully; "still, I know from Trixy the pr mise you and Lady Elinor made to her father to wait twelve months; now her father is dead, and her mother and brother will offer no opposition, so why don't you speak of it to me?"

"I have no right to speak of Lady Elinor as being in any way bound to me. Her father's decision holds good though he is dead; at a specified time I shall give her the option of accepting or refusing me, and I think she will do the latter."

"What a cold-blooded way of going to work! and how hard on you to feel all this time—or to fear rather—that some one is trying to alienate her from you. It can't be true these reports that I have read, that she is—that there is a chance of her marrying Lord Charldale. Knowing what I did from Trixy about you, I felt it couldn't —it couldn't be true; but now that you have told me this, I'm afraid. Is it true?"

"I really can't say," he replied, smiling. "I can only rejoice that some one else is not going to marry Lord Charldale."

Constance shivered, then repressed the shiver and drew herself up.

"It was different with me," she said; "but she has

had you to think of and to know that you are thinking of her all the time. It can't be true, of course it can't! And she's so beautiful too, grown more beautiful than ever; how proud you must be of her."

"I don't see that she has grown more beautiful," Don said.

"I can fancy that she has, under the influence of deep feeling," Constance went on, compelling herself to discuss the subject of Lady Elinor in all its most painful bearings without further delay.

"Will you let me come with my sisters to Woodside?" he asked, being desirous of introducing a new topic.

"Will I let you? What a reproach to my hospitality to put it in that way! I am always hard at work trying to make Woodside as perfect as my dear father and mother meant it to be, and you shall come and tell me how I can further improve it. Perhaps by-and-by, when you're married, Lady Elinor and you will come and stay with me, and you'll see then what a methodical, managing, staid mistress of a house I have become."

This was a little beyond what he could bring himself to bear.

"Even should it ever come about that I have the right to take Lady Elinor anywhere, which is an extreme improbability, I shall never take her to Woodside," he said impatiently.

"Don't you wish your wife to be friendly with me?" she asked, a little surprised at his sudden outburst of pettishness. Then she went on to point out to him how inevitably they would all be "mixed up" in the future through Trixy's marriage with Lord Timerton. I'm too much like one of the family to be left out of Trixy's arrangements. I'm to be the old maid-aunt of the family, and Woodside is to be the place where the family are to come and recruit their faded health and spirits, when any of them are done up by gaiety or work."

He did not answer her. He would not encourage her to put a further strain upon herself, for he saw that she was suffering a good deal in the effort she was making to take a familiar and matter-of-fact view of his probable marriage with Lady Elinor.

So he just sat quiet and silent, and let her talk on as she willed. And if giving up his life would have served her, he would have given it freely, but he would not give her one look of love.

"Do you like my portrait?" she asked presently. "It looks to me much more like the 'Connie' I was a year ago than the 'Miss Fielding' I am now; Maude has always seen the best of me, and she has put in the best she has seen."

"Maude sees very clearly."

"What a lovely picture she will make of Lady Elinor; don't let anyone but Maude paint her, Don. Maude can paint the skin, and indicate the soul at the same time; oughtn't we to be proud of Maude?"

So she went on, innocently identifying herself with his dearest interests.

It was really a relief to him when Maude came in; for, sweet as it was to him to have Constance all to himself in this way, there was danger in the sweetness.

After this there came many happy days at Woodside. Days that were full of sunshine, and flowers, and sweet sounds. Days that were terribly testing ones to poor Don, for Lord Timerton had come down to Clyst to prove to Trixy that there was no obstacle to their marriage, and to make her heart sing with this proof of his loyalty and fidelity. So it came to pass—as the two pairs of engaged lovers had a habit of eliminating themselves from the others—that Miss Fielding and Don were thrown very much together.

"It's useless attempting tennis. Trixy and Lord Timerton play in such a maddeningly limp way now, that they spoil any game, to say nothing of any temper; and Maude makes no pretence of wishing to play. What shall we do, Mr Arminger, when they desert us in this way?" Constance said to him one day when Maude had gone away in one direction with her sketching materials, and Donald Vaughan and Trixy had taken Tennyson's last poem, and Lord Timerton away to the summer-house by the river,—

"Shall we try being idle for a change?"

"No, no; Satan will find some mischief for idlers to talk about; there's danger for everyone in idleness, I'm sure. I suggest that we garden; you shall do the hard part, and I'll do the fancy work."

"There's nothing to be done in this garden," Donald protested. "It's in too perfect order for any of our artistic touches to be visible. I feel no ambition to labour hard when I know there will be no perceptible result."

"There speaks the tempter. You are letting vanity and laziness get the better of you; if the garden doesn't excite your horticultural ambition, perhaps the green-house will? Come and see. There's always plenty to do in a greenhouse; you shall fill the pots, and I'll trans-plant and take cuttings."

"How restless you are; you must always be doing something," Don said, as he followed her to the green-house, but he said it very admiringly.

In spite of his pretence of unwillingness, Don Armin-ger liked his occupation far too well for a semi-engaged man. The programme as arranged by Constance, that he should fill the pots and she put in the cuttings, involved constant and close companionship, for Don felt it to be needful that he should assist in placing the delicate transplants symmetrically in the middle of their new homes. Altogether in her desire to avoid dangerous idleness, Miss Fielding had proposed a more dangerous pastime.

"How's that going to end?" Lord Timerton said to Trixy as they passed the greenhouse, and marked the confidential way in which the pair within were pursuing their calling as gardeners.

"In nothing more than there is at present—in friend-ship, I suppose," Trixy replied.

"Do you know, I hardly think you are justified in

supposing anything of the sort; she is free, and they're desperately in love with one another."

"But you can't say that Don is free?"

"I should consider myself so if I were in Don's case. Elinor is not treating him fairly at all. It's all nonsense her pretending that she is simply abiding by my father's wishes in sticking out for the expiration of the twelve months before she gives her decision. She's holding off to see if Charldale will come back to her, and if he does, she'll throw Don over."

"If you think that, you ought to tell Don so," Trixy says with glowing cheeks. "It's too shameful! Don is too good in every way to be anyone's plaything. Hugh, I shall be so indignant, I shall detest your sister if she treats Don badly, or only marries him because she can't get Lord Charldale."

"My dear Trixy, Elinor is one of the coolest-headed, coolest-hearted girls out; but she did take a fancy to Don, there's no doubt of that. That fancy to a great extent has faded since she went to Crownistown, and discovered that Charldale's wife will have some of the finest diamonds and places in England. She'll always prefer Don to Charldale naturally, but if she marries Don they'll both be wretched. I should urge on the affair with Miss Fielding if I were you."

"Don is so honourable; he will leave it entirely to your sister," Trixy said rather dejectedly, for the idea of Don being either jilted or unhappy in his marriage with Elinor was galling to her.

"May I come and pot some more cuttings to-morrow?" Don asked when he was going away that day.

"No; to-morrow we picnic out in the Berryan Woods, and as we're not going to take any servants with us, you'll have an opportunity of making yourself useful in another way. I'll teach you how to compound a salad on un-English principles, and show you how to lay a cloth and keep it quiet on a breezy slope."

"In fact, under your auspices, I shall become as good

an amateur butler as I already feel myself to be a gardener," he told her ; and Constance said,—

"Yes ; I am very kindly making you useful. Lady Elinor ought to be grateful to me."

Mrs Arminger and three or four of their Clyst friends went with them to this picnic in Berryan Woods, and Constance managed it so that she kept some of her guests with her all the day, and by this means increased Don's feeling of safety, but gave him one of deadly dulness in its place. It was in vain that he tried to tempt her away into flowery shady places on little botanising expeditions. She shook her head, and adhered steadily to the companionship of some rather tedious guests and the path of duty.

But when the day was over, Don descended to strategy, and after packing away his mother and their friends in their respective carriages, contrived to get himself left behind with no means of getting home unless Miss Fielding would give him a seat in her little oak village-cart.

The prospect of doing this, of driving Don home in the soft fading summer light, through long winding lanes whose hedges were wreathed with the wild briony, honeysuckle, and white convolvulus, and rich with briar-roses —those faithful " dog " roses that remain with us so late into the summer—was full of delight for Constance. Indeed, the delight was so keen and vivid that she immediately became conscious that she ought not to give it to herself, Lady Elinor being in the background.

"If I were you I would walk ; the footpath through the woods to Clyst is a mere nothing as to distance, and you can't imagine anything prettier than it is," she said, displaying a degree of earnestness in her description which revealed more than she meant to reveal.

"I can imagine it very well, I've tramped it many a time when I was an usher in Dalzel's school ; the road will have a greater charm and beauty for me this evening than the footpath "

"You are very obstinate, and I am very weak! Get in."

He got into the little carriage by her side, and she started her pony at a pace that promised well for their speedy arrival in Clyst.

"Why are you driving so fast?" he asked presently.

"It's safer," she replied, looking at him steadily ; then she added, "the pony's not nearly so likely to stumble over rough ground if you drive fast. Do you remember Peppercorn?"

"Too well!" he said with a rush, which immediately awakened his repentance.

"So do I, and everything that happened that day when you saved my life."

Her voice softened and broke, and for a moment he was afraid she was going to cry. But she recovered herself quickly, and asked brightly,—

"When are you going away, Mr Arminger?"

"Soon, I think."

"You ought to go soon."

"Why do you say so?"

"You know you ought to go soon. I don't think you have been wrong in coming—there are the lights of Clyst—for we both had a lesson to learn, and we have learnt it by heart, and we shall never forget it ; but now that the lesson is learnt, you ought to go and obey its precepts."

"I cannot act, I can only wait," he said in a low voice, and again Constance felt her heart fill with dangerous pity. Then silence set in, and reigned between them until they reached Clyst, and Don said good-evening to her at his mother's garden-gate.

It seemed as if her words, "You ought to go soon," had been uttered in a spirit of prophecy, when the next day there came a letter from the widowed Lady Timerton, asking him to go and spend a few days with them at Scallow, which had been lent to her by Lady Kenwyn.

"Elinor must mean to bring things to a climax, or she wouldn't have me here," he told himself despondently

But he had "learnt his lesson well," in very truth, and did not dare to show despondency before either his own people or Constance.

"It's clear to me that Nell has given up all hope of Charldale, and now she is going to fall back on Don," Lord Timerton said to his betrothed when he heard of his mother's invitation. "Poor fellow! he would be a hundred times happier with the other one, but I can't counsel a man to jilt my own sister."

CHAPTER XXIV.

ELINOR'S FUTURE HOME.

HER brother had been quite right in his estimate of the depth and sincerity of Elinor's attachment to Don. It was because she had given up all hopes of Lord Charldale, that she had allowed her mother to summon Mr Arminger.

Old Lady Charldale had paid a flying visit to Crowniston once since Lady Timerton and Elinor had been staying at Scallow, and on this occasion she had sought Elinor with flattering celerity, and spoken quite hopefully of her son's improved health and speedy return. But there had been something underlying this apparent hopefulness of hers, which had led Elinor to think it was assumed, and that all was not as well with Lord Charldale as his mother affected to think.

Indeed, poor old Lady Charldale had a heart full of sorrow, and a head full of bewildered trouble at this period. He was her only son, and he was as dear to her as a son could be to a mother. He was her only son, and with him it rested to continue the honour of his father's house, or to cover that honour with shame. She had screened him, helped him, struggled for him against his besetting sin and the worse part of his nature from his boyhood. But now she felt that a wife whom he loved, and of whom he was proud, would execute these tasks better than she—his mother—could ever hope to do. If she could only see him safely anchored to Elinor Divett, her motherly fears would be at rest, and her heart would be right again.

But in these latter days a dreadful report had reached her. The *White Squall*, which she had believed to be safely harboured in some Norwegian port, was at Malta, and Lord Charldale was making himself notorious by a flirtation he was carrying on with a native beauty. The girl was good, pretty, and virtuous, but English society in Malta was cut to the core by his lordship's conduct, and his mother was given to understand that social degradation was in store for her son if he followed his current course of flirtation to the point of marriage.

At last, in despair of getting him home by any other means than by an appeal to his vanity, she wrote,—

"Mr Don Arminger has evidently determined to rival you in every direction. It was his influence which induced Miss Fielding to behave in the infamous way she did; and now I hear that he is actually going to be daring enough to aspire to Elinor; I will not betray the dear girl's feelings even to you, but we all know of what 'a woman scorned' is capable. How people will rave about her when she comes out of her retirement at Scallow! I saw her the other day, and trembled that one unworthy of her may carry off the greatest beauty of the day."

Lord Charldale laughed when he read this letter; but nevertheless he did not like the idea of being cut out of the good graces of "the greatest beauty of the day," more especially by that "fellow Arminger."

His Maltese enchantress felt a marked decline and fall in the temperature of his attentions during the few days that followed the receipt of his mother's letter, and at the end of a week the *White Squall* sailed for England.

But in the days of his infatuation for her, he had

written letters to the Maltese beauty that were worded
more warmly than was wise or well, and when the *White
Squall* sailed away she re-read these letters very carefully,
derived some comfort from them, and then, in unromantic
fashion, handed them over to her papa.

The *White Squall* was in safe waters, but the same
cannot be said of her owner.

When Don Arminger saw Lady Elinor waiting for him
at the station in an innocent-looking little pony-carriage,
he felt that his fate was sealed. Had she desired to stave
off coming to a definite conclusion, she would surely have
abstained from proclaiming her right to be unconventional with him in this pronounced manner. But in this
he was mistaken. Lady Elinor cared very little about
the deductions that might be drawn from her conduct by
the station-master and porters, and these were the only
people to criticise her here.

She did not intend to let this gracious act of coming to
meet him commit her to anything—just yet.

Unquestionably she looked very handsome in her deep
mourning, and Don acknowledged to himself that she
did so, but still felt that he preferred beauty of a warmer
type than hers. After a lengthened perusal of Constance's
expression, and a prolonged study of the poses into which
her graceful figure fell naturally, there was something
a little hard and cold about Elinor, perfectly modelled
and mannered as she was.

And the worst of it was, he felt that her heart was to
match. He knew that it was modelled on the best
principles, and that it would never forget or do discredit
to itself ; but it would no more give itself entirely to him
than—his would give itself to her.

"Did you find it dull at Clyst?" she asked him as
they drove back to Scallow. "I should think you must
have done so. Two pairs of engaged people about one
all day long must be dreadfully trying, especially if they're
fond of one another.

"They didn't try me at all."

"Indeed! Then you must have had some diversion apart from and independent of them," she said, laughing pleasantly at the thought of the power she had to rend him away from his "diversion" whenever it pleased her.

"On the contrary, we were always together."

"Then were you an unwanted fifth?"

"I never felt myself *de trop*."

"Perhaps Miss Fielding saved you from experiencing that sensation? Yes. I read guilt in your eye. Don, you've evidently been improving the time, and flirting with Miss Fielding.

"Miss Fielding is the last woman in the world that I should or could flirt with. What have you been doing by way of improving the time?"

"I am not going to be turned aside from my path of discovery by idle and vain questions," Lady Elinor said placidly. "You may as well tell me as let me find out. Just confess that you would much rather have stayed at Clyst than have come to Scallow? I promise not to be hurt or offended, or any folly of that kind."

"Have you found it dull at Scallow, or have you lighted upon any agreeable neighbours?" he asked, ignoring her question.

"If you think for a moment, you will remember that it is in the order of things that we should find it quiet; in other words, dull anywhere just at present," she said in accents of gentle reproach.

"And if you think for a moment, you will remember that I am never dull with my mother and sisters."

"To say nothing of Miss Fielding?" she put in, laughing good-humouredly.

"To say nothing of Miss Fielding, who is a charming companion."

"Does she ride? Did you ever ride with her?"

"She rides, but I never rode with her."

"Did you ever go for little solitary drives with her?" Lady Elinor persisted.

"Once I did," he replied, with a vivid recollection of that drive home after the picnic in Berryan Woods, when he learnt the whole hard lesson that honour and duty taught him.

"And now having enjoyed your idyll you have come back to me and the prose of life. We shall have to discuss the question of where we shall live sooner or later, so we may as well begin. Mamma wants us to live with her, and I think it a good plan ; don't you?"

"No, I do not," Don said decidedly. "Whatever or wherever our future home may be, I shall prefer being master and your being mistress in it."

"I should be mistress virtually in any home we made with mamma."

"That would be unjust to your mother."

"Then you must let me choose the situation of the house."

"So I will, within certain bounds," Don said guardedly ; but Lady Elinor had made up her mind that he should have nothing to do with the choice of locality.

"When Timerton marries, mamma means to have a house in Portland Place ; it would be pleasant for us to take one near her."

"Camden Town would be as near as I could manage in that direction," he said quietly, and Lady Elinor's eyes sparkled with vexation.

"I am discussing the subject seriously," she said coldly.

"So am I. I assure you I think the subject of where we are to live a very important one, and I'm afraid we shall not agree about it."

"It's always the lady's right to choose the situation of the house, unless the husband is a professional man and obliged to go where he can make a living. I mean to stand on my rights ; but we needn't quarrel about it yet. Wait till we're in town and the choice has to be made."

Now this looked unpromising. Still Don looked at the brightest aspect of affairs, and while he resolved to show all due consideration and respect for Lady Elinor's wishes, he at the same time made up his mind that the situation of their home of the future should be settled by himself.

So without any more words on the actual subject of the marriage, it came to be an understood thing in the family that Lady Elinor and Mr Arminger were engaged properly at last, and Don's mother tried to respond affectionately to the warm entreaty that Elinor penned to her, asking for her " blessing on her new daughter."

Mr Arminger soon brought his visit to Scallow to a close. Now that he was to assume the responsibilities of marriage, it was more necessary than ever that he should provide himself as amply as possible with munitions for carrying on the war. It is true that Lady Elinor had a moderate fortune, but her fortune bore no sort of relative comparison to the way in which she would want to live, and Don had no intention of being assisted in money matters by her brother or mother, during the latter's lifetime. Accordingly he declared it to be needful that he should return to the Great Mart, where presently he assumed certain editorial duties which combined the advantages of largely increasing his income, and greatly occupying his time. And Elinor taught herself to speak triumphantly of his avocations and success, and really believed that she was very proud of the intellectual victories of the man she was finding it expedient to marry.

About October, Scallow became oppressively dull to her, by reason of Crowniston being still unoccupied by any of " the family," and Elinor began instructing her mother that it was time for them to go up to town, and begin to think of making preparations for the wedding. But it was in fact not so much anxiety about getting the wedding outfit under weigh, as it was to finally settle the mootpoint about the house to her own satisfaction.

For the first week after her arrival in London, Elinor held her peace on the subject of the house, and merely discussed different styles of furniture with Don, who found her so reasonable that he began to be hopeful about amicably adjusting their difference of opinion with regard to locality. It is true that her ideas were more conventional and less artistic than those of his sisters. But this mattered little to him. If Elinor had what she liked, and he could compass giving it to her, he would be perfectly satisfied.

But after two or three visits of inspection to the fashionable upholsterers, her ideas expanded under the skilful treatment she experienced from her guides through various departments. Elegancies and artistic touches began to be suggested that outnumbered the hairs of her head. And then Don thought it was time to let it be known that he meant the furniture to be chosen with due regard to his power of paying for it.

"In fact, he said, "before you make any definite selection, you must know where the things are to go, or they may be out of all proportion to the rooms they are to go into."

"I've thought of it and have purposely avoided everything colossal, for I shall be quite satisfied with small rooms, provided the house is in the right locality."

"I'll get a house-agent's list and mark two or three that may do, and then you and Lady Timerton can go and see them," Don said. And Elinor reserved herself till she had seen his selections.

But in the meantime she got a list of houses in the Mayfair district, and inspected a gem of a place, just out of Piccadilly, yet close to and commanding a beautiful view of the Park. The rent was enormous, but this was a detail that Elinor felt sure she should reason Don into disregarding. The arrangement of the house was exquisite, and a conservatory divided the drawing-room from an altogether original morning-room in a way that made her feel she should never regret the glories of Timerton House.

In the evening Don came with his list, and by-and-by they looked at it together.

Elinor sat at the table, her hand supporting her forehead and shading her eyes, so that he, standing by her side, could not see the expression of them. But her tone revealed much to him when she asked,—

"Why have you put this house to be first looked at?"

"Because I think it the one most likely to suit us,

It may save you a good deal of driving about if it does, and we settle to take it."

"Do you see where it is?"

She turned over a page or two of the list, then threw it aside.

"I won't live in any of the places you've marked," she said, speaking with unusual force and decision ; "I won't, Don. Kensington Park Gardens, Upper Westbourne Place, Sussex Gardens, Bayswater. Who ever heard of the places excepting the people who live in them? No. I shall not take such utterly useless journeys in search of them even. I have done much better than you in the time. I've actually seen a house that will suit us in every way."

Then she told him where it was, and depicted the magic charms of the conservatory and morning-room.

"You can't be serious in proposing that we should go there ; the rent would be nearly my income, Elinor. You must be contented with a house in a suburb, and that suburb not one of the most expensive."

"Nothing shall induce me to put my foot into a house in Bayswater," she said petulantly ; and her mood was not improved when he replied,—

"Very well, if you like St John's Wood better, we might get a house and garden."

"Why don't you go and say 'by which means we shall combine the advantages of town and country?' That's what my last maid said when she married a baker at Peckham, and became the proud mistress of a cottage, with a garden containing several rows of early potatoes and sweet-peas. You must find something a little more suitable than Bayswater or St John's Wood, or I shall be driven to the conclusion that you want to make the residence a stumbling-block to the marriage."

"You will never even in anger accuse me of such dishonesty ; but even at the risk of such injustice on your part, I shall decline to take any house for which it impossible I can pay."

'Then if you draw the line so narrowly, I shall think

you very unkind if you won't let mamma provide me with a home fit to live in," she pouted, and Don Arminger gave her to understand that her home, if she came to be his wife, must be provided by him only.

"No one shall say that I live in a way for which I am unable to pay. I will not accept anything for myself which I don't fairly earn; if you are to run in harness with me, the harness must be paid for by me, and me only. You understand?"

"I suppose you will consult the feelings of my family in the matter of our house? You will hardly wish to separate me from them, or to drag them out into what Timerton calls shy places."

"Timerton and Trixy and your mother will come to us wherever we are, and you shall receive them with all the more pleasure because you will feel the home, whatever it may, is our own, and not their gift. Come, Elinor, be reasonable; don't let such an ignominious difficulty be our first one."

"The difficulty may be ignominious, but at the same time it is one that will be a dreadful trouble to me all my life, if I don't combat it now," she said sullenly. "I should be more than half-an-hour driving to the Park from any of those horrible places."

"That's not all the world to you, surely!"

"And when I got there I should always be blown about and dusty and tired, and not fit to be seen, and—in fact, nothing shall take me to any of the places you've marked. If you make a split out of it, I shall know what to think of you, and so will everyone else, and as Timerton and you have always been such friends, I hope your conscience will approve you."

"It will, as it will Timerton also; he has a wholesome manly horror of pretence and debt," Don replied.

Then he busied himself with his house-agent's list again, but failed to find anything that accorded with Lady Elinor's views.

———

CHAPTER XXV.

HEARTSEASE.

IN consequence of the recent death of his father, Lord Timerton's marriage with Trixy was a very quiet one, only his mother and sister from his side of the house being present at it, and the Armingers limiting their invitations to Constance Fielding.

There had been a word or two said as to the advisability of Elinor being married on the same day as her brother, but this word had been said by old Lady Timerton, not by Elinor herself. The question of the house not being settled yet, Elinor advanced two or three reasonable objections to the proposition. And Don did not oppose her.

But though she blew hot and cold in various ways about him, and her marriage with him, she took care when they went to the wedding at Clyst, that it should be seen by all of them that Don was in strict thrall to her; that he was in fact her property, and as such of far greater account than he had ever been before.

They were only thrown together for a day or two, but during that time Lady Elinor rather gave beholders the impression of wishing to be kind and friendly to Constance, as to one who had suffered, and whose suffering had been—innocently—partially caused by Lady Elinor herself. Now this attitude was unquestionably an obnoxious one to Miss Fielding; but she went through the ordeal without flinching, and never once gave Don the additional pain of seeing that his betrothed had the power to hurt her.

Not that Lady Elinor did anything in a coarsely triumphant way, nor that she displayed anything so distinctly ill-bred as ill-nature or spite. But she quietly towered over Constance, and assumed a submissive and disappointed spirit in her which Constance did not possess.

"Trix is a lucky girl in every way," Elinor said, when the bride and bridegroom had gone away. "For one thing, she'll never have the sting of feeling that some other girl has wanted to marry Timerton; that's the hardest thing of all for a good-hearted girl to feel."

"It's a feeling that would never sting me for a moment," Constance said.

"Oh yes, it would; to know yourself prized and adored by a man who is prized and adored by another girl who's quite as good as you in every way, would be awfully painful. Timerton is a very staunch fellow; he never raised false hopes even by accident."

"I think they'll be very happy, as happiness goes in married life," Constance said; and Elinor replied,—

"Yes, I think they will. How cruel we all thought poor papa last year when he put his veto on both Timerton's marriage and mine; and now their affair has come off as placidly as possible, and there seems to be nothing but peace before them."

"And your affair will come off soon, and I hope there will be nothing but peace for you and Mr Arminger," Constance said brightly.

"I shall do my part towards preserving it, but Don is so sensitively alive to what I am sacrificing in marrying him; if I raise the least objection to—to the situation of a house in which I am likely to live all my life, he thinks I'm regretting the step I've taken. There is such a thing as a man's being too much in love—too anxious to smooth all the crumples out of the rose-leaves of the woman he is going to marry."

Lady Elinor said this easily and naturally, but Constance knew that both the sentiment and the words had been well rehearsed.

"You can easily avoid raising those tender fears in his breast by agreeing to the situation of any house he proposes," Constance said merrily.

"No, I can't," Elinor replied petulantly; "my instincts are against certain quarters, and his instincts are not sympathetic. A man really should make some concessions when a girl comes off her pedestal, as I have done at his solicitation."

"But I understood you just now that Mr Arminger was too sensitively eager to please you," Constance said, with a quickly-growing distaste to the tone of the conversation.

"So he is," Elinor replied, with quick consciousness of the lapse she had made.

She had not intended to pass the slightest censure on Don when she began, but the house grievance was the greatest she had ever known, and her judgment grew weak as her wrath rose.

'So he is; but his sensibilities are not keen on the subject of propriety of position, and when I point them out to him, he thinks I am repenting myself of my engagement, and that distresses him."

"Then don't do it," Constance said bluntly, and Lady Elinor solaced herself under the implied rebuke by mentally calling Constance "a local-minded, impertinent girl."

The Dowager Lady Timerton and her daughter went back to town late on the day of the wedding, escorted by Don, who had found this brief glimpse of paradise rather a painful thing.

Painful in spite of Constance's unceasing brave endeavours to rob the situation of all pathos. She made herself as prosaic and as practical as a girl could be, merely addressing him on the veriest common-places, neither shunning him nor seeming to do so, but putting him so perfectly in place as "one of the Arminger family, with whom she was very intimate," that he ought to have been at ease.

But he was not. Indeed, he was man-like and unhero-like enough to let her nonchalance add to his uneasiness.

"Good-bye. I'll let you know when I have taught Mr Arminger the map of London," Lady Elinor whispered when taking leave of Constance.

"And when you've done that, perhaps he will reward

you with a trip to South Africa, the map of which must be much more interesting when learnt on the spot," Constance laughed; and Lady Elinor remarked, as the carriage rolled off from the door,—

"What irritatingly and fatiguingly high spirits the country heiress has, to be sure; she seems to be no more subject to fits of human depression than the horses and dogs, and cattle and pigs by which she has lived exclusively surrounded all her life."

"In which class do you put my mother and sisters?" Mr Arminger asked.

And Lady Elinor made up her mind that, in place of vials of sarcasm, she would pour the smoothest melted butter over Constance Fielding for the future.

"One of my dear children is as safe and happy, humanly speaking, as it is possible for her to be," Mrs Arminger said to Constance when the guests were gone, and they were having a cosy time together in a little room that had been left intact through all the festivities.

"And we'll hope for the best for the others, dear," Constance said cheerily; "Donald Vaughan isn't much more selfish than the majority, and Maude's eyes always fail to see selfishness; he will be as fond of her as Donald Vaughan can be of any one but himself, and he will depend upon her in reality, and make it seem that she depends upon him."

"I can't thwart my dear girl, but I wish she had kept her heart from Donald Vaughan," the mother sighed.

"Dear old friend, that's rubbish; the man a girl's heart goes to, is the man to have it; we can't alter that."

"And Don has disappointed me too," Mrs Arminger said sadly; "Elinor with her cold regularity of social feeling and profound consciousness of what is due to herself, is not the wife my Don ought to have had."

"Perhaps Don knows better about that even than you do; she is very fond of him, and he may well be very proud of her, and there's a great deal of family feeling and interest to bind them together. You're tired, and for once in your life inclined to glance away from the sunny side; but how happy and jolly you and I will be by-and-by, when all these young couples come down upon us, and tell us off to the service of their bairns."

"You speak as if you always meant to be Constance 'Fielding,' and it breaks my heart, my dear," the elder woman said; and the younger one replied,—

"So I do, mother. I've had a little bit of my day of love, and that day is done, but there are plenty of things to excite my interest and keep me full of employment and happiness. You're the very first of all. When these young people have all got themselves together, you and I must get ourselves together. It will be the only duty you've left unperformed to make me happy, and you'll make me that by coming to Woodside."

"Next to my children, you're my nearest, Connie, but I can't make you happy in that way, or rather I can't pretend to do it. To make me happy I must see you doing your best part in the world, and the best part you can play, my dear, is that of a happy wife and mother."

"Give me a pattern and I'll try to follow it," Constance replied. Then she wound her arms round Mrs Arminger's neck and said, "You and I together—together— can do without a pattern."

"Connie, dear, I don't believe in the efficacy of us poor mortals striving to look into our little futurity in this world; but still, I can't help looking ahead a little and hoping and feeling sure that yours won't be a solitary life at Woodside."

"No; it's not in my programme that I am to be solitary, for I mean to haunt you, in order that you may teach me how to treat all the young people who will, God willing, come about us by-and-by. The Timertons and the Donald Vaughans, and Mr Arminger and his wife and all their belongings will come to Woodside in time. And you will help me to make Woodside home-like and pleasant to them."

"Until you are no longer the heart-free and inde-

pendent Miss Fielding. And oh, Connie, how I hope
that day may come soon !"

"It will never come—to rid you of me. It can't, you
see," Constance said frankly. "I launched my little
barque of love, and it sailed away silently into some
far-away sea from whence no sound of it shall ever be
heard again. Then I put out a little boatful of ambition,
and that got wrecked. Now I am going to rest and be
thankful at Woodside, and you must help me."

"That I will," Mrs Arminger said. And that she
did.

It was very easy to help Constance Fielding, for she
had about her such a fund of self-helpfulness. She had
the courage to acknowledge herself defeated on points of
vital interest, and she had the better courage to fight on
in the face of these openly-acknowledged defeats.

"They do say our young lady at Woodside have been
rarely badly treated by her sweethearts," the Clyst people
were in the habit of saying to one another when Miss
Fielding passed through their midst on market-days.
And even her own social set, getting hold of the wrong
end of the stick, as it is the wont of one's social set to
do, belaboured her with pity for having been "shamefully
treated" by both Lord Charldale and Mr Arminger.
"He as used to teach up at Mr Dalzell's," as the villagers
said.

Constance didn't care for these things that were said
of her. Honestly and truly she didn't care. In her
own heart she knew that Don Arminger had never behaved badly about her ; and as for Lord Charldale—well,
she had forgiven him the ignominious difficulty he had
put her in for an hour, in gratitude for her narrow
escape from a life spent with him.

The fact is she was conscience clear herself, and
that to a girl of her calibre is the real balm in Gilead.
She had been "true and fast" all through. Yes,
even to Lord Charldale, who had been unworthy of
her, she had been loyal until that supreme moment
when he had shown himself unable to comprehend,

much less to appreciate, her loyalty. And now, whatever happened, she had done nothing that might aid in the consummation of the mistakes of Don Arminger's life.

Vigorously she threw herself into any employment that presented itself, or that came any way near her. As she had said several times to Maude, she would have been perhaps a happier girl if circumstances had compelled her to work for her living. When one is struggling incessantly for the necessaries of life, one has no time to lament a lost lover.

However, fate having ordained that she should be the possessor of a fair fortune, and having provided her with a beautiful home, duty did not call upon her to strive to increase the one or enrich the other.

But duty did call upon her to take an active and befitting interest in those less favoured fellow-creatures of hers who were abundant about Clyst as everywhere else in this world. And in doing this duty heartily she found the best panacea.

In her gardens and greenhouses every tree, shrub and flower reminded her of Don. Together they had planted the melons which were ripening now in the hotbed, which was held sacred to her experiments. Together they had selected from a neighbouring florist's a vast variety of the rarest and most beautiful pansies, and made a bed of them which was now in full velvety perfection. But there was no heartsease for Constance in contemplating them.

Her two old gardeners, Rill and Staveley, who were at daggers drawn on every other point, were of one accord in this, namely, that they disapproved of and despised all the garden and greenhouse work which had been done by Mr Arminger. Rill conceived his own speciality to be hotbeds, and the treatment of flowers generally. On these two points he took his proudest stand, but he also claimed to have more than common skill and judgment in the treatment of every kind of fruit and vegetable that grows upon the earth. He held Staveley (who was

less pronounced in proclaiming his own great abilities) in
abhorrence.　And Staveley held Rill in contempt.

But against the common foe, the daring gentleman
intruder who had come in and planted melons, and made
a pansy-bed without the aid of either of them, they united
their forces, and made fierce verbal war.

Devoted as they were to their young mistress, lenient
to her "fads," as they called all her suggestions behind
her back, and desirous as they were to see her garden all
other gardens in the region round about excelling, they
still took black-hearted pleasure in seeing the melons, in
the culture of which they had no hand, growing feebly.

They were good old men, pious old men, after their
lights—which were of the Wesleyan persuasion—but
they did nourish feelings of professional envy and malice
against one another, and agreed to differ on every other
subject than that of Mr Arminger's presumptuous ignorance in presuming to plant out melons and make pansy-
beds.

"Mr Arminger he've no conscience," Rill would say to
Miss Fielding, when he would see her gaze disconsolately
at her equally disconsolate-looking melons, and though
Constance knew well what his reply would be, she
humoured the old man's whim by always asking,—

"Why do you say that, Rill?　I think Mr Arminger
a most conscientious gentleman."

"Not about the fruits of the earth, ma'am—not about
the fruits of the earth.　They as plant melons should
water them, else stands to reason that melons which
wants drowning will go frail and not prosper; that's why
I say Mr Arminger have no conscience; there may be
some good about him, 'tisn't for me to say there's not,
for I don't know that there's not for truth; but he've
taken one of the best fruits God has given us, and wasted
it through not watering."

"He is gone away, Rill; he has left you to do the
watering."

"And if he knowed he was going away he shouldn't
ha' taken and planted melons.　I water them, I do, but

I can't give all my time, with winter potatoes and potting for next spring bedding-out on my mind, to watering they melons, which have no call on me, for I didn't plant 'em. Howsumever, I water them, but I don't answer for Staveley. Staveley's that obstinate, it's no use asking him to do what he oughter do unless he feels that way. Staveley have no conscience either, and very little knowledge."

Rill's is the bludgeon blow. Staveley fights with a finer-edged weapon.

"Mr Rill he attend to these here melons, miss, since Mr Arminger went, and left they to theirselves, poor things, so they're all right, let's hope, whatever else in the garden is wrong. They was flagging for want of air just now, and I was just putting my hand to the frame, to give them a breath, but Mr Rill come along, and he being so clever about melons, I let 'em alone, and he wouldn't open the frame, 'cos I was ignorant enough to want to do it, and so, as he knows best, they melons are burnt up and dying."

"Have you weeded my pansy-bed, Staveley?"

"No miss; I'll speak the truth. That pansy-bed, to my mind, is a blot on the garden. Pretty enough in itself 'twould ha' been if it had been laid out by one as knew how pansies should be placed; but lor! there they are—the yaller, and the purple, and the gold-and-blue, and the white-and-blue, and the violet, all meshed up together anyhow. Mr Arminger knowed so much better than any one else that it wasn't for me to tell him he was spoiling the bed, and now, though I'd weed it with pleasure, Mr Rill can do it much better, because I don't know half so much about pansies—which I've cultivated special all my life—than he do, who never touched the cultivation of 'em."

"I'll weed the pansy-bed, and you air and water the melons," Constance said confidentially; and Staveley did take a canful of water up surreptitiously by-and-by, and pour it upon the parched and drooping melons.

CHAPTER XXVI.

ELINOR IS WISE.

LADY ELINOR DIVETT had gone back to town with a strong determination to be amiable about most things. But about the house she thoroughly intended to make a stand.

"Don doesn't seem to recognise any difference between Belgravia and Ball's Pond," she said to her brother when he advised her to leave the selection of locality to Don.

"Don will not go to one or the other extreme," his sister, Lady Timerton, put in, and then Elinor gently reminded Trixy that her experience about such matters was of very recent date.

Meanwhile, Don let the house question drift, and merely worked hard for the means of maintaining a house, if one should be taken and lived in.

But in drifting he came upon what he felt would suit him exactly.

He was spending a leisurely Bohemian Sunday with an artist at the artist's Queen Ann red-brick house, in Bedford Park, when a happy inspiration led him to express approbation of the combined picturesqueness and utility of this new departure in house architecture. And his friend—one of those amiable people who always express a fervent desire to locate every chance acquaintance, much more every friend, in their immediate vicinity —instantly responded to this approbation, by saying,—

"The best built and arranged house in the colony happens just to have been vacated, and is in course of thorough re-decoration; it would be the very thing for you, Arminger. I wish you'd have a look at it. I can get the key in five minutes."

"I think I'll see it," Don said, but his heart misgave him even as he spoke, for he prefigured to himself Lady Elinor's expression when she should hear that he had even so much as looked at it.

Nevertheless, look at it he did, and more than this he looked at it very thoroughly, as one who looked at it in a serious light. From its many-gabled red-brick exterior, through its mediæval glass-doors and windows, up to its lofty narrow chimney-pieces, along its dado'd walls, and Minton tiled fireplaces, Mr Arminger looked at the house observantly, and liked it and its situation well.

"Charming garden and conservatory, not too much of a thing for a moderate gardener with a lad to help to keep in order; and within easy reach of the park; Lady Elinor will be able to drive down to the park, and get the terrace view when both are in perfection on summer evenings, when the blue bloom is over the river, and the Surrey vales and woods," the artist friend remarked encouragingly.

"If the rent doesn't stump me I'll take the house," Don said, with decision, and he hoped that Elinor would be reasonable enough to like the house, which might be made so perfect a one through the efforts of their united tastes.

Unfortunately, or shall it be said, fortunately—it is so extremely difficult to decide which a thing is often that weighs the balance by a hair's-breadth—before Mr Arminger said anything to Lady Elinor about the house in Bedford Park, she heard that the *White Squall* was at Cowes, and that her owner was likely to be in town any day. This she heard from his mother, who added words to the apparently boldly and indifferently-given statement that made Elinor's heart beat.

"If I could only persuade myself that you wouldn't be dull, I should get you to come down to Crowniston with me, Elinor, but an old woman would be no companion for you in solitude. To be sure Charldale will follow me in a few days, and then, I suppose, we shall go in for as much gaiety as is to be had in Cheshire."

Lady Charldale had the decency to avert her eyes as she made this barefaced proposal, but her precaution was a needless one. Elinor's beautiful complexion and expression remained unchanged, unmoved.

"Dear Lady Charldale, it will be very pleasant to find myself at Crowniston with you alone for a few days. I assure you your powers of persuasion won't be very severely taxed to induce me to go."

"Then we'll get away the day after to-morrow," Lady Charldale said, embracing her favourite effusively.

And an hour after a telegram was received by the owner of the *White Squall*, from his mother, to this effect,—

"I go to Crowniston on Wednesday. E. D. will be with me. Join me without delay."

"I'm in for it," was his lordship's comment on this— a comment rather moodily made. Then his noble brow cleared as he thought, "Anyway, I can leave her behind when I go to Malta next year."

This happened on the Monday after that Sunday spent by Don Arminger at Bedford Park. On the Tuesday Don saw his future wife, and suggested to her the expediency of her going with her mother and himself to look at their future home.

"Bedford Park! Is it anywhere near Bedford Square?" she asked.

"You've passed it often, and commented on it on your way to Richmond," Don said, rather surlily, for her affectation of ignorance annoyed him.

"Have I? It's so long since I've been to Richmond. You see we don't go there now; it's so far, it takes up so much time. No, Don, I don't see the least use in my going to look at this house."

"You had better go, as it's the house I've made up my mind to take, Elinor."

"Really, sir knight! Well, as you're courteous to your lady's wishes, I need have no scruple in saying it's a house I've made up my mind not to live in. But we needn't argue any more at present or settle the matter just now, for I find my health giving way so fast that I must—really must—get away to the country for a few days."

Now Timerton House, where the Dowager Lady Tim_

erton and Elinor were for the time, was in course of being replastered, painted, and papered for the young owner and his bride, who were still away in the country, prolonging their honeymoon, and shooting and eating pheasants. Therefore, as the painters, plasterers, and the rest of them were making the house inodorous, to say the least of it, there was reasonableness unquestionably in Elinor's desire to get into a purer atmosphere.

"I suppose, Lady Timerton, you will go down to Scallow?" Don asked ; and as he was in ignorance of the return of the *White Squall* and her owner from warmer waters, he asked the question without any back thought of Lord Charldale.

"No," Elinor said carelessly. "I was going to tell you when you began about that house. I am going to stay with Lady Charldale ; she found me looking so ill yesterday from the smell of the paint, that she said she should carry me off to Crowniston for a breath of fresh air."

"Oh, indeed ! and when are you going?"

"To-morrow ; you see, Don, mamma can't very well leave town now ; some one must stay to see about my things, and I'm really feeling too deadly to do it myself."

"I wouldn't do it, if I were you ; but before you go I must ask you to have a look at this house ; I can go with Lady Timerton and you any time you like, provided I can be back to look in at the office at six ; when you see it, your prejudice against the place will banish, I'm convinced. And I can be getting things on in your absence."

For a moment or two Lady Elinor hesitated. She really had no desire to run this "poor fellow," as she was beginning to call him to herself, into useless expense. At the same time she was not sufficiently sure of Lord Charldale to burn her boats behind her, by breaking with Don definitely. On the whole, she judged it better to show a nice amiable front to the last.

"Very well ; if mamma can go, I will ; but mind, I don't pledge myself to anything by going ; nothing shall induce me to live in a place I don't like, and I know it would be the very desolation of isolation for me at Bedford Park."

"You would know some of the people, and the majority of them are as far removed from being commonplace as even you can desire."

"I don't think I should care for them," Elinor said indifferently. "Clever people—professionally clever people—never do amuse me; the women especially think that if you don't write novels, or paint pictures as they do, you are a fool. Aunt Kenwyn used to be awfully fond of getting such people about her before she took up spiritualism, and I've spent the dullest hours of my life at her house in their company. I'm afraid you'll find that I'm not sympathetic with the surroundings at Bedford Park."

However, in spite of her saying this, she went down in pursuance of her plan of being amiable to the last, and looked at the house, and was fain to confess that it was "very pretty."

"If it were in Green Street or Upper Brook Street, or out near Hyde Park Gate, I'd go into it to-morrow, Don," she said graciously; "but, really, I shouldn't care for Solomon's Temple out here, not if I had to live in it all the year round; the atmosphere of red-brick and sham seventeenth-centuryism would make me sick."

Good-natured Lady Timerton looked at Don deprecatingly.

"I think the smell of the paint has upset Elinor," she murmured; "she does nothing but complain; the Cheshire air will set her up again, and she'll come back quite prepared to like this most charming house, I'm sure."

"Don't be sure of anything of the kind, mamma," Elinor put in angrily; "this house would be all very well if I had one in town and one properly in the country, but as I'm to have but one tent for life, let that at least be pitched near to my fellow-creatures."

Don said not a word, but after handing them into

their carriage in silence, he took off his hat and let them drive off without him.

"My dear child, I'm afraid you've vexed Don," Lady Timerton said reproachfully.

"I can't help it if I have; every day I'm feeling myself a greater fool for having let the engagement be talked about. I can't and I won't be stuck down here, away from all I care for; just ask yourself, mamma, how could I live there day after day all the year round and every year with nothing to do?"

"Duties soon come to young married women."

"Duties! I shouldn't do them, if I had nothing but them to do. Ugh! the very idea of my having to get through the days down there makes me faint."

"I can't help feeling sorry for Don," Lady Timerton said; "it will be such a sad pity if he and you can't agree about where you will live, as you must live together."

"Perhaps we shall agree not to live together at all."

"My dear child, that would make a terrible scandal."

"I mean sometimes I think our engagement will come to a smash," Elinor said.

Then seeing her mother's eyes fill with tears, she turned her head aside, gazed idly at the passers-by, and said no more till the carriage stopped at Timerton House.

"I forgot to tell Don that Lady Charldale and I go off by an early train to-morrow; but it doesn't matter; you can tell him I forgot to do it; the vexed question of the house put it quite out of my head."

The next morning Elinor went off, accompanied by a few dozen exquisite toilettes, with old Lady Charldale to Crowniston.

For two days it seemed that she was to be doomed to yet another disappointment with regard to Lord Charldale, for there was no sound of his coming. Still she sustained an air of being perfectly satisfied with the society of his mother, and the invigorating Cheshire air.

But on the third day he telegraphed for the dog-cart

and luggage-van to meet him at the station at six o'clock. Elinor took care to be out of the way when he arrived, not being sure as to how far it would be prudent to see him immediately after his journey. But she need have had no scruples. His lordship was perfectly presentable.

"Is Elinor with you?" he asked his mother as he kissed her.

"Yes, I rejoice to say she is."

"Did she seem glad to hear I was coming?"

"She is not a simple village maiden to blush and smile forth her delight; in fact, she is as self-possessed as a young queen, but I could see that she was pleased when I read your telegram."

"Do you know, mother, I've been hearing things about her."

"What things?"

"Why, that she is going to marry that fellow Arminger."

"I really know nothing whatever about it; if you want to have her, I should advise you not dragging any other man's name in; of course, there are a hundred people who are jealous of her and of you, and if by idle and malicious innuendoes they can separate you, they will."

"Well, there's plenty of time for me. I'll see what I think of her in a few days," Lord Charldale said, and then he went off to dress for dinner.

On his dressing-table he found a budget of letters which had been given to his man just as they were leaving the yacht in the morning, and which Lord Charldale had not had time to glance over yet.

One was from the young Maltese lady who had cast her glamour over him while the *White Squall* lay in Malta harbour.

The first three pages were couched in terms of such fiery affection, that he made up his mind that, come what would, he would see her pretty, glowing face again. But the last page made him tone down this determination. For in it, though she did not exactly threaten

him, she gave him to understand that if he did not
return to her and give her the opportunity of wearing
the beautiful white lace wedding-dress which she was
having made, that her love would turn to revenge, and
that her "father would take steps."

"Hang their cheek!" his lordship said contemptuously,
as he threw her letter into the fire, and he resolved
to punish Nita for her presumption, by "having it out
and settling it" with Elinor Divett as soon as possible.

What a fool little Nita had been to think that she
could ever be the Countess of Charldale!

Elinor's appearance by-and-by strengthened his resolution concerning her. True, she was in mourning
still, but it was in glittering mourning, composed entirely of bugles, that made her resemble a glittering black
serpent with a white face, blue eyes and golden head.
Lord Charldale quite longed to see the Charldale diamonds
on that head, it was so bright and shapely.

Once more they were in the terra-cotta passage-room
with no one by to hinder their sayings and doings. But
Lady Elinor had learnt to play a better game than she
played last Christmas. Praises of Crowniston no longer
fell from her lips. She only cared to hear and speak of
the yacht.

"How could you tear yourself from the *White Squa'l*
and Malta?" she asked, and he muttered something about
wanting to have a shot at the pheasants.

"I would have a yacht of my own, and emulate Lady
Brassey if I could," she went on ; and he eagerly responded,—

"I wish my mother and you would come over to Cowes
and have a cruise in the *White Squall*, just to see how you
like her."

"No, indeed ; I don't care for tastes of Paradise,"
Elinor said, and then she got up and made as though she
were going back to the drawing-room, where Lady Charldale sat sleeping considerately.

But her hand was taken and held while Lord Charldale
pleaded his cause very briefly.

"I'll give you the yacht and anything else in the world you desire if you'll take me too, Elinor," he whispered; and Elinor surrendered her other hand into his keeping, and gave him to understand very clearly that she would take him, and keep him too.

"We'll go to Malta," Lord Charldale told himself, "and when that goose Nita sees her, Nita'll feel what a little fool she must have been to think I'd make her Lady Charldale."

It was a nuisance, a bitter nuisance, too, to Elinor, to think that etiquette demanded that she should leave Crowniston, now that the owner of it had proposed to her. But she was very correct in her observance of all those points which marked her caste, which distinguished her from the million who might do as they pleased. Still, though it was a bitter nuisance to her, she knew him to be so safely bound to her, that she had no need to feel anything like alarm.

"If you manage Charldale properly, he will be an honour to his country and the peerage, and an excellent husband and father," Lady Charldale said meaningly to Elinor; "but he won't bear neglect, either in seeming or reality."

"He won't have to bear it from me," Elinor said. But inwardly she did hope that Lord Charldale would not be one of those husbands who want a wife to be "perpetually fussing after them."

"I shall give you your wedding-dress; the dress shall be what you please, but the lace will be old point d'Alençon, than which I've never seen anything more beautiful," Lady Charldale said to her just before she was leaving Crowniston, and Elinor thanked her, and smiled faintly, thinking of that other wedding-dress which was already built for her.

Lady Elinor travelled up to town alone—or rather, with only her maid for her companion, for she was resolved to do everything with the most rigid regard for the proprieties. Already she had telegraphed to the Dowager Lady Timerton, announcing her return, and thereby alarming that excellent woman painfully. Accordingly, when she arrived at King's Cross, the brougham was there to meet her.

As she was crossing the platform, Mr Mott jostled against her, then laboriously begged her pardon, and said,—

"I'm due in New York twelve days from now, and I'd like to prove to you that I don't bear malice. It's not the thing for a peeress to be runnin' round alone; let me see you to a cab."

"Thanks," Elinor said sweetly; "it will be so kind if you help my maid with my jewel case to the carriage. If one is robbed at a railway station, people always say now that you've stolen your own things. Farquhar, Mr Mott will help you."

Then she went on and got into the brougham, and when Mr Mott had adjusted the jewel-box comfortably on the seat by her, she called out, "Home!" and with a bow and smile drove off, the wheel grazing Mr Mott's leg, and doing serious damage to that leg's broadcloth as it sped.

"You're the straight outcome of the highest and most bloatedly best spawn of English society," he said savagely, looking after the retreating brougham, and apostrophising its inmate, "and you haven't as much knowledge in your head as a tenpenny nail, or as much warmth in your heart as would hatch the unborn nit of a flea; but all the same, if you ever come across the herring-pond you shall make my fortune by letting those darned republicans see how intimate I am with a peeress who is not a spiritualist."

"I saw your friend, Mr Mott, at a railway station the other day, aunt," Lady Elinor said, in describing this *rencontre* to Lady Kenwyn, "and he jumped at me, and called me 'a peeress,' and altogether I'm afraid he must have been tipsy."

As Mr Mott drank nothing but water, and that by the bucketful, Lady Kenwyn felt that indeed her niece was ceasing from all consideration for her.

In accordance with her custom Elinor was as calm in her method of telling her mother of her new engagement as if she had been speaking of the purchase of a new dress.

"I've come home because Charldale asked me to marry him last night, and I couldn't stay on in the house engaged to him."

"Engaged to him?" Lady Timerton gasped.

"Yes, mamma dear; don't repeat my words, it wastes so much time, and there's such a lot to do between now and the wedding; in fact, more to do than I care to contemplate unless you help me in every way."

"That I will," Lady Timerton said tearfully, "but there are so many things to undo as well as to do, dear child."

"Yes, to be sure," Elinor interrupted; "there's that wedding-dress that we had ordered for one thing. Lady Charldale insists on giving me mine, so the former affair can be turned into a dinner-dress by the aid of wreaths of coloured chrysanthemums. Louise and you can settle all that between you. I shall want ever so many more things, so she won't mind altering a few of the originals; and, mamma, you must see Don Arminger."

"It will break my heart to do it," Lady Timerton said, crying tears of honest anger against her daughter, and honest sympathy with Don.

"No, it won't, nor will it break his heart either; no man who had truly cared for me could have behaved as he has about a house; if you don't make a show of distress, mamma, you will find that he will take the announcement very equably; but I should like it got over as soon as possible, for in a day or two the approaching marriage will be given out."

"You nearly broke your poor father's heart by insisting upon engaging yourself to Don," Lady Timerton whimpered.

"So I did, and now I feel that Providence could never smile upon a union of which a parent so thoroughly disapproved. Cheshire agrees with you so well that you

must promise to spend Christmas at Crowniston with us,
mamma. And you will see about the wedding-dress being turned into a dinner one, and make it all right with
Mr Arminger to-day, won't you?"

CHAPTER XXVII.

DON IS RESIGNED.

"PLAY to her, but death to me," Lady Timerton said,
while discussing her daughter's brilliant marriage prospects with Lady Kenwyn previous to breaking them to
Don Arminger.

"Oh, not at all," Lady Kenwyn said, with placid complacency. "Play to her! Not at all. She is merely
obeying life's serious, earnest instinct, which calls upon
her to cast off Arminger and take Charldale. In time
probably another wave will pass over her, bidding her
leave Charldale and follow some one else."

"Heaven forbid!" the Dowager Lady Timerton
sobbed.

"Yes, as you say. I only suggest that, if it's not providentially forbidden, such may be the result. In the
meantime, don't worry Elinor or yourself; it's always
such a pity to worry one's self about unavoidable
things."

"You haven't to break it to Don Arminger," Lady
Timerton said reproachfully.

"Perhaps he will be more philosophic about it than
you think," Lady Kenwyn rejoined.

But Elinor's mother did not at all approve of that
view of the case. It would be very terrible to her to
witness Don's distress and anguish of mind at losing
Elinor. But it would be even more distressing to see
him callous about it.

Elinor was very busy in these days, though there was
no ignominious house difficulty to be solved this time.

Lord Charldale's residences were all unexceptionally situated. Still, though this harassing matter was finally and satisfactorily settled, Elinor had her hands full, for the marriage was to come off with little delay, and the trousseau that was admirably adapted for Lady Elinor Arminger was quite insufficient for the Countess of Charldale.

"If you don't take care, mamma, Don will see it in the papers before you have told him, and naturally he will think that underhand of you."

"I wish you would write and tell him yourself, Elinor," poor goaded Lady Timerton pleaded.

"Now, mamma, that's really very inconsiderate of you. I literally haven't a minute to myself; in fact, it would be on my conscience if I did anything but look after my dresses. That Catherine de Medicis costume has to be watched inch by inch, or they'd go wrong in it! and as Aunt Kenwyn has given me the jewellery, I quite intend the dress to be up to the mark."

Grievous to relate, something had come between the soul of Lady Kenwyn and the spirit of Catherine de Medicis, so in order that she might not be perpetually reminded of those happier days when they two were one, her ladyship had given the Catherine de Medicis collection of jewellery to her niece Elinor. By so doing, Lady Kenwyn was enabled to give her thoughts exclusively to Marie Antoinette, who had kindly stepped, or glided rather, into the place formerly occupied by the earlier French queen.

"I would rather have it on my conscience that I was neglecting the make of dress than that I was behaving heartlessly to Don Arminger," Lady Timerton protested.

"Well, I wouldn't," Elinor answered coolly; "that dress and its lace and stomacher of gold embroidery and seed-pearls will come to four hundred pounds, and it would be sinful on my part to be negligent about it." Then Lady Elinor got into her victoria, and had herself driven to the place where her heart was—by the side of the embroidered stomacher—and Lady Kenwyn wrote a note entreating Don Arminger to come to her.

It was a busy day with him, and her messenger reached him at a very inopportune hour. Nevertheless, her entreaty that he would go to her without delay was so urgent that he got himself away from his work and went down to Timerton House at once.

She had wrought herself up to a pitch of painful excitement by the time he joined her in that room which she always had devoted to business, and which was the only one in the house that was not under reparation now. Her eyes were full of tears and her voice full of trembling when she greeted him with the words,—

"Don, I have bad news to break to you."

"Nothing wrong with Timerton or Trixy, is there?" he asked in quick, unfeigned alarm, and when Lady Timerton said "No, no," he remembered that he ought to have thought of Elinor first.

"It's about Elinor," Lady Timerton went on, beginning to cry.

"About Elinor?"

"Oh, Don, how shall I—how can I tell you? My poor, dear boy, my heart is aching for you, and I'm so angry with my own child that I've scarcely patience to speak of her."

"She's not ill, then? I feared she was ill."

"Ill! Oh no, but she has behaved so badly, so heartlessly, that I hope you'll feel you are well rid of a girl who could treat you so." (Don's unruly heart began to bound with a sense of relief.) "She has actually come back from Crowniston engaged to Lord Charldale."

The great melancholy fact was communicated to him, and Don actually did not faint, or even totter.

"Don't vex yourself about it," he said, taking Lady Timerton's hand cordially, "she will be infinitely happier in his groove than she would have been in mine; don't mar her happiness by showing displeasure."

"It's of you I'm thinking, my poor boy," she sobbed.

"I must try to get over it," he said, putting a decent

amount of resignation into his tone, but he felt that he was being a little hypocritical in doing even so much.

Then he was anxious to get back and finish the article, in the writing of which he had been interrupted ; but Lady Timerton, having gone through the agony of telling him, and now having come into the possession of peace through his manner of receiving the tidings, felt inclined to detain him in order that she might talk about the sunny side of this golden match, which really (apart from Don) was a gratifying one to her maternal pride.

"As she can be happy with him (how she can have brought herself to it after you), but as she feels she can like him, I ought to be content that my daughter is going to make what is indisputably the best match in the country," she said, rather timidly to Don.

" Indeed, you ought," he assented, with unsentimental, unselfish heartiness. " She'll be thoroughly in her right place, and she'll keep a firm hand on him. Charldale isn't half a bad fellow, and Elinor will make a thorough man of him."

" It will be a great relief to Elinor to find you take it in this way," said Lady Timerton dubiously.

" She must not think that I regard the change lightly ; but she may feel that I honestly believe she would have failed to find happiness as my wife ; and, therefore, what is is best."

" Won't you wait and see her ? She will be in at five."

" Not to-day," Don said, thinking of that unfinished article. " Give her my friendliest love and greeting ; tell her that with all my heart I wish for her happiness."

" Shall I say you forgive her ? "

" No, no, Lady Timerton ; there's no need to say that. She has done nothing that calls for forgiveness ; she has merely emancipated herself from a thrall that would have been irksome to her. Elinor and I shall always be good friends, though we have made the mistake of trying to be lovers for a time."

Lady Timerton shook her head. She could not understand it. Don's resignation looked very real, but might it not be assumed to conceal a broken heart and a suicidal intention?

Don Arminger went back to his work a happier man than he had been for many a month. His heart was more warmly disposed towards Elinor this day than it had ever been before, and he felt almost sorry that he should never dare to tell her what a load she had lifted from him by jilting him.

In spite of his perturbation of spirit, he worked away manfully at his article, and finished it. This he did before he gave himself to the luxury of picturing the way in which Constance would receive the news.

He was undecided as to how he should break it to her. Should he go down and tell out the truth, or should he write it to his mother first, and learn from her whether or not Constance was prepared to receive him in the way in which he wanted to be received? He would take the night to think it over, and with the morning light would come the clear vision of what he ought to do.

But with the morning light came letters, telegrams, printer's devils, and the stern necessity for speedy and incessant work. He had a good many heavy interests hanging upon his shoulders just now, for he was about to make a new departure in journalism, and other men had linked their interests with his. The onus was on him of throwing his most earnest self into the fray. The prose of life demanded him. The poetry of it and Constance must wait.

It was rest—and pleasurably rest, too—to feel that he need no longer go into single combat with graceful Elinor anent a house. The girl had been right all through, he admitted now. What would have become of her if she had been condemned to a suburban existence? It was merely the instinct of self-preservation which had made her hold out against the house in Bedford Park. Elinor would have been out of gear there altogether; nevertheless, he would take the house still, and Constance would show him how to make it perfect.

Work over-mastered him for a few days, then before he had time to write to her, came a letter from his mother.

"Sad changes here," she wrote; "Mr Vaughan has had a stroke. He is ordered to Normandy, and Constance goes with her aunt. Donald remains behind. Indeed, I fear Donald and Maude have made up their minds to be very disobedient. Give my love to your Elinor. My news from Trixy is the happiest the old mother can have. Constance has just come in to wish me good-bye; in her travelling-gear she is the very prettiest creature eyes can rest on."

Don telegraphed at once,—"Send me Miss Fielding's address."

But his mother was vague about it for a week or two, and Constance was well away from the haunts of men before Don got any clue to her whereabouts.

Meantime his business matters multiplied themselves, as it is the wont of business matters to do, and he let the business that was nearest to his heart slide, thinking he could catch it up at any time, after the manner of men.

He felt so sure of her. She was just gone away for a change with her ailing aunt and uncle, and she would come back all the more fit for a life of content and repose with him. This was the idea he formed half unconsciously, and it served to keep him quite satisfied and at ease about her.

Meantime he took the house at Bedford Park, and began filling it gradually with the "earliest" English furniture that combined comfort with high art principles. And while he was doing this, Constance was settling down into a life of quiet usefulness in a little town in Normandy, where Mr Vaughan was trying to recruit his broken strength, and Mrs Vaughan was grumbling at the length of time "wasted" in the process.

The sick man would have preferred having his own daughters to nurse him, deft and thoughtful though Constance was. But the Misses Vaughan had rather gladly availed themselves of an invitation from an aunt of their father, and a half hint from Mrs Vaughan to the effect that she would be best pleased at their accepting the same. So, as Mrs Vaughan was unequal to any tiresome exertion, on Constance devolved the care and charge of nursing the invalid.

There was little to interest her at Etretât, for her services were in too incessant requisition for her to indulge in explorations amidst the surrounding scenery. Mr Vaughan was exacting and capricious, after the manner of convalescents, and his wife had no patience with his caprices, and disregarded his requirements even when they were reasonable. So upon Constance he soon came to rely entirely, and it was almost pitiful to see him so utterly dependent upon her, and at the same time so angry with her still for not having married his son.

"My affliction makes me a terrible burden, a terrible, terrible burden," he would say, with plaintive querulousness, "and it has been brought about by distress of mind."

"It has been laid upon you by the hand of God," Constance would say firmly and kindly, "and you are no burden at all, and I'm happier in being of use to you than I can express."

"All the same, dear neighbour Constance, I'm a terrible trouble to you—I feel it, a terrible trouble to you and a burden to your aunt, and this is the work of others, Connie; if Donald and you had not been wilful and obstinate, I would not have broken down in this way."

"Donald will have one of the best and dearest girls in the world for a wife. When once you can soften your heart enough to give in and see Maude Arminger, you'll love her and bless her for marrying your son."

"No, I won't," he snapped; "they're a pair of fools, and she is a selfish one, for she knows if Donald marries her he will lose Strathlands. I couldn't rest in my grave if I thought that girl was queening it at Strathlands. Donald will rue the day he met her when he finds that Reggie has the old place."

"Mr Vaughan, you're cruel and unjust; how can you

expect that God's mercy will restore you to health when you nourish feelings of hatred and malice against your own son?"

"That girl shall never have Strathlands, and Strathlands is what she and her designing mother have schemed for. Constance, those Armingers have been the cause of all my troubles; that usher fellow was the cause of your wavering about Donald in the first place, and then he didn't care to take what he had won."

"I will not let your words vex me, Mr Vaughan," Constance said good-temperedly, "but for all that they are cruel."

"They are true, Connie; you preferred that fellow to my Donald, a fellow whose sole aim and object in life is self-advarcement. He plotted and schemed to get his former pupil to marry one sister, and he made love to you to get you out of the other sister's way with Donald—"

"I won't hear Don Arminger spoken ill of without protesting," Constance said. But Mr Vaughan's words fell heavily on her heart.

Lady Elinor had really been very anxious to hear the result of her mother's interview with Don. When she came home that day, after an hour's unremitting attention to one of the details of the Catherine de Medicis dress, she felt really curious as to what had transpired.

"I can see you've been crying, mamma, so I suppose you've had it out with Mr Arminger?"

"Yes, he has been here, and I have told him," Lady Timerton said slowly. She could not quite make up her mind as to whether she was pleased or hurt at the calm way in which Don had received the tidings.

"What did he say?"

"He said he thought, or hoped, or something of the kind, that you would be happier with Lord Charldale than you would have been with him. Oh! everything he said was nice and kind, but I'm afraid the wound is a very deep one, and he won't bare it, poor fellow! his pride won't let him."

"I hope it won't," Elinor said candidly. "It would be so awkward if he made a fuss and Charldale heard anything about it. I am so glad you've got it over, mamma dear; now we can get on with things. Some one ought to write and tell Timerton and Trixy. I don't think Timerton will be surprised; he always thought it would be Charldale."

So Lady Elinor was airily off with the old love, and free to proceed apace with the preparations to be legally on with the new. And Constance read of the approaching marriage in high life, as she sat by Mr Vaughan's chair upon wheels on the little beach at Etretât.

It cannot be denied that her heart beat high with hope, that her cheeks flushed with joyful expectation as she read it. She knew now not only that Don cared for her, but she gauged with tolerable correctness the depth of that caring. The lesson taught by honour and learnt so hardly at Woodside in the summer while he was semibound to Elinor, might be unlearnt now!

"Will he come?" This was the question she asked herself with tolerable frequency, for you see she had little to do here save brood over her love and the possibilities surrounding it. It seemed to her the most natural thing in the world that Don should come to her at once, now that he was free. And as day after day passed by, and he neither came nor wrote, she felt cruelly disappointed.

It did not occur to her that to the manly mind there was an insurmountable awkwardness in writing to tell her that having been thrown over by Elinor, he was now ready to take her (Constance). Nor did she think that it was just possible business and work of the utmost importance to himself and others might be keeping him away. She was a woman! and without a tinge of selfishness, she felt that her love ought to be the chief thing in life to the object to it.

CHAPTER XXVIII.

DONALD'S RASHNESS.

ONE day there came to Donald Vaughan a letter from his step-mother telling him of his father's fast increasing weakness, and urging upon Donald the propriety of his coming to them with little delay, and bringing his brother Reginald with him.

"Your father has taken it into his head that Reggie is up to some mischief, and nothing will convince him to the contrary but Reggie's coming. Besides, I really do not think it right that he should be without either of his sons. He is failing fast, and in your own interests I advise your coming to him."

"There's some good in the woman after all," Donald observed when he read this letter to Mrs Arminger and Maude; "she doesn't want me to offend my father, that's clear."

"And it's equally clear that you ought to go to him at once," Maude said; but Donald, who was very much in love in the selfishly absorbent way, demurred at this.

"If I go and leave you behind me, something will happen to part us: I've a presentiment of that, Maude, and I'm as sure as any old woman could be that my presentiments always come true; if you'll marry me I'll go, but I won't start without you."

"My dear Donald!" Mrs Arminger said, with a shudder at the Evil being brought so close to her, "there would be something almost unnatural in what you propose."

"I can't help that," he said doggedly; "Maude has promised to be my wife, and if anything came between us now it would wreck me; if she will go with me I'll go to Etretât, but I'll not go without her."

"The shock might be very injurious to your father."

"He needn't know anything about it till he has been well prepared," the young man pleaded. "Mrs Arminger, you're really wrong in trying to put me off now."

"Mother isn't trying to put you off; she only wants you to be sensible," Maude said soothingly.

"Do you doubt me? Do you fear that I sha'n't make Maude a good husband? Do you think my professions shams and promises idle? With Maude I may be of some account in the world; without her, I shall go to destruction."

"You needn't fear Maude; she will be just as faithfully your own in your absence as now that you are with her daily."

"I won't go without her," Donald said; and Mrs Arminger felt that her nephew had an inexhaustible stock of obstinacy to draw upon.

"How does your own heart prompt you?" Mrs Arminger said to Maude when they were alone.

"To please Donald. But mother, be sure of this, I won't do anything against your wishes."

"It is very terrible for me to have to decide. Donald is utterly unreasonable; it is his plain duty to go to his father at once, and he ought to put aside all thoughts of marriage for a time."

"I know you are right, but I can't think Donald very wrong," Maude said, and then she went to work at her picture in a way that was meant to show her mother that "Art was enough."

But Mrs Arminger was not deceived by Maude's apparent contentment. The mother knew that her child was being harassed hourly almost by entreaties and supplications from Donald, who had the winning art of making his argument appear a true one. So a day or two slipped by in indecision, and then came a more urgent request from Mrs Vaughan that her stepson should come speedily to his father.

This time the request was backed up by a few words from Constance.

"Poor Mr Vaughan pines for his sons, especially for Donald; his daughters seem to be of far less account in his eyes—a state of feeling for which I have no sympathy. Nevertheless, it exists, and it seems heartless of Donald and Reggie to stay away now."

"I believe Reggie is in town, but I'm not sure; however, I'll write to his old address," Donald said, when Maude read this passage from Constance's letter to him.

"That won't be enough; you must go yourself, dear Donald."

"So I will, if you will go with me," Donald replied.

There was a good deal of controversy, of combative argument, and of bewilderment. But it all ended in this —namely, that Mrs Arminger, against the dictates of her heart and head, gave an unwilling consent to a hasty marriage.

Maude was married in her travelling dress, and started with her husband for Etretât within the hour after the ceremony. Only her mother and Mr Dalzel were present, and altogether there was a surreptitious hole-in-corner air about the affair which sorely distressed Mrs Arminger.

But Donald Vaughan was supremely happy and infinitely grateful, and Maude assured her mother that she was perfectly content and had no fear.

The letter directed to the old address found Reginald. The old address was in that penitential precinct where Reginald had lodged for the last two years. Being a younger son with no expectations, he had fared less luxuriously than his brother, for his father had insisted on his " doing something " and living on the income that he made by doing it. His clerkship in the Audit Office did not bring him a stipend on which he could riot in the upper ways of society, but it enabled him to live, and he eked it out by a little desultory writing for some of the sporting and dramatic papers and cheap magazines.

In describing his lodgings to his own people, he always said that his rooms were capitally kept, and his breakfasts (the only meal he had at home) were admirably served by his landlady : "A very good creature—a widow." And this statement was perfectly true, but it was not all the truth.

He did not go on to say that this widow was an extremely pretty, smart little woman, who was so well dowered with discretion that her most anxious friends felt that she was quite safe in having even such a handsome young lodger as Reginald Vaughan.

Probably his friends, had they known anything about it, would not have deemed there was equal safety for him in the arrangement.

Mrs Welton was in the habit of saying that she "had had her ups and downs." This was said with an idea that was intended to convey the idea that mansions and deer parks were the familiar objects to which her youthful eyes had been accustomed. Whereas, in truth, when she emerged from the dense obscurity of her early years, it was to occupy the (to her) then dazzling position of barmaid at the Welsh Harp, Hendon.

A sharp winter and hard frost in her first season there, sent down swarms of skaters, and one of these—Percy Welton, a young actor—skated into the affections of the pretty barmaid, and married her.

Being in receipt of a fair salary, he made a comfortable home in Gower Street, and furnished it well for his young wife. So that when he died, five years after their marriage, leaving her childless, she wisely turned her well-ordered house to profitable account by letting lodgings.

A conversation that took place between her and Reginald Vaughan, after the receipt of Donald's letter, inviting Reginald to accompany him (Donald) to their father's dying bed, will serve to show what terms the widow and her lodger were on.

"Mind you're prudent, Reggie ; and, above all things, don't confide in your brother. He would be only too glad to give your father a hint that you were going to marry me, and get you out of the will altogether."

'I'll be as close as wax," Reginald promised.   'But

look here, Adelaide, I'm not going to keep you dark, as
I were ashamed of you, much longer."

"No, no ; that's all right ; only be prudent," the practical little woman replied gaily.   "While you're away I
shall have more time to see about getting the furniture
polished up and renovated ; and I can look out for a
house."

For Mrs Welton had no intention of starting afresh in
life, as Mrs Reginald Vaughan, in the region where she
had been known as a lodging-house keeper.

When the brothers met at the railway station, Donald
drew Reginald aside.

"You'll hardly be surprised when I tell you I'm
married."

"The deuce you are !   To whom ?"

"To Maude, of course.   Come and see her."

"Whew ! a runaway match is the last thing I should
have supposed cousin Maude would have been guilty of."

"It wasn't runaway ; it was all plain straightforward
sailing.   We were married by old Dalzel this morning,
and her mother gave her away."

"The governor will go cracky himself, and want to
shut you up in an asylum," Reginald laughed, as he went
to the waiting-room to congratulate and salute his new
sister.

Maude was not given to being feebly retrospective,
therefore she did not say that she thought the deed she
had done that morning a rash and unwise one.   It was
done ; and by no word or look of hers would she ever
reproach Donald with having tempted her to the doing.
But, nevertheless, as they journeyed on, her heart sank a
little whenever Reginald made a joking allusion to the
kind of reception Donald and his bride were likely to
meet with.

They stayed a few hours at Dieppe to recruit Maude's
strength, which had gone from her considerably in the
crossing.   And then they went on—the happy pair with
their hearts in their mouths, and Reginald in a state of
self-complacency anent his superior prudence.

" Constance will be on our side," Donald whispered to Maude, when at last they entered the hotel where his father was, and he tried to whisper it reassuringly.

But Maude had an intuitive feeling that Constance would not only disapprove of what they had done, but would manifest her disapproval.

As soon as she heard of their arrival, Constance came flying down to meet them, glad to see Maude beyond the power of words to express, but distressed visibly at the manner of Maude's presence.

" Married ! You, Maude, of all people in the world to have gone in this untoward way into life's difficulties. Donald, you can never repay her for the trust she has shown in you."

" Oh, I don't know that," Donald said. He was very proud and fond of Maude, but he was even prouder of that mental prowess of his which had enabled him to conquer Maude's scruples, and he was by no means disposed to be disparaged in the lightest degree.

Then Constance told them that their father was much worse, speechless now, and powerless to move, but still sensible, and able to comprehend all that was said to him.

Presently Mrs Vaughan came, crying, not so much because her husband was dying, as because she had been unconsciously taught from her earliest years that it was the right thing to cry when death was near, and to her next was the tale of the marriage told.

She kissed Maude and welcomed her with what really was loving warmth from Mrs Vaughan, and cheered both her stepson and his bride with encouraging words relative to the way in which his father would receive them.

" He is shockingly altered, and quite unable to speak, but he can understand all you say to him. Go to him, Donald, and when he is used to your presence, tell him honestly of your marriage, and then break it to him that Maude is here.

This was wonderfully sound advice, considering that it came from Mrs Vaughan, and Reginald urged his brother to act upon it at once.

That Mr Vaughan was made infinitely happy by the presence of his eldest son there could be no manner of doubt, though he was not able to give verbal expression to his feelings.   But a look of content came into his poor drawn face when Donald laid his hand on his father's, that had long been a stranger there.

Still Donald delayed telling the great truth that had to be told.

By nightfall both the sons had seen their father. But still no mention had been made of Maude, the bride.

Each one shrank from the task of telling, and meanwhile Maude sat down below with Constance, and tried to think that she was content with the current state of things.

At last Constance could bear it for her no longer.

"They're all afraid of spectres of their own creating," she said impatiently.   "I will go up and tell him that he's entertaining an angel unawares.   He's not a bad-hearted man, and now that he knows he is dying, he will cast out the devil of bitterness that he has nourished for so many years."

So Constance went up, fraught with this good intent; and when she came to the bedside, the poor weary eyes of the dying man lighted up with a pleased smile.

He was still able to move one hand a little, and presently he motioned for Constance, and Donald to kneel down.   Then he drew their hands together, and clasped them in his feeble one, and was closing his eyes in peace, when Donald started up, saying,—

"Oh! father, I am married to Maude—my cousin Maude!" Donald cried, drawing his hand away, as if it had been burnt by this momentary contact with Constance's.   And then Constance, able and capable, clear-headed and kind, as it was her wont to be, told the story out with lucid, loving vehemence.

Who can tell what anguish filled the speechless, help-less father's soul in that dark hour? For he knew, he remembered well the will he had made, and all its cruel conditions, and now he would have given his little space of life to have altered them.

But they could not understand his feeble signs, his inarticulate utterances. In vain they strained eye and ear and mind: his meaning was hidden from them by a veil they could not rend.

But, when Maude was brought to him, he held the hand she laid in his closely, and looked at her with kindness, after she had kissed him, and made them all to know, as well as he could, that he was pleased and at peace with her.

Still, that agony of trying to make them comprehend something which they could not, was upon him.

If he could only speak for a minute now and tell them that he would have that rash codicil revoked, whereby he disinherited his eldest son, if that son should ever marry Maude Arminger. But he co ll not—he could not, and so his anguished spirit struggled away in pain and incapacity.

And all the while Reginald was regretting that he had not married his Adelaide, and introduced her to his family in the same courageous and successful way in which his brother had introduced Maude.

That darkened hour!—who can tell the misery of it? Clear in mind as he had ever been, but physically powerless to make one iota of that mind clear to others, with a softened heart and a repentant soul, the wretched father laid there, knowing that he had ruined his first-born.

What fervent, earnest prayers he offered now, but for one minute's power to speak—one minute—only one minute would enable him to undo the great wrong.

But the minute was not granted to him. He died with that codicil uncancelled.

CHAPTER XXIX.

WEAK VESSELS.

"CHARLDALE has broken loose again." This is what a few of the friends who knew him best were saying to one another ten days or a fortnight before the date fixed for his marriage with Lady Elinor Divett. His mother had done her best. She had kept him quiet at Crowniston until the time was nearly ripe for her to render him up to the younger, stronger hands that were to mould him henceforth. But now he was up in London, and it was true he had broken loose again!

His mother was sorely distressed. His faults were grievous, and she knew them, and admitted the galling truth about them, but he was her son, and her heart ached for him, and she crowded on all the canvas she could in hopes of sailing him into the safe harbour of matrimony with Elinor Divett.

It was an awful time for the poor heart-wrung, loving mother. If he had been merely a sot and a brute perhaps, even she, his mother, would have recoiled from him. But he had his redeeming qualities, and she loved him, and would have sacrificed every other human being for him. And now, just as she had thought he was so safe, he had broken loose again.

He was her boy still, though he got drunk now and again. Though he brutalised himself, he was her fair-haired, high-spirited, bold, beautiful boy still, and she did rage against every hindrance to the marriage that was to save him.

In her distress she did the wisest thing she could have done, and her doing it proved that she had gauged Elinor correctly. She took her son's betrothed into the frankest confidence respecting his failings.

"Charldale is acting very imprudently; he is drinking a great deal more than is good for him," she said to

Elinor, with such earnestness that Elinor felt convinced he must be acting imprudently indeed.

"I can't speak to him yet," Elinor replied.

"Can't you get your brother to say a word, and be with him a good deal? Charldale is easily influenced for good, and I know he has a great respect for Lord Timerton."

"Timerton's the worst person in the world to deal with a matter of this sort; he'd get disgusted so soon," Elinor said.

"I shall not breathe freely till you are married; once married, I feel sure you'll manage the poor boy; but the day before the marriage will be full of anxiety for me, Elinor. I shall never forget what I suffered on a former occasion," Lady Charldale said, with a shudder.

"I suppose there was some truth in those reports?" Elinor asked.

"Yes, my dear, a great deal too much truth, I'm sorry to say, not but what Miss Fielding behaved iniquitously in making such a scene and scandal, still I must admit that Charldale forgot himself terribly. I only pray your influence may be excited beneficially this time."

Undoubtedly, this was rather hard on Lady Elinor that she should be expected to keep her lover straight the day before the marriage. But she knew that this was what was expected of her, and she determined to do it, or to get it done.

To get it done, and by Don Arminger. That was the resolution she came to as soon as the responsibility was thrust upon her by Lord Charldale's mother.

Some people would have seen a certain amount of indelicacy in asking a cast-off lover to mount guard over a promoted one. But Elinor had no foolish feeling of this kind with regard to Don. He was the one man in her circle of friends and acquaintances on whom she knew she could rely. And she was not going to let the fact of her having been engaged to marry him at one time stand in the way of her seeking his aid now.

Accordingly she wrote to him, and told him that, in an emergency which had arisen, she turned to him as her truest and wisest friend, and added,—

"I know well that no small feeling will keep you from coming to help me now."

"Sensible girl she is," Don said approvingly as he pocketed her letter, and prepared to obey her summons.

She was delightfully unembarrassed when she saw him, and went on with her occupation of drawing a design for the floral embellishment of her wedding-cake, just as if no other relations than those of free and easy friendship had ever existed between them.

"I'm not going to have a single ornament excepting white German asters and chrysanthemums on my cake," she said, pointing to her work; "don't you think it will be the best taste?"

"They won't show well up against the white sugar, will they?" he asked critically.

"Oh yes, they will, with a border of maidenhair fern all round them."

Then she held her design off at arm's length, and was well satisfied with it.

"Is it about the cake you want to consult me?" he said presently, and she laughed at the idea for a moment, then grew suddenly serious, and said,—

"No, of course it's not the cake; it's about Charldale."

"He's all right, I hope?"

"Well, no; scarcely all right, I'm afraid. You know, of course everybody knows, what happened when he was going to marry Miss Fielding. Now it mustn't happen again. When I'm married I can manage for myself, I'm sure. But now, before the wedding I want your help. Will you give it to me, Don?"

"With all my heart, Elinor."

"Then do this for me : get hold of Charldale; you can do it easily, for he has a great idea of your cleverness and power; and the day before the wedding impress him into keeping quite—quite as he ought to be."

"I'll do all that man can do in such a case," Don said

"but Lord Charldale is more than likely to repel any advances I may make."

"No, he won't; his mother is going to ask you to dinner, and you can interest him about travelling. Put him on his mettle by taking it for granted that he means to explore and travel intelligently, and let him think that you'd like to have him for a fellow-voyager, and you'll win his heart, and get influence over him; then the rest is easy."

"I don't care about the difficulties, and if the deed is to be done I'll do it," Don promised. And Elinor had no further anxiety as to what might happen the day before the wedding.

"It will be a great comfort to Timerton and Trixy to find everything so pleasant between us, Don," she said in her friendliest way.

"They need never have feared anything else."

"Oh, I don't know! some men would have been nasty and spiteful about it, but I felt sure it wasn't in you to be that. I was good to set my face against that house in Bedford Park; if I had let you run into that expense it would have been an unpardonable shame."

"I've taken the house, and I hope Lord Charldale and you will visit it often."

"You're not going to live there alone?"

"Probably not."

"Is it Miss Fielding?"

"Miss Fielding is abroad, and I have neither seen nor heard from her since I saw you last."

"I'm glad of that; it wouldn't have been like you—it wouldn't have been good taste if you had turned to any-one else so soon," she said approvingly, and then gave him an interesting description of the Catherine de Medici costume, and he found her a far more entertaining and agreeable companion than she had ever been in the days of their engagement.

In accordance with Elinor's desire, Don Arminger did go to dinner with old Lady Charldale, and did contrive to ingratiate himself with her son so successfully that he soon had no difficulty in securing a good deal of Lord Charldale's society to himself.

The day before the wedding he found that a sudden need had arisen in a journal over which he had sway, for a paper on yachting, and this he got Lord Charldale to do for him. They dined together that night, and Lord Charldale, whose mind had been fully and fairly exercised all day, went to bed tired, well content with himself, and sober.

Nothing marred the perfect propriety of the wedding ceremonies on the following day, for which happy state of things the newly-made countess thanked her old friend Don very heartily.

"The first thing I do will be to get rid of that man of his—Morris," she confided to Don. "There will be a tussle over it, I know, but I won't be the one to give in."

Mr Vaughan was brought home to Strathlands to be buried, and the will whereby Donald was disinherited under certain conditions, and Reginald made to reign in his stead was brought into force.

In spite of his rapturous regard for his young and pretty wife, poor Donald Vaughan took his downfall very dismally.

The conditions of the codicil by which he was cast out were very cruel. If he married Maude Arminger he was not only to lose Strathlands, but he was not to have a shilling of his father's money. The only thing that was left to him was his share—a fourth of his mother's fortune, and on this it was impossible that he and his wife could live.

He did not say much about this bitter blight to his brother, for Reginald proffered but the scantiest sympathy, and took his unexpected exaltation so entirely as a matter of course, that a root of bitterness was planted in Donald's heart against him.

Reginald was the head of the house now, the master of Strathlands, and all appertaining unto it, and he took care to very soon manifest his power.

When his father had been buried about three days, he

thought that it was time to make an end of inactive mourning, and he was prompted to this course by frequent and urgent letters from Mrs Welton.

"Understand," that enterprising woman wrote, "I'll have no mothers-in-law, especially one that's nothing but a 'step,' about my house. The sooner you settle all that, and let me come down and see about getting the house comfortable and straight after my own way, the better for us all."

Accordingly, one evening, just before they were about to go to bed, Reginald introduced the subject rather abruptly.

"What day are you thinking of going to your own house, Mrs Vaughan? There'll be a good deal to do to this place before I settle down, and I want to begin as soon as possible."

Now this was staggering to Mrs Vaughan, for though she was comfortably dowered with a fair income, and a pleasant small house in Clyst Street, she had not contemplated cutting herself off from the glories of Strathlands so soon.

"I can go at any time, but I thought perhaps, as you have no idea of marrying yet a while, that you might like me to stay and superintend the house till you do marry."

"That's it exactly. I am engaged to a—a lady in London, and I shall marry as soon as I have this house ready to bring her to."

"Oh, I can leave to-morrow," Mrs Vaughan said, in a huff; and Constance put in sensibly,—

"No, aunt, you can't leave to-morrow, or for many days, in fact. You must have time to furnish and arrange your house. Reginald, I'm sure you can't wish to put my aunt to inconvenience in the way she proposes."

"Mrs Vaughan is welcome to stay here any reasonable time," he said sullenly.

"Maude and I quite intended to be off to-morrow," Donald said hastily.

"And I have no doubt Constance will have me at

Woodside," Mrs Vaughan murmured, but Constance did not feel disposed to instal her aunt at Woodside again.

"That would be giving you the trouble of two moves within a short time instead of one, aunt," she said; "I'll help you to get your own house in order, and Rill and Staveley shall begin upon your garden to-morrow. You've been too long mistress in your own house to find it pleasant to live in another person's now."

" I hardly know what belongs to me here and what does not," Mrs Vaughan wailed.

"Settle your own way," Reginald said, getting up and taking his candle, "you're welcome to stay here a reasonable time, as I told you before, Mrs Vaughan, and I don't think you can say I'm unreasonable about it; and you're welcome to take whatever belongs to you from here, and any little trifle that doesn't belong to you I'll give you with pleasure if you fancy it. Good-night to you all," so saying the young squire of Clyst marched off to bed.

"I'll never put my foot inside Strathlands after the day I leave it," Mrs Vaughan cried; "going to be married too! Ah, to some low creature he was obliged to keep in the background during his poor father's life. Donald, my heart bleeds for you, positively bleeds for you."

" Donald has promised to be very contented," Maude said brightly, "and while he is that I can do plenty of work, and we shall be very happy."

"I can never be happy when I think of the mess I've got you into," poor Donald said mournfully, and then he indulged in a jeremiade against Reginald and selfishness generally.

"Has he told you anything about this person he is going to marry?" Mrs Vaughan asked Donald.

"No, never alluded to her before to-night; ashamed of her probably; my poor father, if he could only know how bitterly he is being paid out for his injustice to me!"

"That's the most sorrowful thought to me, Donald," Constance said softly; "if his spirit will know through all eternity that he has wronged you, how sad, how unutterably sad it is to think of!"

"Donald will be happy, and we'll both work," Maude said encouragingly. But Donald shook his head, and said that he had never been brought up to the idea of work, and he feared he was too old to begin to think about it now.

"Something will come in the way that you can do, be sure of that, if you give your mind steadily to finding something," Constance said.

But Donald could not take a hopeful view of his capabilities and chances of a career just yet. The wound made in his spirit was too new and raw, and it seemed as if Maude, his wife, would have a querulous husband as well as poverty to deal with.

Mrs Vaughan did not make light of her difficulties at this juncture. When she came to look over the Strathlands house with the view of collecting her own goods and chattels and removing them to the dower-house in the village, she gave Reginald a great deal more trouble than he liked. For she clung with ivy-like tenacity to every article which had been brought into the house since her marriage.

"It would be hard, indeed, if I couldn't retain possession of my own bedroom furniture," she said plaintively, pointing to the exquisitely artistic suite which Mr Vaughan had ordered on his second marriage.

"My father has left the furniture to me with the house," Reginald said doggedly.

"There is a great deal of my work in the drawing-room. The *portières* and window-curtain borders, the chimney boards and curtains, and a great many of the chairs I embroidered with my own hands," Mrs Vaughan said in an aggrieved tone.

"You can take your own work away, of course," Reginald said munificently.

"Do you mean that I am to rip it off the curtains and chairs?"

"I mean you can do as you like about taking it or

leaving it; if you take it, it will have to be ripped off, I suppose, as the chairs will certainly remain where they are."

"And I only hope, with all my heart, that your wife will have the good taste to cover them properly," Mrs Vaughan spit out in wounded pride.

"Thanks! my wife that is to be has a very fair notion of doing things well. I don't think your work would be her style, so perhaps it will save contention and bother if I order it to be taken off the furniture at once."

Mrs Vaughan acquiesced, and choked for a moment or two. Then she said,—

"Donald and you have always been attached brothers; you are not going to let him want and suffer all that he will have to want and suffer if you act on your father's will—a will he repented of bitterly at the last, I am sure."

"Donald has shown the most gross disregard for my father's wishes in the matter of his marriage."

"Reggie, be just! Are you going to marry in a way that would please your father were he still alive?"

"No; don't suppose I should," Reggie said dauntlessly; "but you see my father isn't alive to be vexed or pleased, and I'm master here now, therefore it doesn't matter much whether other people are vexed or pleased with my arrangements."

Power is a wonderful instrument for developing brutality in some natures.

"Maude, my darling! don't you think you should have a studio in town?" Donald said to his wife one day; "your brother could help you if you were up there, and Lady Charldale and a host of people."

"Please never say to me that any one can help me with my pictures," Maude pleaded; "they are my own; bad, good, or indifferent, they are mine, and by them I stand or fall. I can't be helped."

CHAPTER XXX.

MRS WELTON'S VIEWS.

Mrs VAUGHAN's little house was rapidly assuming a habitable appearance under Constance's vigilant supervision, and the garden was soon metamorphosed from the weedy wilderness it had been to a neat, well-planted and ordered plot of content.

"We can't make you gay with annuals till next spring, aunt, but I'll have a lot of chrysanthemums and German asters in flower carefully transplanted from my garden to yours. They'll brighten the place up a bit," Constance said.

"Nothing will ever make any place bright to me now," Mrs Vaughan said, for she had started a theory, founded on fiction, that she was lamenting her husband grievously, and she would not allow this fiction to be ignored, much less gainsaid.

"Oh yes, flowers will," Constance said brightly, and Mrs Vaughan shook her head, and murmured,—

"Not after such a loss as mine!"

In truth, it was a sorry change, this, from Strathlands and plenteousness to the little house in the village street, and an income that would only suffice to keep the little house up in a modest way.

Unfortunately, too, her sufferings were aggravated by the fact of Strathlands being visible from all her front windows, and further, by her house lying in the direct road that led from the railway station to Strathlands. For big packing cases, containing new furniture for Strathlands—furniture that had been selected, ordered, and sent down by that unknown but already well-hated intruder, whom Reginald was going to marry—were constantly passing Mrs Vaughan's windows. And though the sight made her blood boil, and congeal, and run cold, and do a variety of other extraordinary things, she averred still she had not the moral courage to either keep away from the window or pull the blinds down, and shut the hateful spectacle out.

In her anger against Reginald, on her own account, Mrs Vaughan sided heartily with Donald, and uttered rather ferocious denunciations of Reginald's conduct, quite regardless of the liability there was of Reginald's hearing them again with piquant additions.

Indeed, Reginald's cool acceptance of all that his father had to leave, and his callousness regarding his brother, touched others besides Mrs Vaughan into partisanship with Donald. Mr Dalzel ventured for one to remark on the subject.

"I hope, Reginald," he said, "that you are not going to let your brother and that poor girl suffer altogether by that will, of which it's my firm belief your father bitterly repented before he died."

"Donald is better off than I should have been if he had come into the property; he can get a clerkship, and his wife can make money. I should have had only the clerkship."

"It's rather a mean thing to suggest that he is to live on his wife's talent."

"He needn't live on it; he can take a clerkship as I did. Besides, whether it's mean or not, Maude can make money; but that's not the point. I only mention it to show you that my brother has really not as much to complain of as I should have had if our positions had been reversed."

After this exposition of his selfish intentions, Mr Dalzel could not bring himself to treat Reginald other than coolly, though he was the squire and great man of the parish; and this coolness Reginald attributed to party-feeling, to partisanship for Donald, and accused Donald of trying to "undermine" him in the place; so the breach between the brothers widened.

Until they could come to something like a definite decision as to what it would be best for them to do, Mr and Mrs Donald Vaughan stayed with her mother at the Grange, Maude spending the days in hard, unceasing work, and Donald hindering her a good deal by grumbling at his changed fortunes and the severity of his fate.

There were difficulties and unpleasantnesses, too, about the two sisters, the Misses Vaughan. Their father had expressed a wish, but had not uttered it as a command, that they should continue to live on under the protection of their stepmother, paying her fair remuneration for their maintenance; but to this they demurred. Life had been dull enough for them at Strathlands; at Clyst it would be quite unendurable, they affirmed, and on her side Mrs Vaughan was not anxious to have them.

Still, they could not remain on a visit to their great-aunt for ever, and in default of anything better turning up, they accepted Reginald's offer of "a home with him for as long as they could all go on comfortably together." This offer he made, and they accepted before they had become acquainted with Mrs Welton.

"But I'd rather you didn't come down till after I'm married and settled in at Strathlands," Mr Reginald Vaughan wrote, at the dictation of his bride-elect, who had a shrewd conviction that they "should not all go along comfortably" for any length of time.

There was no lack of the shrewd discretion which teaches a woman how to take care of herself about Mrs Welton. But she was not constrained by conventionalities where her interests were concerned. So now, in her eager desire to see her future home and to see that it was being fitted suitably for her occupation, she came down to Clyst without note of warning, thereby causing much annoyance to Reginald, and considerable conversation and scandal in the village.

"What on earth made you do this, Adelaide?" was Mr Reginald Vaughan's greeting when smart Mrs Welton drove up in boisterous spirits.

"Why, I wanted to see the place, to be sure," she replied, in no wise taken aback or put down by the manner of her reception. "What a fine 'all! And, my! Reggie, what a number of servants a 'ouse like this will require."

Reginald groaned in spirit, but showed a manly front

to the group of wondering, amused servants. Never before had the dropped h's fallen upon him with such ponderous, cruel weight.

"Come out and see the conservatories," he said, glad to get her away from the observation of his shrewd retainers.

"You can't stay here, you know," he began, as they got out of earshot of the servants.

"Bring your stepmother back for a day or two."

"She wouldn't come. Don't you see what you've done? You've given them a handle to turn against you by your rashness. Why on earth you couldn't wait till we were married I can't think."

"That's rubbish!" she said coolly. "You thought nothing of my going to look about for a house, and leaving all the arrangements to me before you came into this and got so grand ; and now I'm going to act the same, just as I did then. If I can't stay here I'll stay at the inn at Clyst; but stay I will, to see the house put into order."

And stay she did, superintending and interfering, and giving her orders, "just for all the world as if she had been master's wife already," the servants said.

In his distress and desire to put the best aspect on her imprudence, he threw himself at the feet of the enemy, as it were. First he called at the Dower House, as Mrs Vaughan had named her abode, and begged his father's widow to call on Mrs Welton at the inn.

But Mrs Vaughan was quite void of generous feeling about the matter. The memory of the slights and injuries which she believed herself to have received at his hands rose up and steeled her heart against his appeal.

"In my broken state of health it is quite impossible for me to think of seeing a stranger. I couldn't dream of doing so. I feel I should sink under the effort."

"If you won't go to the inn and call on her, will you let me bring her here? It's so deuced awkward for her as it is, and if she is not received properly it will set every brutal tongue in the village wagging."

"She should have thought of that before she came," Mrs Vaughan said sententiously.

"It's no use saying what she should have done; the question is what are we to do now; you don't want to cast a slur on her, and damage her, I suppose? For by doing that you'll damage me."

"Really, I feel quite unequal to continuing this most painful conversation," Mrs Vaughan said in a low, suffering voice. "You must remember that this is the first visit you have paid me, the first time I have seen you since I left Strathlands under most trying circumstances. The only thing I feel equal to, is to go and lie down and rest."

"And it will be my last visit, I can tell you that," Reginald said savagely, catching up his hat and departing.

Then he bethought himself of his brother and his brother's wife. "Maude won't bear malice! it isn't in her; and I should think Donald would do it for me."

It always seemed to Reginald to be a right and natural thing that everyone should make concessions, and do doughty deeds for him.

Mrs Arminger was not at home when he got to the Grange, and her absence deprived him of a true ally. Maude was painting and "wouldn't be disturbed," Donald said, and then he added drearily, "her work is all we have to depend on now, and we both feel that it would be almost dishonest on her part to waste a minute."

"That's rather rough on Maude, isn't it?" Reginald asked.

"It is, but the roughness of it is none of my making." Then there was a pause, for Reginald felt that the opening remarks were not propitious to the forwarding of his request.

At last he made the effort and blurted out his wishes.

"I'm sorry I can't see Maude; it's awfully unfortunate, in fact, for I wanted to ask her to call on Mrs Welton, who is staying at the inn for a day or two."

"Mrs Welton is—"

"The lady I am going to marry," Reginald interrupted hastily. "Naturally, I want Maude and you to call on her. Mrs Vaughan, with her usual cat-like contrary spirit, makes out that she's too ill to make the effort : that's humbug, I know."

"Maude can't stir from her work, it's no use asking her ; we have to make up a sum of money before we can start in London, even in the little mean pettifogging way we are going to start."

"This only means that you'll do me and mine all the damage you can. Well, I shall know how to thank you for it," Reginald said, speaking and making his exit in the same manner he had done from the Dower House.

His last hope was in Constance.

"I suppose you've heard that Mrs Welton has come down stupidly enough. Will you be good-natured and go and call on her ?"

"Yes, certainly, I'll go and call, it's no great stretch of good nature that ; I'll get Maude to go with me."

"Donald won't let her," he said, and then he went on to tell her of the vile disregard which both his step-mother and his brother had shown for his wishes.

"I may succeed where you failed. Donald won't keep me out of Maude's studio, and Maude will feel with me that we have no right to make Mrs Welton, who is innocent of all offence against Donald, suffer for his father's injustice to him ; anyway, I'll go and speak to Maude on my way to the village."

After all Reginald went back to Mrs Welton with more charitable feelings than those which pervaded him when he left her.

Mrs Welton prepared for the reception of her promised visitors with a mixture of glee and grandeur that galled and irritated Reginald. How was it that this demeanour of hers, which was no new thing, had never struck discordantly upon him in the lodging-house ? It was useless asking himself that question. It struck discordantly upon him now.

"I hope they don't think it a condescension to call on

me?" she questioned pugnaciously. "Because I don't feel myself honoured, I can tell you. When I've got to Strathlands, they'll be glad enough to come as often as I'll have them, I expect."

"Both Miss Fielding and my brother's wife have always been in the best county society. You'll not find either of them 'glad' to go anywhere."

"Then why, if she's a swell, did your father set his face against her being your brother's wife?"

"Family reasons. Maude was my mother's niece, and besides his dislike to cousins marrying, my father wanted to make up a match between Donald and Miss Fielding."

"Well, I hope they won't be stiff; I 'ate your stiff folks," said Mrs Welton, with that fatal barmaid volubility, which was so sure to tell against herself in the coming time of her being put upon her trial by the neighbourhood.

"I hope you won't be noisy."

"I shall be just what I like," she said, tossing her head. "I was good enough in manners and everything else for you when you lived in my house, and asked me to marry you, and I'm good enough now for them, I should think."

Then she went up to her room and set off her pretty smart little person with the most stylish costume she had brought with her, and in spite of her defiant assertion, trained her tones down to quietness in unconscious homage to the refinement of her coming guests.

But after all Constance came alone, having been completely circumvented by Donald.

He had not been able to keep her out of Maude's studio; indeed, he had not tried to do so, for no premonition of what errand Miss Fielding had come upon, warned him to keep her out. But he had gone into the room with her, thrown cold water on her wishes, and made Maude to feel that it would wring his heart to breaking-point if she went into the enemy's camp.

"Mrs Welton has never harmed you," Constance argued.

"It would look to all the world as if Maude were flying in my face, and siding with my brother, if she went," Donald said angrily.

"I should fly in your face fast enough in this case," Constance said honestly ; "I can't stand vindictiveness ; you're making Maude seem spiteful, when she hasn't a particle of it in her ; why gall this woman whom your brother is going to marry ?"

"Because my brother is going to marry her," he replied, and as he would not stir from the position he had taken up, Constance had to go on her social way without Maude after all.

All Mrs Welton's professional ease and vivacity came into play for Constance's benefit on this their first interview. She told Miss Fielding how many offers she had received since Mr Welton's death, and how she had "stood out" against all these ardent swains, preferring "her freedom, and to do what she liked with what was her own, till Reggie came along." She also assured Miss Fielding that she should come to Strathlands determining "not to be still with anyone," but that if any of the old country fogies tried on their airs with her she should let them know who was who, and what was what.

In fact her conversation, together with her pronounced and faulty style, took Miss Fielding's breath away to such an extent that, from sheer inability to keep the ball rolling, she slided into silence, and so fell under the ban of Mrs Welton's displeasure.

For the first time Constance thought with pity of the poor ambitious father, whose whole heart and soul had been bound up in the hope that the son who inherited Strathlands should make a fitting marriage. Now this was the end of it. Mrs Welton was to reign there.

CHAPTER XXXI.

HINDRANCES.

Two or three times during those weeks that followed Mr Vaughan's death and the reconstruction of things at Strathlands, Don Arminger had been on the point of going down to his mother's house at Clyst, and asking Constance to tell him that she felt the time had come for them to begin life together.

They had both wasted a great deal of time in making mistakes, but they had redeemed that time by rectifying them. At least Constance had done so, and Lady Elinor had, for her own ends, kindly rectified Don's.

But whenever Don thought of going to Clyst, the reflection that Donald Vaughan was now installed there as a son of the house deterred him.

Not that he disliked Donald Vaughan as a friend or cousin, but the thought of him as a brother-in-law supinely giving way to temper and idleness because he had been cruelly wronged by his father's will, was an irritating one to Don. And even more irritating to Maude's brother was the knowledge (obtained from others, not from her) that her husband had it in his mind to leave their future fortunes to be worked out by Maude's talent.

On the whole, Don told himself that it would be more conducive to peace and pleasantness in the family if he stayed away from Clyst Grange while Donald Vaughan was there.

That he should stay away was not very surprising to Constance Fielding, for she had an unfeminine habit of looking at things from several sides, and she was quite able to view Donald Vaughan's conduct from Don's point. Therefore she did not feel aggrieved at his staying away from daily contemplation of that which was obnoxious to him. But what she did feel aggrieved at was his not writing to her.

And all the while he was so perfectly unconscious that he was being guilty of a sin of omission in not doing this. He judged it better that he should speak to her than he should write, and as he meant to speak to her soon, he was innocent of all offence in thus keeping silence.

At length Donald Vaughan began to feel that he was not doing well in remaining in Clyst. He had stayed on at first because he had a faint-hearted intention of contesting the claim with his brother, and of trying to upset his father's will; but, after taking sound and friendly legal advice, he knew this was not to be done. Then he had stayed on, hoping that the sight of him might induce Reginald to offer him honourable reparation; but Reginald was evidently a stranger to anything approaching to either fraternal feeling or remorse, and so Donald Vaughan began to think the time was come for him to take his wife away.

The Mrs Welton episode hastened matters, for Reginald, being very wroth with her for her imprudence, and not caring to betray the anger he felt to her, "kicked where he dared," and made it a matter of quarrel with Donald that neither he nor Maude had called on Mrs Welton.

"I made a very reasonable and civil excuse for Maude's not calling," Donald said.

"All the same, I knew it was an excuse merely, and so did Mrs Welton, and she won't forget it."

"As far as we're concerned, she is perfectly welcome to remember it. Indeed, I wish now that I had told the blunt truth, and not made any excuse at all, since my complaisance in doing so is questioned."

"Perhaps you'll not care to go so far as to tell me what the blunt truth is?" Reginald asked, with rising choler.

"Yes, if you care to hear it."

"Out with it, then," said the younger brother, and the elder one replied,—

"Well, the truth is, that I don't mean my wife to know Mrs Welton."

After this there was undeclared war to the knife between the two brothers, and Maude's high kind heart was wrung hourly by the wrathful and vindictive speeches which her husband was constantly making about Reginald.

"You'd get better into harness if you were up in town, wouldn't you, Maude?" he said to her one day, and she, hoping that a removal from Clyst might bring peace to his troubled spirit, assented at once.

"Shall we go up and look after a place? I suppose your sister can take us in for a few days?"

"I'll write and ask Trixy," Maude said.

"You haven't a doubt about it, have you? You don't think that she and Timerton will want to give us the cold shoulder, do you?"

"Trixy never cold-shouldered any one in her life," Maude said, laughing at the idea, and yet vexed at the element of suspicion in it.

"Ah, but she hasn't been Lady Timerton all her life. At any rate, write and inquire. If she makes any excuse—well, the sooner we know our friends from our foes the sooner we shall learn to rely entirely on ourselves. Self-reliance is the grandest quality out," Donald Vaughan said, looking round at his audience (consisting of his wife and her mother) for approval of the sentiment.

Maude heaved a patient sigh. She had come to understand that all the self-reliance displayed by the Donald-and-Maude-Vaughan firm must be displayed by herself.

But Mrs Arminger tried to bring him up to his bridle by saying briskly,—

"I'm glad to hear you speak in that way, Donald. I've felt sure you would take that line when you had overcome your first very natural feeling of discomfiture. And now, as we are upon the subject, and as Maude and you have taken me into your confidence, I will ask you, what do you purpose doing?"

"The first thing I do will be to secure a house in London, where Maude can work under easy and pleasant conditions; to settle her in a studio that will be not merely a workshop but an aid to her in her work, is my first desire."

Donald said this rather heroically, and Maude found herself heartily admiring the sympathy and foresight which caused him to make the facilitating her work his chief object and aim.

Mrs Arminger was not quite so deeply impressed with the sympathy expressed in the intention as was her daughter.

"That is really very praiseworthy and considerate of you, Donald, as far as Maude's work is concerned; but you have to think of yourself. You must not forget your own career in seeking to forward hers, for Maude's is established," the mother wound up proudly.

"I don't believe I shall ever be able to do a stroke of work of any kind, indeed I don't," Donald said so plaintively, that Maude felt ready to weep as she listened to this unconscious plaint against the ill-usage to which he had been subjected. "I'm too old for any Civil Service appointment, and, upon my word, I don't know that I'm capable of doing any of the things by which money is made. It's deuced unfortunate altogether."

"It is," Mrs Arminger assented gravely.

"Yes; unless Don and Timerton between them do anything for me. Of course, if they please, they can make an effort in my behalf, and get a decent appointment for me."

"If you'll tell me what you would call a good appointment, I will write and ask Don if he can bring any influence to bear upon getting it for you," Mrs Arminger said timidly.

"Thanks, no; I don't think I'll ask you to do that; I'll wait till I go up, and then I'll speak to Timerton first; he's more likely to be in the way of hearing of a thing that might suit me than Don is; besides, there's no hurry, for a time I shall be occupied in getting things comfortable for Maude; her work must be the first consideration, and as she'll have to pursue it pretty arduously, I feel I am bound to make all the conditions surrounding it as agreeable to her as possible. Eh, dear Maude?"

"Yes, I'm sure you will," Maude said gratefully, while her mother thought—

"My child, under the guise of a considerate adviser, will have an exacting task-master in her husband," but though she thought this, Mrs Arminger was far too discreet, and far too fond of her daughter to let the thought find expression in any way.

The letter was written to Trixy, asking her if she could receive Maude and her husband at Timerton House for a few days, while Donald was looking out for a suitable house, and the answer was awaited in loving expectancy by Maude, in cynical doubt by Donald.

"She ought to reply to that letter by return of post, considering my delicate position," Donald said, thinking of himself first, as usual with him.

"So Trixy will, if she's in town," Maude said in affectionate confidence.

"So Trixy might; but will Lady Timerton be equally prompt? My dear Maude, I'm not imputing anything like snobbishness to your sister, but you must remember that she is occupying a position she never could have dreamt of occupying; we, through a most cruelly adverse fate, and certainly through no fault of mine, but only because of my fondness for you, are occupying a much humbler one. If you had been Mrs Vaughan of Strathlands, you would have received an invitation to Timerton House long before this."

Maude did not like to tell her husband that she didn't believe him, but she did not do so, though she kept silence.

Trixy's heart had been an open book to her all Trixy's life. The mere fact of their altered positions—of the difference in their relative states, would make no difference in Trixy's heart—Maude knew right well.

Still days passed and no answer came, and Maude began to grow anxious. And this was the reason of it.

Lord and Lady Timerton had gone off, without giving any sign of their sudden movement, to Malta, whither Lord Timerton had been summoned by his sister, Lady Charldale.

In an hour of ill-timed bravado, Lord Charldale had carried his wife there in the *White Squall.* They were hardly at anchor before a boat put off to and boarded them, while Lord Charldale and his bride were dining, and the first notification they had of the arrival of their unexpected and extremely unwelcome visitors, was given by a handsome girl flashing down the steps into the saloon, flinging her arms round Lord Charldale's neck, and assuring him that she had always said she knew he would return to her.

As the handsome girl was followed by a keen-eyed business-like looking papa this was awkward.

It was in vain that Lady Charldale drew herself up to her haughtiest heights, and iced her words till they fell like chilled shot on her husband's ears. It was equally in vain that Lord Charldale strove to restore the order of decorum by explaining that the lady opposite to him at the table was his wife, the Countess of Charldale. It was little Nita's day of vengeance and reign of terror, and she reigned ferociously.

Her accents rose high above his; she would not hear, nor would she suffer anyone else to hear his proclamation of Elinor as his wife, the Countess of Charldale. Nita deemed it the best policy to rave and be blind. She turned her back on Lady Charldale, while she (Nita) clung convulsively to Lord Charldale's arms and coat-collar, and all the while she was doing this she was shrilly apostrophising him as her dearest, her truest, her own.

Meanwhile her father, much affected, stood in the background and wiped his eyes now and again, during which occupation he took keen "sights" at Lady Charldale.

Presently Elinor, who was not angry, or even amused, got tired of the situation, and then the vehement young native Maltese lady wished herself on her island home again.

"Have that woman put into a boat and sent on shore under proper control, Charldale," she said, so quietly that Nita felt herself compelled to stop her transports, and listen to those cool cutting accents; "I think as our dinner has been disturbed in this way, I'll go to my own cabin. Come and speak to me when that woman has been put off the yacht."

With that Lady Charldale amiably left the saloon, and Lord Charldale disencumbered himself of the native beauty with the same shuddering violence he would have displayed towards an adder.

"Won't you save your daughter from degrading herself any further, sir?" he asked, turning towards Nita's father.

But that gentleman merely shrugged his shoulders and observed,—

"She is your promised wife. There is no degradation to her in finding a female on board."

Altercation ensued, and altogether the yacht's crew had a good deal of excitement and amusement that evening. Especially they liked their work of rowing the infuriated native beauty and her incensed sire on shore, where a select company of English residents sauntered past and slighted them.

Lady Charldale, eating ices and reading an instalment of an amusing novel in her own cabin, took it all very quietly. When Nita and her father had been handed overboard, Lord Charldale came to her in an apologetic mood, but Lady Charldale would have none of it. She knew that if once she treated the "Nita" business seriously, it might grow to be a serious business for her. At present her one anxiety was that Charldale should not grow nervous, and feel himself in need of Dutch courage.

"I needn't say that I wouldn't have had this occur for the world, Elinor," he began. "Let me explain—"

"No, no, dear; you needn't," she interrupted. "The tiresome woman—half a savage, I see—has evidently over-estimated some trifling attentions on your part. I ought to be the last person in the world to blame her for doing that, or to find it astonishing that she should have done so."

Lady Charldale was quite willing to tickle his self-love, if the doing so would keep him from seeking any more ignoble solace.

"Shall we make sail away from here to-morrow morning?" he asked earnestly, but for once she was un-wise enough to underrate a difficulty, and declared in favour of staying on.

"If we went off in that way it would look as if you were afraid. and I know you're not that. I want to have some silk lace made while I'm here; it's all new to me remember; I have not had your pleasant experiences of Malta."

"It shall be as you please, but I think we had better go, Elinor."

"If it's as I please, we stay for a few days at any rate; directly the yacht moves I shall be sick, and I don't want either to be sick or to go home yet."

"As you like," he assented, but all the time he did wish that she would let him sail away from the atmo-sphere of Nita without delay.

Not that he was afraid of succumbing to Nita's in-fluence again.   He was too much in love with his wife to fear that. but he knew that Nita was quite capable of bringing turmoil into his life, "the little sensational beast!" he called her to himself now.   And as for her father, "By Jove! I believe he's a Greek," Lord Charl-dale muttered.

All this time there was a struggle going on that was deadly though silent, between Morris, Lord Charldale's "old and attached" first valet, and his lordship's young and attached wife. It had been borne in upon her strongly, partly from her own observation. and partly from hints that had been dropped by the dowager countess, that this man exercised a secret and deleterious influence over Lord Charldale's life.   "Get rid of

Morris," the mother had whispered to the young bride when the latter was departing on her wedding-day, and the young bride had emphatically answered,—

"I will."

But up to the day of this distressing scene, which marred the harmony of the dinner-hour on board the *White Squall*, Elinor had failed to detach Morris from his master.

But now from sundry signs which her acute senses had learnt to understand since her marriage, she knew that Lord Charldale was thrown just sufficiently off his balance by the exciting event of the evening, to fall an easy prey to the wiles of the tempter. And alas! for her she knew too well what form the temptation would take.

She had literally no experience, but she had a clear head, a heart that never tore her to tatters, and a strong will. These she resolved to put in battle array against the snare and the snarer this night.

Until ten o'clock her husband stayed up talking to her in her own saloon cabin. Then he rose up, yawning, saying he had a headache, and should go to his berth.

"All right," she said affably. "I know what's best for a headache that comes from bother; when you're in your berth comfortably tucked up, I'll come and blow eau de Cologne over your forehead; and then I'll read you a jolly letter I've had from Trixy Timerton. Trixy's out-and-out the best letter-writer I know."

"I couldn't stand a bit of modernised Mrs Chapone," he says petulantly, for he wants to have himself to himself and Morris for the night.

"I shall make you listen to the whole of Trixy's letter now, in order to prove to you that she isn't Chaponish."

Then she called to Morris, who was hanging about, and said,—

"Lord Charldale wishes you to call me to read to him as soon as he is settled for the night; don't forget it."

"No, your ladyship," the man said promptly. But all the same, Elinor was not called that night, and even she lacked the courage to intrude upon the orgie of the master and the man.

She made a resolution, and as her husband was a gentleman, she knew that he would back her up in it. She would go to him in the morning, and tell him that Morris, that evil panderer to his lower craving, must leave his service, or that she, his wife, would fling up her duty in the face of all society, and leave him.

But in the morning both he and Morris were incapable of understanding her. Morris was in a comfortable state of hazy torpor. Lord Charldale had "what they call the horrors, my lady," one of the crew told her. Then she sent at once for her brother and his wife.

CHAPTER XXXII.

JAR AND FRET.

It need not be said that Lady Charldale did not lose her head in this emergency. She wore such an air of unruffled serenity that even her favoured maid did not venture to proffer her anything remotely approaching to sympathy. She issued her orders and made arrangements for the day just exactly as if Lord Charldale had only been a "little indisposed," as she said he was, instead of being frightfully and dangerously ill, as was the fact.

She received the distinguished English residents, who came off from the island to do her homage, with the same calm grace she would have displayed had her husband not been suffering from a fierce attack of delirium tremens in his own saloon.

And one other thing she did, which was perhaps the best act of all. She ordered Morris's portmanteau to be packed and put into the already lowered boat, gave directions that the full amount of his wages, up to a month a-head, should be paid to him, and that he should then be compelled to follow his portmanteau, and conveyed to the landing-steps, where he was to be left to his own devices.

It was in vain that the man whined and whimpered, protested and defended himself; in vain that he cast himself on his knees at her feet and vowed such an offence should never occur again. Lady Charldale took no more heed of his plaints than she did of the screech of the seagulls. Lord Charldale's attack was a short though a sharp one. When he came to himself he found his wife sitting by his side. He looked at her languidly, and asked for Morris.

"I have provided you with a new man—an officer's servant, who understands what his duties are much better than Morris did," she said good-humouredly.

"Where is Morris?" he repeated.

"I have dismissed him; he was not a good servant."

"Elinor, I've been a brute to you," he said humbly; "to bring you here and behave to you as I have done was too beastly caddish a thing for me ever to forgive myself for."

"You must forget it all, as I have done. And now you must get up and help me with invitations to open luncheons on board the yacht every day of our stay here," she said grandly. Then she left him with the new servant, and Lord Charldale prepared to obey her with grateful feelings.

By the time Lord and Lady Timerton arrived, festive peace was reigning on board the yacht. Lady Charldale's daily open luncheons had conquered Malta society, and the threats and execrations of the Maltese native beauty fell unheeded on society's ears.

But at the same time her papa gave the Earl of Charldale to clearly understand that Nita intended to proceed against his lordship for breach of promise of marriage; and Lord Charldale's soul was sick within him at the prospect of some of his letters being read in open court.

For in some of them, if his memory served him correctly, he had been very indiscreet.

"Why do you stay here?" Lord Timerton asked his

sister. "You're constantly hearing through side winds what that girl is doing and saying and meaning to do. You never go on shore but she throws herself in your way, and pantomimically assures Charldale that her torrid love is unchanged; she'll take him off with her one fine day if you fool about here any longer."

"I am staying here to give Charldale a lesson he will never forget; in former days, if he could leave the scene of an orgie such as that he indulged in when we came here first, he thought people forgot all about it. Now he can't think that, and the shame of it is wholesome. Besides, he must be taught that I only consider that woman and her claims despicable. What does it matter to us whether she brings an action and gets damages or not! Her trying it only proves that she wants money so badly that she would degrade herself to any extent in order to get it. And that will rebound on her head, for it will injure her father's mercantile credit. That's the view of the case which I am circulating. It gives me no trouble to do it, for a word or a hint from me dropped at the luncheon table is repeated with additions as original surmises of their own, by all the people all over the place. Nita's papa will find his credit gone before he is aware of it."

This, then, was the reason why Lady Timerton did not answer her sister's letter before. When the answer did reach Clyst it was all that was loving and kind.

"We shall not be home just yet," Trixy said; "but, darling, make Timerton House your headquarters for just exactly as long as it suits you. Dear old Maude, it would be odd indeed if my home wasn't yours whenever you pleased."

"She doesn't say a word about me," Donald grumbled plaintively.

"Dear Donald, she takes you for granted, of course; wherever I am welcome you may be sure that you are also."

"I am not at all so sure of that," Donald said, shaking his head; "the omission of my name looks rather pointed; in fact, I'm not sure that I shall trespass on Lady Timerton's hospitality at all."

"If you don't go, naturally I shall not either, Donald," Maude said sadly; "and then Trixy will be dreadfully hurt."

"As it is I am hurt, but not dreadfully; I can still hold my head above these paltry slights and rebuffs."

"If I were Maude I should feel inclined to give your head a punch, Donald," Constance, who was present when the subject was being discussed, said impatiently. "Find fault with the faulty ones of the earth if you please, but don't pick holes in the perfect ones."

"I don't know any such."

"I do; many who are as perfect as it's possible for humanity to be; your wife is one, and her mother and sister are two more, and I'm a third, if you'll only believe it; but I shall cease from being nice soon, and get so out of temper with you, that I shall grow cross and quarrelsome."

"Oh, I've no doubt you'll find it convenient to drop us in time, like the rest of the world," Donald said, and Maude, instead of being disgusted and annoyed with his carping, querulous spirit, was happy enough to be able to pity and pardon it.

"Dear me!" Constance thought, as she went on from the Grange to her aunt's house in the village, "if I had the misfortune to be endowed with a duplicate of Donald Vaughan's spirit I should be savage by this time with Don for not having come to claim what he is so sure of."

Then she cross-questioned herself, and found that "no really" she had neither doubt nor fear concerning Don. All she felt was a wholesomely jealous desire to see him.

She seemed doomed this day to have other people's petty little troubles laid frettingly upon her. Donald Arminger had chafed her far more than he had chafed his wife by that display of fractious sensitiveness which he had made anent Trixy's invitation. And now when she reached the Dower House she was met by her aunt in the passage, with a cold in her head, and a shawl over it.

"I'm glad you've come at last, Constance," Mrs Vaughan began as rebukingly as if Constance had caused her (Mrs Vaughan) to miss a train, or a new song by Marzials at a ballad concert, or the best bit in Gilbert's last fairy comedy. "I'm glad you've come at last, Constance ; those gardeners of yours are so trying about the sea-kale and celery."

"Between them they're sure to get it right," Constance said cheerfully. "Come in out of this cold passage. You'll get neuralgia if you stay here any longer."

"I have it already, and toothache too : and worse than that, Constance—worse than that, I have the deplorable feeling upon me that I'm no longer looked up to in this place. I went out just now, hearing Rill and Staveley disputing in a very painful way, a way that was extremely painful for me to listen to, and spoke to them of the duty of exercising Christian forbearance and charity towards each other, and—you'll hardly credit me, but it's true—I saw Staveley's shoulders shaking, and Rill I caught winking—yes, winking—at the man he had been quarrelling with a moment before."

"It's part of the joy of their lives to dispute and be cranky with each other, aunt. Naturally they'd resent any effort to rob them of that harmless amusement. Let us see how the greenhouse is getting on."

"Rill assures me that all the flowers that have been transplanted here from Woodside are dying for want of nourishment, and I can't help seeing that he holds Staveley to blame for this."

"Of course he does, aunt ; and Staveley holds Rill to blame for those flowers having been transplanted at this time of year at all. You don't know how amicably they agree to differ. Don't worry yourself about them ; it's only on garden ground they fight. They're as pacific as possible over their pipes and beer in Rill's lodge or in the kitchen at Woodside."

"I can't pass over the nasty contentious spirit they

displayed before me, lightly as you do, Constance. No; I can't, and I won't. I know too well what it means. They have no respect for me now since I have been put away here to end my days. If they had come to do a day's work for me at Strathlands, their behaviour would have been very different."

"Perhaps so. Then they would have quarrelled with your gardeners instead of with each other."

"No, they wouldn't, Constance," Mrs Vaughan said, drifting into a lazy-looking arm-chair by the side of a cheerfully-burning fire. "They wouldn't have presumed to do anything so unseemly; but naturally, now, when they see me huddled out of my own home by Reginald in his indecent haste to instal that despicable woman there as—"

"You've no right to call her despicable; you've no right to blame Reginald for wishing to instal his wife in her own home," Constance said judicially.

"Yes, I have, Constance; I have every right in the world to do so, considering what that wife is. She has sprung from the mud—"

"If she has sprung and cleared herself, all the more credit to her," Constance interrupted. "We have nothing to do with that; we have to do with her as Reginald's wife, and I mean to treat her as Reginald's wife ought to be treated."

"Reginald has not even sent me a bit of cake. How am I to know they're married?"

"Because they have announced it very fully in several papers."

"I am surprised at your upholding her, Constance."

"I'm not upholding her; I'm only meting out the barest justice. All my heart is alive with sympathy for Donald Vaughan's fate, because Maude's lot is linked with his; but my loving sympathy for them doesn't make me splenetic about the woman who has not designedly superseded them. You have no right—we have none of us any right—to spit fire at Mrs Reginald Vaughan, simply because she has been more fortunate than the ones we love have been."

"Oh, I don't for a moment pretend that I love Donald Vaughan," his stepmother avowed with hesitation : "but Reginald behaved so badly about the bedroom furniture and the things I covered with my own work in the drawing-room, that I shall never forgive him—never."

"Perhaps if we all treat Reginald and his wife nicely and kindly, he will in time do what is just and brotherly by Donald. Reggie was not a bad-hearted boy, only a little wayward and selfish," Constance said encouragingly.

"My dear Constance, both the boys were dreadfully wayward and selfish, just like their poor, dear father, and so were the girls, too, for that matter. I pity those poor things now for having to live with Reginald's wife, though they never did show much affection or consideration for me. They're disregarding their poor father's wishes, too, in not living with me."

"But you're rather glad they're not going to live with you, aunt?"

"Certainly I am; but that doesn't alter the fact that their poor father wished them to do it; but I always did say, and I always will say, that root and branch the Vaughans are eaten up with selfishness."

"The carpenter is coming down presently, aunt, to take the measurements for putting up a little conservatory to open out of this room," Constance said, striving to divert the conversation into a happier channel.

"My dear Connie, you are very kind, very good and kind, and I am very grateful to you; but I don't suppose I shall live to see the conservatory put up; the change from Strathlands, which has been my home for so long, to this place where I'm overlooked, and, no doubt, criticised and gossipped about by all Clyst, has tried me terribly, and Reginald's heartlessness and insults have all told upon me, though I've said nothing."

"It's so much better to say nothing," Constance said.

"Ah, my dear, it's all very well for you, full of youth and health, and happiness and riches, to say that; it's very easy for you to be silent and content; but I'm a poor, old, neglected woman, for whom anything is thought good enough. If Reginald could have his way, I've no doubt I should be shoved into the humblest cottage on the estate. As it is, I try to be grateful and content."

As Mrs Vaughan's house was comfortably designed, admirably built, and exquisitely furnished, the casual observer might have been forgiven for supposing that she had every reason to be content.

"To be sure you do, dear aunt; I've come to dine with you if you'll have me, to-night, there's no cook in all the region round turns out such sweet little dinners as yours."

"Ah, I'm not likely to keep her long; Reginald knows what a good cook she is, and Mrs Reginald will take her from me as a matter of course."

"I don't think so, aunt; I should rather think she'll prefer new servants to the old ones."

"Well, perhaps so. But it's not much cooking I shall require in a little time; there's something in the atmosphere here that robs me of all appetite. I really think it's the close rooms, Constance, and the sight of those people's yellow blinds opposite. They make me feel quite bilious."

"Stretch Madras muslin over your own windows; then you won't see their yellow blinds."

"No, I couldn't do that. Fresh air is a luxury still left to me; and with Madras muslin tightly stretched and fastened down in front of my windows, I couldn't have enough of it. That carpenter is a long time coming, Constance. Ah, dear, when I was at Strathlands the tradesmen were much more prompt in waiting upon me!"

That night as she was being driven home, Constance did ask herself a trifle wearily,—

"Is my life to be worn away amidst this jar and fret?"

Soon after this, Reginald and his bride came home, and Clyst (being unanimously possessed by the spirit of the Vicar of Bray) made them very welcome with evergreen arches and sentences expressive of good feeling in red and white camelias. Mrs Reginald dressed for the occasion capitally, and bowed her head with royal impartiality to the right and left as they drove through the village.

"I saw the 'step' peeping behind the curtains as we passed; didn't you, Reggie? And my! didn't she look as if she could have eaten me!"

"Let her alone; she has a nasty tongue, and if she can, she'll set people against you," Reginald said curtly.

"I'm not afraid of her, nor of anyone else, as far as that goes. I've got a tongue too."

"I should advise you not to use it in the way of being nasty."

"Miss Fielding gave me a nice friendly smile as we passed. Do you know, Reggie, I like that girl; I shall take her up."

"If she will be friendly with you, I shall be very glad."

"Oh, I always know how to make myself agreeable," Mrs Reginald Vaughan said, with a vivid recollection of the triumphs and successes of her barmaid days.

CHAPTER XXXIII.

WHISPERED WORDS CAN POISON TRUTH.

It was the saddest day Mrs Arminger had known since competency had been her portion, and her children had grown up, this one on which Donald Vaughan took his wife away, in order, as he expressed it, that "they might fight the battle of life together."

For though Mrs Arminger did not exactly distrust her nephew, she did to a certain extent doubt his being possessed of either the will or the ability to do much fighting on the dull battle-field of every-day life. And she did fear pitifully that Maude her daughter would be over-weighted in the race which she would be compelled to run.

Donald had so far got over his chagrin at being un-mentioned in Lady Timerton's letter that he had agreed to go to Lady Timerton's house while they were looking about for a place with a suitable studio, "a studio that would be conducive to Maude's successful work," he explained. Now in this arrangement Mrs Arminger foresaw much that would be trying and exasperating, for Donald would be sure to detect indifference to his comfort and wishes in the demeanour of all who came in contact, and even the cat of the house would have to deport her-self, if she would avoid offending the rather sensitive Mr Vaughan.

The two brothers had not met since Reginald's mar-riage, and of this fact Mrs Reginald Vaughan made a great deal of noisy empty fun, pretending to everyone to whom she spoke on the subject that Reggie's brother jumped over hedges and ditches in the roads to avoid her, and slunk up back-ways into obscure purlieus when they met in the village.

The Timertons were not back yet. They were staying on at Malta in order to give the weight of their presence to the crushing force with which Lady Charldale was putting down the presumptuousness of Miss Nita and her adherents. But though they were not at home, Timerton House was perfectly ordered for their use and service, and Donald Vaughan might have been happy had he pleased.

But it did not please him to be so. Having scrupu-lously avoided letting any of his old friends and associates know of his sojourn in town, he was now deeply grieved at none of them seeking him. And his deep aggrieve-ment was all the more manifest because he strove to veil it under the garb of perfect satisfaction.

"I'm really delighted that we are able to be quiet; social interruptions would have been a great nuisance just now," he would say, as he sat down to dinner with

Maude opposite to him in solemn state. And then he would go on to inquire: "Any callers while I have been out to-day, Maude dear?"

"Only Don. So far as I know we haven't any other friends in town," Maude would say with unaffected resignation to their absence.

"You're about right there. We've very few friends left in town or anywhere else as far as I can see. Don is engaged on something of importance to himself, I suppose?"

"He didn't say so."

"Oh! I only presumed that he was, as he doesn't seem to be bestirring himself about anything for me. Your poor mother! She has such a pitiably exaggerated idea of Don's influence; all I can say is, if it's within his scope to do for me all she implies he can do, he ought to be ashamed of himself for leaving it undone."

"I am sure Don isn't forgetful of your interests; he was only saying this morning that he thought if Timerton exerted himself you might get the secretaryship of a club," Maude said hopefully.

"And Timerton doesn't care to exert himself, that's the long and the short of it. At the same time, considering Don is your brother, and Timerton only your brother-in-law, I don't see why Don is to expect Timerton to take all the trouble."

"He only said he thought Timerton was more likely to be able to assist you than he was," Maude said, apologetically.

"If he ever uses that word 'assist' again, I shall decline his interference in my concerns. It's a little too much when Don Arminger proffers his assistance to me! He ought to bear the cause of my downfall in mind, and not offer me uncalled-for insults about it."

"Donald," Maude said, her sweet, noble, generous spirit driven into revolt at last, "if I am the cause of your downfall, my brother will take care that, should my own powers fail, I shall still never be a burden to you."

"It's cruel on your part to insinuate that I've ever

regarded you as one," Donald whined complainingly, "and you've no right to expect your brother to maintain you and the children you may have. It's our duty to do that, not his, and I won't shirk my part of it."

But though he said this spiritedly enough, and made his wife miserable by the statements he made relative to the lowly nature of the work he was prepared to undertake, he made no efforts to get a situation for himself, contenting himself with abusing Don and Lord Timerton for what he called "the laxity they displayed in his interests."

Maude during the two past seasons had been making a good name for herself as a cattle painter, and the prices her pictures commanded were remunerative to a degree she had never in her real artistic humility dared to dream of. Accordingly she was anxious to settle in a house of her own in which the conditions should be favourable to her work.

She did not want either a perfectly appointed or a unique residence. The conditions she asked for were good drainage, good air, moderately good-sized rooms, and a good light. With these she would be happy and content, and under these she felt she could do good work pleasantly.

But Donald, her husband, had "ideas," and these "ideas," as he had not the means of gratifying them himself, he thought it was her bounden duty to exert herself to fulfil.

"Your brother can't possibly want that house of his in Bedford Park; if he had an ounce of that pure fraternal feeling your poor mother is always ascribing to him, he would offer you the use of it till we light upon something suitable," he would say.

"Then we should have to turn out when he married," Maude would reply. "No; I'd rather go straight into a home of my own where I shall feel settled."

Then she went on to describe to him a house which she had seen at Hampstead, a house that was almost on the breezy health-giving heath.

And Donald was pleased to be pleased with her description of it. So pleased indeed that he went to see it, liked it better than he had anticipated, and took it on the spot.

While this phase of intense satisfaction with the house reigned, he made a point of speaking of it as if he had been the discoverer and selector of it. That he should do this did not disturb Maude in the least. She liked her pretty, airy, commodious house, and set about furnishing it with funds provided by herself with the heartiest grace and graciousness.

Meantime the Timertons came home, and with them the Charldales. Between them the two countesses had utterly extinguished anything like ill-natured reports about Lord Charldale in Malta. With two such women quietly fighting his battles, he soon came to be considered quite a worthy and justifiable "cause."

His gratitude to his wife for the course she had pursued with regard to his troubles was really deep and sincere. And now that he was free from the debasing thrall he had been under to the servant who had pandered to his master's weakness till that weakness and the servant had become Lord Charldale's masters, the young husband was thankful to his wife for having so summarily dismissed Morris.

There was no doubt about it, Elinor managed him admirably; and she quite agreed with Don Arminger and Lord Charldale himself in thinking his marriage with her the wisest act of his life.

Only at times old Lady Timerton had doubts as to whether there might not be "a worm i' the bud" in Don's case. It seemed incredible to her that he should be as patiently resigned to the loss of her daughter as he appeared to be. So she bestowed a fair portion of superfluous pity upon him, and told Elinor that she was "heedlessly endangering Don's peace of mind by seeing so much of him."

"I'm afraid I can't lay the flattering unction to my soul that he has ever given one really tender thought to me in the whole course of his life, mamma," Lady Charldale says truthfully. "He has always been more or less in love with Miss Fielding—generally more—and now he has gone down to Clyst to tell her so, I suppose."

Lady Charldale's conjecture was a correct one. Don had gone down to Clyst to upset Constance's hardly-sustained life of industry and contentment, and to take her into the bustle and raree-show which agitate mankind below, away from the monotonous peacefulness of Woodside.

He reached his mother's house in Clyst on a bright star-lighted winter's night, and during dinner, without any sentimental reticence, he made his mother acquainted with the reason of his being there.

"I've come down to ask Constance when she will marry me. Trixy wants to have us at Christmas, so we haven't much time to lose."

"My dear boy, are you not taking her acceptance a little too much for granted ?"

With all her heart she hoped, with all her faith she believed, that Constance would soon say, "I will" to Don, but though his mother had Don's happiness very greatly at heart, she had Constance's dignity there also, and she did not like to hear anything that sounded like an easy concession from the young lady being taken for granted.

"I only take this much for granted : Constance is too distinctly noble a woman to let a man see that she likes him well enough to marry him if all were clear and free between them. Now she has done this, and all is clear and free between us, and when I ask her to be my wife there will be no shilly-shallying on her part, she will say 'yes' at once, and then we can settle the time."

"The last time you saw her you were engaged to Lady Elinor, remember."

"My dear mother, neither Constance nor I are likely to forget that fact,—it made us very unhappy during my last visit."

"I suppose you will see her to-morrow, dear boy?"

"I shall see her to-night, dear mother; you and I will walk up there presently, and while you are overhauling any work she may have in hand, I shall ask her to be my wife."

"I'm a goose to go out in the cold night air," Mrs Arminger said gleefully, getting up to look for a bonnet and cloak with the activity of a girl, or of a mother who wanted to further her son's wishes and help him on to happiness.

Through the keen, bracing, wintry air, under the star-studded heavens, the mother and son presently stepped out buoyantly. But before they had cleared the Grange grounds this changeable climate destroyed their expectations of a pleasant, exhilarating walk.

The stars disappeared behind clouds, the fresh keen air became cutting and windy, there was a positive rasp in the way it eddied round corners, and caught one a slap in the face when one thought it was behind one.

By the time they reached the Dower House, where the widowed Mrs Vaughan dwelt, Mrs Arminger's cloak was wafted over her head, and ballooned out behind her. The cloudy darkness was increasing rapidly, and altogether it was bidding fair to be a foul night.

"Hadn't we better go back, Don?" she asked.

And one of Mrs Vaughan's maid-servants, standing at that far too universal dark entry which gives access to the backs of so many houses, heard the question, recognised the questioned by his name, and failed to distinguish the questioner.

"Are you afraid? No. Surely not afraid with me," her son said to Mrs Arminger affectionately, and the moral soul of the listening maid-servant was outraged, yet contradictorily enough it craved for more.

"Do let me go back, dear Don. How weak I was to let you delude me out on a night like this," Mrs Arminger laughed half complainingly, half in amusement, and then Don turned, put his arm over the ballooning-cloak round her waist, and said he would take

her safely back, he would not have the sin of keeping her
out against her will on his conscience.

The listening maid-servant was, as it happened, that
useful person one frequently finds in a small establishment who combines the offices of house and parlour
maid, and attendant on her mistress in herself. So this
night when Mrs Vaughan got herself away to her own
chamber, feeling dull and dispirited by reason of not
having heard one single ill-natured rumour regarding her
successor, Mrs Reginald, during the day, her waiting-
woman met her with a countenance that promised something succulent in the way of a morsel of gossip.

"I'm all of a tremble," the girl began, as with rather
too demonstrative a show of nervous agitation she pulled
down her mistress's sparse locks, thereby hurting her
mistress's time-honoured head.

"Don't be awkward! you're pulling my hair. What
is it, Jane? for I see you're dying to tell me something."

"I shouldn't think of mentioning anything unless you
asked me, ma'am," Jane said humbly, for her mistress's
mood was slippery as ice, and Jane had to venture
warily upon it.

"Nonsense," Mrs Vaughan said more good-temperedly,
in dread of the succulent morsel of gossip vanishing
from her hungry gaze. "I wish you to confide in me;
if you have heard anything that distresses you, it is my
duty to get you to confide it to me while you live under
my roof."

"It isn't so much anything that distresses me, ma'am;
leastways I've no call to be distressed about it, any more
than through feeling for you."

"I suppose Mrs Reginald has been doing something
ridiculous or extraordinary again," Mrs Vaughan cried.
"Ah, Jane! I'm quite prepared for the worst I can
hear about Mrs Reginald, I'm sorry to say; nothing bad
about her would surprise me for a moment, for what do
I know about her? What does any one in Clyst know
about her? Depend upon it, Jane, where there is secrecy
there is sin."

"It ain't Mrs Reginald this time," Jane said, with an air that seemed to promise direful things anent Mrs Reginald at no distant date. "It is Mr Arminger as has been courting Miss Constance all these years. But there, I hardly like to tell you, ma'am, you've got trials enough a'ready."

"Much as I abhor scandal, I will bring myself to listen to it this once, for Miss Fielding's sake," Mrs Vaughan said firmly.

Then a good dish of gossip was served up to her, as she settled herself more comfortably in the chair before the cheerful fire, and her maid brushed away at her hair.

"He had his arm that tight round her waist that I thought I should have shrook," Jane said in an outburst of offended purity, "and he told her not to be afraid with him, and called her 'dear,' and said he'd like to see her safely home; and that's your Mr Arminger, ma'am, who's thought so much of here by Miss Constance and others, and whose ma doesn't think the ground he treads on good enough for him!"

"It grieves me to hear all this," Mrs Vaughan said self-pityingly.

Inwardly she was rejoicing, for Don's final downfall in her niece's estimation would probably mean her (Mrs Vaughan's) re-establishment at Woodside, and though she might never hope to reign absolutely at Woodside again, as she had done of yore in the days of Constance's childhood, still the prospect of a home there in a prominent position was a pleasant one to her.

The next morning Mrs Vaughan got up early. It was an effort for her to do this; therefore she thought the doing it partook somehow or other of the nature of a religious sacrifice, and sanctified all that might otherwise have been malicious in her intention and action. She got up early and walked to Woodside, catching Constance in her brightest morning mood.

"Come out with me to the conservatories, aunt," she said. "I'm having them all re-arranged for my party for the bride."

"Do you mean to tell me, Constance, that you have asked me to meet that woman?"

"Which one? I've asked you to meet several."

"The one I mean is Reginald's wife."

"Certainly I have. You might reasonably have been vexed, dear aunt, if I had left you out."

"I suppose I may as well come; but we are living in dreadful days," Mrs Vaughan said vehemently.

And then she detailed Don's iniquities, as observed and reported by Jane last night.

CHAPTER XXXIV.

LAND IN SIGHT.

THE tale that Jane had told to her mistress finally got itself repeated by that mistress to Constance, with many a suggestion, innuendo, and almost imperceptible addition, and Constance listened to it so patiently that Mrs Vaughan inwardly congratulated herself on her niece's eyes being "fully opened at last."

When Constance spoke it was to say,—

"Jane saw Mr Arminger so distinctly that it seems rather strange that she should have been unable to distinguish his companion."

"Jane couldn't exactly distinguish her, but she saw enough to satisfy herself that the person looked like a superior shop-girl," Mrs Vaughan said.

Now, it may be remembered that in Jane's narrative there had been no mention of anything of this kind.

"I've seen several hundred shop-girls in my life in 'superior' London shops, but as they were all widely dissimilar the one from the other, I confess I should have some difficulty in recognising any girl in the dark as belonging to the genus. Jane seems to have great powers of observation, aunt. Don't you think it a great improvement making that window out from the drawing room into the conservatory?"

"It's pretty, certainly it's pretty, but you're spending a great deal of money on the place, Constance," Mrs Vaughan assented.

Then she determined that her subject, her dark grievance against Don Arminger, should not escape her without having a little more worrying.

"After what I have told you, I suppose you will not receive Mr Arminger again, Constance ?"

"Yes, I shall."

"My dear child, that will be very undignified."

"Then I shall be undignified."

"It will really look as if you took a lax view of moral obligations."

"I shall be sorry for that, for I certainly do not take a lax view of them."

"Then with consistency you can't receive Mr Arminger here, as he disregards them."

"I don't know that he does disregard them yet."

"I'm not accustomed to have my word doubted, Constance."

"It's not your word, it's Jane's word, and though I don't doubt its truthful intention, I do distrust its accuracy."

"Ah, you're bent on ganging your own gait like the rest of the young people, without let or hindrance from those who are older and wiser than you."

"Jane may be older, but she certainly is not wiser. Now come and look, I've had the tea-room arranged for my party night."

"You will not ask the county people to meet Mrs Reginald ?"

"Whom else should I ask than my own friends ? "

"My dear Constance, I see nothing but ruin before you, now you have embraced these radical notions."

"Now, aunt, be logical, if I omitted my own class from the invitation-list, and went in for inviting business and tradespeople to meet Reginald and his wife, you might call me a radical."

"You'll rue the day you make yourself into a cork

jacket to float that woman into society," Mrs Vaughan wound up angrily, for her heart was still sore at the thought of that ripped-off work which had erst-while decorated the drawing-room at Strathlands. However, though she said this, Mrs Vaughan surveyed all her niece's preparations for what was to be a great social event in Clyst, and heard of novelties that were to be created for the supper with keen interest. Having done this, she found that Constance would not give her so much as a conversational interstice into which she could insert the thin edge of the wedge of scandal she had raised against Don Arminger.

Now, when her aunt was gone, Constance did permit her thoughts to linger about the subject of Jane's communication a little. That Don should be in Clyst, and make no sign of his presence to her, seemed altogether so strange and incomprehensible a thing that she could not keep herself from wondering about it. Over and over again she told herself that it hadn't been Don at all. But she found no comfort in this expression of unbelief, for she could not verify it. Then she strove to persuade herself that it must have been one of his sisters. But reason promptly upset this hope, for it told that neither Maude nor Lady Timerton would have left her in ignorance of their being at home again, up to this hour of the day, after their arrival.

"This hour" was only the noontide one. Still, it seemed late in the day for her not to have heard of Don's return from Don himself.

"I'll go on just as if I didn't think he was so near," the girl resolved, and she went about seeing to the draping of some cretonne on the walls of a little room, that was to be transformed into a tent-like boudoir on the night of her party ; and as she was getting really interested in the task of arrangement, Mr Arminger was announced.

He came towards her so happily and confidently that even the memory of Jane's report fled from her mind on the instant, and the delight of seeing him was so enhanced and intensified by his long absence that she forgave him on the spot for having stayed away so long.

"My mother thought of coming with me, but the cold vanquishes her in the morning. She freezes for the day unless she sits down in her own cosy nook by the fire directly after breakfast," he explained to Constance; but he never thought of adding that his mother had started for Woodside. The present was quite enough for him—the present, and the bright future it promised. He would not go back one hour into the past.

"Come down and let me look at you," he said, for she was still standing on a high pair of steps festooning the wall draperies according to her own idea.

She gave him her hand, and jumped down willingly, happily. And he kept her hand, and drew her nearer to him, and kissed her.

"After all we've settled it very quickly and sensibly, haven't we?" he asked, and Constance answered,—

"Yes, and all the hard lesson was learnt for nothing."

"No, not for nothing; you would not be the prize you are now, if you hadn't revealed yourself to me as you did when you ordered me to learn that lesson."

"Now, Don, confess that the order was a very necessary one? Lady Elinor's chains were around you, and you persisted in not feeling them now and then. Did you slip into your engagement with her as easily as you have into this with me?"

"I don't know. I only know that Lady Charldale is one of the nicest and best women that ever breathed; you'll never be jealous of my love and respect for her, for I shall proclaim it openly everywhere."

"Trix says she worked wonders with her husband."

"So she has, and that without any offensive display of patience or forbearance. She has put him on his mettle, and taken it for granted that he feels as a man ought to feel about things."

"She and I having reversed our experiences, exactly as we have done, will never fall into the feminine pitfall of sympathising with one another; but for all that we shall be good friends, though I did express a hope that she might be taken away to savage countries when I said good-bye to her at Trixy's wedding."

"She was quite right about that house at Bedford Park; nevertheless I mean you to live there a good many months in the year, Connie."

" You won't give up Woodside altogether, will you ?" she asked a little anxiously.

"You'd give me up if I suggested doing it ?"

" No, I wouldn't; you would find that I carried out my own theories of subordinating place to people, if you tried me."

"I'll never try you, so help me Heaven!" he said fervently, and at the moment a reminiscence of Jane's scandal against him flashed into Constance's mind, and she felt all the happy scorn against the libeller that is born of perfect trust in the libelled.

"Shall I come with you, and tell mother at once ?" Constance asked him presently, "we're dreadfully in the way here, for somehow or other I'd rather be talking to you than putting up *portières*, and I know mother has been waiting to hear this for several months; so, shall we go and tell her?"

He assented, and they walked off together to the Grange through the village street. And they were much looked at and commented upon, for Jane had visited several cottages and the two village shops this morning, and her tale had grown several inches each time she repeated it.

By the time they reached the Grange the rumour of the audacious, iniquitous publicity of their progress had reached the ears of Mrs Reginald Vaughan. For Jane's sister was scullery-maid at Strathlands, and the system of communication between the two houses was unceasing, even if of necessity a little imperfect. The rumour reached the ears of Mrs Reginald Vaughan, and she was delighted. For Mrs Fielding was (to use Mrs Reginald's own phrase) "the only one who had the pluck to take her up." And Mrs Reginald had in her the elementary flavour of crude gratitude.

"I say, Reggie," she said, stopping her ponies to speak to him as she met him at the lodge-gates; "they're saying unkind things about that awfully nice Miss Fielding, so I'm just going up to show her I stand by her whatever other folks do."

"Unkind things of Constance!" He could not help it. For the moment he was so true to the family fealty to Constance, that he felt in a rage with his wife for presuming to tell him that "unkind things" were being said about her.

"Yes, about Miss Fielding," Mrs Reginald went on eagerly. "You see, it isn't only we that gets stones thrown at her. They say Miss Fielding is running after Mr Don Arminger, walking and talking with him just as if they quite understood each other. And last night he was out in the street with his arm round another young woman's waist. going on with her, and disgracing himself, as far as Miss Fielding is concerned."

"Don's beastly successful, but he was never a sneak or a cad, and he'd be both if he tried to humbug Constance now," Reginald said scornfully. "Just be guided by me, Adelaide. Accept Miss Fielding's invitation, but let Miss Fielding's affairs alone. She's trying to do you a good turn; don't you render her efforts null and void by your own stupidity."

But Mrs Reginald was in no mood to be guided by her husband this day. Indeed, to tell the truth, she rarely was in one now, for she had learnt that she had but to stand out for her own way in order to get it.

She cast a brief exultant glance at Mrs Vaughan's decorously curtained windows as she passed them. For she well understood that by this time the "step," as she always insisted on calling the widow, was girding in her narrow soul against the honour shortly to be done to Mrs Reginald by Miss Fielding of Woodside.

"Nasty old spiteful thing!" the bride said as she took her ready ponies by, they were "ready," therefore very easy to drive, "it's her mean, low ways that have taught her servants to be spies on her own niece's lover; if I'm not able to crow over her before I've done with her, my name's not Adelaide Vaughan."

Out of evil sometimes comes good. Mrs Reginald was so bent on proving Jane's tale a malicious one, that she set Jane's sister (her own scullery-maid) to work to root out contrary evidence and confute it. She had no special object in doing this, unless dislike to Mrs Vaughan may be accepted as one. But all the same she worked with a will in all sorts of obscure directions to prove the scandal unfounded before even Don Arminger had heard of it.

Meantime the trio at the Grange had been having a very happy time of it. Constance had insisted on dragging Mrs Arminger out for a walk in the snow, in order that they might together look over that little cottage garden-gate through which Don had been carried after his adventure with the bull.

"And I followed, howling, if you remember," she said, "and the poor Vaughans came and picked me up, and made decorous moan over me, not because I had been nearly killed, but because I had offered to love Don all my life."

"And I saw this end then, as I put you away, and pretended I did not wish you to love my boy," Mrs Arminger said.

"Ah! but, mother, your pretence never deceived me. Now all is right and fair, and my engagement to Don shall be given out the night of my party for Mrs Reginald, the bride."

CHAPTER XXXV.

MRS REGINALD SCORES ONE.

CONSTANCE FIELDING'S determination to show fitting social consideration and honour to Reginald Vaughan's wife was conceived in a generous spirit of justice, and carried out with a brave disregard of the littlenesses of time-serving opinion.

Constance would not hold the woman guilty of a high society misdemeanour because she had married the man when he came into power, to whom she had been engaged while he was in poverty. Nor would Miss Fielding regard Mrs Reginald as despicable, because the latter lived in the house that was legally her husband's, surrounded by all that appertained to the glory of the race that had long reigned at Strathlands.

There was wrong in her so reigning there unquestionably, but the wrong had not been wrought by Mrs Reginald. She had not forced herself, but had been forced by her dead father-in-law's will, and her living husband's wish, into the position. That she did not adorn it was not her fault, but her misfortune.

"Still, Connie, don't you think it a little rash to force her into contact with people who side vehemently with Donald, simply because they look upon Reginald as a cuckoo?" even Mrs Arminger (who was very tolerant) asked.

"It may be rash, but I know it's right; their children will be true Vaughans, received and treated as such, and what will those children be if they grow up with the knowledge that their mother has been scouted, or at least lightly looked upon by people who are glad to know them because their father is Vaughan of Strathlands? Why, they would be the worst kind of snobs! They would either despise or tolerate their mother! Their mother! think of that."

"My dear Con, you are contemplating and warring against a contingency that may never occur," Mrs Arminger hinted.

"But as it may occur, I'll provide against it as far as in me lies," Constance said; "it's a horribly cruel and unjust thing that Donald Vaughan should be cut out of Strathlands, but Mrs Reginald Vaughan has had nothing to do with the cruel injustice of it. She is Reggie's wife, and she ought to have her chance just the same as all the wives of the bygone Vaughans have had."

"My poor sister lived a life of barren honour at Strathlands, I fear, from all I've heard and seen; especially after circumstances brought me here," Mrs Arminger said, and the blood mounted to Constance's forehead at the remembrance of all the insults she had heard poured out upon the Armingers by old Mr Vaughan.

Woodside was a good place to hold high festival in Spacious, well-appointed, and with abundance of well-trained servants in it, there was no lack of either room, accommodation, or good attendance. On the night of Constance's party for the bride it was looking its best, for it was wreathed with hot-house flowers, flooded with light, and brilliant with beautifully-dressed women.

Conspicuous among these was Mrs Reginald Vaughan. Her husband had suffered many a qualm and doubt as to the way in which she would pass through the ordeal of her first introduction to the county set. He had fumed in silence for several days, and at length he began to fidget openly.

"Don't dress yourself loudly," he said to her on the night of the party, when she rose from the table at which they had just dined in speechless gloom.

"I know what to put on, and how to put it on as well as any woman does," she replied sharply. And, indeed, she had some cause for feeling annoyed at the implied doubt of her taste; for in the matter of apparel Mrs Reginald invariably evinced discernment.

When she came down by-and-by ready to start, her husband was gratified to see that she looked excellently well. Her dress of opal-tinted plush was well made, and well put on, and her throatlet, earrings, and bracelets of diamonds and opals, brightened her up judiciously without being too flashing or brilliant.

She would not ask him how she looked, but she saw that her appearance pleased him, and she hoped that he was going to let well alone, and not disturb her by any further hints as to what she should do or leave undone this night. But as they drove along he disappointed her by saying,—

"If you let yourself be perfectly easy and natural you'll do splendidly to-night, Adelaide. Don't make any advances to any of the women who will be there; but if they seem cordially disposed towards you just meet them half-way."

"One would think to hear you talk, Reggie, that I had been brought up among Hottentots or heathens!" she exclaimed resentfully.

"I only want to make things as pleasant as possible for you," he said apologetically; but in his heart he thought the educational influence of the "Welsh Harp" and the Gower Street boarding-house an infinitely worse one than that of either order of mankind which she had mentioned.

"I won't put on any 'side' to them if they don't begin to do it to me," she said complacently; and he fell into the futile error of imploring her not to indulge in slang.

"Why, the highest in the land use it, Reggie."

"How do you know that?"

"Because I've heard that they do from scores of young fellows. There was a young earl used to come out skating to Hendon that I've chaffed with dozens of times, and he used to say I was out of it altogether, compared to a Lady Victoria somebody he knew."

"Well, you see, you're not Lady Victoria somebody," Reginald said testily, for these barmaid reminiscences galled him horribly. Months ago, while he was boarding in her house, and not looking forward to ever boarding in a better one, they had not galled him at all. But times were changed with Reginald, and he felt disgusted with his wife because she had not changed with them.

"Now be careful, Adelaide, be easy and natural, but don't be flippant, or you'll do for yourself," was his final injunction as his wife, a little incited by the novelty of the situation, and a little bewildered by his manifold directions, was about to step out of the carriage.

His tone set her quick temper aflame. Looking up indignantly, she was about to remonstrate with him for his ill-timed warning, when her foot caught in the lace festoon, which was the chief glory of the right side of her dress. Silently but heavily she fell prone on her face on the sleet-saddened ground, and when she got up she was very grimy and a little bruised, and Reginald was exceedingly angry with her.

"What in the world did you do that for?" he asked savagely; and Adelaide could not help remembering that if she had fallen headlong out of a cab six months ago, Reginald would have overflowed with sympathy, and would have put her in a state of grateful confusion by his offers of assistance.

"Perhaps I did it to please myself and displease you, for a change," she said defiantly; and the servants who were gathered around the door were able to report that Mr and Mrs Reginald Vaughan were quarrelling like cat and dog, as they entered the house.

It was a good representative social gathering this, which Miss Fielding had called together, in order to do kindly womanly honour to the woman who was Reginald Vaughan's wife. Everyone who could lay claim to be in the county set in the region round had been invited, and the majority had accepted the invitation and come gladly, more especially those who had sons among them; for Constance was not yet publicly known to be engaged, and Woodside had its charms even for her wealthier neighbours.

The neighbouring clergy and their wives and families had assembled in great force, and it was really curious to see how some of the former, who in their respective pulpits were quite eloquent on the subject of humility, meekness, and true Christian charity, held aloof from and ignored Reginald and his wife, until they saw which way the wind blew from titled quarters. Indeed, Mrs Reginald fell into the error of mistaking the arrogant wife of a pluralist broad-church rector for a duchess who was reported to be there, and mentioned her suspicion to a gentle, gracious-mannered little old lady by whom she (Mrs Reginald) was sitting.

When this same gentle and gracious little elderly dame turned out to be the duchess in question, Reginald's irritation knew no bounds, and he told his wife that he should always look upon her stupidity as the cause of his not gaining admission to the dukery over which that duchess reigned.

As for Constance, she did her hospitable part in such a high-spirited way, that her guests soon came to feel that if slights were to be offered to Mrs Reginald Vaughan, another place than Woodside must be chosen as the scene of the offering. And so, on the whole, the early part of the evening wore away pleasantly enough for Mrs Reginald, though her conversational efforts did not meet with any great success.

" Why do you look perpetually as if you were racking your brains for ' something to say next,' when any one speaks to you ? " her husband took an opportunity of whispering to her once.

" I declare, if you watch me, I won't speak again : and if any one looks surprised, I'll tell them that you're afraid if I open my mouth I shall disgrace myself," she replied angrily. " Goodness me ! if good society is made up of the likes of you, I shall never want to be in it."

After this Reginald ceased to worry his wife with hints, suggestions, or directions. But she had been shaken by her fall, and made nervous by his comments, and she was a novice in the art of self-control. Accordingly, she looked what she felt—nervous, cross, and unhappy. The music and singing, which was as distinctly bearable as amateur music and singing generally is, failed to please or attract her. The topics of the coterie in which she found herself were sealed books to her, and she was tenaciously alive to every glance or gesture that might be construed into a slight to her.

But still terribly out of gear as the poor woman was

through her husband's injudicious attempts to improve her, she was full of gratitude to Miss Fielding and Don Arminger, who treated her, she keenly observed, precisely as he did any other lady in the room. She knew that there were many present who believed the scandal respecting him, which had been promulgated by Mrs Vaughan's thick-brained, sharp-tongued maid Jane. And Mrs Reginald, having fully informed herself on that point, longed for an opportunity of refuting that scandal and proclaiming everyone wrong but Don Arminger.

The announcement of the engagement between their "charming hostess and our old friend Mr Don Arminger," was made by Mr Dalzel, the rector, at supper, and this announcement was so rapturously received by everyone (excepting the widowed Mrs Vaughan), that Adelaide found some difficulty in believing the evidence of her own ears, which during the evening had overheard many a caustic remark to Don's disadvantage.

In fact, the raptures at this happy result were so great that Mrs Reginald was disappointed for the time of clearing Don in the triumphant and public way in which she had proposed to herself to do it.

But when Miss Fielding's other guests were beginning to disperse, cordial Constance came up to Mrs Reginald, and begged her to stay on a little later.

"I look upon Reginald and you as belonging to the family, and you must show that you feel you do so by staying on cosily with my aunt, and Mrs Arminger, and Don, and the Dalzels, just to talk the party over, and agree as to how it has gone off," Constance said, and Mrs Reginald acceded to the proposition gratefully, and wondered whether the widowed Mrs Vaughan would speak to her when they were thrust into such close contact.

So when the others had gone these few got themselves into a pretty little room, where a little, light, private supper had been prepared for them; and over it Constance tried to inaugurate the reign of family good-feeling and cordiality.

But her aunt would not second or aid her in any way. Indeed, old Mrs Vaughan was in one of the most malignant moods that she had ever allowed to overcome her. It was as the root of bitterness to her to see her niece—her own niece Constance—going out of her way to do kindness and honour to that woman who had married Reginald, and been the cause of the work of years being ripped off the drawing-room chairs at Strathlands. And further, it was a stinging blow to her that Constance should be openly engaged to Don Arminger after she (Mrs Vaughan) had secretly denounced him as unworthy.

Accordingly her mood was as full of acidity and spite as it could be within the decent observance of social amenities. But by-and-by it burst through the bonds both of civility and prudence, and goaded by some laughing allusion made by Constance to Don's future mastership at Woodside, Mrs Vaughan selected a sudden lull in which to snap out,—

"I suppose, now that you are properly engaged, Mr Arminger, you will leave off roaming about Clyst streets at night with young women you're ashamed to be seen speaking to in open day?"

He regarded her in sorrow and amazement for a few moments, thinking that the unwonted excitement of the evening had been too much for the poor old lady's venerable but weak head.

Then he said quietly,—

"I never roamed in Clyst streets or any other street at night with a young woman yet; but I shall hope to do so often now." And as he spoke he took Constance's hand with a quiet air of happy, sure proprietorship, that added oil to the flame of Mrs Vaughan's wrath.

"Constance shall have fair warning whether she chooses to take it or not," she cried, quivering with nervous fury. "You can't deny it, for my Jane has sworn solemnly on the Bible that she saw you with your arm round a young woman's waist, late at night, opposite my side-door, the day you came down from London. Jane is a pious girl.

and knows the nature of an oath; you can't deny her evidence."

There was a pause, and painful confusion for a few moments. The charge was so unexpected, so unseemly, so ridiculous, and at the same time so serious, that for the life of him Don could not recall at the instant what he really had done on the night of his return from London. The only thing he felt certain of was that he had not put his arm round a young woman's waist in Clyst streets in the dark.

"You are making some dangerous, wretched mistake, Mrs Vaughan," his mother said presently.

She knew that she could answer for her son as she could for herself, and all her pure soul was in revolt at the idea of the imputation of a piece of coarse, low, idle gallantry being cast upon him.

"No, it's only a stupid mistake after all, a stupid mistake made by some one who wants to damage Mr Don," Mrs Reginald said eagerly, and while her husband stared at her in angry amazement at her thus daring to take part in the fray, she went on dauntlessly, supported now by a feeling of gratitude to both Constance and Don. "It's rather a compliment to you, Mrs Arminger, that they should say such things. You're so young looking in figure, and light in your way of stepping, that it's easy enough to take you for a young woman in the day, let alone in the dark; but before Jane went to work so piously to help her mistress to prove that you were not worthy of Miss Fielding, she might have taken the trouble to find out that it was his mother out with Mr Don that night."

The unexpected partisan, and her simple, truthful elucidation of the mystery, were greeted with ringing rejoinders of approbation from all present, with the exception of old Mrs Vaughan. The latter could not bring herself all at once to feel or even to simulate pleasure or satisfaction in the discovery of the fact that Don was not a villain.

If you have a proper regard for Constance, instead

of crowing over me or laughing at me, you'll feel humbly glad and grateful that I have her interests and happiness so truly at heart," she said to Don, and he tried to convince her that he believed she had meant it all for the best, and thanked her for her zealous watchfulness over Constance's weal.

"The very way you say all that shows me that you look upon me as an interfering old woman. Well, I sha'n't be here very long to trouble any of you. When an old woman like me is turned out of her natural home, and put into a place that never can be like a home to her, what with the draughts and passers-by staring in at her windows, she can't look for or hope for length of days."

"Dear aunt, you shall ask the whole party of us to dinner with you on the first anniversary of my wedding-day, and you shall be as happy as a queen," Constance said soothingly.

But Mrs Vaughan could not come round for a long time, and her sense of defeat was bitterly augmented by the fact of her having been worsted by Mrs Reginald.

On their way home that night Reginald was much more affable.

"You scored one by bowling out that wretched old woman's scandal, Adelaide," he said graciously. "Indeed, on the whole, I think you've done capitally to-night. Some of those brutes were inclined to be stiff-necked at first, but they soon followed the best lead. Now it only remains for us to see if they invite us."

"I don't care whether they do or not ; I don't care to know any of them but Miss Fielding and Mrs Arminger," Adelaide said.

"But I do care—care very much indeed," her husband replied sternly. "I don't want Donald to be able to go on sneering at my inability to take my proper place as owner of Strathlands. What I was going to say when you interrupted me was this : when once those people have given me a chance by inviting us, I'll outdo them all in my entertainments. I'll give better dinners and better balls, and better lunches and better tennis-parties than any of them. If they think I don't know how to do things quite as well as my elder brother, they shall soon find their mistake."

"Don't you be a silly spendthrift, Reggie," she said, and he replied,—

"Don't you be a niggardly fool, Adelaide; leave me to take care of myself."

CHAPTER XXXVI.

NEW PEOPLE AT STRATHLANDS.

In pursuance of his avowed intention of doing his duty manfully, Donald Vaughan, after a few months' idleness, consented to accept the secretaryship of a club, which situation Lord Timerton carried for him at the point of the sword, it might almost be said.

It was a good situation, the salary being four hundred a-year, and many privileges appertaining to it. But Donald took it, and performed his duties as if he felt he was setting the seal to his own humiliation. Dozens of better men had fought for, and sighed for it; but Lord Timerton's influence had been great, and had been exercised unsparingly, and now this was the end! Donald had got the situation, and found its duties to be the reverse of either onerous or unpleasant, and he was profoundly discontented with it.

Meantime the house out near the edge of the breezy Hampstead Heath had grown to be one of the prettiest and most charming homes in that region, even where charming and pretty homes abound. Maude, its mistress, found time to be frequently touching it up and beautifying it, and this without stealing a minute of time she felt she ought to give to her profession. Her house grew very dear to her, as a house is apt to grow to one who decorates doors and dados, and even shutters, and window-sills, and lintels, with her own brush and artistic fancies. She was very happy in it, in spite of that habit Donald had of seeing the murkiest side of everything, and of propping up a difficulty if it seemed to be fading away under her treatment.

There was no lack of funds in the establishment, and undoubtedly a generous stream of vile dross flowing into it does add considerably to the pleasant atmosphere of a house. Nor was there a prospect of any lack; for, as has been said, Maude was working hard, and making good prices for her pictures, and Donald had a safe and good salary.

But the house at Hampstead, charming as it was in the eyes of others, was not Strathlands. And Donald Vaughan could not forget Strathlands ; and the thought that his brother was reigning there unrighteously in his stead was like an aching wound to him.

He dwelt upon the idea that he was an ill-used and singularly unfortunate man until it assumed Brobdignagian proportions, and threatened to overwhelm him at times. He scented difficulties afar off, and saw slights and forgetfulnesses, and contemptuous overlookings of himself and his desserts where they did not exist. And whenever he felt one of these stings, he complained of the " inconveniences of the house at Hampstead," and reproached his father's memory for having left him in such sore and ignominious straits.

The alliance that existed between the Timertons, Charldales, and themselves he made a source of misery to himself, and to Maude when she had time to give attention to the subject. He would grow huffy as an idle, exacting, vain woman, if he found that Lady Timerton had not included them in the list of those invited to what he chose to consider the best dinner she had given during the week. And when he was huffy he would revile Trixy to her sister.

“When I think of the way Trixy was brought up, and now see the airs my lady the countess gives herself, I am amused,” he said once to Maude, who replied,—

“Donald, you really are ‘cranky,’ as Don says. Trixy never gave herself an air in her life; you mustn’t pick holes in her. You said the other day, when she asked us five days in the week, that she was treating us like poor relations. Now you’re angry that she didn’t ask us yesterday.”

“Oh no, not angry, don’t mistake me. I’m only amused, intensely amused. I wouldn’t have mentioned the matter to you if I had thought you were going to take it up so fiercely. As for Lady Charldale, I’ll not give her an opportunity of cutting me again.”

“Has she cut you once, Donald?”

“Distinctly. She was waiting outside the club for Charldale yesterday, and I passed out with a man she doesn’t know; she looked clear over my head, and I resolved that the next time I waited for her to bow I should deserve the snub she’d be ready to offer.”

“I don’t believe she saw you,” Maude said indignantly, “she was here half-an-hour ago, planning how we would all go down to Don’s wedding. Constance has invited the Charldales in such a charming note, you must know, and I will say that, dearly as I love Constance, I find Lady Charldale’s note of acceptance equally charming and good.”

“You don’t mean to tell me that you expect me to go down there again, Maude?”

“To Don’s wedding? Certainly I do!”

“Expect me to go down to see that insufferably low woman queening it in my place? I must say, Maude, you don’t bestow much thought or care on what I have to endure.”

“Throw off that resentful spirit, dear,” she said encouragingly; “you can, if you will, put away that idea that always seems to me to be fraught with injustice—that the eldest son is of more account than the second; be satisfied. Strathlands hasn’t passed out of your family. Your brother has it, and you are very well off; what more could either of us desire than we have—each other and a lovely home?"

"Why don't you go on and tell me to be grateful to Lady Timerton for acknowledging you as her sister, and to Lady Charldale for contemplating admitting us to the delights of social intercourse with her in an obscure country place like Clyst?" he asked.

"Because I wouldn't be so cynically silly on any account," she answered. "Lady Charldale has just been here to ask us to her big 'Royal personage' party next week. Can she show more consideration for us than this?"

"There you go—how unfair you are," he expostulated. "You begin by telling me that Lady Charldale simply came out here to plan how she could, with the greatest convenience to herself, go to your brother's wedding. When I have expressed myself—mildly enough—disgusted with her shallow selfish pretence of friendship, you suddenly tell me that she came on another and more polite mission. Really, Maude, it seems to me that you, in common with the rest of the world, take a delight in making sport of me."

"Oh, my poor darling," Maude sighed to herself, "if you could but take a kinder view of other people's motives, how much kinder you would be to me, and to yourself."

Day by day Donald's grievance against the existing order of things grew, until at last it came to this pass with him, that he actually regarded himself as injured, because his home was on Hampstead Heath, and his daily duties were in Pall Mall.

He fatigued himself as little as possible, chartering a hansom daily to take him to the scene of his congenial labours. But for all this expenditure of money, self-consideration, and prudence, he soon found his suburban home a daily difficulty as regarding reaching it.

"It was solely for your sake that I consented to come here at all; you seemed to have set your heart upon the place, and I'm not the man to thwart a woman in any reasonable desire; but, of course, now it adds considerably both to my fatigue and my expenses to be so far from the scene of my labours," he said to Maude, coming in upon her as she was striving to limn forth on canvas a beautiful recollection she had of the muscular crest of a young bull she had seen out Edgeware village way on the previous day.

"Let us give up the house, Donald," she said promptly.

"What nonsense you talk; just if a man could give up a house as easily as he can throw aside an old glove; besides, I've spent too much about the house to care to give it up lightly; if you don't value the painting you've lavished on all these doors, I do; I thought at the time you were doing them that you were very foolish to waste so much time on what we couldn't either turn to money account, or take away with us when we left; however, I said nothing; it's not my way to say anything; only now when I hear you so carelessly and thoughtlessly proposing that we should 'give up the house' I must speak."

"I only want to do what pleases you, what you think best," Maude said, and with all her sweetness there was mixed this much of strength, she would not permit herself to think her husband in the wrong.

It must be conceded though that old Mr Vaughan's perniciously cruel and ambitious will was not bearing good and kindly fruit in this, the direction of his eldest son.

Constance's wedding-day was not a cloudless one, either atmospherically or socially, for it rained a good deal, and the humble concourse of spectators outside the churchyard-gate got very wet, and many among them partook too freely of the flowing bowl afterwards in the vain hope of drying themselves thereby. And the brothers Vaughan quarrelled bitterly, and said unbrotherly things to one another. Donald declaring that Reginald had cheated and robbed him, and Reginald re torting that for the sake of that accusation neither Donald nor the children that might come after him should ever benefit by a penny made from a Strathland acre.

But for all these trifling *contretemps* of rain and unfraternal feeling, Don Arminger and the girl whom he had saved from the reckless addresses of the bull years ago were made man and wife, sure and fast, and Lord Charldale, with really hearty, manly, generous joy, saw Constance given to Don Arminger on the very spot where once he—Lord Charldale—had, with many a stumble and totter, striven to take her to himself.

But his days of stumbling and tottering, and falling away from his own dignity and manhood, were over now, and he could look not only all men, but his stately, beautiful wife firmly in the face as he advanced to wish the bride joy, and to clasp the richest of all the presents she had received round her wrist.

Dear old Lady Timerton was at the wedding, overcome with tearful emotion at the sight of " dear Don trying to console himself for the loss of dear Elinor." It was in vain that her daughter strove to comfort the maternal heart with assurances of the length and lastingness of Don's attachment to his bride.

Old Lady Timerton knew better.

"The wound is there, Elinor, I know well, but he'll never bare it. Don is one to suffer in secret; he will never, never bare it."

" I wish the whole world—or at least all the people I like—were as happy as Don is now, mother," Lady Charldale said seriously.

But at this dear old Lady Timerton only wept the more, declaring that she, "better than any one else, knew what Don had lost in losing Elinor."

"You see, dear," she argued with her daughter, " that unless you have sufficient mediumistic power to see into the hearts of those about you in the future, you can never tell what those hearts are making them suffer, or where those hearts are leading them. I'm sure, if any one had told me, ten months ago, that this would be the end of your Aunt Kenwyn's friendship for Mr Mott, I should have blankly declined to believe that person."

"You don't mean to tell me that Lady Kenwyn is going to be fool enough to marry that man?" Lady Charldale asked hurriedly.

"My dear, it is what I have expected her to do all the time, ever since I first saw them together; their souls were so perfectly attuned, they were in such perfect harmony, they never were off as though they were with us. It seemed to be enough for them to sit and know that higher spiritualistic influences were about them, unseen, unheard, unfelt."

"I'll never go near Lady Kenwyn again if she marries that vulgar brute," Lady Charldale interrupted hastily. "What can Vie be about to permit her mother to make such a fool of herself?"

"But Lady Kenwyn isn't going to marry him," Lady Timerton put in perplexedly. "Didn't I tell you? Didn't I explain? It's that new maid of hers, Raybroke, the pretty young woman that Vie found out and insisted on her mother taking. Raybroke turns out to be wonderfully clever, and very mediumistic, and Mr Mott has been told by the spirits that he is to be Raybroke's husband, so, of course, as Lady Kenwyn gives her a thousand pounds for her wedding portion, what better can they do than marry? But I own I am surprised."

"Clever Vie!" said Lady Charldale admiringly. "Mother, if you pick up an enterprising American medium, I shall instantly pick up a pretty maid for you. I forgive Mott now for having stumbled over me at a railway station, and called me a peeress before I was one."

In reply to a congratulatory letter to Lady Victoria Gardiner on the subject of her mother's emancipation, Lady Charldale had the following reply from her cousin :—

"My dear Nell,—I was always rather good in light comedy you'll admit, but I had to go in for melodrama the few days previous to Mott's marriage with Raybroke. They were such greedy beasts, that besides that thousand pounds which I consented to their screwing out of mamma by means of repeated messages from Marie Antoinette, they wanted a regular annuity. Towards this end they positively bombarded her with messages from the spheres, and as they were two, and worked together admirably, I had hard work to frustrate their knavish tricks. At last I did it, by sending Raybroke into a room where Alice Cunningham (who is blest with a duplicate of my figure, and hair the colour of mine) was lying on her face, in my clothes, on the sofa, representing me in a swoon. While Raybroke was proceeding coolly to investigate Alice under the supposition that she was me, I suddenly appeared at Raybroke's elbow in a white diaphonous robe, touched up with phosphorous, and in my natural voice (which frightened her ten times more than any sepulchral one could have done) told her that unless she ceased her nefarious designs on my mother's purse, my spirit, which was emancipated from my body (I pointed to Alice on the sofa as I spoke) would haunt her closely and visibly through all time. Raybroke was so frightened that she promised all I asked, and fled to her Mott, and with her Mott and the thousand pounds ; and may we never hear of either of them again. Mamma is quite sick of spiritualism, and says if you like to have the Marie Antoinette costume for your next fancy ball you're welcome to it."

Don Arminger and his wife stayed away from Woodside for more than twelve months after their marriage, for Constance had a real desire to learn the map of South Africa on the spot, and Don was anxious to gratify that desire as far as lay in his power.

They found that many things had gone awry with some of those with whom they had to do in their absence, notably with Reginald Vaughan.

The latter's ambition of being received by, and in return entertaining and trying to dazzle, the county people to whom by birth he belonged, but from whom he had been estranged by circumstances, had been realised.

For every dinner which had been given for his wife and himself he had given in return three or four, on a scale which made everyone declare that he knew "how to do it." He had given a ball, and spent many hundreds of pounds in the floral decorations alone. He had heaped jewellery on his wife until rumour had it that he was putting every penny he had into precious stones, in order that when the time came he might run away with them the more conveniently. He had started a pack of hounds, and outdone everyone in the magnificence of his hunt-breakfasts, when he had a lawn meet at Strathlands. He had improved the house and grounds till no one recognised either. And now he was in "queer street" every one averred, and still the reckless expenditure went on !

At last, just after Don Arminger and Constance came back to Woodside, the ugly truth was laid bare. The second son, to whom it had been left, had wrecked the property, and Strathlands was for sale.

There was a great auction of all the household effects, but before the day of the sale Reginald had disappeared, and not even his wife—who, to do her justice, would have been quite ready to accompany him into poverty and obscurity—could tell whither he had gone or what was to become of him. It is supposed that, recklessly as he had lived at Strathlands, so recklessly he lived and died abroad, for some one recognised him in a couriers haunt in Paris once, and he had slunk out of that some one's observation, as one who feels that he has disgraced himself.

So the father's unjust will did not bear good fruit as far as the second son, who was unrighteously elevated to his brother's place, was concerned.

The proceeds of the sale did not do more than half cover Reginald Vaughan's personal debts, and so there was nothing left for his wife.　But she would take help from no man now the one who should have helped her had deserted her.　She made no moan, but went back with lessened means to her old way of life, and to this day keeps one of the best managed boarding-houses in Bloomsbury.

When Strathlands itself " came to the hammer," it was bought by people who were on the fair side of every one's favour in that neighbourhood, and there was great and genuine rejoicing.

Only Donald Vaughan said to his wife,—

" It's just like that fellow, your brother Don, to come in for the best of everything.　How furious my poor father was when Don came to Clyst as an usher ! and now he has married Constance and bought Strathlands ! "

THE END.

COLSTON AND SON, PRINTERS, EDINBURGH.

www.ingramcontent.com/pod-product-compliance
Lightning Source LLC
Chambersburg PA
CBHW031021120726
47905CB00007B/1995